TALES
OF THE
GRAND
TOUR

TOR BOOKS BY BEN BOVA

As on a Darkling Plain
The Astral Mirror
Battle Station
The Best of the Nebulas (editor)
Challenges
Colony
Cyberbooks
Escape Plus
Gremlins Go Home (with Gordon R. Dickson)
Jupiter
The Kinsman Saga
The Multiple Man
Orion
Orion Among the Stars
Orion and the Conqueror
Orion in the Dying Time
Out of the Sun
Peacekeepers
The Precipice
Privateers
Prometheans
The Rock Rats
Saturn
Star Peace: Assured Survival
The Starcrossed
Tales of the Grand Tour
Test of Fire
To Fear the Light (with A. J. Austin)
To Save the Sun (with A. J. Austin)
The Trikon Deception (with Bill Pogue)
Triumph
Vengeance of Orion
Venus
Voyagers
Voyagers II: The Alien Within
Voyagers III: Star Brothers
The Winds of Altair

TALES
OF THE
GRAND
TOUR

BEN BOVA

TOR®

A TOM DOHERTY ASSOCIATES BOOK
NEW YORK

TALES OF THE GRAND TOUR

Copyright © 2004 by Ben Bova

This book is printed on acid-free paper.

Edited by Patrick Nielsen Hayden

A Tor Book
Published by Tom Doherty Associates, LLC
175 Fifth Avenue
New York, NY 10010

www.tor.com

Tor® is a registered trademark of Tom Doherty Associates, LLC.

ISBN 0-765-30722-7

First Edition: January 2004

Printed in the United States of America

0 9 8 7 6 5 4 3 2 1

To my colleagues of the Arizona Astronomy Board,
with special thanks to Peter Wehinger

CONTENTS

INTRODUCTION

The land was ours before we were the land's . . .
Such as we were we gave ourselves outright
(The deed of gift was many deeds of war)
To the land vaguely realizing westward,
But still unstoried, artless, unenhanced,
Such as she was, such as she would become.

—Robert Frost
"The Gift Outright"

For the past fifteen years I have been writing a series of novels about humankind's expansion through the solar system, a saga about the people who move out into space: who they are, why they leave Earth, their loves and fears and hopes and rivalries. Readers have dubbed the series the Grand Tour.

It began in 1988, when I started living on Mars.

Well, not exactly Mars. My wife and I moved to northern New Mexico because the dry, mountainous country there reminded me of the pictures of the Martian landscape sent back by the *Viking* spacecraft that had landed on the surface of the red planet a dozen years earlier.

I wanted to write a novel about Mars, a completely realistic novel about the first human explorers of that strange yet familiar world. For weeks on end I soaked up the clear dry atmosphere, the sun-baked desert, the *feel* of the region. I learned a bit about the Navaho, and that peculiar blend of Hispanic, Navaho, and Anglo traditions that makes up the Southwestern culture.

Yet, try as I might, I could not get the novel properly started. Every morning I sat at my keyboard and worked at it. The pages that accumulated were dull, lifeless. Only after many weeks of struggle did I realize that the protagonist of my novel, Jamie Waterman, had to be part Navaho. I was trying to make him an ordinary "white bread" geologist. He isn't. Jamie's father was Navaho, his mother a descendant of the *Mayflower* pilgrims. The two planets, Earth and Mars, the blue world and the red one, represent the two conflicting sides of Jamie's soul. Only when I finally understood this could I begin to write the novel in earnest.

What I didn't realize, even then, was that I had started on a journey that is still unfinished, even after more than fifteen years, a journey that has taken me to Mars twice (so far), that would make me partake in the founding of the first permanent human settlement off-Earth (Moonbase, later to become the nation of Selene), that would send me to Venus, to Jupiter, Saturn, and to the Asteroid Belt several times.

This interrelated series of novels is now known as the Grand Tour. And that's what they are: a grand tour of the solar system, as it is, and as it will be.

In each of the Grand Tour novels, the background setting is as accurate and up-to-date as today's Internet news. Thanks to modern communications and to many good and patient friends both within NASA and outside the space agency, the physical settings of my novels are based solidly on what is known about the other worlds in our solar system.

But these are works of fiction, so they go beyond the scientists' current knowledge to explore what humans will find when they venture back to the Moon and outward to Mars, Venus, and beyond. And what they will find is not restricted to scientific facts and figures. For they will learn that they bring their human passions along with them, no matter how far they travel: love and fear, greed and heroism, hatred and heart-stopping adventure accompany us wherever we dare to go, because they are inside us, part of the human condition.

The Grand Tour novels are actually an extensive, multihued, vibrant canvas on which I am painting the vast saga of the human race's expansion across the breadth of the solar system. These are the stories of who goes to these strange and alien new worlds, and why; who remains back on Earth, and why; how human consciousness changes as we expand our habitat beyond the confines of the world that gave us birth.

That question of *why* is what novels are all about. What would motivate people to journey hundreds of millions of miles to a strange and inhospitable world, where quick death awaits the slightest error in judgment or competence?

In my Grand Tour novels, this question of motivation takes on two different but complimentary facets:

What attracts certain men and women to explore the unknown, to seek their fortunes and risk their lives in strange and alien places? Is it the excitement? The thrill of being the first, of literally going where no one has gone before? Could it be the lure of fame, or wealth, or just plain egotism?

On the other hand, what drives explorers and entrepreneurs away from the safe and comfortable world in which they were born and nurtured? What forces them to leave the normal life and head off for parts unknown?

Attraction and repulsion. Pull and push. It takes both to make an explorer, a risk-taking entrepreneur, a believable character in a realistic novel. In my Grand Tour novels we journey to distant worlds, but we keep one eye on Earth, as well, because what happens on Earth determines to a major extent how far our space-farers are willing to go, how far they are driven to go.

It might seem strange to think of a novel about worlds as unknown as Jupiter or Venus as being realistic, but I have tried my best to show these worlds as accurately as possible. I want my characters to face these alien planets as they really are, no punches pulled, no tricks of fantasy to ease their problems. The worlds in my novels are based on what planetary astronomers have learned about them. I've invented plenty, because we really don't know anywhere near enough to write a good novel about those distant worlds. But everything I've invented is consistent with what is known.

These stories are called science fiction, but I prefer to think of them as historical fiction—history that has not yet happened. But it surely will.

The human race will expand through the solar system. It is as inevitable as the European expansion into the New World, starting five hundred years ago. And it will happen for much the same reason.

There are about six billion people on Earth today, with a quarter-million more born every day. The tensions, the wars, the terrorism, the ecological degradation that we see today are all rooted in the fact that the human race is growing faster than our ability to feed, house, clothe, and educate its growing numbers.

When will the breaking point come? At seven billion? Ten? *Has it already come, and we simply haven't recognized its knell?*

If population continues to grow, wars and terrorism will continue and even worsen. More frightening, perhaps, is the damage that our growing numbers are doing to the global environment. Tropical forests are being stripped away. Fisheries that once fed whole continents are now depleted. Global warming is threatening climate disasters that could flood coastal cities and alter climate everywhere in the world.

How can we stop global population growth? By government restrictions? By force? By asking the wealthy nations to reduce their consumption so that their resources can be shared with the poor?

The Harvard biologist E. O. Wilson estimated that in order to bring the standard of living for everyone in the world up to the level of the average American's, we would need the natural resources of four planet Earths. He regarded that as manifestly impossible, and urged that the wealthy cut back and share their riches with the poor. Yet even if this could be accomplished it would inevitably make everyone equally poor.

The time-proven way to slow population growth is to make people rich. Wealthy people do not have as many children as poor people. But where could we find the resources to make everyone wealthy? How can we create such an abundance to equal four times planet Earth's natural resources?

It's out there.

We have seen, photographed, even measured *thousands* of times the resources of planet Earth. Enormous wealths of energy and natural resources lie waiting for us in space. We have only to go out there and begin developing them.

That is what the Grand Tour novels are all about: expanding the human race's habitat throughout the solar system, developing those resources, and changing human society.

This will happen. It has already begun, although in a very small way. As the decades of this new century unfold, though, the human race will reach into space to tap the incredibly rich resources of energy and raw materials that wait for us on those distant, fascinating, alien worlds: all the true wealth we need to build a flourishing, fair, and free interplanetary society.

Thus will we continue the old, old struggle against humankind's ancient and remorseless enemies: hunger, poverty, ignorance, and death. We will continue this struggle for one brutally simple reason: survival.

The Grand Tour novels portray this struggle and the coming era of humankind's expansion through the solar system.

The shorter tales that are in this book are part of the Grand Tour, as well. Some of these stories have been excerpted from the novels. Others were written independently of the novels. All of them are collected in this one volume for the first time.

Here you will visit Mars, Venus, the Moon, and other worlds— including Earth. Here you will meet the men and women who are driven to go farther, to dream larger dreams, driven to push the frontier of human daring and human achievement outward, toward the stars.

Welcome to these *Tales of the Grand Tour*.

Ben Bova
Naples, Florida
December 2002

THE GRAND TOUR NOVELS

Mars, Bantam Books, 1992

Empire Builders, Tor Books, 1993

Moonrise, Avon Books, 1996

Moonwar, Avon Books, 1998

Return to Mars, Avon Books, 1999

Venus, Tor Books, 2000

Jupiter, Tor Books, 2001

The Precipice:
Book I of the Asteroid Wars, Tor Books, 2001

The Rock Rats:
Book II of the Asteroid Wars, Tor Books, 2002

Saturn, Tor Books, 2003

TALES
OF THE
GRAND
TOUR

Sam Gunn has appeared in many of my shorter works of fiction.[1] Sam is a "little guy," a sawed-off, fast-talking rogue, a rascal, a womanizing scoundrel who just happens to have a heart as big as the solar system. He's charming, loyal to his friends, and the first true entrepreneur in space. He is constantly making fortunes—and losing them—as he battles the "big guys" of the government and the multinational corporations.

Sam was crazy enough to go out to the Asteroid Belt before anyone else did, an escapade that cost him two years of grief and left him broke. But he showed that it was possible to begin developing the vast resources of the Belt. Others followed, in time, which eventually led to the Asteroid Wars.

In this story, Sam returns to the Belt for reasons other than business. In fact, Sam has several reasons for leaving his bride-to-be waiting for him on Earth while he tries to find the solar system's most dangerous man—all in the service of the solar system's most beautiful woman.

---

1. Sam's tales have been collected in two books, *Sam Gunn, Unlimited* (Bantam 1993) and *Sam Gunn Forever* (Avon 1998).

SAM AND THE FLYING DUTCHMAN

ushered her into Sam's office and helped her out of the bulky dark coat she was wearing. Once she let the hood fall back I damned near dropped the coat. I recognized her. Who could forget her? She was exquisite, so stunningly beautiful that even irrepressible Sam Gunn was struck speechless. More beautiful than any woman I had ever seen.

But haunted.

It was more than her big, soulful eyes. More than the almost frightened way she had of glancing all around as she entered Sam's office, as if expecting someone to leap out of hiding at her. She looked *tragic*, lovely and doomed and tragic.

"Mr. Gunn, I need your help," she said to Sam. Those were the first words she spoke, even before she took the chair that I was holding for her. Her voice was like the sigh of a breeze in a midnight forest.

Sam was standing behind his desk, on the hidden little platform back there that makes him look taller than his real 165 centimeters. As I said, even Sam was speechless. Leather-tongued, clatter-mouthed Sam Gunn simply stood and stared at her in stupified awe.

Then he found his voice. "Anything," he said, in a choked whisper. "I'd do anything for you."

Despite the fact that Sam was getting married in just three weeks' time, it was obvious that he'd tumbled head over heels for Amanda Cunningham the minute he saw her. Instantly. Sam Gunn was always falling in love, even more often than he made fortunes of money and lost them again. But this time it looked as if he'd really been struck by the thunderbolt.

If she weren't so beautiful, so troubled, seeing the two of them together would have been almost ludicrous. Amanda Cunningham looked like a Greek goddess, except that her shoulder-length hair was radiant golden blond. She wore a modest knee-length sheath of delicate pink that couldn't hide the curves of her ample body. And those eyes! They were bright china blue, but deep, terribly troubled, unbearably sad.

And there was Sam: stubby as a worn old pencil, with a bristle of red hair and his gap-toothed mouth hanging open. Sam had the kind of electricity in him that made it almost impossible for him to stand still for more than thirty seconds at a time. Yet he stood gaping at Amanda Cunningham, as tongue-tied as a teenager on his first date.

And me. Compared to Sam I'm a rugged outdoorsy type of guy. Of course, I wear lifts in my boots and a tummy tingler that helps keep my gut flat. Women have told me that my face is kind of cute in a cherubic sort of way, and I believe them—until I look in the mirror and see the pouchy eyes and the trim black beard that covers my receding chin. What did it matter? Amanda Cunningham didn't even glance at me; her attention was focused completely on Sam.

It was really comical. Yet I wasn't laughing.

Sam just stared at her, transfixed. Bewitched. I was still holding one of the leather-covered chairs for her. She sat down without looking at it, as if she were accustomed to there being a chair wherever she chose to sit.

"You must understand, Mr. Gunn," she said softly. "What I ask is very dangerous . . ."

Still standing in front of his high-backed swivel chair, his eyes never leaving hers, Sam waved one hand as if to scoff at the thought of danger.

"It involves flying out to the Belt," she continued.

"Anywhere," Sam said. "For you."

"To find my husband."

That broke the spell. Definitely.

Sam's company was S. Gunn Enterprises, Unlimited. He was involved in a lot of different operations, including hauling freight between the Earth and Moon, and transporting equipment out to the Asteroid Belt. He was also dickering to build a gambling casino and hotel on the Moon, but that's another story.

"To find your husband?" Sam asked her, his face sagging with disappointment.

"My ex-husband," said Amanda Cunningham. "We were divorced several years ago."

"Oh." Sam brightened.

"My current husband is Martin Humphries," she went on, her voice sinking lower.

"Oh," Sam repeated, plopping down into his chair like a man shot in the heart. "Amanda Cunningham Humphries."

"Yes," she said.

"*The* Martin Humphries?"

"Yes," she repeated, almost whispering it.

Mrs. Martin Humphries. I'd seen pictures of her, of course, and vids on the society nets. I'd even glimpsed her in person once, across a ballroom crowded with the very wealthiest of the wealthy. Even in the midst of all that glitter and opulence she had glowed like a beautiful princess in a cave full of trolls. Martin Humphries was towing her around the party like an Olympic trophy. I popped my monocle and almost forgot the phony German accent I'd been using all evening. That was a couple of years ago, when I'd been working the society circuit selling shares of nonexistent tritium mines. On Mars, yet. The richer they are, the easier they bite.

Martin Humphries was probably the richest person in the solar system, founder and chief of Humphries Space Systems, and well-known to be a prime S.O.B. I'd never try to scam him. If he bit on my bait, it could be fatal. So that's why she looks so miserable, I thought. Married to him. I felt sorry for Amanda Cunningham Humphries.

But sorry or not, this could be the break I'd been waiting for. Amanda Cunningham Humphries was the wife of the richest sumbitch in the solar system. She could buy anything she wanted, including Sam's whole ramshackle company, which was teetering on the brink of bankruptcy. As usual. Yet she was asking Sam for help, like a lady in distress. She was scared.

"Martin Humphries," Sam repeated.

She nodded wordlessly. She certainly did not look happy about being married to Martin Humphries.

Sam swallowed visibly, his Adam's apple bobbing up and down twice. Then he got to his feet again and said, as brightly as he could manage, "Why don't we discuss this over lunch?"

Sam's office in those days was on the L-5 habitat *Beethoven.* Funny name for a space structure that housed some fifty thousand people, I know. It was built by a consortium of American, European, Russian, and Japanese corporations. The only name they could agree on was Beethoven's, thanks to the fact that the head of Yamagata Corp. had always wanted to be a symphony orchestra conductor.

To his credit, Sam's office was not grand or imposing. He said he didn't want to waste his money on furniture or real estate. Not that he had any money to waste, at the time. The suite was compact, tastefully decorated, with wall screens that showed idyllic scenes of woods and waterfalls. Sam had a sort of picture gallery on the wall behind his desk, S. Gunn with the great and powerful figures of the day—most of whom were out to sue him, if not have him murdered—plus several photos of Sam with various beauties in revealing attire.

I, as his "special consultant and advisor," sat off to one side of his teak-and-chrome desk, where I could swivel from Sam to his visitor and back again.

Amanda Humphries shook her lovely head. "I can't go out to lunch with you, Mr. Gunn. I shouldn't be seen in public with you."

Before Sam could react to that, she added, "It's nothing personal. It's just . . . I don't want my husband to know that I've turned to you."

Undeterred, Sam put on a lopsided grin and said, "Well, we could have lunch sent in here." He turned to me. "Gar, why don't you rustle us up some grub?"

I made a smile at his sudden Western folksiness. Sam was a con man, and everybody knew it. That made it all the easier for me to con him. I'm a scam artist, myself, par excellence, and it ain't bragging if you can do it. Still, I'd been very roundabout in approaching Sam. Conning a con man takes some finesse, let me tell you.

About a year ago I talked myself into a job with the Honorable Jill Myers, former U.S. senator and American representative on the International Court of Justice. Judge Myers was an old, old friend of Sam's, dating back to the early days when they'd both been astronauts working for the old NASA.

I had passed myself off to Myers's people as Garret G. Garrison III, the penniless son of one of the oldest families in Texas. I had doctored up a biography and a dozen or so phony news media reports. With just a bit of money in the right hands, when Myers's people checked me out in the various web nets, there was enough in place to convince them that I was poor but bright, talented, and honest.

Three out of four ain't bad. I was certainly poor, bright, and talented. Jill Myers wanted to marry Sam. Why, I'll never figure out. Sam was—is!—a philandering, womanizing, skirt-chasing bundle of testosterone who falls in love the way Pavlov's dogs salivated when they heard a bell ring. But Jill Myers wanted to marry the little scoundrel, and Sam had even proposed to her—once he ran out of all the other sources of funding that he could think of. Did I mention that Judge Myers comes from Old Money? She does: the kind of New England family that still has the first nickel they made in the molasses-for-rum-for-slaves triangle trade back in precolonial days.

Anyway, I had sweet-talked my way into Judge Myers's confidence (and worked damned hard for her, too, I might add). So when they set a date for the wedding, she asked me to join Sam's staff and keep an eye on him. She didn't want him to disappear and leave her standing at the altar.

Sam took me in without a qualm, gave me the title of "special consultant and advisor to the CEO," and put me in the office next to his. He knew I was Justice Myers's enforcer, but it didn't seem to bother him a bit.

Sam and I got along beautifully, like kindred souls, really. Once I told him the long, sad (and totally false) story of my life, he took to me like a big brother.

"Gar," he told me more than once, "we're two of a kind. Always trying to get out from under the big guys."

I agreed fervently.

I've been a grifter all my life, ever since I sweet-talked Sister Agonista into overlooking the fact that she caught me cheating on the year-end exams in sixth grade. It was a neat scam for an eleven-year-old: I let her catch me, I let her think she had scared me onto the path of righteousness, and she was so happy about it that she never tumbled to the fact that I had sold answer sheets to half the kids in the school.

Anyway, life was always kind of rough-and-tumble for me. You hit it big here, and the next time you barely get out with the hide on your back. I had been at it long enough so that by now I was slowing down, getting a little tired, looking for the one big score that would let me wrap it all up and live the rest of my life in ill-gotten ease. I knew Sam Gunn was the con man's con man: The little rogue had made more fortunes than the New York Stock Exchange—and lost them just as quickly as he could go chasing after some new rainbow. I figured that if I cozied up real close to Sam I could snatch his next pot of gold before he had a chance to piss it away.

So when Judge Myers asked me to keep an eye on Sam I went out to the *Beethoven* habitat that same day, alert and ready for my big chance to nail the last and best score.

Amanda Cunningham Humphries might just be that opportunity, I realized.

So now I'm bringing a tray of lunch in for Sam and Mrs. Humphries, setting it all out on Sam's desk while they chatted, and then retreating to my own little office so they could talk in privacy.

Privacy, hah! I slipped the acoustic amplifier out of my desk drawer and stuck it on the wall that my office shared with Sam's. Once I had wormed the earplug in, I could hear everything they said.

Which wasn't all that much. Mrs. Humphries was very guarded about it all.

"I have a coded video chip that I want you to deliver to my ex-husband," she told Sam.

"Okay," he said, "but you could have a courier service make the delivery, even out to the Belt. I don't see why—"

"My ex-husband is Lars Fuchs."

Bingo! I don't know how Sam reacted to that news but I nearly jumped out of my chair to turn a somersault. Her first husband was Lars Fuchs! Fuchs the pirate. Fuchs the renegade. Fuchs and Humphries had fought a minor war out there in the Belt a few years earlier. It had ended when Humphries's mercenaries had finally captured Fuchs and the people of Ceres had exiled him for life.

For years now Fuchs had wandered through the Belt, an exile eking out a living as a miner, a rock rat. Making a legend of himself. The Flying Dutchman of the Asteroid Belt.

It must have been right after he was exiled, I guessed, that Amanda Cunningham had divorced Fuchs and married his bitter rival, Humphries. I later found out that I was right. That's exactly what had happened. But with a twist. She divorced Fuchs and married Humphries on the condition that Humphries would stop trying to track Fuchs down and have him killed. Exile was punishment enough, she convinced Humphries. But the price for that tender mercy was her body. From the haunted look of her, maybe the price included her soul.

Now she wanted to send a message to her ex. Why? What was in the message? Humphries would pay a small fortune to find out. No, I decided; he'd pay a *large* fortune. To me.

Mrs. Humphries didn't have all that much more to say and she left the office immediately after they finished their lunch, bundled once more into that shapeless black coat with its hood pulled up to hide her face.

I bounced back into Sam's office. He was sitting back in his chair, the expression on his face somewhere between exalted and terrified.

"She needs my help," Sam murmured, as if talking in his sleep.

"Our help," I corrected.

Sam blinked, shook himself, and sat up erect. He nodded and grinned at me. "I knew I could count on you, Gar."

Then I remembered that I was supposed to be working for Judge Myers.

"He's going out to the Belt?" Judge Myers's chestnut-brown eyes snapped at me. "And you're letting him do it?"

Some people called Jill Myers plain, or even unattractive (behind her back, of course), but I always thought of her as kind of cute. In a way, she looked almost like Sam's sister might: Her face was round as a pie, with a stubby little nose and a sprinkling of freckles. Her hair was light brown and straight as can be; she kept it in a short, no-nonsense bob and refused to let stylists fancy it up for her.

Her image in my desk screen clearly showed, though, that she was angry. Not at Sam. At me.

"Garrison, I sent you to keep that little so-and-so on track for our wedding, and now you're going out to the Belt with him?"

"It'll only be for a few days," I said. Truthfully, that's all I expected at that point.

Her anger abated a skosh; suspicion replaced it.

"What's this all about, Gar?"

If I told her that Sam had gone bonkers over Amanda Humphries she'd be up at *Beethoven* on the next shuttle, so I temporized a little.

"He's looking into a new business opportunity at Ceres. It should only take a few days."

Fusion torch ships could zip out to the Belt at a constant acceleration. They cost an arm and two legs, but Sam was in his "spare no expenses" mode, and I agreed with him. We could zip out to the Belt in four days, deliver the message, and be home again in time for the wedding. We'd even have a day or so to spare, I thought.

One thing about Judge Myers: She couldn't stay angry for more than a few minutes at a time. But from the expression on her face, she remained highly suspicious.

"I want a call from you every day, Gar," she said. "I know you can't keep Sam on a leash; nobody can. But I want to know where you are and what you're doing."

"Yes, ma'am. Of course."

"Every day."

"Right."

Easier said than done.

Sam rented a torch ship, the smallest he could find, just a set of fusion engines and propellant tanks with a crew pod attached. It was called *Achernar*, and its accommodations were really Spartan. Sam piloted it himself.

"That's why I keep my astronaut's qualifications up to date with the chickenshit IAA," he told me, with a mischievous wink. "No sense spending money on a pilot when I can fly these birds myself."

For four days we raced out to Ceres, accelerating at a half-gee most of the time, then decelerating at a gee-and-a-half. Sam wanted to go even faster, but the IAA wouldn't approve his original plan, and he had no choice. If he didn't follow their flight plan the IAA controllers at Ceres would impound *Achernar* and send us back to Earth for a disciplinary hearing.

So Sam stuck to their rules, fussing and fidgeting every centimeter of the way. He hated bureaucracies and bureaucrats. He especially loathed being forced to do things their way instead of his own.

The trip out was less than luxurious, let me tell you. But the deceleration was absolute agony for me; I felt as if I weighed about a ton and I was scared even to try to stand up.

Sam took the strain cheerfully. "Double-strength jockstrap, Gar," he told me, grinning. "That's the secret of my success."

I stayed seated as much as possible. I even slept in the copilot's reclinable chair, wishing that the ship had been primitive enough to include a relief tube among its equipment fixtures.

People who don't know any better think that the rock rats out in the Belt are a bunch of rough-and-tumble, crusty, hard-fisted prospectors and miners. Well, sure, there are some like that, but most of the rock rats are university-educated engineers and technicians. After all, they work with spacecraft and teleoperated machinery out at the frontier of human civilization. They're out there in the dark, cold, mostly empty Asteroid Belt, on their own, the nearest help usually so far away that it's useless to them. They don't use mules and shovels, and they don't have barroom brawls or shootouts.

Most nights, that is.

Sam's first stop after we docked at the habitat *Chrysalis* was the bar.

The *Chrysalis* habitat, by the way, was something like a circular, rotating junkyard. The rock rats had built it over the years by putting used or abandoned spacecraft together, hooking them up like a Tinkertoy merry-go-round, and spinning the whole contraption to produce an artificial gravity inside. It was better than living in Ceres itself, with its minuscule gravity and the constant haze of dust that you stirred up with every move you made. The earliest rock rats actually did live inside Ceres. That's why they built the ramshackle *Chrysalis* as quickly as they could.

I worried about hard radiation, but Sam told me the habitat had a superconducting shield, the same as spacecraft use.

"You're as safe as you'd be on Earth," Sam assured me. "Just about."

It was the "just about" that scared me.

"Why are we going to the bar?" I asked, striding along beside him down the habitat's central corridor. Well, maybe "central corridor" is an overstatement. We were walking down the main passageway of one of the spacecraft that made up *Chrysalis*. Up ahead was a hatch that connected to the next spacecraft component. And so on. We could walk a complete circle and come back to the airlock where *Achernar* was docked, if we'd wanted to.

"Gonna meet the mayor," said Sam.

The mayor?

Well, anyway, we go straight to the bar. I had expected a kind of rough place, maybe like a biker joint. Instead the place looked like a sophisticated cocktail lounge.

It was called the Crystal Palace, and it was as quiet and subdued as one of those high-class watering holes in Old Manhattan. Soft lighting, plush faux-leather wall coverings, muted Mozart coming through the speakers set in the overhead. It was midafternoon and there were only about a dozen people in the place, a few at the bar, the rest in high-backed booths that gave them plenty of privacy.

Sam sauntered up to the bar and perched on one of the swiveling stools. He spun around a few times, taking in the local scenery. The only woman in the place was the human bartender, and she wasn't much better looking than the robots that trundled drinks out to the guys in the booths.

"What's fer yew?" she asked. She looked like she was into weightlifting. The gray sweatshirt she was wearing had the sleeves cut off; plenty of muscle in her arms. The expression on her squarish face was no-nonsense, unsmiling.

"West Tennessee," said Sam. "Right?"

The bartender looked surprised. "Huntsville, 'Bama."

"Heart of the Tennessee Valley," Sam said. "I come from the bluegrass country, myself."

Which was a complete lie. Sam was born in either Nevada or Pennsylvania, according to which of his dossiers you read. Or maybe Luzon, in the Philippines.

Well, in less than six minutes Sam's got the bartender laughing and trading redneck jokes with him. Her name was Belinda. I just sat beside him and watched the master at work. He could charm the devil out of hell, Sam could.

Sam ordered Tennessee corn mash for both of us. While he chatted up the bartender, though, I noticed that the place was emptying out. The three guys at the bar got up and left first, one by one. Then, out of the corner of my eye, I saw the guys in the booths heading for the door. No big rush, but within a few minutes they had all walked out. On tiptoes.

I said nothing, but soon enough Sam realized we were alone.

"What happened?" he asked Belinda. "We chased everybody out?"

She shook her head. "Rock rats worry about strangers. They prob'ly think you're maybe a tax assessor or a safety inspector from the IAA."

Sam laughed. "Me? From the IAA? Hell, no. I'm Sam Gunn. Maybe you've heard of me?"

"No! Sam Gunn? You couldn't be!"

"That's me," Sam said, with his Huckleberry Finn grin.

"You were the first guy out here in the Belt," said Belinda, real admiration glowing in her eyes.

"Yep. Captured a nickel/iron asteroid and towed her back to Earth orbit."

"Pittsburgh. I heard about it. Took you a couple of years, didn't it?"

Sam nodded. He was enjoying the adulation.

"That was a long time ago," Belinda said. "I thought you'd be a lot older."

"I am."

She laughed, a hearty roar that made the glasses on the back bar rattle. "Rejuve therapy, right?"

"Why not?"

Just then a red-haired mountain strode into the bar. One of the biggest men I've ever seen. He didn't look fat, either: just *big*, with a shaggy mane of brick-red hair and a shaggier beard to match.

He walked right up to us.

"You're Sam Gunn." It wasn't a question.

"Right," said Sam. Swiveling toward me, he added, "And this young fellow here is Garret G. Garrison III."

"The third, huh?" the redhead huffed at me. "What happened to the first two?"

"Hung for stealin' horses," I lied, putting on my thickest Wild West accent.

Belinda laughed at that. The redhead simply huffed.

"You're George Ambrose, right?" Sam asked.

"Big George, that's me."

"The mayor of this fair community," Sam added.

"They elected me th' fookin' chief," Big George said, almost belligerently. "Now, whattaya want to see me about?"

"About Lars Fuchs."

George's eyes went cold and narrow. Belinda backed away from us and went down the bar, suddenly busy with the glassware.

"What about Lars Fuchs?" George asked.

"I want to meet him. I've got a business proposition for him."

George folded his beefy arms across his massive chest. "Fuchs is an exile. Hasn't been anywhere near Ceres for dog's years. Hell, this fookin' habitat wasn't even finished when we tossed him out. We were still livin' down inside th' rock."

Sam rested his elbows on the bar and smiled disarmingly at Big George. "Well, I've got a business proposition for Fuchs and I need to talk to him."

"What kind of a business proposition?"

With a perfectly straight face Sam answered, "I'm thinking of starting a tourist service here in the Belt. You know, visit Ceres, see a mining operation at work on one of the asteroids, go out in a suit and chip some gold or diamonds to bring back home. That kind of thing."

George said nothing, but I could see the wheels turning behind that wild red mane of his.

"It could mean an influx of money for your people," Sam went on, in his best snake-oil spiel. "A hotel here in orbit around Ceres, rich tourists flooding in. Lots of money."

George unbent his arms, but he still remained standing. "What's all this got to do with Fuchs?"

"Shiploads full of rich tourists might make a tempting target for a pirate."

"Bullshit."

"You don't think he'd attack tour ships?"

"Lars wouldn't do that. He's not a fookin' pirate. Not in that sense, anyway."

"I'd rather hear that from him," Sam said. "In fact, I've got to have his personal assurance before my backers will invest in the scheme."

George stared at Sam for a long moment, deep suspicion written clearly on his face. "Nobody knows where Lars is," he said at last. "You might as well go back home. Nobody here's gonna give you any help."

We left the bar with Big George glowering at our backs so hard I could feel the heat. Following the maps on the wall screens in the passageways, we found the adjoining rooms that I had booked for us.

"Now what?" I asked Sam as I unpacked my travel bag.

"Now we wait."

Sam had simply tossed his bag on the bed of his room and barged through the connecting door into mine. We had packed for only a three-day stay at Ceres, although we had more gear stowed in *Achernar*. Something had to happen pretty quick, I thought.

"Wait for what?" I asked.

"Developments."

I put my carefully folded clothes in a drawer, hung my extra pair of wrinkle-proof slacks in the closet, and set up my toiletries in the lavatory. Sam made himself comfortable in the room's only chair, a recliner designed to look like an astronaut's couch. He cranked it down so far I thought he was going to take a nap.

Sitting on the bed, I told him, "Sam, I've got to call Judge
"Go right ahead," he said.
"What should I tell her?"
"Tell her we'll be back in time for the wedding."
I doubted that.

Two days passed without a word from anyone. Sam even tried to date
Belinda, he was getting so desperate, but she wouldn't have anything to
do with him.

"They all know Fuchs," Sam said to me. "They like him and they're
protecting him."

It was common knowledge that Humphries had sworn to kill Fuchs,
but Amanda had married Humphries on the condition that he leave
Fuchs alone. Everybody in Ceres, from Belinda the barmaid to the last
rock rat, thought that we were working for Humphries, trying to find
Fuchs and murder him. Or at least locate him, so one of Humphries's
hired killers could knock him off. Fuchs was out there in the Belt somewhere, cruising through that dark emptiness like some Flying Dutchman,
alone, taking a strangely measured kind of vengeance on unmanned
Humphries ships.

I had other fish to fry, though. I wanted to find out what was on the
chip that Amanda had given Sam. Her message to her ex-husband. What
did she want to tell him? Fuchs was a thorn in Humphries's side; maybe
only a small thorn, but he drew blood, nonetheless. Humphries would
pay a fortune for that message, and I intended to sell it to him.

But I had to get it away from Sam first.

Judge Myers was not happy with my equivocating reports to her. Definitely not happy.

There's no way to have a conversation in real time between Ceres
and Earth; the distance makes it impossible. It takes nearly half an hour
for a message to cross one-way, even when the two bodies are at their closest. So I sent reports to Judge Myers and—usually within an hour—I'd
get a response from her.

After my first report she had a wry grin on her face when she called
back. "Garrison, I know it's about as easy to keep Sam in line as nailing
tapioca to a wall in zero-gee. But all the plans for the wedding are set; it's

going to be the biggest social event of the year. You've got to make sure that he's here. I'm depending on you, Garrison."

A day later, her smile had disappeared. "The wedding's only a week from now, Garrison," she said after my second call to her. "I want that little scoundrel at the altar!"

Third call, the next day: "I don't care what he's doing! Get him back here! Now!"

That's when Sam came up with his bright idea.

"Pack up your duds, Gar," he announced brightly. "We're going to take a little spin around the Belt."

I was too surprised to ask questions. In less than an hour we were back in *Achernar* and heading out from Ceres. Sam had already filed a flight plan with the IAA controllers. As far as they were concerned, Sam was going to visit three specific asteroids, which might be used as tourist stops if and when he started his operation in the Belt. Of course, I knew that once we cleared Ceres there was no one and nothing that could hold him to that plan.

"What are we doing?" I asked, sitting in the right-hand seat of the cockpit. "Where are we going?"

"To meet Fuchs," said Sam.

"You've made contact with him?"

"Nope," Sam replied, grinning as if he knew something nobody else knew. "But I'm willing to bet *somebody* has. Maybe Big George. Fuchs saved his life once, did you know that?"

"But how—?"

"It's simple," Sam answered before I could finish the question. "We let it be known that we want to see Fuchs. Everybody says they don't know where he is. We go out into the Belt, away from everything, including snoops who might rat out Fuchs to Martin Humphries. Somebody from *Chrysalis* calls Fuchs and tells him about us. Fuchs intercepts our ship to see what I want. I give him Amanda's message chip. Q.E.D."

It made a certain amount of sense. But I had my doubts.

"What if Fuchs just blasts us?"

"Not his style. He's only attacked unmanned ships."

"He wiped out an HSS base on Vesta, didn't he? Killed dozens."

"That was during the war between him and Humphries. Ancient history. He hasn't attacked a crewed ship since he's been exiled."

"But suppose—"

The communications console pinged.

"Hah!" Sam gloated. "There he is now."

But the image that took form on the comm screen wasn't Lars Fuchs's face. It was Jill Myers.

She was beaming a smile that could've lit up Selene City for a month. "Sam, I've got a marvelous idea. I know you're wrapped up in some kind of mysterious mission out there in the Belt, and the wedding's only a few days off so . . ."

She hesitated, like somebody about to spring a big surprise. "So instead of you coming back Earthside for the wedding, I'm bringing the wedding out to you! All the guests and everything. In fact, I'm on the torch ship *Statendaam* right now! We break Earth orbit in about an hour. I'll see you in five days, Sam, and we can be married just as we planned!"

To say Sam was surprised would be like saying Napoleon was disturbed by Waterloo. Or McKenzie was inconvenienced when his spacecraft crashed into the Lunar Apennines. Or—well, you get the idea.

Sam looked stunned, as if he'd been poleaxed between the eyes. He just slumped in the pilot's chair, dazed, his eyes unfocused for several minutes.

"She can't come out here," he muttered at last.

"She's already on her way," I said.

"But she'll ruin everything. If she comes barging out here Fuchs'll never come within a lightyear and a half of us."

"How're you going to stop her?"

Sam thought about that for all of a half-second. "I can't stop her. But I don't have to make it easy for her to find me."

"What do you mean?"

"Run silent, run deep." With deft finger, Sam turned off the ship's tracking beacon and telemetry transmitter.

"Sam! The controllers at Ceres will think we've been destroyed!"

He grinned wickedly. "Let 'em. If they don't know where we are, they can't point Jill at us."

"But Fuchs won't know where we are."

"Oh yes he will," Sam insisted. "Somebody at Ceres has already given him our flight plan. Big George, probably."

"Sam," I said patiently, "you filed that flight plan with the IAA. They'll tell Judge Myers. She'll come out looking for you."

"Yeah, but she'll be several days behind. By that time the IAA controllers'll tell her we've disappeared. She'll go home and weep for me."

"Or start searching for your remains."

He shot me an annoyed glance. "Anyway, we'll meet with Fuchs before she gets here, most likely."

"You hope."

His grin wobbled a little.

I thought the most likely scenario was that Fuchs would ignore us and Judge Myers would search for us, hoping that Sam's disappearance didn't mean he was dead. Once she found us, I figured, she'd kill Sam herself.

It was eerie, out there in the Belt. Flatlanders back on Earth think that the Asteroid Belt is a dangerous region, a-chock with boulders, so crowded that you have to maneuver like a kid in a computer game to avoid getting smashed.

Actually, it's empty. Dark and cold and four times farther from the Sun than the Earth is. Most of the asteroids are the size of dust flakes. The valuable ones, maybe a few meters to a kilometer or so across, are so few and far between that you have to hunt for them. You can cruise through the Belt blindfolded and your chances of getting hit even by a pebble-sized 'roid are pretty close to nil.

Of course, a pebble could shatter your ship if it hits you with enough velocity.

So we were running silent, but following the flight plan Sam had registered with the IAA. We got to the first rock Sam had scheduled and loitered around it for half a day. No sign of Fuchs. If he was anywhere nearby, he was running as silently as we were.

"He's gotta be somewhere around here," Sam said as we broke orbit and headed for the next asteroid on his list. "He's gotta be."

I could tell that Sam was feeling Judge Myers's eager breath on the back of his neck.

Me, I had a different problem. I wanted to get that message chip away from him long enough to send a copy of it to Martin Humphries. With a suitable request for compensation, of course. Fifty million would do nicely, I thought. A hundred mil would be even better.

But how to get the chip out of Sam's pocket? He kept it on his person all the time; even slept with it.

So it floored me when, as we were eating breakfast in *Achernar's* cramped little galley on our third day out, Sam fished the fingernail-sized chip out of his breast pocket and handed it to me.

"Gar," he said solemnly, "I want you to hide this someplace where *nobody* can find it, not even me."

I was staggered. "Why . . . ?"

"Just a precaution," he said, his face more serious than I'd ever seen it before. "When Fuchs shows up things might get rough. I don't want to know where the chip is."

"But the whole point of this flight is to deliver it to him."

He nodded warily. "Yeah, Humphries must know we're looking for Fuchs. He's got IAA people on his payroll. Hell, half the people in Ceres might be willing to rat on us. Money talks, pal. Humphries might not know why we're looking for Fuchs, but he knows we're trying to find him."

"Humphries wants to find Fuchs, too," I said. "And kill him, no matter what he promised his wife."

"Damned right. I wouldn't be surprised if he has a ship tailing us."

"I haven't seen anything on the radar plot."

"So what? A stealth ship could avoid radar. But not the hair on the back of my neck."

"You think we're being followed?"

"I'm sure of it."

By the seven sinners of Cincinnati, I thought. This is starting to look like a class reunion! We're jinking around in the Belt, looking for Fuchs. Judge Myers is on her way, with a complete wedding party. And now Sam thinks there's an HSS stealth ship lurking out there somewhere, waiting for us to find Fuchs so they can pounce on him.

But all that paled into insignificance for me as I stared down at the tiny chip Sam had placed in the palm of my hand.

I had it in my grasp! Now the trick was to contact Humphries without letting Sam know of it.

I couldn't sleep that night. We were approaching the second asteroid on Sam's itinerary on a dead-reckoning trajectory. No active signals going out from the ship except for the short-range collision avoidance radar.

We'd take up a parking orbit around the unnamed rock midmorning tomorrow.

I waited until my eyes were adapted to the darkness of the sleeping compartment, then peeked down over the edge of my bunk to see if Sam was really asleep. He was on his side, face to the bulkhead, his legs pulled up slightly in a sort of fetal position. Breathing deep and regular.

He's asleep, I told myself. As quietly as a wraith I slipped out of my bunk and tiptoed in my bare feet to the cockpit, carefully shutting the hatches of the sleeping compartment and the galley, so there'd be no noise to waken Sam.

I'm pretty good at decrypting messages. It's a useful talent for a con man, and I had spent long hours at computers during my one and only jail stretch to learn the tricks of the trade.

Of course, I could just offer the chip for sale to Humphries without knowing what was on it. He'd pay handsomely for a message that his wife wanted to give to Lars Fuchs.

But if I knew the contents of the message, I reasoned, I could most likely double or triple the price. So I started to work on decrypting it. How hard could it be? I asked myself as I slipped the chip into the ship's main computer. She probably did the encoding herself, not trusting anybody around her. She'd been an astronaut in her earlier years, I knew, but not particularly a computer freak. Should be easy.

It wasn't. It took all night and I still didn't get all the way through the trapdoors and blind alleys she'd built into her message. Smart woman, I realized, my respect for Amanda Cunningham Humphries notching up with every bead of sweat I oozed.

At last the hash that had been filling the central screen on the cockpit control panel cleared away, replaced by an image of her face.

That face. I just stared at her. She was so beautiful, so sad and vulnerable. It brought a lump to my throat. I've seen beautiful women, plenty of them, and bedded more than my share. But gazing at Amanda's face, there in the quiet hum of the dimmed cockpit, I felt something more than desire, more than animal hunger.

Could it be love? I shook my head like a man who's just been knocked down by a punch. Don't be an idiot! I snarled at myself. You've been hanging around Sam too long, you're becoming a romantic jackass just like he is.

Love has nothing to do with this. That beautiful face is going to earn you millions, I told myself, as soon as you decrypt this message of hers.

And then I smelled the fragrance of coffee brewing. Sam was in the galley, right behind the closed hatch of the cockpit, clattering dishes and silverware. In a weird way I felt almost relieved. Quickly I popped the chip out of the computer and slipped it into the waistband of the under-shorts I was wearing.

Just in time. Sam pushed the hatch open and handed me a steaming mug of coffee.

"You're up early," he said, with a groggy smile.

"Couldn't sleep," I answered truthfully. That's where the truth ended. "I've been trying to think of where I could stash the chip."

He nodded and scratched at his wiry, tousled red hair. "Find a good spot, Gar. I think we're going to have plenty of fireworks before this job is finished."

Truer words, as they say, were never spoken.

The three asteroids Sam had chosen were samples of the three differ-ent types of 'roids in the Belt. The first one had been a rocky type. It looked like a lumpy potato, pockmarked with craterlets from the impacts of smaller rocks. The one we were approaching was a chondritic type, a loose collection of primeval pebbles that barely held itself together. Sam called it a beanbag.

He was saving the best one for last. The third and last asteroid on Sam's list was a metallic beauty, the one that some Latin American sculp-tress had carved into a monumental history of her Native American peo-ple; she called it "The Rememberer." Sam had been involved in that, years ago, I knew. He had shacked up with the sculptress for a while. Just like Sam.

As we approached the beanbag, our collision-avoidance radar started going crazy.

"It's surrounded by smaller chunks of rock," Sam muttered, studying the screen.

From the copilot's chair I could see the main body of the asteroid through the cockpit window. It looked hazy, indistinct, more like a puff of smoke than a solid object.

"If we're going to orbit that cloud of pebbles," I said, "it'd better be at a good distance from it. Otherwise we'll get dinged up pretty heavily."

Sam nodded and tapped in the commands for an orbit that looped a respectful distance from the beanbag.

"How long are we going to hang around here?" I asked him.

He made a small shrug. "Give it a day or two. Then we'll head off for 'The Rememberer.'"

"Sam, your wedding is in two days." Speaking of remembering, I thought.

He gave me a lopsided grin. "Jill's smart enough to figure it out. We'll get married at 'The Rememberer,' outside, in suits, with the sculpture for a background. It'll make terrific publicity for my tour service."

I felt my eyebrows go up. "You're really thinking of starting tourist runs out here to the Belt?"

"Sure. Why not?"

"I thought that was just your cover story."

"It was," he admitted. "But the more I think about it, the more sense it makes."

"Who's going to pay the fare for coming all the way out here, just to see a few rocks?"

"Gar, you just don't understand how business works, do you?"

"But—"

"How did space tourism start, in the first place?" Before I could even start thinking about an answer, he went on, "With a few bored rich guys paying millions for a few days in orbit."

"Not much of a market," I said.

He waggled a finger at me. "Not at first, but it got people interested. The publicity was important. Within a few years there was enough of a demand so that a real tourist industry took off. Small, at first, but it grew."

I recalled, "You started a honeymoon hotel in Earth orbit back then, didn't you?"

His face clouded. "It went under. Most of the honeymooners got space sick their first day in weightlessness. Horrible publicity. I went broke."

"And sold it to Rockledge Industries, right?"

He got even more somber. "Yeah, right."

Rockledge made a success of the orbital hotel after buying Sam out, mainly because they'd developed a medication for space sickness. The facility is still there in low Earth orbit, part hotel, part museum. Sam was a pioneer, all right. An ornament to his profession, as far as I was concerned. But that's another story.

"And now you think you can make a tourist line to the Belt pay off?"

Before he could answer, three things happened virtually simultaneously. The navigation computer chimed and announced, "Parking orbit established." At that instant we felt a slight lurch. Spacecraft don't lurch, not unless something bad has happened to them, like hitting a rock or getting your airtight hull punctured.

Sure enough, the maintenance program sang out, "Main thruster disabled. Repair facilities urgently required."

Before we could do more than look at each other, our mouths hanging open, a fourth thing happened.

The comm speaker rumbled with a deep, snarling voice. "Who are you and what are you doing here?"

The screen showed a dark, scowling face: jowly, almost pudgy, dark hair pulled straight back from a broad forehead, tiny deepset eyes that burned into you. A vicious slash of a mouth turned down angrily. Irritation and suspicion were written across every line of that face. He radiated power, strength, and the cold-blooded ruthlessness of a killer. Lars Fuchs.

"Answer me or my next shot will blow away your crew pod."

I felt an urgent need to go to the bathroom. But Sam stayed cool as a polar bear.

"This is Sam Gunn. I've been trying to find you, Fuchs."

"Why?"

"I have a message for you."

"From Humphries? I'm not interested in hearing what he has to say."

Sam glanced at me, then said, "The message is from Mrs. Humphries."

I didn't think it was possible, but Fuchs's face went harder still. Then, in an even meaner tone, he said, "I'm not interested in anything she has to say, either."

"She seemed very anxious to get this message to you, sir," Sam wheedled. "She hired us to come all the way out to the Belt to deliver it to you personally."

He fell silent. I could feel my heart thumping against my ribs. Then Fuchs snarled, "It seems more likely to me that you're bait for a trap Humphries wants to spring on me. My former wife hasn't anything to say to me."

"But—"

"No buts! I'm not going to let you set me up for an ambush." I could practically *feel* the suspicion in his voice, his scowling face. And something more. Something really ugly. Hatred. Hatred for Humphries and everything associated with Humphries. Including his wife.

"I'm no Judas goat," Sam snarled back. I was surprised at how incensed he seemed to be. You can never tell, with Sam, but he seemed really teed off.

"I'm Sam Gunn, goddammit, not some sneaking decoy. I don't take orders from Martin Humphries or anybody else in the whole twirling solar system and if you think . . ."

While Sam was talking, I glanced at the search radar, to see if it had locked onto Fuchs's ship. Either his ship was super stealthy or it was much farther away than I had thought. He must be a damned good shot with that laser, I realized.

Sam was jabbering, cajoling, talking a mile a minute, trying to get Fuchs to trust him enough to let us deliver the chip to him.

Fuchs answered, "Don't you think I know that the chip you're carrying has a homing beacon built into it? I take the chip and a dozen Humphries ships come after me, following the signal the chip emits."

"No, it's not like that at all," Sam pleaded. "She wants you to see this message. She wouldn't try to harm you."

"She already has," he snapped.

I began to wonder if maybe he wasn't right. Was she working for her present husband to trap her ex-husband? Had she turned against the man whose life she had saved?

It couldn't be, I thought, remembering how haunted, how frightened she had looked. She couldn't be a Judas to him; she had married Humphries to save Fuchs's life, from all that I'd heard.

Then a worse thought popped into my head. If Sam gives the chip to Fuchs I'll have nothing to offer Humphries! All that money would fly out of my grasp!

I had tried to copy the chip but it wouldn't allow the ship's computer to make a copy. Suddenly I was on Fuchs's side of the argument: Don't take the chip! Don't come anywhere near it!

Fate, as they say, intervened.

The comm system pinged again and suddenly the screen split. The other half showed Judge Myers, all smiles, obviously in a compartment aboard a spacecraft.

"Sam, we're here!" she said brightly. "At 'The Rememberer.' It was so brilliant of you to pick the sculpture for our wedding ceremony!"

"Who the hell is that?" Fuchs roared.

For once in his life, Sam actually looked embarrassed. "Um . . . my, uh, fiancée," he stumbled. "I'm supposed to be getting married in two days."

The expression on Fuchs's face was almost comical. Here he's threatening to blow us into a cloud of ionized gas and all of a sudden he's got an impatient bride-to-be on the same communications frequency.

"Married?" he bellowed.

"It's a long story," said Sam, red-cheeked.

Fuchs glared and glowered while Judge Myers's round freckled face looked puzzled. "Sam? Why don't you answer? I know where you are. If you don't come out to 'The Rememberer' I'm going to bring the whole wedding party to you, minister and boys' choir and all."

"I'm busy, Jill," Sam said.

"Boys' choir?" Fuchs ranted. "Minister?"

Not even Sam could carry on two conversations at the same time, I thought. But I was wrong.

"Jill, I'm in the middle of something," he said, then immediately switched to Fuchs: "I can't hang around here, I've got to get to my wedding."

"Who are you talking to?" Judge Myers asked.

"What wedding?" Fuchs demanded. "Do you mean to tell me you're getting married out here in the Belt?"

"That's exactly what I mean to tell you," Sam replied to him.

"Tell who?" Judge Myers asked. "What's going on, Sam?"

"Bah!" Fuchs snapped. "You're crazy! All of you!"

I saw a flash of light out of the corner of my eye. Through the cockpit's forward window I watched a small, stiletto-slim spacecraft slowly emerge from the cloud of pebbles surrounding the asteroid, plasma exhaust pulsing from its thruster and a bloodred pencilbeam of laser light probing out ahead of it.

Fuchs bellowed, "I knew it!" and let loose a string of curses that would make an angel vomit.

Sam was swearing too. "Those sonsofbitches! They knew we'd be here and they were just laying in wait in case Fuchs showed up."

"I'll get you for this, Gunn!" Fuchs howled.

"I didn't know!" Sam yelled back.

Judge Myers looked somewhere between puzzled and alarmed. "Sam, what's happening? What's going on?"

The ambush craft was rising out of the rubble cloud that surrounded the asteroid. I could see Fuchs's ship through the window now because he was shooting back at the ambusher, his own red pencilbeam of a spotting laser lighting up the cloud of pebbles like a Christmas ornament.

"We'd better get out of here, Sam," I suggested at the top of my lungs.

"How?" he snapped. "Fuchs took out the thruster."

"You mean we're stuck here?"

"Smack in the middle of their battle," he answered, nodding. "And our orbit's taking us between the two of them."

"Do something!" I screamed. "They're both shooting at us!"

Sam dove for the hatch. "Get into your suit, Gar. Quick."

I never suited up quicker. But it seemed to take hours. With our main thruster shot away, dear old *Achernar* was locked into its orbit around the asteroid. Fuchs and the ambusher were slugging it out, maneuvering and firing at each other with us in the middle. I don't think they were deliberately trying to hit us, but they weren't going out of their way to avoid us, either. While I wriggled into my spacesuit and fumbled through the checkout procedure *Achernar* lurched and quivered again and again.

"They're slicing us to ribbons," I said, trying to keep from babbling.

Sam was fully suited up; just the visor of his helmet was open. "You got the chip on you?"

For an instant I thought I'd left it in the cockpit. I nearly panicked. Then I remembered it was still in the waistband of my shorts. At least I hoped it was still there.

"Yeah," I said. "I've got it."

Sam snapped his visor closed, then reached over to me and slammed mine shut. With a gloved hand he motioned for me to follow him to the airlock.

"We're going outside?" I squeaked. I was really scared. A guy could get killed!

"You want to stay here while they take potshots at us?" Sam's voice crackled in my helmet earphones.

"But why are they shooting at us?" I asked. Actually, I was talking, babbling really, because if I didn't I probably would've started screeching like a demented baboon.

"Fuchs thinks we led him into a trap," Sam said, pushing me into the airlock, "and the bastard who's trying to bushwhack him doesn't want any living witnesses."

He squeezed into the airlock with me, cycled it, and pushed me through the outer hatch when it opened.

All of a sudden I was hanging in emptiness. My stomach heaved, my eyes blurred. I mean there was nothing out there except a zillion stars but they were so far away and I was falling, I could feel it, falling all the way to infinity. I think I screamed. Or at least gasped like a drowning man.

"It's okay, Gar," Sam said, "I've got you."

He grasped me by the wrist and, using the jetpack on his suit's back, towed me away from the riddled hulk of *Achernar*. We glided into the cloud of pebbles surrounding the asteroid. I could feel them pinging off my suit's hard shell; one of them banged into my visor, but it was a fairly gentle collision, no damage—except to the back of my head: I flinched so sharply that I whacked my head against the helmet hard enough to give me a concussion, almost, despite the helmet's padded interior.

Sam hunkered us down into the loose pile of rubble that was the main body of the asteroid. "Safer here than in the ship," he told me.

I burrowed into that beanbag as deeply as I could, scooping out pebbles with both hands, digging like a terrified gopher on speed. I would've dug all the way back to Earth if I could have.

Fuchs and the ambusher were still duking it out, with a spare laser blast now and then hitting *Achernar* as it swung slowly around the 'roid. The ship looked like a shambles, big gouges torn through its hull, chunks torn off and spinning lazily alongside its main structure.

They hadn't destroyed the radio, though. In my helmet earphones I could hear Judge Myers's voice, harsh with static:

"Sam, if this is another scheme of yours . . ."

Sam tried to explain to her what was happening, but I don't think he got through. She kept asking what was going on and then, after a while, her voice cut off altogether.

Sam said to me, "Either she's sore at me and she's leaving the Belt, or she's worried about me and she's coming here to see what's happening."

I hoped for the latter, of course. Our suits had air regenerators, I knew, but they weren't reliable for more than twenty-four hours, at best.

From the looks of poor old *Achernar*, we were going to need rescuing and damned soon, too.

We still couldn't really see Fuchs's ship, it was either too far away in that dark emptiness or he was jinking around too much for us to get a visual fix on him. I saw flashes of light that might have been puffs from maneuvering thrusters, or they might have been hits from the other guy's laser. The ambusher's craft was close enough for us to make out, most of the time. He was viffing and slewing this way and that, bobbing and weaving like a prizefighter trying to avoid his opponent's punches.

But then the stiletto flared into sudden brilliance, a flash so bright it hurt my eyes. I squeezed my eyes shut and saw the afterimage burning against my closed lids.

"Got a propellant tank," Sam said, matter-of-factly. "Fuchs'll close in for the kill now."

I opened my eyes again. The stiletto was deeply gashed along its rear half, tumbling and spinning out of control. Gradually it pulled itself onto an even keel, then turned slowly and began to head away from the asteroid. I could see hot plasma streaming from one thruster nozzle, the other was dark and cold.

"He's letting him get away," Sam said, sounding surprised. "Fuchs is letting him limp back to Ceres or wherever he came from."

"Maybe Fuchs is too badly damaged himself to chase him down," I said.

"Maybe." Sam didn't sound at all sure of that.

We waited for another hour, huddled inside our suits in the beanbag of an asteroid. Finally Sam said, "Let's get back to the ship and see what's left of her."

There wasn't much. The hull had been punctured in half a dozen places. Propulsion was gone. Life support shot. Communications marginal.

We clumped to the cockpit. It was in tatters; the main window was shot out, a long ugly scar from a laser burn right across the control panel. The pilot's chair was ripped, too. It was tough to sit in the bulky spacesuits, and we were in zero gravity, to boot. Sam just hovered a few centimeters above his chair. I realized that my stomach had calmed down. I had adjusted to zero-gee. After what we had just been through, zero-gee seemed downright comfortable.

"We'll have to live in the suits," Sam told me.

"How long can we last?"

"There are four extra air regenerators in stores," Sam said. "If they're not damaged we can hold out for another forty-eight, maybe sixty hours."

"Time enough for somebody to come and get us," I said hopefully.

I could see his freckled face bobbing up and down inside his helmet. "Yep . . . provided anybody's heard our distress call."

The emergency radio beacon seemed to be functioning. I kept telling myself we'd be all right. Sam seemed to feel that way; he was positively cheerful.

"You really think we'll be okay?" I asked him. "You're not just trying to keep my hopes up?"

"We'll be fine, Gar," he answered. "We'll probably smell pretty ripe by the time we can get out of these suits, but except for that I don't see anything to worry about."

Then he added, "Except . . ."

"Except?" I yelped. "Except what?"

He grinned wickedly. "Except that I'll miss the wedding." He made an exaggerated sigh. "Too bad."

So we lived inside the suits for the next day and a half. It wasn't all that bad, except we couldn't eat any solid food. Water and fruit juices, that was all we could get through the feeder tube. I started to feel like a Hindu ascetic on a hunger strike.

We tried the comm system, but it was intermittent, at best. The emergency beacon was faithfully sending out our distress call, of course, with our position. It could be heard all the way back to Ceres, I was sure. Somebody would come for us. Nothing to worry about. We'll get out of this okay. Someday we'll look back on this and laugh. Or maybe shudder. Good thing we had to stay in the suits; otherwise I would have gnawed all my fingernails down to the wrist.

And then the earphones in my helmet suddenly blurted to life.

"Sam! Do you read me? We can see your craft!" It was Judge Myers. I was so overjoyed that I would have married her myself.

Her ship was close enough so that our suit radios could pick up her transmission.

"We'll be there in less than an hour, Sam," she said.

"Great!" he called back. "But hold your nose when we start peeling out of these suits."

Judge Myers laughed and she and Sam chatted away like a pair of teenagers. But then Sam looked up at me and winked.

"Jill, I'm sorry this has messed up the wedding," he said, making his voice husky, sad. "I know you were looking forward to—"

"You haven't messed up a thing, Sam," she replied brightly. "After we've picked you up—and cleaned you up—we're going back to 'The Rememberer' and have the ceremony as planned."

Sam's forehead wrinkled. "But haven't your guests gone back home? What about the boys' choir? And the caterers?"

She laughed. "The guests are all still here. As for the entertainment and the caterers, so I'll have to pay them for a few extra days. Hang the expense, Sam. This is our wedding we're talking about! Money is no object."

Sam groaned.

In a matter of hours we were aboard Judge Myers's ship, *Parthia*, showered, shaved, clothed, and fed, heading to 'The Rememberer' and Sam's wedding. Sam was like Jekyll and Hyde: While he and I were alone together he was morose and mumbling, like a guy about to face a firing squad in the morning. When Judge Myers joined us for dinner, though, Sam was chipper and charming, telling jokes and spinning tall tales about old exploits. It was quite a performance; if Sam ever goes into acting he'll win awards, I'm sure.

After dinner Sam and Judge Myers strolled off together to her quarters. I went back to the compartment they had given me, locked the door, and took out the chip.

It was easier this time, since I remembered the keys to the encryption. In less than an hour I had Amanda's hauntingly beautiful face on the display of my compartment's computer. I wormed a plug into my ear, taking no chances that somebody might eavesdrop on me.

The video was focused tightly on her face. For I don't know how long I just gazed at her, hardly breathing. Then I shook myself out of the trance and touched the key that would run her message.

"Lars," she said softly, almost whispering, as if she were afraid somebody would overhear her, "I'm going to have a baby."

Holy mother in heaven! It's a good thing we didn't deliver this message to Fuchs. He would've probably cut us into little pieces and roasted them on a spit.

Amanda Cunningham Humphries went on, "Martin wants another son, he already has a five-year-old boy by a previous wife."

She hesitated, looked over her shoulder. Then, in an even lower voice, "I want you to know, Lars, that it will be your son that I bear, not his. I've had myself implanted with one of the embryos we froze at Selene, back before all these troubles started."

I felt my jaw drop down to my knees.

"I love you, Lars," Amanda said. "I've always loved you. I married Martin because he promised he'd stop trying to kill you if I did. I'll have a son, and Martin will think it's his, but it will be your son, Lars. Yours and mine. I want you to know that, dearest. Your son."

Humphries would pay a billion for that, I figured.

And he'd have the baby Amanda was carrying aborted. Maybe he'd kill her, too.

"So what are you going to do about it, Gar?"

I whirled around in my chair. Sam was standing in the doorway.

"I thought I locked—"

"You did. I unlocked it." He stepped into my compartment and carefully slid the door shut again. "So, Gar, what are you going to do?"

I popped the chip out of the computer and handed it to Sam.

He refused to take it. "I read her message the first night on our way to the Belt," Sam said, sitting on the edge of my bed. "I figured you'd try to get it off me, one way or another."

"So you gave it to me."

Sam nodded gravely. "So now you know what her message is. The question is, what are you going to do about it?"

I offered him the chip again. "Take it, Sam. I don't want it."

"It's worth a lot of money, Gar."

"I don't want it!" I repeated, a little stronger.

Sam reached out and took the chip from me. Then, "But you know what she's doing. You could tell Humphries about it. He'd pay a lot to know."

I started to reply, but to my surprise I found that I had to swallow hard before I could get any words out. "I couldn't do that to her," I said.

Sam looked squarely into my eyes. "You certain of that?"

I almost laughed. "What's a few hundred million bucks? I don't need that kind of money."

"You're certain?"

"Yes, dammit, I'm certain!" I snapped. It wasn't easy tossing away all that money, and Sam was starting to irritate me.

"Okay," he said, breaking into that lopsided smile of his. "I believe you."

Sam got to his feet, his right fist closed around the chip.

"What will you do with it?" I asked.

"Pop it out an airlock. A few days in hard UV should degrade it so badly that even if somebody found it in all this emptiness they'd never be able to read it."

I got up from my desk chair. "I'll go with you," I said.

So the two of us marched down to the nearest airlock and got rid of the chip. I had a slight pang when I realized how much money we had just tossed out into space, but then I realized I had saved Amanda's life, most likely, and certainly the life of her baby. Hers and Fuchs's.

"Fuchs will never know," Sam said. "I feel kind of sorry for him."

"I feel sorry for her," I said.

"Yeah. Me, too."

As we walked down the passageway back toward my compartment, curiosity got the better of me.

"Sam," I asked, "what if you weren't sure that I'd keep her message to myself? What if you thought I'd sneak off to Humphries and tell him what was on that chip?"

He glanced up at me. "I've never killed a man," he said quietly, "but I'd sure stuff you into a lifeboat and set you adrift. With no radio."

I blinked at him. He was dead serious.

"I wouldn't last long," I said.

"Probably not. Your ship would drift through the Belt for a long time, though. Eons. You'd be a real Flying Dutchman."

"I'm glad you trust me."

"I'm glad I can trust you, Gar." He gave me a funny look, then added, "You're in love with her, too, aren't you?"

It took me a few moments to reply, "Who wouldn't be?"

●   ●   ●

So we flew to "The Rememberer" with Judge Myers and all the wedding guests and the minister and boys' choir, the caterers and all the food and drink for a huge celebration. Six different news nets were waiting for us: The wedding was going to be a major story.

Sam snuck away, of course. He didn't marry Jill Myers after all. She was so furious that she . . .

But that's another story.

While the Grand Tour novels are set on other worlds, for the most part, the driving force behind these stories comes from what is happening on Earth. Here is a tale of one fairly ordinary man, driven to extraordinary deeds — literally driven off the Earth, in order to help save the world.

MONSTER SLAYER

his is the way the legend began.

He was called Harry Twelvetoes because, like all the men in his family, he was born with six toes on each foot. The white doctor who worked at the clinic on the reservation said the extra toes should be removed right away, so his parents allowed the whites to cut the toes off, even though his great-uncle Cloud Eagle pointed out that Harry's father, and his father's fathers as far back as anyone could remember, had gone through life perfectly well with twelve toes on their feet.

His secret tribal name, of course, was something that no white was ever told. Even in his wildest drunken sprees Harry never spoke it. The truth is, he was embarrassed by it. For the family had named him Monster Slayer, a heavy burden to lay across the shoulders of a little boy, or even the strong young man he grew up to be.

On the day that the white laws said he was old enough to take a job, his great-uncle Cloud Eagle told him to leave the reservation and seek his path in the world beyond.

"Why should I leave?" Harry asked his great-uncle.

Cloud Eagle closed his sad eyes for a moment, then said to Harry, "Look around you, nephew."

Harry looked and saw the tribal lands as he had always seen them, brown desert dotted with mesquite and cactus, steep bluffs worn and furrowed as great-uncle's face, turquoise blue sky and blazing Father Sun baking the land. Yet there was no denying that the land was changing. Off in the distance stood the green fields of the new farms and the tiny dark shapes of the square houses the whites were building. And there were gray rain clouds rising over the mountains.

Refugees were pouring into the high desert. The greenhouse warming that gutted the farms of the whites with drought also brought rains that were filling the dry arroyos of the tribal lands. The desert would be gone one day, the white scientists predicted, turned green and bountiful. So the whites were moving into the reservation.

"This land has been ours since the time of First Man and First Woman," Great-uncle said. "But now the whites are swarming in. There is no stopping them. Soon there will be no place of our own left to us. Go. Find your way in the world beyond. It is your destiny."

Reluctantly, Harry left the reservation and his family.

In the noisy, hurried world of the whites jobs were easy to find, but good jobs were not. With so many cities flooded by the greenhouse warming, they were frantically building new housing, whole new villages and towns. Harry got a job with a construction firm in Colorado, where the government was putting up huge tracts of developments for the hordes of refugees from the drowned coastal cities. He started as a lowly laborer, but soon enough worked himself up to a pretty handy worker, a jack-of-all-trades.

He drank most of his pay, although he always sent some of it back to his parents.

One cold, blustery morning, when Harry's head was thundering so badly from a hangover that even the icy wind felt good to him, his supervisor called him over to her heated hut.

"You're gonna kill yourself with this drinking, Harry," said the supervisor, not unkindly.

Harry said nothing. He simply looked past the supervisor's ear at the calendar tacked to the corkboard. The picture showed San Francisco the way it looked before the floods and the rioting.

"You listening to me?" the supervisor asked, more sharply. "This morning you nearly ran the backhoe into the excavation pit, for chrissake."

"I stopped in plenty time," Harry mumbled.

The supervisor just shook her head and told Harry to get back to work. Harry knew from the hard expression on the woman's face that his days with this crew were numbered.

Sure enough, at the shape-up a few mornings later the super took Harry aside and said, "Harry, you Indians have a reputation for being good at high steel work."

Harry's head was thundering again. He drank as much as any two men, but he had enough pride to show up on the job no matter how bad he felt. Can't slay monsters laying in bed, he would tell himself, forcing himself to his feet and out to work. Besides, no work, no money. And no money, no beer. No whiskey. No girls who danced on your lap or stripped off their clothes to the rhythm of synthesizer music.

Harry knew that it was the Mohawks back East who were once famous for their steelwork on skyscrapers, but he said nothing to the supervisor except, "That's what I heard, too."

"Must be in your blood, huh?" said the super, squinting at Harry from under her hard hat.

Harry nodded, even though it made his head feel as if some old medicine man was inside there thumping on a drum.

"I got a cousin who needs high steel workers," the super told him. "Over in Greater Denver. He's willing to train newbies. Interested?"

Harry shuffled his feet a little. It was really cold, this early in the morning.

"Well?" the super demanded. "You interested or not?"

"I guess I'm interested," Harry said. It was better than getting fired outright.

As he left the construction site, with the name and number of the super's cousin in his cold-numbed fist, he could hear a few of the other workers snickering.

"There goes old Twelvetoes."

"He'll need all twelve to hold onto those girders up in the wind."

They started making bets on how soon Harry would kill himself.

But Harry became a very good high steel worker, scrambling along the steel girders that formed the skeletons of the new high-rise towers. He cut down on the drinking: Alcohol and altitude didn't mix. He traveled from Greater Denver to Las Vegas and all the way down to Texas, where the Gulf of Mexico had swallowed up Galveston and half of Houston.

When he'd been a little boy, his great-uncle had often told Harry that he was destined to do great things. "What great things?" Harry would ask. "You'll see," his great-uncle would say. "You'll know when you find it."

"But what is it?" Harry would insist. "What great things will I do?"

Cloud Eagle replied, "Every man has his own right path, Harry. When you find yours, your life will be in harmony and you'll achieve greatness."

Before he left his childhood home to find his way in the world, his great-uncle gave him a totem, a tiny black carving of a spider.

"The spider has wisdom," he told Harry. "Listen to the wisdom of the spider whenever you have a problem."

Harry shrugged and stuffed the little piece of obsidian into the pocket of his jeans. Then he took the bus that led out of the reservation.

As a grown, hard-fisted man, Harry hardly ever thought of those silly ideas. He didn't have time to think about them when he was working fifty, sixty, seventy stories high with nothing between him and the ground except thin air that blew in gusts strong enough to knock a man off his feet if he wasn't careful.

He didn't think about his great-uncle's prophecy when he went roaring through the bars and girlie joints on the weekends. He didn't think about anything when he got so drunk that he fell down and slept like a dead man.

But he kept the spider totem. More than once his pockets had been emptied while he slept in a drunken stupor, but no one ever took the spider from him.

And sometimes the spider did speak to him. It usually happened when he was good and drunk. In a thin, scratchy voice the spider would say, "No more drinking tonight, Harry. You've had enough. Sleep all through tomorrow, be ready for work on Monday."

Most of the time he listened to the totem's whispers. Sometimes he didn't, and those times almost always worked out badly. Like the time in New Houston when three Japanese engineers beat the hell out of him in the alley behind the cat house. They didn't rob him, though. And when Harry came to, in a mess of his own blood and vomit and garbage, the spider was wise enough to refrain from saying, "I told you not to get them angry."

He bounced from job to job, always learning new tricks of the trades, never finding the true path that would bring him peace and harmony. The days blurred into an unending sameness: crawl out of bed, clamber along the girders of a new high-rise, wait for the end of the week. The nights were a blur, too: beer, booze, women he hardly ever saw more than once.

Now and then Harry wondered where he was going. "There's more to life than this," the spider whispered to him in his sleep. "Yeah, sure," Harry whispered back. "But what? How do I find it?"

One night, while Harry was working on the big Atlanta Renewal Project, the high steel crew threw a going-away party for Jesse Ali, the best welder in the gang.

"So where's Jesse going?" Harry asked a buddy, beer in hand.

The buddy took a swig of his own beer, then laughed. "He's got a good job, Harry. Great job. It's out of this world." Then he laughed as if he'd made a joke.

"But where is it? Are they hiring?"

"Go ask him," the buddy said.

Harry wormed his way through the gang clustered at the bar and finally made it to Jesse's side.

"Gonna miss you, Jess," he said. Shouted, actually, over the noise of the raucous crowd.

Ali smiled brightly. "Christ, Harry, that's the longest sentence you ever said to me, man."

Harry looked down at the steel-tipped toes of his brogans. He had never been much for conversation, and his curiosity about Jesse's new job was butting its head against his natural reticence. But the spider in his pocket whispered, "Ask him. Don't be afraid. Ask him."

Harry summoned up his courage. "Where you goin'?"

Ali's grin got wider. He pointed a long skinny finger straight up in the air.

Harry said nothing, but the puzzlement must have shown clearly on his face.

"In space, man," Ali explained. "They're building a great big habitat in orbit. Miles long. It'll take years to finish. I'll be able to retire by the time the job's done."

Harry digested that information. "It'll take that long?"

The black man laughed. "Naw. But the pay's that good."

"They lookin' for people?"

With a nod, Ali said, "Yeah. You hafta go through a couple months' training first. Half pay."

"Okay."

"No beer up there, Harry. No gravity, either. I don't think you'd like it."

"Maybe," said Harry.

"No bars. No strip joints."

"They got women, though, don't they?"

"Like Yablonski," said Ali, naming one of the crew who was tougher than any two of the guys.

Harry nodded. "I seen worse."

Ali threw his head back and roared with laughter. Harry drifted away, had a few more beers, then walked slowly through the magnolia-scented evening back to the barracks where most of the construction crew was housed.

Before he drifted to sleep the spider urged him, "Go apply for the job. What do you have to lose?"

It was tough, every step of the way. The woman behind the desk where Harry applied for a position with the space construction outfit clearly didn't like him. She frowned at him and she scowled at her computer screen when his dossier came up. But she passed him on to a man who sat in a private cubicle and had pictures of his wife and kids pinned to the partitions.

"We are an equal opportunity employer," he said, with a brittle smile on his face.

Then he waited for Harry to say something. But Harry didn't know what he should say, so he remained silent.

The man's smile faded. "You'll be living for months at a time in zero gravity, you know," he said. "It affects your bones, your heart. You might not be fit to work again when you return to Earth."

Harry just shrugged, thinking that these whites were trying to scare him.

They put him through a whole day of physical examinations. Then two days of tests. Not like tests in school; they were interested in his physical stamina and his knowledge of welding and construction techniques.

They hired Harry, after warning him that he had to endure two months of training at half the pay he would start making if he finished the training okay. Half pay was still a little more than Harry was making on the Atlanta Renewal Project. He signed on the dotted line.

So Harry flew to Hunstville, Alabama, in a company tiltrotor plane. They gave him a private room, all to himself, in a seedy-looking six-story apartment building on the edge of what had once been a big base for the space agency, before the government sold it off to private interests.

His training was intense. Like being in the army, almost, although all Harry knew about being in the army was what he'd heard from other construction workers. The deal was, they told you something only once. You either got it or you flunked out. No second chances.

"Up there in orbit," the instructors would hammer home, time and again, "there won't be a second chance. You screw up, you're dead. And probably a lot of other people get killed, too."

Harry began to understand why there was no beer up there. Nor was there any at the training center. He missed it, missed the comfort of a night out with the gang, missed the laughs and the eventual oblivion where nobody could bother him and everything was dark and quiet and peaceful and even the spider kept silent.

The first time they put him in the water tank Harry nearly freaked. It was *deep*, like maybe as deep as his apartment building was high. He was zipped into a white space suit, like a mummy with a bubble helmet on top, and there were three or four guys swimming around him in trunks and scuba gear. But to a man who grew up in the desert, this much water was scary.

"We use the buoyancy tank to simulate the microgravity you'll experience in orbit," the instructor told the class. "You will practice construction techniques in the tank."

As he sank into the water for the first time, almost petrified with fear, the spider told Harry, "This is an ordeal you must pass. Be brave. Show no fear."

For days on end Harry suited up and sank into the deep, clear water to work on make-believe pieces of the structure he'd be building up in space. Each day started with fear, but he battled against it and tried to do the work they wanted him to do. The fear never went away, but Harry completed every task they gave him.

When his two months of training ended, the man in charge of the operation called Harry into his office. He was an Asian of some sort: Chinese, Japanese, maybe Korean.

"To tell you the truth, Harry," he said, "I didn't think you'd make it. You have a reputation for being a carouser, you know."

Harry said nothing. The pictures on the man's wall, behind his desk, were all of rockets taking off on pillars of flame and smoke.

The man broke into a reluctant smile. "But you passed every test we threw at you." He got to his feet and stretched his hand out over his desk. "Congratulations, Harry. You're one of us now."

Harry took his proffered hand. He left the office feeling pretty good about himself. He thought about going off the base and finding a nice friendly bar someplace. But as he dug his hand into his pants pocket and felt the obsidian spider there, he decided against it. That night, as he was drowsing off to sleep, the spider told him, "Now you face the biggest test of all."

Launching off the Earth was like nothing Harry had ever even dreamed of. The Clippership rocket was a squat cone; its shape reminded Harry of a big teepee made of gleaming metal. Inside, the circular passenger compartment was decked out like an airliner's, with six short rows of padded reclinable chairs, each of them occupied by a worker riding up to orbit. There was even a pair of flight attendants, one man and one woman.

As he clicked the safety harness over his shoulders and lap, Harry expected they would be blasted off the ground like a bullet fired from a thirty-aught. It wasn't that bad, though in some ways it was worse. The rockets lit off with a roar that rattled Harry deep inside his bones. He felt pressed down into his seat while the land outside the little round window three seats away tilted and then seemed to fly away.

The roaring and rattling wouldn't stop. For the flash of a moment Harry wondered if this was the demon he was supposed to slay, a dragon made of metal and plastic with the fiery breath of its rockets pushing it off the Earth.

And then it all ended. The noise and shaking suddenly cut off and Harry felt his stomach drop away. For an instant Harry felt himself falling, dropping off into nothingness. Then he took a breath and saw that his arms had floated up from the seat's armrests. Zero-gee. The instructors always called it microgravity, but to Harry it was zero-gee. And it felt good.

At the school they had tried to scare him about zero-gee with stories of how you get sick and heave and get so dizzy you can't move your head without feeling like it's going to burst. Harry didn't feel any of that. He felt as if he were floating in the water tank again, but this was better, much better. There wasn't any water. He couldn't help grinning. This is great, he said to himself.

But not everybody felt so good. Looking around, Harry saw plenty of gray faces, even green. Somebody behind him was gagging. Then somebody upchucked. The smell made Harry queasy. Another passenger retched, up front. Then another. It was like a contagious bug, the sound and stench was getting to everyone in the passenger compartment. Harry took the retch bag from the seat pocket in front of him and held it over his mouth and nose. Its cold sterile smell was better than the reek of vomit that was filling the compartment. There was nothing Harry could do about the noise except to tell himself that these were whites who were so weak. He wasn't going to sink to their level.

"You'll get used to it," the male flight attendant said, grinning at them from up at the front of the compartment. "It might take a day or so, but you'll get accustomed to zero-gee."

Harry was already accustomed to it. The smell, though, was something else. The flight attendants turned up the air blowers and handed out fresh retch bags, floating through the aisles as if they were swimming in air. Harry noticed they had filters in their nostrils; that's how they handle the stink, he thought.

He couldn't see much of anything as the ship approached the construction site, although he felt the slight thump when they docked. The flight attendants had told everybody to stay in their seats and keep buckled in until they gave the word that it was okay to get up. Harry waited quietly and watched his arms floating a good five centimeters off the armrests of his chair. It took a conscious effort to force them down onto the rests.

When they finally told everybody to get up, Harry clicked the release on his harness and pushed to his feet. And sailed right up into the overhead, banging his head with a thump. Everybody laughed. Harry did, too, to hide his embarrassment.

He didn't really see the construction site for three whole days. They shuffled the newcomers through a windowless access tunnel, then down a long sloping corridor and into what looked like a processing center, where clerks checked in each new arrival and assigned them to living quarters. Harry saw that there were no chairs anywhere in sight. Tables and desks were chest-high, and everybody stood up, with their feet in little loops that were fastened to the floor. That's how they keep from banging their heads on the ceiling, Harry figured.

Their living quarters were about the size of anemic telephone booths, little more than a closet with a mesh sleeping bag tacked to one wall.

"We sleep standing up?" Harry asked the guy who was showing them the facilities.

The guy smirked at him. "Standing up, on your head, sideways, or inside-out. Makes no difference in zero-gee."

Harry nodded. I should have known that, he said to himself. They told us about it back at the training base.

Three days of orientation, learning how to move and walk and eat and even crap in zero-gee. Harry thought that maybe the bosses were also using the three days to see who got accustomed to zero-gee well enough to be allowed to work, and who they'd have to send home.

Harry loved zero-gee. He got a kick out of propelling himself down a corridor like a human torpedo, just flicking his fingertips against the walls every few meters as he sailed along. He never got dizzy, never got disoriented. The food tasted pretty bland, but he hadn't come up here for the food. He laughed the first time he sat on the toilet and realized he had to buckle up the seat belt or he'd take off like a slow, lumbering rocket.

He slept okay, except he kept waking up every hour or so. The second day, during the routine medical exam, the doc asked him if he found it uncomfortable to sleep with a headband. Before Harry could answer, though, the doctor said, "Oh, that's right. You're probably used to wearing a headband, aren't you?"

Harry grunted. When he got back to his cubicle he checked out the orientation video on the computer built into the compartment's wall. The headband was to keep your head from nodding back and forth in your sleep. In microgravity, the video explained, blood pumping through the arteries in your neck made your head bob up and down while you slept, unless you attached the headband to the wall. Harry slept through the night from then on.

Their crew supervisor was a pugnacious little Irishman with thinning red hair and fire in his eyes. After their three days' orientation, he called the dozen newcomers to a big metal-walled enclosure with a high ceiling ribbed with steel girders. The place looked like an empty airplane hangar to Harry.

"You know many people have killed themselves on this project so far?" he snarled at the assembled newbies.

"Eighteen," he answered his own question. "Eighteen assholes who didn't follow procedures. Dead. One of them took four other guys with him."

Nobody said a word. They just stood in front of the super with their feet secured by floor loops, weaving slightly like long grasses in a gentle breeze.

"You know how many of *my* crew have killed themselves?" he demanded. "None. Zip. Zero. And you know why? I'll tell you. Because I'll rip the lungs out of any jerkoff asshole who goes one millionth of a millimeter off the authorized procedures."

Harry thought the guy was pretty small for such tough talk, but what the hell, he's just trying to scare us.

"There's a right way and a wrong way to do anything," the super went on, his face getting splotchy red. "The right way is what I tell you. Anything else is wrong. Anything! Got that?"

A couple of people replied with "Yes, sir," and "Got it." Most just mumbled. Harry said nothing.

"You," the super snapped, pointing at Harry. "Twelvetoes. You got that?"

"I got it," Harry muttered.

"I didn't hear you."

Harry tapped his temple lightly. "It's all right here, chief."

The supervisor glared at him. Harry stood his ground, quiet and impassive. But inwardly he was asking the spider, "Is this the monster I'm gonna slay?"

The spider did not answer.

"All right," the super said at last. "Time for you rookies to see what you're in for."

He led the twelve of them, bobbing like corks in water, out of the hangar and down a long, narrow, tubular corridor. To Harry it seemed more like a tunnel, except that the floor and curving walls were made of what looked like smooth, polished aluminum. Maybe not. He put out a hand and brushed his fingertips against the surface. Feels more like plastic than metal, Harry thought.

"Okay, stop here," said the super.

Stopping was easier said than done, in zero-gee. People bumped into one another and jostled around a bit while the super hovered at the head of the group, hands on hips, and glowered at them. Harry, back near the end of the queue, managed to brush against one of the better-looking women, a Hispanic with big dark eyes and a well-rounded figure.

"Sorry," he muttered to her.

"*Da nada,*" she replied, with a smile that might have been shy. Harry read the name tag pinned above her left breast pocket: Marta Santos.

"All right now," the super called to them, tugging a palmcomp from the hip pocket of his coveralls. "Take a look."

He pecked at the handheld, and suddenly the opaque tube became as transparent as glass. Everybody gasped.

They were hanging in the middle of a gigantic spiderwork of curving metal girders, like being inside a dirigible's frame, except that the girders went on and on for miles. And beyond it Harry saw the immense curving bulk of Earth, deep blue gleaming ocean, brighter than the purest turquoise, and streams of clouds so white it hurt his eyes to look at them. He blinked, then looked again. He saw long rows of waves flowing across the ocean, and the cloud-etched edge of land, with gray wrinkles of mountains off in the distance. Beyond the flank of the curving world and its thin glowing skin of air was the utterly black emptiness of space.

We're in space! Harry realized. He had known it, in his head, but now he felt it in his guts, where reality lived. I'm in space, he said to himself, lost in the wonder of it. I'm no longer on Earth.

Abruptly the tunnel walls went opaque again. The view shut off. An audible sigh of disappointment gusted through the crew.

"That's enough for now," the super said, with a grin that was somewhere between smug and nasty. "Tomorrow you clowns go out there and start earning your pay."

Harry licked his lips in anticipation.

The suits were a pain. The one thing they couldn't prepare you for on Earth was working inside the goddamned space suits. Not even the water tank could simulate the zero pressure of vacuum. The suit's torso, arms, and leggings were hard-shell cermet, but the joints and the gloves had to be flexible, which meant they were made of fabric, which meant they ballooned and got stiff, tough to flex and move when you went out-side. The gloves were especially stubborn. They had tiny little servomo-tors on the back that were supposed to amplify your natural muscle power and help you move the fingers. Sometimes that helped, but when it came to handling tools it was mostly a waste of time.

Harry got used to the clunky gloves, and the new-car smell of his suit. He never quite got used to hanging in the middle of nothing, sur-rounded by the growing framework of the miles-long habitat with the huge and glowing Earth spread out before his eyes. Sometimes he thought it was below him, sometimes it seemed as if it was hanging overhead. Either way, Harry could gawk at it like a hungry kid looking through a restaurant window, watching it, fascinated, as it slid past, ever-changing, a whole world passing in panoramic review before his staring eyes.

"Stop your goofin', Twelvetoes, and get back to work!" The super's voice grated in Harry's helmet earphones.

Harry grinned sheepishly and nodded inside his helmet. It was awfully easy to get lost in wonder, watching the world turn.

They worked a six-day week. There was no alcohol in the habitat, not even on Sundays. There was a cafeteria, and the crews socialized there. Everybody complained about the soggy sandwiches and bland fruit juices that the food and drink machines dispensed. You didn't have to put money into them; their internal computers docked your pay auto-matically.

Harry was scanning the menu of available dishes, wishing they'd bring up somebody who knew how to cook with spices, when a woman suggested, "Try the chicken soup. It's not bad."

She introduced herself: Liza Goldman, from the engineering office. She was slightly taller than Harry, on the skinny side, he thought. But she looked pretty when she smiled. Light brown hair piled up on top of her head. She and Harry carried their trays to one of the chest-high tables. Harry took a swig from the squeeze bulb of soup. It was lukewarm.

Goldman chattered away as if they were old friends. At first Harry wondered why she had picked him to share a meal with, but pretty soon he was enjoying her company enough to try to make conversation. It wasn't easy. Small talk was not one of his skills.

"You'd think they'd be able to keep the hot foods hot," Goldman was saying, "and the cold foods cold. Instead, once they're in the dispensers they all go blah. Entropy, I guess."

Harry wrinkled his brow and heard himself ask, "You know what I wonder about?"

"No. What?"

"How come they got food dispensers and automated systems for life support and computers all over the place, but they still need us construction jocks?"

Goldman's brows rose. "To build the habitat. What else?"

"I mean, why don't they have automated machines to do the construction work? Why do we hafta go outside and do it? They could have machines doin' it, couldn't they?"

She smiled at him. "I suppose."

"Like, they have rovers exploring Mars, don't they? All automated. The scientists run them from their station in orbit around Mars, don't they?"

"Teleoperated, yes."

"Then why do they need guys like me up here?"

Goldman gave him a long, thoughtful look. "Because, Harry, you're cheaper than teleoperated equipment."

Harry was surprised. "Cheaper?"

"Sure. You construction people are a lot cheaper than developing teleoperated machinery. And more flexible."

"Not in those damned suits," Harry grumbled.

With an understanding laugh, Goldman said, "Harry, if they spent the money to develop teleoperated equipment, they'd still have to bring people up here to run the machines. And more people to fix them when they break down. You guys are cheaper."

Harry needed to think about that.

Goldman invited him to her quarters. She had an actual room to herself; not a big room, but there was a stand-up desk and a closet with a folding door and a smart screen along one wall and even a sink of her own. Harry saw that her sleeping mesh was pinned to the ceiling. The mesh would stretch enough to accommodate two, he figured.

"What do you miss most, up here?" Goldman asked him.

Without thinking, Harry said, "Beer."

Her eyes went wide with surprise for a moment, then she threw her head back and laughed heartily. Harry realized that he had given her the wrong answer.

She unpinned her hair and it spread out like a fan, floating weightlessly.

"I don't have beer, Harry, but I've got something just as good. Maybe better."

"Yeah?"

Goldman slid back the closet door and unzipped a faux leather bag hanging inside. She glided back to Harry and held out one hand. He saw there were two gelatin capsules in her palm.

"The guys in the chem lab cook this up," she said. "It's better than beer."

Harry hesitated. He was on-shift in the morning.

"No side effects," Goldman coaxed. "No hangover. It's just a recreational compound. There's no law against it."

He looked into her tawny eyes. She was offering a lot more than a high.

Her smile turned slightly malicious. "I thought you Native Americans were into peyote and junk like that."

Thinking he'd rather have a beer, Harry took the capsule and swallowed it. As it turned out, they didn't need the sleeping bag. They floated in the middle of the room, bumping into a wall now and then, but who the hell cared?

The next morning Harry felt fine, better than he had in months. He was grinning and humming to himself as he suited up for work.

Then he noticed the super was suiting up, too, a couple of spaces down the bench.

Catching Harry's puzzled look, the super grumbled, "Mitsuo called in sick. I'm goin' out with you."

It was a long, difficult shift, especially with the super dogging him every half-second:

"Be careful with those beams, hotshot! Just 'cause they don't weigh anything doesn't mean they can't squash you like a bug."

Harry nodded inside his helmet and wrestled the big, weightless girder into place so the welders could start on it while the supervisor went into a long harangue about the fact that zero-gee didn't erase a girder's mass.

"You let it bang into you and you'll get crushed just like you would down on Earth."

He went on like that for the whole shift. Harry tried to tune him out, wishing he had the powers of meditation that his great-uncle had talked about, back home. But it was impossible to escape the super's screechy voice yammering in his helmet earphones. Little by little, though, Harry began to realize that the super was trying to educate him, trying to teach him how to survive in zero-gee, giving him tips that the training manuals never mentioned.

Instead of ignoring the little man's insistent voice, Harry started to listen. Hard. The guy knew a lot more about this work than Harry did, and Harry decided he might as well learn if the super was willing to teach.

By the time they went back inside and began to worm themselves out of the spacesuits, Harry was grinning broadly.

The super scowled at him. "What's so funny?"

Peeling off his sweat-soaked thermal undergarment, Harry shook his head. "Not funny. Just happy."

"Happy? You sure don't smell happy!"

Harry laughed. "Neither do you, chief."

The super grumbled something too low for Harry to catch.

"Thanks, chief," Harry said.

"For what?"

"For all that stuff you were telling me out there. Thanks."

For once, the supervisor was speechless.

Days and weeks blurred into months of endless drudgery. Harry worked six days each week, the monotony of handling the big girders broken only by the never-ending thrill of watching the always-changing Earth sliding along below. Now and then the super would give him another impromptu lecture, but once they were inside again the super never socialized with Harry, nor with any of his crew.

"I don't make friends with the lunks who work for me," he explained gruffly. "I don't want to be your friend. I'm your boss."

Harry thought it over and decided the little guy was right. Most of the others on the crew were counting the days until their contracts were fulfilled and they could go back to Earth and never see the super again. Harry was toying with the idea of signing up for another tour when this one was finished. There was still plenty of work to do on the habitat, and there was talk of other habitats being started.

He spent some of his evenings with Goldman, more of them with the chemists who cooked up the recreational drugs. Goldman had spoken straight: The capsules were better than beer, a great high with no hangovers, no sickness.

He didn't notice that he was actually craving the stuff, at first. Several months went by before Harry realized his insides got jumpy if he went a few days without popping a pill. And the highs seemed flatter. He started taking two at a time and felt better.

Then the morning came when his guts were so fluttery he wondered if he could crawl out of his sleeping bag. His hands shook noticeably. He called in sick.

"Yeah, the same thing happened to me," Goldman said that evening, as they had dinner in her room. "I had to go to the infirmary and get my system cleaned out."

"They do that?" Harry asked, surprised.

She tilted her head slightly. "They're not supposed to. The regulations say they should report drug use, and the user has to be sent back Earthside for treatment."

He looked at her. "But they didn't send you back."

"No," said Goldman. "The guy I went to kept it quiet and treated me off the record."

Harry could tell from the look on her face that the treatment wasn't for free.

"I don't have anything to pay him with," he said.

Goldman said, "That's okay, Harry. I'll pay him. I got you into this shit, I'll help you get off it."

Harry shook his head. "I can't do that."

"I don't mind," she said. "He's not a bad lay."

"I can't do it."

She grasped both his ears and looked at him so closely that their noses touched. "Harry, sooner or later you'll have to do something. It doesn't get better all by itself. Addiction always gets worse."

He shook his head again. "I'll beat it on my own."

He stayed away from the pills for nearly a whole week. By the fifth day, though, his supervisor ordered him to go to the infirmary.

"I'm not going to let you kill yourself out there," the super snarled at him. "Or anybody else, either."

"But they'll send me back Earthside," Harry said. Pleaded, really.

"They ought to shoot you out of a mother-humping cannon," the super growled.

"I'll beat it. Give me a chance."

"The way your hands are shaking? The way your eyes look? You think I'm crazy?"

"Please," Harry begged. It was the hardest word he had ever spoken in his whole life.

The super stared at him, his face splotchy red with anger, his eyes smoldering. At last he said, "You work alone. You kill yourself, that's your problem, but I'm not going to let you kill anybody else."

"Okay," Harry agreed.

"And if you don't start shaping up damned soon, you're finished. Understand?"

"Yeah, but—"

"No buts. You shape up or I'll fire your ass back to Earth so fast they'll hear the sonic boom on Mars."

So Harry got all the solo jobs: setting up packages of tools at the sites where the crew would be working next; hauling emergency tanks of oxygen; plugging in electronics boards in a new section after the crew finished putting it together; spraying heat-reflecting paint on slabs of the habitat's outer skin. He worked slowly, methodically, because his hands were shaking most of the time and his vision went blurry now and then. He fought for control of his own body inside the confines of his space suit, which didn't smell like a new car anymore; it smelled of sweat and piss and teeth-gritting agony.

He spent his nights alone, too, in his closet-sized quarters, fighting the need to down a few pills. Just a few. A couple, even; that's all I need. Maybe just one would do it. Just one, for tonight. Just to get me through the night. I'll be banging my head against the wall if I don't get something to help me.

But the spider would tell him, "Fight the monster, Harry. Nobody said it would be easy. Fight it."

The rest of the crew gave him odd looks in the mornings when he showed up for work. Harry thought it was because he looked so lousy, but finally one of the women asked him why the super was picking on him.

"Pickin' on me?" Harry echoed, truly nonplussed.

"He's giving you all the shit jobs, Twelvetoes."

Harry couldn't explain it to her. "I don't mind," he said, trying to make it sound cheerful.

She shook her head. "You're the only Native American on the crew and you're being kept separate from the rest of us, every shift. You should complain to the committee—"

"I got no complaints," Harry said firmly.

"Then I'll bring it up," she flared.

"Don't do me any favors."

After that he was truly isolated. None of the crew would talk to him. They think I'm a coward, Harry said to himself. They think I'm letting the super shit on me.

He accepted their disdain. I've earned it, I guess, he told the spider. The spider agreed.

When the accident happened, Harry was literally a mile away. The crew was working on the habitat's endcap assembly, where the curving girders came together and had to be welded precisely in place. The supervisor had Harry installing the big, thin, flexible sheets of honeycomb metal that served as a protective shield against micrometeoroid hits. Thin as they were, the bumpers would still adsorb the impact of a pebble-sized meteoroid and keep it from puncturing the habitat's skin.

Harry heard yelling in his helmet earphones, then a high-pitched scream. He spun himself around and pushed off as far as his tether would allow. Nothing seemed amiss as far as he could see along the immense curving flank of the habitat. But voices were hollering on the intercom frequency, several at the same time.

Suddenly the earphones went dead silent. Then the controller's voice, pitched high with tension: "EMERGENCY. THIS IS AN EMERGENCY. ALL OUTSIDE PERSONNEL PROCEED TO ENDCAP IMMEDIATELY. REPEAT. EMERGENCY AT ENDCAP."

The endcap, Harry knew, was where the rest of the crew was working.

Without hesitation, without even thinking about it, Harry pulled himself along his tether until he was at the cleat where it was fastened. He unclipped it and started dashing along the habitat's skin, flicking his gloved fingers from one handhold to the next, his legs stretched out behind him, batting along the curving flank of the massive structure like a silver barracuda.

Voices erupted in his earphones again, but after a few seconds somebody inside cut off the intercom frequency. Probably the controller, Harry thought. As he flew along he stabbed at the keyboard on the wrist of his suit to switch to the crew's exclusive frequency. The super warned them never to use that frequency unless he told them to, but this was an emergency.

Sure enough, he heard the super's voice rasping, "I'm suiting up; I'll be out there in a few minutes. By the numbers, report in."

As he listened to the others counting off, the shakes suddenly turned Harry's insides to burning acid. He fought back the urge to retch, squeezed his eyes tight shut, clamped his teeth together so hard his jaws hurt. His bowels rumbled. Don't let me crap in the suit! he prayed. He missed a handhold and nearly soared out of reach of the next one, but he righted himself and kept racing toward the scene of the accident, whatever it was, blind with pain and fear. When his turn on the roll call came he gasped out, "Twelvetoes, on my way to endcap."

"Harry! You stay out of this!" the super roared. "We got enough trouble here already!"

Harry shuddered inside his suit and obediently slowed his pace along the handholds. He had to blink several times to clear up his vision, and then he saw, off in the distance, what had happened.

The flitter that was carrying the endcap girders must have misfired its rocket thruster. Girders were strewn all over the place, some of them jammed into the skeleton of the endcap's unfinished structure, others spinning in slow motion out and away from the habitat. Harry couldn't see the flitter itself; probably it was jammed inside the mess of girders sticking out where the endcap was supposed to be.

Edging closer hand over hand, Harry began to count the spacesuited figures of his crew, some floating inertly at the ends of their tethers, either unconscious or hurt or maybe dead. Four, five. Others were clinging to the smashed-up pile of girders. Seven, eight. Then he saw one spinning away from the habitat, its tether gone, tumbling head over heels into empty space.

Harry clambered along the handholds to a spot where he had delivered emergency oxygen tanks a few days earlier. Fighting down the bile burning in his gut, he yanked one of the tanks loose and straddled it with his legs. The tumbling, flailing figure was dwindling fast, outlined against a spiral sweep of gray clouds spread across the ocean below. A tropical storm, Harry realized. He could even see its eye, almost in the middle of the swirl.

Monster storm, he thought as he opened the oxy tank's valve and went jetting after the drifting figure. But instead of flying straight and true, the tank started spinning wildly, whirling around like an insane pinwheel. Harry hung on like a cowboy clinging to a bucking bronco.

The earphones were absolutely silent, nothing but a background hiss. Harry guessed that the super had blanked all their outgoing calls, keeping the frequency available for himself to give orders. He tried to talk to the super, but he was speaking into a dead microphone.

He's cut me off. He doesn't want me in this, Harry realized.

Then the earphones erupted. "Who the hell is that? Harry, you shithead, is that you? Get your ass back here!"

Harry really wanted to, but he couldn't. He was clinging as hard as he could to the whirling oxy tank, his eyes squeezed shut again. The bile was burning up his throat. When he opened his eyes he saw that he was riding the spinning tank into the eye of the monster storm down on Earth.

He gagged. Then retched. Dry heaves, hot acid bile spattering against the inside of his bubble helmet. Death'll be easy after this, Harry thought.

The space-suited figure of the other worker was closer, though. Close enough to grab, almost. Desperately, Harry fired a few quick squirts of the oxygen, trying to stop his own spinning or at least slow it down some.

It didn't help much, but then he rammed into the other worker and grabbed with both hands. The oxygen tank almost slipped out from between his legs, but Harry clamped hard onto it. His life depended on it. His, and the other guy's.

"Harry? Is that you?"

It was Marta Santos, Harry saw, looking into her helmet. With their helmets touching, Harry could hear her trembling voice, shocked and scared.

"We're going to die, aren't we?"

He had to swallow down acid before he could say, "Hold on."

She clung to him as if they were racing a Harley through heavy traffic. Harry fumbled with the oxy tank's nozzle, trying to get them moving back toward the habitat. At his back the mammoth tropical storm swirled and pulsated like a thing alive, beckoning to Harry, trying to pull him down into its spinning heart.

"For chrissake," the super's voice screeched, "how long does it take to get a rescue flitter going? I got four injured people here and two more streakin' out to friggin' Costa Rica!"

Harry couldn't be certain, but it seemed that the habitat was getting larger. Maybe we're getting closer to it, he thought. At least we're heading in the right direction. I think.

He couldn't really control the oxygen tank. Every time he opened the valve for another squirt of gas the damned tank started spinning wildly. Harry heard Marta sobbing as she clung to him. The habitat was whirling around, from Harry's point of view, but it was getting closer.

"Whattaya mean it'll take another ten minutes?" the super's voice snarled. "You're supposed to be a rescue vehicle. Get out there and rescue them!"

Whoever was talking to the super, Harry couldn't hear it. The supervisor had blocked out everything except his own outgoing calls.

"By the time you shitheads get into your friggin' suits my guys'll be dead!" the super shrieked. Harry wished he could turn off the radio altogether but to do that he'd have to let go of the tank and if he did *that* he'd probably go flying off the tank completely. So he held on and listened to the super screaming at the rescue team.

The habitat was definitely getting closer. Harry could see space-suited figures floating near the endcap and the big mess of girders jammed into the skeletal structure there. Some of the girders were still floating loose, tumbling slowly end over end like enormous throwing sticks.

"Harry!"

Marta's shriek of warning came too late. Harry turned his head inside the fishbowl helmet and saw one of those big, massive girders looming off to his left, slightly behind him, swinging down on him like a giant tree falling.

Automatically, Harry opened the oxy tank valve again. It was the only thing he could think to do as the ponderous steel girder swung down on him like the arm of an avenging god. He felt the tank spurt briefly, then the shadow of the girder blotted out everything and Marta was screaming behind him and then he could feel his leg crush like a berry bursting between his teeth and the pain hit so hard that he felt like he was being roasted alive and he had one last glimpse of the mammoth storm down on Earth before everything went black.

When Harry woke he was pretty sure he was dead. But if this was the next world, he slowly realized, it smells an awful lot like a hospital. Then he heard the faint, regular beeps of monitors and saw that he was in a hospital, or at least the habitat's infirmary. Must be the infirmary, Harry decided, once he recognized that he was floating without support, tethered only by a light cord tied around his waist.

And his left leg was gone.

His leg ended halfway down the thigh. Just a bandaged stump there. His right leg was heavily bandaged, too, but it was all there, down to his toes.

Harry Sixtoes now, he said to himself. For the first time since his mother had died he felt like crying. But he didn't. He felt like screaming or pounding the walls. But he didn't do that, either. He just lay there, floating in the middle of the antiseptic white cubicle, and listened to the beeping of the monitors that were keeping watch over him.

He drifted into sleep, and when he awoke the supervisor was standing beside him, feet encased in the floor loops, his wiry body bobbing slightly, the expression on his face grim.

Harry blinked several times. "Hi, chief."

"That was a damned fool thing you did," the super said quietly.

"Yeah. Guess so."

"You saved Marta's life. The frickin' rescue team took half an hour to get outside. She'd a' been gone by then."

"My leg . . ."

The super shook his head. "Mashed to a pulp. No way to save it."

Harry let out a long, weary breath.

"They got therapies back Earthside," the super said. "Stem cells and stuff. Maybe they can grow the leg back again."

"Workman's insurance cover that?"

The super didn't answer for a moment. Then, "We'll take up a collection for you, Harry. I'll raise whatever it takes."

"No," Harry said. "No charity."

"It's not charity, it's—"

"Besides, a guy doesn't need his legs up here. I can get around just as well without it."

"You can't stay here!"

"Why not?" Harry said. "I can still work. I don't need the leg."

"Company rules," the super mumbled.

Harry was about to say, "Fuck the company rules." Instead, he heard himself say, "Change 'em."

The super stared at him.

Hours after the supervisor left, a young doctor in a white jacket came into Harry's cubicle.

"We did a routine tox screen on your blood sample," he said.

Harry said nothing. He knew what was coming.

"You had some pretty fancy stuff in you," said the doctor, smiling.

"Guess so."

The doctor pursed his lips, as if he were trying to come to a decision. At last he said, "Your blood-work report is going to get lost, Harry. We'll detox you here before we release you. All off the record."

That's when it hit Harry.

"You're Liza's friend."

"I'm not doing this for Liza. I'm doing it for you. You're a hero, Harry. You saved a life."

"Then I can stay?" Harry asked hopefully.

"Nobody's going to throw you out because of drugs," said the doctor. "And if you can prove you can still work, even with only one leg, I'll recommend you be allowed to stay."

And the legend began. One-legged Harry Twelvetoes. He never returned to Earth. When the habitat was finished, he joined a new crew that worked on the next habitat. And he started working on a dream, as well. As the years turned into decades and the legend of Harry Twelvetoes spread all across the orbital construction sites, even out to the cities that were being built on the Moon, Harry worked on his dream until it started to come true.

He lived long enough to see the start of construction for a habitat for his own people, a man-man world where his tribe could live in their own way, in their own desert environment, safe from encroachment, free to live as they chose to live.

He buried his great-uncle there, and the tribal elders named the habitat after him: Cloud Eagle.

Harry never quite figured out what the monster was that he was supposed to slay. But he knew he had somehow found his path, and he lived a long life in harmony with the great world around him. When his great-grandchildren laid him to rest beside Cloud Eagle, he was at peace.

And his legend lived long after him.

This is one of my earliest short stories, written in the mid-1960s, when the Cold War between the United States and Soviet Russia was at its most dangerous.

Strictly speaking, the "historical" background of this story does not match the general background of the Grand Tour, but Chet Kinsman's struggle to carry a fellow astronaut to safety gives a realistic picture, I believe, of what it's like to travel across the barren, airless surface of the Moon.

And some emotional kick, as well.

FIFTEEN MILES

Sen. Anderson: Does that mean that man's mobility on the moon will be severely limited?
Mr. Webb: Yes, sir; it is going to be severely limited, Mr. Chairman. The moon is a rather hostile place.

U.S. Senate Hearings on National Space Goals
August 23, 1965

A ny word from him yet?"
"Huh? No, nothing."
Kinsman swore to himself as he stood on the open platform of the little lunar rocket-jumper.
"Say, where are you now?" The astronomer's voice sounded gritty with static in Kinsman's helmet earphones.
"Up on the rim. He must've gone inside the damned crater."
"The rim? How'd you get—"
"Found a flat spot for the jumper. Don't think I walked this far, do you? I'm not as nutty as the priest."
"But you're supposed to stay down here on the plain! The crater's off limits!"
"Tell it to our holy friar. He's the one who marched up here. I'm just following the seismic rigs he's been planting every three-four miles."
He could sense Bok shaking his head. "Kinsman, if there're twenty officially approved ways to do a job, I swear you'll pick the twenty-second."
"If the first twenty-one are lousy."
"You're not going inside the crater, are you? It's too risky."
Kinsman almost laughed. "You think sitting in that aluminum casket of ours is *safe?*"

The earphones went silent. With a scowl, Kinsman wished for the tenth time in the past hour that he could scratch his twelve-day beard. Get zipped up in the suit and the itches start. He didn't need a mirror to know that his face was haggard, sleepless, and his black beard was mean-looking.

He stepped down from the jumper—a rocket motor with a railed platform and some equipment on it, nothing more—and planted his boots on the dust-covered rock of the ringwall's crest. With a twist of his shoulders to settle the weight of the spacesuit's bulky backpack, he shambled over to the packet of seismic instruments and fluorescent marker that the priest had left there.

"He came right up to the top and now he's off on the yellow brick road, playing moon explorer. Stupid bastard."

Reluctantly, he looked into the mammoth crater Alphonsus. The brutally short horizon cut across its middle, but the central peak stuck its worn head up among the solemn stars. Beyond it was nothing but dizzying blackness, an abrupt end to the solid world and the beginning of infinity.

Damn the priest! God's gift to geology . . . and I've got to play guardian angel for him.

"Any sign of him?"

Kinsman turned back and looked outward from the crater, across the broad dark basalt plain of the Mare Nubium. The Sea of Clouds, he thought. There hasn't been a cloud or a drop of water here in four billion years or more. He could see the lighted radio mast and their squat return rocket, far below on the plain. He even convinced himself he could see the mound of rubble marking their buried base shelter, where Bok lay curled safely in his bunk. It was two days before sunrise, but the Earthlight lit the plain well enough.

"Sure," Kinsman answered. "He left me a big map with an X to mark the treasure."

"Don't get sore at me!"

"Why not? You're sitting inside. I've got to find our fearless geologist."

"Regulations say one man's got to be in the base at all times."

But not the same one man, Kinsman flashed silently.

"Anyway," Bok went on, "he's got a few hours' oxygen left. Let him putter around inside the crater for a while. He'll come back."

"Not before his air runs out. Besides, he's officially missing. Missed two check-in calls. I'm supposed to scout his last known position. Another of those sweet regs."

Silence again. Bok didn't like being alone in the base, Kinsman knew.

"Why don't you come on back," the astronomer's voice returned, "until he calls in. Then you can get him with the jumper. You'll be running out of air yourself before you can find him inside the crater."

"I'm supposed to try."

"But why? You sure don't think much of him. You've been tripping all over yourself trying to stay clear of him when he's inside the base."

Kinsman suddenly shuddered. It shows! If you're not careful you'll tip them both off.

Aloud, he said, "I'm going to look around. Give me an hour. Better call Earthside and tell them what's going on. Stay in the shelter until I come back." Or until the relief crew shows up.

"You're wasting your time. And taking an unnecessary chance."

"Wish me luck," Kinsman answered.

"Good luck. I'll sit tight here."

Despite himself, Kinsman grinned. Shutting off the radio, he said to himself, "I know damned well you'll sit tight. Two scientific adventurers. One goes over the hill and the other stays in his bunk two weeks straight."

He gazed out at the bleak landscape, surrounded by starry emptiness. Something caught at his memory.

"They can't scare me with their empty spaces," he muttered. There was more to the verse but he couldn't recall it.

"Can't scare me," he repeated softly, shuffling to the inner rim. He walked very carefully and tried, from inside the cumbersome helmet, to see exactly where he was placing his feet.

The barren slopes fell gently away in terraced steps until, more than half a mile below, they melted into the crater floor. Looks easy . . . too easy. With a shrug that was weighted down by the space suit, Kinsman started to descend into the crater.

He picked his way across the gravelly terraces and crawled, booted feet first, down the breaks between them. The dust-covered rocks were slippery, although sometimes sharp. Kinsman went slowly, step by step, careful not to puncture the aluminized fabric of his suit.

His world was cut off now by the dark rocks. The only sounds he knew were the creakings of the suit's joints, the electrical hum of its pump motor, the faint whir of the helmet's air blower, and his own labored breathing. Alone, all alone. A solitary microcosm. One living creature in the one universe.

> They cannot scare me with their empty spaces
> Between stars — on stars where no human race is.

There was still more to it: the tag line that he couldn't remember.

Finally he had to stop. The suit was heating up too much from his exertion. He took a marker beacon from the backpack and planted it on the broken ground. The Moon's soil, churned by meteorites and whipped into a frozen froth, had an unfinished look to it, as though somebody had been black-topping the place but stopped before he could apply the final smoothing touches.

From a pouch on his belt Kinsman took a small spool of wire. Plugging one end into the radio outlet on his helmet, he held the spool at arm's length and released the catch. He couldn't see it in the dim light, but he felt the spring fire the wire antenna a hundred yards or so upward and out into the crater.

"Father Lemoyne," he called as the antenna drifted in the moon's easy gravity. "Father Lemoyne, can you hear me? This is Kinsman."

No answer.

Okay. Down another flight.

After two more stops and nearly an hour of sweaty descent, Kinsman got his answer.

"Here . . . I'm here . . ."

"Where?" Kinsman snapped. "Do something. Make a light."

". . . can't . . ." The voice faded out.

Kinsman reeled in the antenna and fired it out again. "Where in hell are you?"

A cough, with pain behind it. "Shouldn't have done it. Disobeyed. And no water. Nothing."

Great! Kinsman frowned. He's either hysterical or delirious. Or both.

After firing the spool antenna again, Kinsman flicked on the lamp atop his helmet and looked at the radio direction-finder dial on his forearm. The priest had his suit radio open and the carrier beam was coming through even though he was not talking. The gauges alongside the direction-finder reminded Kinsman that he was almost halfway down on his oxygen, and more than an hour had elapsed since he had spoken to Bok.

"I'm trying to zero in on you," Kinsman said. "Are you hurt? Can you—"

"Don't, don't, don't. I disobeyed and now I've got to pay for it. Don't trap yourself too . . ." The heavy, reproachful voice lapsed into a mumble that Kinsman couldn't understand.

Trapped. Kinsman could picture it. The priest was using a canister-suit: a one-man walking cabin, a big, plexidomed rigid can with flexible arms and legs sticking out of it. You could live in it for days at a time—but it was too clumsy for climbing. Which is why the crater was off limits.

He must've fallen and now he's stuck.

"The sin of pride," he heard the priest babbling. "God forgive us our pride. I wanted to find water, the greatest discovery a man can make on the moon . . . . Pride, nothing but pride . . ."

Kinsman walked slowly, shifting his eyes from the direction-finder to the roiled, pocked ground underfoot. He jumped across an eight-foot drop between terraces. The finder's needle snapped to zero.

"Your radio still on?"

"No use . . . go back . . ."

The needle stayed fixed. Either I busted it or I'm right on top of him.

He turned full circle, scanning the rough ground as far as his light could reach. No sign of the canister. Kinsman stepped to the terrace edge. Kneeling with deliberate care, so that his backpack wouldn't unbalance him and send him sprawling down the tumbled rocks, he peered over.

In a zigzag fissure a few yards below him was the priest, a giant, armored insect gleaming white in the glare of the lamp, feebly waving its one free arm.

"Can you get up?" Kinsman saw that all the weight of the cumbersome suit was on the pinned arm. Banged up his backpack, too.

The priest was mumbling again. It sounded like Latin.

"Can you get up?" Kinsman repeated.

"Trying to find the secrets of natural creation . . . storming heaven with rockets. . . . We say we're seeking knowledge, but what we're really after is our own glory."

Kinsman frowned. He couldn't make out the older man's face behind the canister's heavily tinted dome.

"I'll have to get the jumper down here."

The priest rambled on, coughing spasmodically. Kinsman started back across the terrace.

"Pride leads to death," he heard in his earphones. "You know that, Kinsman. It's pride that makes us murderers."

The shock boggled Kinsman's knees. He turned, trembling. "What . . . did you say?"

"It's hidden. The water's here, hidden . . . frozen in fissures. Strike the rock and bring forth water . . . like Moses. Not even God himself was going to hide this secret from me."

"What did you say," Kinsman whispered, completely cold inside, "about murder?"

"I know you, Kinsman . . . anger and pride. . . . Destroy not my soul with men of blood . . . whose right hands are . . . are . . ."

Kinsman ran away. He fought back toward the crater's rim, storming the rock terraces blindly, scrabbling up inclines with twelve-foot-high jumps. Twice he had to turn up the air blower in his helmet to clear away the sweaty fog from his faceplate. He didn't dare stop. He raced on, breath racking his lungs, heart pounding until he could hear nothing else.

But in his mind he still saw those savage few minutes in orbit, when he had been with the Air Force, when he became a killer. He had won a medal for the secret mission, a medal and a conscience that never slept.

Finally he reached the crest. Collapsing on the deck of the jumper, he forced himself to breathe normally again, forced himself to sound normal as he called Bok.

The astronomer said guardedly, "It sounds as though he's dying."

"I think his regenerator's shot. His air must be pretty foul by now."

"No sense going back for him, I guess."

Kinsman hesitated. "Maybe I can get the jumper down close to him." *He found out about me!*

"You'll never get him back in time. And you're not supposed to take the jumper near the crater, let alone inside it. It's too dangerous."

"You want to just let him die?" *He's hysterical. If he babbles about me where Bok can hear it . . .*

"Listen," said the astronomer, his voice rising, "you can't leave me stuck here with both of you gone! I know the regulations, Kinsman. You're not allowed to risk yourself or the third man on the team in an effort to help a man in trouble."

"I know. I know." But it wouldn't look right for me to start minding regulations now. Even Bok doesn't expect me to.

"You don't have enough oxygen in your suit to get down there and back again," Bok insisted.

"I can tap some from the jumper's propellant tank."

"But that's crazy! You'll get yourself stranded!"

"Maybe." It's an Air Force secret. No discharge; just transferred to the space agency. If they find out about it now I'll be finished. Everybody'll know. No place to hide . . . newspapers, TV, everybody!

"You're going to kill yourself over that priest. And you'll be killing me, too!"

"He's probably dead by now," Kinsman said. "I'll just put a marker beacon there so another crew can get him when the time comes. I won't be long."

"But the regulations!"

"They were written Earthside. The brass never planned on something like this. I've got to go back, just to make sure."

He flew the jumper back down the crater's terraced inner slope, leaning over the platform railing to look for his marker beacons as well as listening to their tinny radio beeping. His radio link with Bok was cut off now that he was inside the crater. In a few minutes he was easing the spraddle-legged platform down on the last terrace before the helpless priest.

"Father Lemoyne."

Kinsman stepped off the jumper and made it to the edge of the fissure in four lunar strides. The white shell was inert, the lone arm unmoving.

"Father Lemoyne!"

Kinsman held his breath and listened. Nothing . . . wait . . . the faintest, faintest breathing noise. More like gasping. Quick, shallow, desperate.

"You're dead," Kinsman heard himself mutter. "Give it up. You're finished. Even if I could get you out of there, you'd be dead before I could get you back to the base."

The plastic dome atop the suit was opaque to him; he only saw the reflected spot of his own helmet lamp. But his mind filled with the shocked face he once saw in another visor, a face that had just realized it was dead.

He looked away, out to the too-close horizon and the uncompromising stars beyond. Then he remembered the rest of it.

> They cannot scare me with their empty spaces
> Between stars—on stars where no human race is.
> I have it in me so much nearer home
> To scare myself with my own desert places.

Like an automaton Kinsman turned back to the jumper. His mind was blank now. Without thought, without even feeling, he rigged a line from the jumper's tiny winch to the metal lugs protruding from the canister-suit's chest. Then he took apart the platform railing and wedged three rejoined sections into the fissure above the fallen man, to form a hoisting angle. Looping the line over the projecting arm, he started the winch.

He climbed down into the fissure and set himself as solidly as he could on the scoured-smooth rock. He grabbed the priest's armored shoulders and guided the oversized canister up from the crevice while the winch strained silently.

The railing arm gave way when the priest was only partway up and Kinsman felt the full weight of the monstrous suit crush down on him. He sank to his knees, gritting his teeth to keep from crying out.

Then the winch took up the slack. Grunting, fumbling, pushing, Kinsman scrabbled up the rocky slope with his arms wrapped halfway around the big canister's middle. He let the winch drag them both to the jumper's edge, then reached out an arm almost numb from exertion and shut the motor.

With only a hard breath's pause, Kinsman snapped down the suit's supporting legs so the priest could stay upright even though unconscious. Then he clambered onto the platform and took the oxygen line from the rocket engine's tankage. Kneeling at the bulbous suit's shoulders, he plugged the line into the priest's emergency air tank.

The older man coughed once. That was all.

Kinsman leaned back on his heels. His faceplate was fogging over again, or was it fatigue blurring his sight?

The regenerator was hopelessly smashed, he saw. The old bird must've been breathing his own juices. When the emergency tank registered full, he disconnected the oxygen line and plugged into the special fitting below the regenerator.

"If you're dead, this is probably going to kill me, too," Kinsman said. He purged the entire suit, forcing the contaminated fumes out and replacing them with oxygen that the jumper's rocket needed to get them back to the base.

He was close enough now to see through the canister's tinted dome. The priest's face was grizzled, eyes closed. Its usual smile was gone; the mouth hung open limply.

Kinsman hauled him up onto the railless platform and strapped him down onto the deck. Then he went to the control podium and inched the throttle forward just enough to give them the barest minimum of life.

The jumper almost made it to the crest before its rocket engine died and bumped them gently on one of the terraces. There was a small emergency tank of oxygen that could have carried them a little farther, Kinsman knew. But he and the priest would need it for breathing.

"Wonder how many Jesuits have been carried home on their shields?" he asked himself as he unbolted the section of decking that the priest was lying on. By threading the winch line through the bolt holes he made a sort of sled, which he carefully lowered to the ground. Then he took down the emergency oxygen tank and strapped it to the deck section, too.

Kinsman wrapped the line around his fists and leaned against the burden. Even in the moon's light gravity it was like trying to haul a truck.

"Down to less than one horsepower," he grunted, straining forward.

For once he was glad that the rocks had been scoured smooth by micrometeors. He would climb a few steps, wedge himself as firmly as he could, then drag the sled up to him. It took a painful half-hour to reach the ringwall crest.

He could see the base again, tiny and remote as a dream. "All downhill from here," he mumbled.

He thought he heard a groan.

"That's it," he said, pushing the sled over the crest, down the gentle outward slope. "That's it. Stay with it. Don't you die on me. Don't you put me through this for nothing."

"Kinsman!" Bok's voice. "Are you all right?"

The sled skidded against a yard-high rock. Scrambling after it, Kinsman answered, "I'm bringing him in. Just shut up and leave us alone. I think he's alive. Now stop wasting my breath."

Pull it free. Push to get it started downhill again. Strain to hold it back . . . don't let it get away from you. Haul it out of craterlets. Watch your step, don't fall.

"Too damned much uphill in this downhill."

Once he sprawled flat and knocked his helmet against the edge of the improvised sled. He must have blacked out for a moment. Weakly, he dragged himself up to the oxygen tank and refilled his suit's supply. Then he checked the priest's suit and topped off his tank.

"Can't do that again," he said to the silent priest. "Don't know if we'll make it. Maybe we can. If neither one of us has sprung a leak. Maybe . . ."

Time slid away from him. The past and future dissolved into an endless now, a forever of pain and struggle, with the heat of his toil welling up in Kinsman drenchingly.

"Why don't you say something?" Kinsman panted at the priest. "You can't die. Understand me? You can't die! I've got to explain it to you. . . . I didn't mean to kill her. I didn't even know she was a woman. You can't tell, can't even see a face until you're too close. She must've been just as scared as I was. She tried to kill me. I was inspecting their satellite . . . how'd I know their cosmonaut was just a scared kid? I could've pushed her off, didn't have to kill her. But the first thing I knew I was ripping her air line open. I didn't know she was a woman, not until it was too late. It doesn't make any difference, but I didn't know. I didn't know."

They reached the foot of the ringwall and Kinsman dropped to his knees. "Couple more miles now . . . straightaway . . . only a couple more . . . miles." His vision blurred and something in his head was buzzing angrily.

Staggering to his feet, he lifted the line over his shoulder and slogged ahead. He could just make out the lighted tip of the base's radio mast.

"Leave him, Chet," Bok's voice pleaded from somewhere. "You can't make it unless you leave him."

"Shut . . . up."

One step after another. Don't think, don't count. Blank your mind. Be a mindless plow horse. Plod along. One step at a time. Steer for the radio mast. . . . Just a few . . . more . . . miles.

"Don't die on me. Don't you . . . die on me. You're my ticket back. Don't die on me, priest . . . don't die . . ."

It all went dark. First in spots, then totally. Kinsman caught a glimpse of the barren landscape tilting weirdly, then the grave stars slid across his field of view, then darkness.

"I tried," he heard himself say in a far, far distant voice. "I tried."

For a heartbeat or two he felt himself falling, dropping effortlessly into blackness. Then even that sensation died and he felt nothing at all.

A faint vibration buzzed at him. The darkness started to shift, turn gray at the edges. Kinsman opened his eyes and saw the low, curved ceiling of the underground base. The noise was the electrical machinery that lit and warmed and pumped good air through the tight little shelter.

"You okay?" Bok leaned over him, his chubby face frowning with worry.

Kinsman weakly nodded.

"Father Lemoyne's going to pull through," Bok said, stepping out of the cramped space between bunks. The priest was awake but unmoving, his eyes staring blankly upward. His canister suit had been removed and one arm was covered with a plastic cast.

Bok explained, "I've been getting instructions from the medics Earthside. They're sending a team up on a high-g burn, should be here in another thirty hours. He's in shock, and his arm's broken. Otherwise he seems pretty good . . . exhausted, but no permanent damage."

Kinsman pulled himself up to a sitting position on the bunk and leaned his back against the curving metal wall. His helmet and boots were off, but he was still wearing the rest of his space suit.

"You went out and got us," he realized.

Bok nodded. "You were less than a mile away. I could hear you on the radio. Then you stopped talking. I had to go out."

"You saved my life."

"And you saved the priest's."

Kinsman stopped a moment, remembering. "I did a lot of raving out there, didn't I?"

"Uh . . . yeah."

"Any of it intelligible?"

Bok wormed his shoulders uncomfortably. "Sort of. It's, uh . . . it all went back to Houston, you know. All radio conversations. It's automatic. Nothing I could do about it."

That's it. Now everybody knows.

"You haven't heard the best of it," Bok said, trying to brighten up. He went to the shelf at the end of the priest's bunk and took a little plastic container. "Look at this."

Kinsman took the container in both his hands. Inside was a tiny fragment of ice, half melted into water.

"It was stuck in the cleats of one of his boots. It's really water! Tests out okay. I even snuck a taste of it. It's water all right."

"He found it after all," Kinsman said. "He'll get into the history books now." And he'll have to watch his pride even more.

Bok sank into the shelter's only chair. "Chet, about what you said out there . . ."

Kinsman expected tension, but instead felt only numb. "I know. They heard it Earthside."

"There've been rumors about an Air Force guy killing a cosmonaut during one of the military missions, but I never thought . . . I mean . . ."

"The priest figured it out," said Kinsman. "Or at least he guessed it."

"It must've been rough on you."

"Not as rough as what happened to her."

"What'll they do about you?"

Kinsman shrugged. "I don't know. It might get out to the media. Somebody'll leak it. Probably I'll be grounded. Unstable. It could get nasty."

"I'm . . . sorry." Bok's voice trailed off helplessly.

"It doesn't matter."

Surprised, Kinsman realized that he meant it. He sat up straight. "It doesn't matter anymore. They can do whatever they want to. I can handle it. Even if they ground me and throw me to the news media . . . I think I can deal with it. I did it, and it's over with, and I can take whatever I have to take."

Father Lemoyne's free arm moved slightly. "It's all right," he whispered hoarsely. "It's all right. I thought we were in hell, but it was only purgatory."

The priest turned his face toward Kinsman. His gaze moved from the astronaut's eyes to the plastic container still in Kinsman's hands. "It's all right," he repeated, smiling. Then he closed his eyes and relaxed into sleep. But the smile remained, strangely gentle in that bearded, haggard face, ready to meet the world or eternity.

This excerpt from my novel Mars *was originally written as an independent short story. Its protagonist is Jamie Waterman, the Navaho-Yankee geologist who is striving to be picked for the first human expedition to the red planet.*

It's an incredibly tough competition, trying to be the one person out of all the geologists on Earth to win that coveted appointment. Jamie—and all the other Mars hopefuls—must face all kinds of physical and psychological tests, from desert survival trials to stints in Antarctica to mandatory appendectomies.

Even after he's on the inside track for the Mars expedition there are hurdles he must overcome. As here, in the search for Muzhestvo.

MUZHESTVO

As they drove along the river, Yuri Zavgorodny gestured with his free hand.

"Like your New Mexico, no?" he asked in his hesitant English.

Jamie Waterman unconsciously rubbed his side. They had taken the stitches out only yesterday and the incision still felt sore.

"New Mexico," Zavgorodny repeated. "Like this? Yes?"

Jamie almost answered, "No." But the mission administrators had warned them all to be as diplomatic as possible with the Russians—and everyone else.

"Sort of," Jamie murmured.

"Yes?" asked Zavgorodny over the rush of the searing wind blowing through the car windows.

"Yes," said Jamie.

The flat brown countryside stretching out beyond the river looked nothing like New Mexico. The sky was a washed-out pale blue, the desert bleak and empty in every direction. This is an old, tired land, Jamie said to himself as he squinted against the baking hot wind. Used up. Dried out. Nothing like the vivid mountains and bold skies of his home. New Mexico was a new land, raw and magic and mystical. This dull dusty desert out here is ancient; it's been worn flat by too many armies marching across it.

"Like Mars," said one of the other Russians. His voice was a deep rumble, where Zavgorodny's was reedy, like a snake-charmer's flute. Jamie had been quickly introduced to all four of them but the only name that stuck was Zavgorodny's.

Christ, I hope Mars isn't this dull, Jamie said to himself.

Yesterday Jamie had been at Bethesda Naval Hospital, having the stitches from his appendectomy removed. All the Mars mission trainees had their appendixes taken out. Mission regulations. No sense risking an attack of appendicitis twenty million miles from the nearest hospital. Even though the decisions about who would actually go to Mars had not been made yet, everyone lost his or her appendix.

"Where are we going?" Jamie asked. "Where are you taking me?"

It was Sunday, supposedly a day of rest even for the men and women who were training to fly to Mars. Especially for a new arrival, jet-lagged and bearing a fresh scar on his belly. But the four cosmonauts had roused Jamie from his bed at the hotel and insisted that he come with them.

"Airport," said the deep-voiced cosmonaut on Jamie's left. He was jammed into the backseat, sandwiched between two of the Russians, sweaty, body odor pungent despite the sharp scent of strong soap. Two more rode up front, Zavgorodny at the wheel.

Like a gang of Mafia hit men taking me for a ride, Jamie thought. The Russians smiled at one another a lot, grinning as they talked among themselves and hiking their eyebrows significantly. Something was up. And they were not going to tell the American geologist about it until they were damned good and ready.

They were solidly built men, all four of them. Short and thickset. Like Jamie himself, although the Russians were much lighter in complexion than Jamie's half-Navaho skin.

"Is this official business?" he had asked them when they pounded on his hotel door at the crack of dawn.

"No business," Zavgorodny had replied while the other three grinned broadly. "Pleasure. Fun."

Fun for them, maybe, Jamie grumbled to himself as the car hummed along the concrete of the empty highway. The river curved off to their left. The wind carried the smell of sun-baked dust. The old town of Tyuratam and Leninsk, the new city built for the space engineers and cosmonauts, was miles behind them now.

"Why are we going to the airport?" Jamie asked.

The one on his right side laughed aloud. "For fun. You will see."

"Yes," said the one on his left. "For much fun."

Jamie had been a Mars trainee for little more than six months. This was his first trip to Russia—to Kazakhstan, really—although his schedule had already whisked him to Australia, Alaska, French Guiana, and Spain. There had been endless physical examinations, tests of his reflexes, his strength, his eyesight, his judgment. They had probed his teeth and pronounced them in excellent shape, then sliced his appendix out of him.

And now a quartet of cosmonauts he'd never met before was taking him in the early morning hours of a quiet Sunday for a drive to Outer Nowhere, Kazakhstan.

For much fun.

There had been precious little fun in the training for Mars. A lot of competition among the scientists, since only sixteen would eventually make the flight: sixteen out of more than two hundred trainees. Jamie realized that the competition must be equally fierce among the cosmonauts and astronauts.

"Have you all had your appendixes removed?" he asked.

The grins faded. The cosmonaut beside him answered, "No. Is not necessary. We do not go to Mars."

"You're not going?"

"We are instructors," Zavgorodny said over his shoulder. "We have already been turned down for the flight mission."

Jamie wanted to ask why, but he thought better of it. This was not a pleasant topic of conversation.

"Your appendix?" asked the man on his left. He ran a finger across his throat.

Jamie nodded. "They took the stitches out yesterday." He realized it had actually been Friday in Bethesda and now it was Sunday but it felt like yesterday.

"You are an American Indian?"

"Half Navaho."

"The other half?"

"Anglo," said Jamie. He saw that the word meant nothing to the Russians. "White. English."

The man sitting up front beside Zavgorodny turned to face him. "When they took out your appendix—you had a medicine man with painted face to rattle gourds over you?"

All four of the Russians burst into uproarious laughter. The car swerved on the empty highway, Zavgorodny laughed so hard.

Jamie made himself grin back at them. "No, I had anesthesia, just as you would."

The Russians chattered among themselves. Jamie got a vision of jokes about Indians, maybe about a red man wanting to go to the red planet. There was no nastiness in it, he felt, just four beer-drinking fliers having some fun with a new acquaintance.

Wish I understood Russian, he said to himself. Wish I knew what these four clowns are up to. Much fun.

Then he remembered that none of these men could even hope to get to Mars anymore. They had been relegated to the role of instructors. I've still got a chance to make the mission. Do they hold that against me? Just what in the hell are they planning to do?

Zavgorodny swung the car off the main highway and down a two-lane dirt road that paralleled a tall wire fence. Jamie could see, far in the distance, hangars and planes parked haphazardly. So we really are going to an airport, he realized.

They drove through an unguarded gate and out to a far corner of the sprawling, silent airport where a single small hangar stood all by itself, like an outcast or an afterthought. A high-wing, twin-engine plane sat on squat tricycle landing gear on the concrete apron in front of the hangar. To Jamie it looked like a Russian version of a Twin Otter, a plane he had flown in during his week's stint in Alaska's frigid Brooks Range.

"You like to fly?" Zavgorodny asked as they piled out of the car.

Jamie stretched his arms and back, glad to be no longer squeezed into the car's backseat. It was not even nine o'clock yet, but the sunshine felt hot and good as it baked into his shoulders.

"I enjoy flying," he said. "I don't have a pilot's license, though. I'm not qualified—"

Zavgorodny laughed. "Good thing! We are four pilots. That is three too many."

The four cosmonauts were already wearing one-piece flight suits of faded, well-worn tan. Jamie had pulled on a white short-sleeved knit shirt and a pair of denims when they had roused him from his hotel bed. He followed the others into the sudden cool darkness of the hangar. It smelled of machine oil and gasoline. Two of the cosmonauts went clattering up a flight of metal stairs to an office perched on the catwalk above.

Zavgorodny beckoned Jamie to a long table where a row of parachute packs sat big and lumpy, with straps spread out like the limp arms of octopi.

"We must all wear parachutes," Zavgorodny said. "Regulations."

"To fly in that?" Jamie jabbed a thumb toward the plane.

"Yes. Military plane. Regulations. Must wear chutes."

Zavgorodny picked up one of the cumbersome chute packs and handed it to Jamie like a laborer passing a sack of cement.

"Where are we flying to?" Jamie asked.

"A surprise," the Russian said. "You will see."

"Much fun," said the other cosmonaut, already buckling the groin straps of his chute.

Much fun for who? Jamie asked silently. But he worked his arms through the shoulder straps of the chute and leaned over to click the groin straps together and pull them tight.

The other two came down the metal steps, boots echoing in the nearly empty hangar. Jamie followed the quartet of cosmonauts out into the baking sunshine toward the plane. A wide metal hatch had been cut into its side. There were no stairs. When he hiked his foot up to the rim of the hatch Jamie's side twinged with pain. He grabbed the sides of the hatch and pulled himself inside the plane. Without help. Without wincing.

It was like an oven inside. Two rows of bucket seats, bare, unpadded. The two men who had been sitting in the back of the car with Jamie pushed past him and went into the cockpit. The pilot's and co-pilot's chairs were thick with padding; they looked comfortable.

Zavgorodny gestured Jamie to the seat directly behind the pilot. He sat himself in the opposite seat and pulled the safety harness across his shoulders and thighs. Jamie did the same, making certain the straps were tight. The parachute pack served as a sort of cushion, but it felt awkward to Jamie: like underwear that had gotten twisted.

One by one, the engines coughed, sputtered, then blasted into life. The plane shook like a palsied old man. As the propellers whirred to invisible blurs, Jamie heard all sorts of rattling noises, as if the plane was going to fall apart at any moment. Something creaked, something moaned horribly. The plane rolled forward.

The two pilots had clamped earphones over their heads, but if they were in contact with the control tower, Jamie could not hear a word they spoke over the roar of the engines and the wind blowing fine sandpapery dust through the cabin. The fourth cosmonaut was sitting behind Jamie. No one had shut the hatch. Twisting around in his seat, Jamie saw that there was no door for the hatch: They were going to fly with it wide open.

The gritty wind roared through as the plane gathered speed down the runway, skidding slightly first one way and then the other.

Awfully long run for a plane this size, Jamie thought. He glanced across at Zavgorodny. The Russian grinned at him.

And then they were off the ground. The sandblasting ended; the wind was clean now. Jamie saw the airport dwindling away out his window, the parked planes and buildings shrinking into toys. The land spread out, brown and dead-dry beneath the cloudless pale blue sky. The engines settled into a rumbling growl; the wind howled so loudly that Jamie had to lean across the aisle and shout into Zavgorodny's ear:

"So where are we going?"

Zavgorodny shouted back, "To find Muzhestvo."

"Moo . . . what?"

"Muzhestvo!" the cosmonaut yelled louder.

"Where is it? How far away?"

The Russian laughed. "You will see."

They climbed steadily for what seemed like an hour. Can't be more than ten thousand feet, Jamie said to himself. It was difficult to judge vertical distances, but they would have to go on oxygen if they flew much beyond ten thousand feet, he thought. It was getting cold. Jamie wished he had brought his windbreaker. They should have told me, he complained silently. They should have warned me.

The co-pilot looked back over his shoulder, staring directly at Jamie. He grinned, then put a hand over his mouth and hollered, "Hoo-hoo-hoo!" His version of an Indian war whoop. Jamie kept his face expressionless.

Suddenly the plane dipped and skidded leftward. Jamie was slammed against the curving skin of the fuselage and almost banged his head against the window. He stared out at the brown landscape beneath him, wrinkled with hills and a single sparkling lake far below, as the plane seemed to hang on its left wingtip and slowly, slowly revolve.

Then it dove and pulled upward, squeezing Jamie down into his seat. The plane climbed awkwardly, waddling in the air, then flipped over onto its back. Jamie felt all weight leave him; he was hanging by his seat harness but weighed practically nothing. It dived again and weight returned, heavy, crushing, as the plane hurtled toward those brown bare hills, engines screaming, wind whistling through the shaking, rattling cabin.

And then it leveled off, engines purring, everything as normal as a commuter flight.

Zavgorodny was staring at Jamie. The co-pilot glanced back over his shoulder. And Jamie understood. They were ragging him. He was the new kid on the block and they were seeing if they could scare him. Their own little version of the Vomit Comet, Jamie said to himself. See if they can make me turn green or get me to puke. Much fun.

Every tribe has its initiation rites, he realized. He had never been properly initiated as a Navaho; his parents had been too Anglicized to allow it. But these guys are going to make up for that.

Jamie made himself grin at Zavgorodny. "That was fun," he yelled, hoping that the other three could hear him over the engines and the wind. "I didn't know you could loop an old crate like this."

Zavgorodny bobbed his head up and down. "Not recommended. Maybe the wings come off."

Jamie shrugged inside his seat harness. "What's next?"

"Muzhestvo."

They flew peacefully for another quarter-hour or so, no aerobatics, no conversation. Jamie realized they had made one wide circling turn and were starting another. He looked out the window. The ground below was flat and empty, as desolate as Mars except for a single narrow road running straight across the brown barren wasteland.

Zavgorodny unbuckled his safety harness and stood up. He had to crouch slightly because the of the cabin's low overhead as he stepped out into the aisle and back toward the big, wide, still-open hatch.

Jamie turned in his seat and saw that the other cosmonaut was on his feet, too, and standing at the hatch.

Christ, one lurch of this crate and he'll go ass over teakettle out the door!

Zavgorodny stood beside the other Russian with one hand firmly gripping a slim metal rod that ran the length of the cabin's ceiling. They seemed to be chatting, heads close together, nodding as if they were at their favorite bar holding a casual conversation. With ten thousand feet of empty air just one step away.

Zavgorodny beckoned to Jamie with his free hand, gesturing him to come up and join them. Jamie felt a cold knot in his stomach. I don't want to go over there. I don't want to.

But he found himself unbuckling the seat harness and walking unsteadily toward the two men near the open hatch. The plane bucked slightly and Jamie grabbed that overhead rod with both fists.

"Parachute range." Zavgorodny pointed out the hatch. "We make practice jumps here."

"Today? Now?"

"Yes."

The other cosmonaut pulled a plastic helmet onto his head. He slid the tinted visor down over his eyes, yelled something in Russian, and jumped out of the plane.

Jamie gripped the overhead rod even tighter.

"Look!" Zavgorodny yelled at him, pointing. "Watch!"

Cautiously Jamie peered through the gaping hatch. The cosmonaut was falling like a stone, arms and legs outstretched, dwindling into a tiny tan dot against the deeper brown of the land so far below.

"Is much fun," Zavgorodny hollered into Jamie's ear.

Jamie shivered, not merely from the icy wind slicing through his lightweight shirt.

Zavgorodny pushed a helmet into his hands. Jamie stared at it. The plastic was scratched and pitted, its red and white colors almost completely worn off.

"I've never jumped," he said.

"We know."

"But I . . ." He wanted to say that he had just had the stitches removed from his side, that he knew you could break both your legs parachute jumping, that there was absolutely no way they were going to get him to step out of this airplane.

Yet he put the helmet on and strapped it tight under his chin.

"Is easy," Zavgorodny said. "You have done gymnastics. It is on your file. Just land with knees bent and roll over. Easy."

Jamie was shaking. The helmet felt as if it weighed three hundred pounds. His left hand was wrapped around that overhead rod in a death grip. His right was fumbling along the parachute harness straps, searching blindly for the D-ring that would release the chute.

Zavgorodny looked quite serious now. The plane was banking slightly, tilting them toward the open, yawning hole in the plane's side. Jamie planted his feet as solidly as he could, glad that he had worn a sturdy pair of boots.

The Russian took Jamie's searching right hand and placed it on the D-ring. The metal felt cold as death.

"Not to worry," Zavgorodny shouted, his voice muffled by Jamie's helmet. "I attach static line to overhead. It opens chute automatically. No problem."

"Yeah." Jamie's voice was shaky. His insides were boiling. He could feel sweat trickling down his ribs even though he felt shivering cold.

"You step out. You count to twenty. Understand? If chute has not opened by then you pull ring. Understand?"

Jamie nodded.

"I will follow behind you. If you die I will bury you." His grin returned. Jamie felt like puking.

Zavgorodny gave him a probing look. "You want to go back and sit down?"

Every atom in Jamie's being wanted to answer a fervent, "Hell yes!" But he shook his head and took a hesitant, frightened step toward the open hatch.

The Russian reached up and slid the visor over Jamie's eyes. "Count to twenty slowly. I will see you on ground in two minutes. Maybe three."

Jamie swallowed hard and let Zavgorodny position him squarely at the lip of the hatch. The ground looked iron-hard and very, very far below. They were in shadow, the overhead wing was shading them, the propeller too far forward to be any danger. Jamie took that all in with a single wild glance.

A tap on his shoulder. Jamie hesitated a heartbeat, then pushed off with both feet.

Nothing. No motion. No sound except the thrum of wind rushing past. Jamie suddenly felt that he was in a dream, just hanging in emptiness, floating, waiting to wake up safe and somehow disappointed in bed. The plane had disappeared somewhere behind and above him. The ground was miles below, revolving slowly, not getting noticeably closer.

He was spinning, turning lazily as he floated in midair. It was almost pleasant. Fun, nearly. Just hanging in nothingness, separated from the entire world, alone, totally alone and free.

It was as if he had no body, no physical existence at all. Nothing but pure spirit, clean and light as the air itself. He remembered the old legends his grandfather had told him about Navaho heroes who had traveled across the bridge of the rainbow. Must be like this, he thought, high above the world, floating, floating. Like Coyote when he hitched a ride on a comet.

He realized with a heart-stopping lurch that he had forgotten to count. And his hand had come off the D-ring. He fumbled awkwardly, seeing now that the hard baked ground was rushing up to smash him, pulverize him, kill him dead, dead, dead.

A gigantic hand grabbed him and nearly snapped his head off. He twisted in midair as new sounds erupted all around him. Like the snapping of a sail, the parachute unfolded and spread above him, leaving Jamie hanging in the straps, floating gently down toward the barren ground.

His heart was hammering in his ears, yet he felt disappointed. Like a kid who had gone through the terrors of his first roller-coaster ride and now was sad that it had ended. Far down below he could see the tiny figure of a man gathering up a dirty white parachute.

I did it! Jamie thought. I made the jump. He wanted to give out a real Indian victory whoop.

But the sober side of his mind warned: You've still got to land without breaking your ankles. Or popping that damned incision.

The ground was really rushing up now. Relax. Bend your knees. Let your legs absorb the shock.

He hit hard, rolled over twice, and then felt the hot wind tugging at his billowing chute. Suddenly Zavgorodny was at his side pulling on the cords, and the other cosmonaut was wrapping his arms around the chute itself like a man trying to get a ton of wrapping paper back inside a box.

Jamie got to his feet shakily. They helped him wriggle out of the chute harness. The plane circled lazily overhead.

"You did hokay," Zavgorodny said, smiling broadly now.

"How'd you get down so fast?" Jamie asked.

"I did free-fall, went past you. You didn't see me? I was like a rocket!"

"Yuri is free-fall champion," said the other cosmonaut, his arms filled with Jamie's parachute.

The plane was coming in to land, flaps down, engines coughing. Its wheels hit the ground and kicked up enormous plumes of dust.

"So now we go to Muzhestvo?" Jamie asked Zavgorodny.

The Russian shook his head. "We have found it already. *Muzhestvo* means in English courage. You have courage, James Waterman. I am glad."

Jamie took a deep breath. "Me, too."

"We four," Zavgorodny said, "we will not go to Mars. But some of our friends will. We will not allow anyone who does not show courage to go to Mars."

"How can you . . . ?"

"Others test you for knowledge, for health, for working with necessary equipment. We test for courage. No one without courage goes to Mars. It would make danger for our fellow cosmonauts."

"Muzhestvo," Jamie said.

Zavgorodny laughed and slapped him on the back and they started walking across the bare dusty ground toward the waiting plane.

Muzhestvo, Jamie repeated to himself. Their version of a sacred ritual. Like a Navaho purifying rite. I'm one of them now. I've proved it to them. I've proved it to myself.

Jamie Waterman returns to Mars on the second expedition to the red planet, this one financed largely by private investors who expect to see a profitable return on their money. Jamie, with the Navaho part of his mind dead set against the exploitation of this new land, is pitted against Dex Trumball, son of the man who put up most of the expedition's funding.

This excerpt from Return to Mars shows what it's like to face one of the planetary-scale dust storms that often sweep across the cold, dry, iron-rust deserts of Mars.

Despite all that technology can do for us, when we face a real challenge what is important is what's inside us: brains, heart, and guts. On the frontier they are more vital than ever.

RED SKY AT MORNING

The gentle winds wafted ghostlike across the rust red desert of Mars as they had for uncounted millions of years, hardly stirring the dusty ground. Across plains pitted by meteor craters they swirled, along deep yawning gorges, around the flanks of massive shield volcanoes and across fields of rocks strewn like the scattered toys of careless children.

Across the entire planet, nothing had changed in ages. Except for one place, on the western end of Lunae Planum, where the rocky ground begins to rise toward the great Tharsis bulge. There stood a strangely incongruous structure, a pair of plastic domes, surrounded by cleat treads of tractors and boot prints of human explorers, visitors from distant Earth.

Morning sunlight streamed through the main dome's lower sides. Above the transparent layer the dome was opaque, reinforced with foam gel to absorb the impact of stray meteoroids. After sunset even the transparent layer was darkened by a polarizing electric current, to keep the dome's interior heat from leaking out into the frigid Martian night. The frail strangers from the blue planet could not survive in the cold of the red planet's night.

"It will be lonesome around here," Stacy Dezhurova said over breakfast.

"We won't be gone that long," Dex Trumball said. "Four weeks, tops."

They were sitting around the long table in the galley: Dezhurova, Trumball, Jamie Waterman, and Possum Craig. The Russian cosmonaut seemed almost melancholy, which surprised Jamie. Usually Stacy was impassive, businesslike. She was a solid, thickset woman with a broad, chunky face and a sandy-blond pageboy that looked as if somebody had put a bowl over her head and chopped away.

"The dome will be quiet," she said, turning her glance from Trumball to Craig. "First Mitsuo and Tómas fly out to the volcano, now you two are leaving us."

Dex grinned at her. "Yeah, but when we come back we'll have the old Pathfinder hardware with us. And the little Sojourner wagon, too."

Dex was handsome, with movie-star looks: dark curly hair, lively blue-green eyes the color of a tropical sea, and a crooked little grin that hovered between self-confidence and cockiness.

Craig was just the opposite: a jowly, shaggy, good-natured bear of a former oil-field geologist with a prominent snoot and permanent five-o'clock shadow.

Jamie inwardly worried that they were biting off more than they could chew. Dex had insisted on adding this long excursion to the mission. For what? Jamie asked himself. So that they could retrieve the Pathfinder/Sojourner spacecraft and auction them off to a museum or private collector. The money people who funded the Second Martian Expedition backed the idea whole-heartedly, of course. Including Dex's father, who was the biggest money guy of them all.

Despite Jamie's misgivings, the expedition controllers had okayed Dex's plan. So now he and Craig were off on a four-week-long jaunt to Ares Vallis in the old rover they had recovered from the first expedition and refurbished with spare parts from their stores.

And they had to launch their backup fuel generator all the way out to Xanthe Terra, to the halfway point in Dex's excursion, so that he and Craig could refuel their rover on the way out and the way back again.

It's not good planning, Jamie told himself. There's no margin for error. It's not smart, not safe. And it certainly isn't good science. Dex is stealing four weeks from his geology work and Craig's . . . for what? To make money. To get glory for himself.

But there was nothing he could do about it. He had objected as strongly as he knew how. His objections were noted back on Earth. And overruled.

So the morning's work would be: First, launch the generator and land it safely in Xanthe. Second, get Dex and Craig off on their jaunt—if the generator lands safely where it's supposed to.

A big morning.

Everyone crowded into the comm center as Dezhurova made the final preparations to launch the generator. Everyone except Jamie, who suited up and went through the airlock to watch the launch with his own eyes.

He walked alone to the crest of the little ridge formed by the rim of an ancient crater. From this vantage he could see the rocket booster standing on the horizon, the fuel generator still sitting at its top, as always. But now its propellant tanks were filled with liquified methane and oxygen. Jamie could see a wisp of white vapor wafting from a vent halfway up the rocket's cylindrical body. But there was no condensation frost on the booster's skin; there simply was not enough moisture in the Martian air for that.

In his helmet earphones Jamie heard the automated countdown ticking off, "Four . . . three . . . two . . . one . . ."

A flash of light burst from the rocket's base and the booster was immediately lost in a dirty pink-gray cloud of vapor and dust. For a heartbeat Jamie thought it had exploded, but then the booster rose up through the cloud and he heard—even through his helmet—the growling roar of the rocket engines.

Higher and higher the rocket rose, swifter and swifter into the bright pink sky. Jamie bent back as far as his hard suit would allow, saw the rocket dwindle to a speck in the sky. And then it was lost to sight.

By the time he had come back through the airlock and taken off his suit, there were whoops and cheers coming from the comm center. Leaving the suit to be vacuumed later, Jamie hurried to join the crowd.

"Down . . . the . . . pipe," Dezhurova was saying. She sat hunched before a display screen, her thick-fingered hands poised over the keyboard like a concert pianist's ready to play.

But she did not touch the keys. She did not have to. The screen showed a plot of the rocket's planned descent trajectory in red, next to a plot in green of its actual course. The two lines overlapped almost completely.

"The wind is stiffer than we expected," Dezhurova said. "But *neh problemeh.*"

Vijay Shektar, the expedition doctor, was sitting beside Stacy, filling in as her assistant. The others were clustered behind the two women, huddled together like a shorthanded football team.

"Fifteen seconds to touchdown," Vijay called out.

"Looks good," Dezhurova said tightly.

"Lookin' *great,*" shouted Possum Craig.

"Ten . . . nine . . ."

"I told you the spot was clear of boulders," Dex Trumball said, to no one in particular.

Jamie saw that he was standing behind Vijay, his hand on her shoulder. He felt his nostrils flare with barely suppressed anger.

And he remembered what Vijay had told him the first night after they had landed, her almond eyes so serious, so lustrous. She always disconcerted Jamie, with her exotic dark Hindu looks and flippant, almost caustic Aussie accent. That night she had rattled him even more than usual.

"Dex is an alpha male, y'know. Just like you. You're both natural leaders. You both *have to* be top dog. It's a prescription for trouble. Maybe disaster."

Maybe disaster, Jamie thought as the countdown ticked off. Maybe I'm sending the two of them off to their deaths. And it would be my fault if it happens; not the money people who made the decision to let them go, not the expedition controllers who agreed to do it—my fault.

"Four . . . three . . . two . . . touchdown!" Vijay announced.

"She is down, safe and sound," said Dezhurova. She swivelled her chair around and swept her headset off with a flourish.

"We're set for the run out to the Sagan site," Dex crowed, beaming with satisfaction.

"Not till we check out the fuel generator, partner," Craig warned. "That contraption's gotta be perkin' right before we go traipsin' all the way out there."

"Yeah, sure," Dex replied, his triumphant grin shrinking only a little.

Within an hour they had all the data they needed. The drill had hit permafrost and the fuel generator was working just as if it had never been moved, already replenishing the booster's propellant tanks.

Trumball and Craig were suiting up; Jamie and Vijay were checking them out: Jamie with Possum, Vijay with Dex.

"Hope we can get the VR rig working right," Dex said as he lifted his helmet from its shelf. Even encased in the bulky suit he radiated excitement, practically quivering, like a kid on Christmas morning.

"Well, I'll finally get enough time to really tear her innards apart and see what th' hell's wrong with her," Craig said.

Their plan was for Possum to work on the faulty VR rig during the long hours of the trek when he was not driving the rover.

Jamie was helping him put on his suit's backpack. Craig backed into it and Jamie clicked the connecting latches shut. Then Possum stepped away from the rack on which the backpack had rested.

"Electrical connects okay?" Jamie asked.

Craig peered at the display panel on his right wrist. "All green," he reported.

"Good." Jamie plugged the air hose into Craig's neck ring.

"You're ready for your radio check," Vijay said to Trumball.

Dex slid his visor down and sealed it. Jamie could hear his muffled voice calling to Stacy Dezhurova, who was manning the communications center, as usual. After a moment he slid the visor up again and made a thumbs-up signal.

"Radio okay."

It took Craig another few minutes to get his suit sealed up and check out its radio. Trumball paced up and down restlessly. In the suit and thick-soled boots he reminded Jamie of Frankenstein's monster waiting impatiently for a bus.

"We're all set," Dex said once Craig's radio check was done. He turned toward the airlock hatch.

"Hold on a second," Jamie said.

Trumball stopped, but did not turn back to face Jamie. Craig did.

"I know you've checked out the rover from here to hell and back," Jamie said, "but I want you to remember that it's an old piece of hardware and it's been sitting out in the cold for six years."

"We know that," Trumball said to the airlock hatch.

"The first sign of trouble, I want you to turn back," Jamie instructed. "Do you understand me? The hardware you're setting out to retrieve isn't worth a man's life, no matter how much money it might bring in on Earth."

"Sure," Dex said impatiently.

"Don't worry, I ain't no hero," Craig added.

Jamie took in a deep breath. "Possum, I'm putting you in charge of this excursion. You're the boss. Dex, you follow his orders at all times. Understand?"

Now Trumball turned toward Jamie, slowly, ponderously in the cumbersome hard suit.

"What kind of bullshit is this?" he asked, his voice low and even.

"It's chain of command, Dex. Possum's older and he's had a lot more experience living out in the field than either one of us has. He's in charge. Anytime you two don't agree on something, Possum is the winner."

Trumball's face went through a whole skein of emotions within the flash of a moment. Jamie waited for an explosion.

But then Dex broke into a boyish grin. "Okay, chief. Possum's the medicine man and I'm just a lowly brave. I can live with that."

"Good," Jamie said, refusing to let Trumball see how much he hated Dex's sneering at his Navaho heritage.

Gesturing toward the hatch with a gloved hand, Trumball said to Craig, "Okay, boss, I guess you should go through the airlock first."

Craig glanced at Jamie, then pulled down his visor and clomped to the hatch.

Vijay said, "Good luck."

"Yeah, right," answered Trumball. Craig waved silently as he stepped over the sill of the open hatch.

The three of them stood in uncomfortable silence while the airlock cycled. When its panel light turned green again, Trumball opened the hatch and stepped in.

Before closing it, though, he turned back to Jamie and Vijay.

"By the way, Jamie, I didn't get a chance to say so long to my father. Would you give him a buzz and tell him I'm on my way?"

"Certainly," Jamie said, surprised at the sweet reasonableness in Trumball's voice.

The hatch slid shut. Jamie started toward the comm center, Shektar walking alongside him.

Vijay asked, "Did you have to do that?"

"What?" Jamie asked.

"Humiliate him."

"Humiliate?" Jamie felt a pang, but it wasn't surprise. It was disappointment that Vijay saw his decision this way.

"Making him officially subordinate to Possum," she went on. "That's belittling him."

Striding along the partitions that marked off the team's sleeping cubicles, Jamie said, "I didn't do it *to* Dex, I did it *for* Possum."

"Really?"

"Dex would try to steamroller Possum whenever they had a difference of opinion. This way, Possum's got the clout to make the final decisions. That might save both their lives."

"Really?" she said again.

"Yes, really."

He looked down at her. Her expression showed a great deal of disbelief.

By the time they reached the comm center, Craig and Trumball had climbed into the rover and started up its electrical generator.

"The boss is going to let me drive," Dex exclaimed, his radio voice brimming with mock delight. "Goodie, goodie."

Stacy Dezhurova went down the rover checklist with him, then cleared them for departure.

"We're off to see the Wizard," Dex said. "Be back in a month or so."

In Dezhurova's display screen Jamie saw the rover shudder to life, then lurch into motion. It rolled forward slowly at first, then turned a quarter-circle and headed off toward the east.

"Oh, Jamie," Trumball called as they trundled toward the horizon, "please don't forget to call my dad, okay?"

"You can call him yourself, right now," Jamie responded.

"No, I want to concentrate on my driving. You do it for me, huh? Please?"

Jamie said, "Sure. I'll send him a message right away."

"Thanks a lot, chief."

Jamie went to his quarters and sent a brief message Earthward, telling Darryl C. Trumball that his son was on his way to Ares Vallis and wanted him to know that everything was going well.

As he looked up from his laptop screen, he saw Stacy Dezhurova at his open doorway. She looked even moodier than she had at breakfast, almost worried.

"What's the matter, Stacy?"

The cosmonaut stepped into Jamie's cubicle but didn't take the empty desk chair. She remained standing.

With a shake of her head that made her pageboy flutter, she answered, "I can't help thinking that I should be out in that rover with them."

Jamie shut down his computer and closed its lid. "Stacy, we went over that a couple of hundred times. You can't be everyplace."

"The safety regulations say an astronaut must be on every excursion."

"I know, but this trek of Dex's is an extra task that we didn't plan on."

"Still . . ."

"Sit down," Jamie said, pointing to the desk chair. He immediately felt silly; there was no other chair in the cubicle.

She sat heavily, like a tired old woman, and Jamie leaned toward her from the edge of his bunk. "We just don't have enough people to send you along with them. You know that."

"Yes."

"And Possum's about as good as they come—for a guy who's not an astronaut."

"Yes," she said again.

"They'll be okay."

"But if something happens," she said, "I will feel responsible. It is my job to go out with the scientists and make certain they don't get themselves killed."

Jamie sat up straighter. "If something happens, it's my responsibility, not yours. I made the decision, Stacy."

"I know, but . . ." Her voice trailed off.

"Look: Tómas had to go with Mitsuo, there was no way around that. We need you here at the base. We don't have any other astronauts! What do you expect me to do, clone you?"

She let a small grin break her dour expression. "I understand. But I don't like it."

"They'll be okay. Possum's no daredevil."

"I suppose so."

Is she sore because Tómas got to fly to Olympus Mons instead of her? Jamie wondered. But she knew that's how it would be. God, we made that decision before we left Earth.

All during the weeks that Rodriguez had been test-flying the rocket plane, taking it out on jaunts that started with a simple circle around their base camp and gradually extended as far as Olympus Mons and back again, never once did Stacy ask to fly the plane. Never once did she show that she was unhappy that Tómas would be the pilot while she "flew" the comm console here at the base.

Only now was she showing how unhappy it made her. Astronauts are fliers, Jamie realized. She's a pilot and she's not being allowed to fly. He remembered how he had felt when it looked as if he would not be selected for the expedition to Mars.

Leaning closer to her, Jamie said, "Stacy, the Navaho teach that each person has to find the right path for his life. Or hers. I'm sorry that your path is keeping you on the ground while Tómas gets to fly. But there'll be other flights, other missions. You'll get into the air before we leave Mars, I promise you."

She brightened only slightly. "I know. I am being selfish. But still . . . damn! I wish it was me."

"You're too important to us right now to risk on an excursion. We need you here, Stacy. I need you here."

Dezhurova blinked with surprise. "You do?"

"I do," Jamie said.

"I didn't think of it that way."

"Find the right path, Stacy. Find the balance that brings beauty to your life."

"That is the Navaho way, eh?"

"It's the way that works."

DOSSIER: ANASTASIA DEZHUROVA

It was the Americans who called her Stacy. Her father's pet name for her was Nastasia.

Her father was a rocket engineer, a hard-working, sober, humorless man whose work took him away from their Moscow apartment for long months at a time. He travelled mostly to the mammoth launch facility in the dreary dust-brown desert of Kazakhstan and returned home tired and sour, but always with a doll or some other present for his baby daughter. Nastasia was his one joy in life.

Anastasia's mother was a concert cellist who played in the Moscow symphony, a bright and intelligent woman who learned very early in her marriage that life was more enjoyable when her husband was a thousand kilometers away. She could give parties in their apartment then; people would laugh and play music. Often one of the men would remain the night.

As Nastasia grew into awareness and understanding, her mother swore her to secrecy. "We don't want to hurt your father's feelings," she would tell her ten-year-old daughter. Later, when Nastasia was a teenager, her mother would say, "And do you think he remains faithful during all those months he's away? Men are not like that."

Nastasia discovered what men are like while she was in secondary school. One of the male students invited her to a party. On the way home, he stopped the car (his father's) and began to maul her. When Nastasia resisted, he tore her clothing and raped her.

Her mother cried with her and then called the police. The investigators made Nastasia feel as if she had committed the crime, not the boy. Her attacker was not punished and she was stigmatized. Even her father turned against her, saying that she must have given the boy the impression she was available.

When she was selected for the technical university in Novosibersk she left Moscow willingly, gladly, and buried herself in her studies. She avoided all socializing with men, and found that love and warmth and safety could be had with other women.

She also found that she was very bright, and very capable. She began to delight in beating men in areas where they thought they were supreme. She learned to fly and went on to become a cosmonaut: Not merely a cosmonaut but the first woman cosmonaut to command an orbital team of twelve men; the first woman cosmonaut to set a new endurance record for months spent aboard a space station; the first woman cosmonaut to go to Mars.

The Second Mars Expedition included two small tractors for hauling heavy loads and two larger, segmented rover vehicles for overland traverses. The rovers were externally the same as those used in the first expedition: Each was a trio of cylindrical aluminum modules, mounted on springy, loose-jointed wheels that could crawl over fair-sized rocks without upsetting the vehicle. They represented a considerable financial savings for the expedition: The cost of developing and testing them had already been absorbed by the first expedition. The second expedition merely had to buy two of them off the shelf.

One of the cylindrical modules was the fuel tank, big enough to keep the vehicle out in the field for two weeks or more. The middle segment usually held equipment and supplies, although it could be modified and pressurized to serve as a small mobile laboratory if necessary. The front segment, largest of the three, was pressurized like a spacecraft so people could live in it in their shirtsleeves. There was an airlock at its rear, where it linked with the second module. Its front end was a bulbous transparent canopy, which made the entire assembly look something like a giant metallic caterpillar.

Each rover was designed to carry four in reasonable comfort, although the entire complement of eight explorers could be squeezed into one in an emergency.

The rover that Craig and Trumball were using, however, was an old one, left abandoned by the first expedition after it had sunk into a crater filled with treacherous dust. At Dex's insistence, they had found the rover, towed it back to the base camp, and refurbished it for this trek to the Sagan site at Ares Vallis.

It was already night on the broad rolling plain of Lunae Planum, yet Possum Craig was still driving the old rover—cautiously, at a mere ten kilometers per hour. He and Dex Trumball had agreed that they could mooch out a little extra mileage after sunset, before they stopped for the night.

Trumball had the radio set to the general comm frequency, so they heard Rodriguez's and Fuchida's landing at Olympus Mons at the same time the four in the base camp did.

"Those two poor bastards gotta live in their suits until they get back to th' dome," Craig said.

"Look on the bright side, Wiley. They get to test the FES." Dex had bestowed the nickname Wiley J. Coyote on Craig during the five-month-long flight from Earth, for the older man's nearly mystical ability to fix any kind of machinery.

The hard suits had a special fitting that was supposed to make an airtight connection to the chemical toilet seat. The engineers called it the Fecal Elimination System.

"The ol' trapdoor," Craig muttered. "I bet they wind up usin' Kaopectate."

"Or getting hemorrhoids."

Craig whooped with laughter.

Sitting beside him in the cockpit, Dex added with a grin, "While we've got all the comforts of home."

Craig made a thoughtful face. "For an old clunker, this travelin' machine is doin' purty well. No complaints."

"Not yet."

Dex had spent most of the day in his hard suit. They had stopped the rover every hundred klicks for him to go outside and plant geology/meteorology beacons. Now he sat relaxed in his coveralls, watching the scant slice of ground illuminated by the rover's headlights.

"You could goose her up to twenty," Dex prodded.

"Yeah, and I could slide 'er into a crater before we had time to stop or turn away," Craig shot back. He tapped a forefinger on the digital clock display. "Time to call it a day, anyway."

"You tired already?"

"Nope, and I don't want to drive when I am tired."

"I could drive for a while," said Dex.

Pressing gently on the brake pedals, Craig said, "Let's just call it a day, buddy. We've made good time. Enough is enough."

Trumball seemed to think it over for a moment, then pulled himself out of the cockpit chair. "Okay. You're the boss."

Craig laughed. "Shore I am."

"Now, what's that supposed to mean?" Trumball asked over his shoulder as he headed back to the minuscule galley.

Craig slid the plastic heat-retaining screen across the windshield, then got up and stretched so hard that Dex could hear his tendons pop.

"It means that I'm th' boss long's you want to be agreeable."

"I'm agreeable," Dex said.

"Then ever'thing's fine and dandy."

Sliding one of the prepackaged meals from its freezer tray, Trumball said to the older man, "No, seriously, Wiley. Jamie put you in charge. I've got no bitch with that."

Still stretching, his hands scraping the curved overhead, Craig said, "Okay. Fine."

"Something bugging you?"

"Naw. Forget it."

As he put the meal tray into the microwave cooker, Dex said, "Hey, come on, Wiley. It's just you and me out here. If something's wrong, tell me about it."

Craig made a face somewhere between annoyed and sheepish. "Well, it's kinda silly, I guess."

"What is it, for chrissakes?"

With a tired puff of breath, Craig sank onto his bunk.

"Well, I'm kinda pissed about bein' a second-class citizen around here."

Trumball stared at him in amazement. "Second-class citizen?"

"Yeah, you know—they all think I'm nothin' more'n a repairman, for shit's sake."

"Well—"

"I'm a scientist, just like you and the rest of y'all," Craig grumbled. "Maybe I didn't get my degree from a big-name school, and maybe I've spent most of my time workin' for oil companies . . ." he pronounced *oil* as *awl* ". . . but I was smart enough to get picked over a lotta guys with fancier pedigrees."

"Sure you are."

"That Fuchida. Damned Jap's so uptight I think if he sneezed he'd come apart. Looks at me like I'm a servant or something."

"That's just his way."

"And the women! They act like I'm a grandfather or somethin'. Hell, I'm younger'n Jamie. I'm younger than Stacy is, did you know that?"

For the first time, Dex Trumball understood that Craig was hurting. And vulnerable. This jowly, shaggy, good-natured bear of a man with the prominent snoot and permanent five-o'clock shadow wants to be treated with some respect. That makes him usable, Dex realized.

"Listen, Wiley," Dex began, "I didn't know that we were hurting your feelings."

"Not you, so much. It's the rest of 'em. They think I'm just here to be their bleepin' repairman. Least you call me Wiley. Never did like bein' called Possum. My name's Peter J. Craig."

The microwave oven chimed. Dex ignored it and sat on his own bunk, opposite Craig's. "I'll get them to call you Wiley, then. Or Peter, if you prefer."

"Wiley is fine."

A smile crept across Trumball's face. "Okay, then. It's going to be Wiley from now on. I'll make certain that Jamie and the others get the word."

Looking embarrassed, Craig mumbled, "Kinda silly, ain't it?"

"No, no," Dex said. "If Jamie and the others are bothering you, you've got a right to complain about it."

To himself Trumball thought, If and when we get to a place where I've got to out-gun Jamie, I'll need Wiley on my side. Wiley, and as many of the others as I can round up.

DOSSIER: C. DEXTER TRUMBALL

No matter how well he did, no matter what he accomplished, Dex Trumball could never satisfy his coldly indifferent father.

Darryl C. Trumball was a self-made man, he firmly proclaimed to anyone and everyone. One of Dex's firmest memories was his father cornering a U.S. senator at a house party and tapping him on the shoulder with each and every word as he declared with quiet insistence, "I started with nothing but my bare hands and my brain, and I built a fortune for myself."

In truth, the old man had started with a meager inheritance: A decrepit auto body shop that was on the verge of bankruptcy when Dex's grandfather died of a massive stroke in the middle of his fourth beer at the neighborhood bar.

Dex had been just a baby then, an only child. His mother was pretty, frail, and ineffectual: totally unable to stand up to her hard-driving husband. Dex's father, blade-slim, fast, and agile, had attended Holy Cross on a track scholarship. He never graduated; he had to take over the family business instead. His dream of going to the Boston College Law School, as he had been promised, was shattered, leaving him bitter and resentful.

And filled with an icy, relentless energy.

Darryl C. Trumball quickly learned that business depends on politics. Although the body shop was practically worthless, the land on which it stood could become extremely valuable if it could be converted to upscale condominiums for the white-collar types who worked in Boston's financial district. He pushed feverishly to get the old neighborhood rezoned, then sold the shop and his mother's house for a sizable sum.

By the time Dex was ready for college, his father was very wealthy, and known in the financial community for his cold-blooded ruthlessness. Money was important to him, and he spent every waking hour striving to increase his net worth. When Dex expressed an interest in science, the elder Trumball snorted disdainfully: "You'll never be able to support yourself that way! Why, when I was your age I was taking care of your grandmother, your two aunts, your mother, and *you*."

Dex listened obediently and registered anyway for physics at Yale. His high school grades (and his father's money) were good enough to be acceptable to Harvard and half a dozen other Ivy League schools, but

Dex decided on Yale. New Haven was close enough to Boston for him to get home easily, yet far enough away for him to be free of his father's chilling presence.

Dex had always found school to be ridiculously easy. Where others pored over textbooks and sweated out exams, Dex breezed through with a near-photographic memory and a clever ability to tell his teachers exactly what they wanted to hear. His relationships with his peers were much the same: They did what he wanted, almost always. Dex got the brilliant ideas and his friends got into trouble carrying them out. Yet they never complained; they admired his dash and felt grateful when he noticed them at all.

Sex was equally easy for him, even on campuses electrified by charges of harassment. Dex had his pick of the women: The more intelligent they were, the more they seemed to bask in the temporary sunshine of his affection. And they never complained afterward.

Physics was not for Dex, but he found himself drawn to geophysics: the study of the Earth, its interior and its atmosphere. His grades were well-nigh perfect. He was a campus leader in everything from the school television station to the tennis team. Yet his father was never pleased.

"An educated bum, that's what you are," his father taunted. "I'll have to support you all my life and keep on supporting you even after I'm gone."

Which suited Dex just fine. But deep within, he longed to hear one approving word from his father. He ached to have the callous old man smile at him.

His life changed forever at a planetarium show. Dex liked to take his dates to the planetarium. It was cheap, it impressed young women with his seriousness and intelligence, and it was the darkest place in town. Very romantic, really, sitting in the back row with the splendors of the heavens spangled above.

One particular show was about the planet Mars. After several failures, an automated spacecraft had successfully returned actual samples of Martian rocks and soil to a laboratory in orbit around the Earth. Now there was talk of sending human explorers there. Suddenly Dex stopped fondling the young woman who had accompanied him and sat up straight in his chair.

"There's more than one planet to study!" he said aloud, eliciting a chorus of shushing hisses from around him, and the utter humiliation of his date.

Dex spent that summer at the University of Nevada, taking a special course in geology. The next summer he went to a seminar on planetary geology in Berkeley.

By the time the first expedition had returned from Mars, triumphantly bearing samples of living Martian organisms, Dex had degrees from Yale and Berkeley. He went to the struggling Moonbase settlement for six months to do fieldwork on the massive meteorites that lay buried deep beneath Mare Nubium and Mare Imbrium.

Much to his father's dismay.

"I give the government fortunes of tax money for this space stuff," the old man complained bitterly. "What damned good is it?"

Dex's father was a real-estate tycoon now, with long fingers in several New England–based banks and business interests in Europe, Asia, and Latin America. He kept in touch with his far-flung associates through satellite-relayed electronic links and even leased space in an orbital factory that manufactured ultrapure pharmaceuticals.

Dex smiled brightly for his father. "Don't be a flathead, Dad. I want to be on the next expedition to Mars."

His father stared at him coldly. "When are you going to start bringing some money *in* to this family, instead of spending it like it's water?"

Challenged, wanting to please his father and win his approval for once, Dex blurted, "We could make money from Mars."

His father was neither surprised nor stopped by the younger man's assertion. He simply asked one question: "How?"

That was when Dex began planning an expedition to Mars that would be funded by private donors. To be sure, a good deal of taxpayers' money went into the pot. But once Dex enlisted the interest and drive of his profit-oriented father, funding for the Second Martian Expedition came mainly from private sources.

Dex was determined to make the expedition profitable. He wanted his father's praise, just once. Then he could tell the old man to go bust a blood vessel and drop dead.

Jamie spent nearly an hour after dinner talking with Rodriguez and Fuchida out atop Olympus Mons. They were spending the night in their seats in the plane's cockpit. Like trying to sleep in an airliner, Jamie thought. Tourist class. In the hard suits. He did not envy them their creature comforts.

Still in the comm center, he scrolled through the messages that had accumulated through the long, eventful, draining day. It took more than another hour to deal with them: everything from a request for more VR sessions from the International Council of Science Teachers to a reminder that his mission status report for the week was due in the morning.

One message was from Darryl C. Trumball. Since it was marked PERSONAL AND CONFIDENTIAL, Jamie saved it, planning to go to his own quarters before he looked at it.

But when he finished all the other messages, he glanced up from the comm screen and saw that the dome was darkened for the night. Suddenly it seemed chilly, as if the frigid cold of the Martian night were seeping through the dome's plastic walls.

No one seemed to be about. No voices, only the background sounds of the machinery and, if he listened carefully enough, the soft sighing of the night wind outside.

So he opened Trumball's personal message.

Darryl C. Trumball's eyes were blazing, his skull-like face grim as death.

"Who in the hell gave you the authority to send my son out on this excursion to the Sagan site?" he began, furious, with no preamble.

"Goddammit to hell and back, Waterman, I specifically gave orders *not* to allow Dex out on that excursion!"

And so it went, for nearly fifteen blistering minutes. Jamie watched Trumball's angry face, flabbergasted at first, then growing angry.

But as the older man blathered on, Jamie's anger slowly dissolved. Behind Trumball's bluster, he saw a man worried about his son's safety, a man accustomed to power and authority, but totally frustrated now because there was no way he could control the men and women on Mars. No way he could control his own son.

He can't even talk to us face-to-face, Jamie knew. All he can do is rant and rave and wait to see if we respond to him.

Trumball finally wound down and finished with, "I want you to know, Waterman, that you can't countermand my orders and get away with it. You'll pay for this! And if anything happens to my son, you'll pay with your goddamned blood!"

The screen went blank. Jamie reran the whole message, then froze Trumball's angry, snarling image at its end.

Leaning back in the squeaking little wheeled chair, Jamie wondered if he should be firm or conciliatory. A soft answer may turneth away wrath, he thought, but Trumball won't be diverted that easily.

There's more involved here than a squabble between Trumball and me, he told himself. That old man is a primary force behind the funding for this expedition—and the next. If you want a smooth road for the next expedition, Jamie told himself, you've got to keep Trumball on the team.

Yet as he stared at the coldly furious image on the screen, anger simmered anew within Jamie. Trumball has no right to scream at me or anybody else like that. If he's sore at his son he should take it out on Dex, not me. And if I give him the impression that he can push me around, he'll start making more demands. He's a bully; the more I give in to him the more he'll take.

What's the best path, Grandfather? How can I do this without causing more pain?

He took a deep breath, then pressed the key that activated the computer's tiny camera. Jamie saw its red eye come on, just atop Trumball's stilled image on the screen.

"Mr. Trumball," he began slowly, "I can understand your concern for your son's safety. I had no idea you sent a message that Dex was not to go on the excursion to pick up the Pathfinder hardware. There was no such message addressed to me. And with all due respect, sir, you are not in command of this expedition. I am. You are not in a position to give orders."

Jamie looked directly into the camera's unblinking red eye and continued, "Neither Dex nor anyone else here will receive any special privileges. The idea for picking up Pathfinder was his, and he certainly wanted to go out on the excursion. Even had I known of your wishes, I'm afraid I would have had to go against them. This is Dex's job, and I'm sure he'll do it without trouble.

"He's got the best man we have along with him: Dr. Craig. If they run into any difficulties, they will return to base. I had—I have, no intention of taking foolish risks with anyone's life."

Unconsciously hunching closer to the camera, Jamie concluded, "I know that you helped to raise most of the money for this expedition, and we're all very grateful for that. But that doesn't give you the authority to make decisions about our work here. You can go to the ICU and complain to them if you want to. But frankly, I don't see what even they could do for you. We're here, more than a hundred million kilometers from Earth, and we have to make our own decisions.

"I'm sorry this particular decision has you so upset and worried. Maybe when Dex comes back with the Pathfinder and Sojourner you'll feel differently. Good night."

He tapped the keyboard twice: once to turn off the camera, the other to transmit his message to Trumball. Only then did he blank the old man's image from the screen.

"I would've told him to stick it up his arse."

Jamie wheeled around and saw Vijay leaning against the partition doorway, holding a steaming mug in both hands, as if she were trying to warm herself with it.

"How long have you been there?"

She came in and sat down beside him. "I was getting myself a cuppa when I heard Dex's dad ranting."

She was in her bulky coral-red turtleneck sweater and loose-fitting jeans instead of the usual coveralls, sitting so close to him that Jamie caught the delicate scent of the herbal tea she was drinking, sensed its warmth.

He said, "The old man must've told Dex he didn't want him going out on this excursion and Dex never informed me about it."

Vijay took a sip from the steaming mug. "Should he have?"

"It would've helped."

"Maybe he was afraid you'd nix the excursion if you knew."

Jamie shook his head. "I couldn't do that. Let somebody like Trumball think he can boss you around and you'll never hear the last of him."

She dipped her chin in agreement. "There is that."

"I just hope nothing happens while he's out there," Jamie said.

"Didn't you hope that anyway? Before Trumball's blast, I mean."

"Yeah, sure, but . . . you know what I mean."

"Yes, I suppose I do."

Jamie blurted, "You slept with him, didn't you?"

"With Dex?"

"During the flight." Jamie was shocked that he mentioned it. The words had come out before he realized what he was going to say.

Vijay nodded, her expression fathomless. "Yes. Once."

"Once," he repeated.

With an odd little smile, Vijay said, "You get to know a lot about a man when he's got his pants down."

Jamie ran out of words.

"I told you he was an alpha male," she said. "Same as you are."

He nodded glumly.

"I'm attracted to alpha males."

"So you're attracted to him."

"I was. Now I'm attracted to you."

"Me?"

She broke into a smile. "Do you see anybody else around here?"

Jamie felt off-balance. *She's teasing me. She must be teasing.*

Placing her mug on the corner of the console desk, Vijay said, "You're attracted to me, aren't you?"

"Um, sure."

She got to her feet and put her hand out to him. "So the only question remaining is, your place or mine?"

Jamie stood up slowly, not certain his legs would support him. "It's not that simple, Vijay."

She planted her hands on her hips. "My god, Jamie, you're as bad as most Aussie blokes!"

"I didn't mean—"

She stepped up to him and slid her arms around his neck. "Don't you ever feel lonely?" she whispered. "Or scared? We're so alone out here. So far from home. Doesn't it ever get to you?"

Her voice wasn't teasing now. He held her tightly and could feel her trembling. Beneath all the flip talk she was tense with anxiety.

"I don't want to be alone tonight, Jamie."

"Neither do I," he admitted at last. "Neither do I."

Pale morning sun slanted through the rover's curved windshield as Dex drove steadily across the rolling, rock-strewn plain. Each pebble and gully cast long early morning shadows. *The sunlight looks different here,* Dex thought. *Weaker, pinker . . . something.*

He and Craig had been underway for nearly an hour when Dex saw a red light suddenly glare up from the control panel.

"Hey, Wiley," he called over his shoulder. "We've got a problem here."

Craig shuffled into the cockpit and sat in the right seat, muttering, "What's this 'we,' white man?"

Dex jabbed a finger at the telltale.

"Oh-oh," said Craig.

"That doesn't sound so good, Wiley."

"Fuel cells're discharging. They shouldn't oughtta do that."

"We don't have to stop, do we?"

"Naw," said Craig. "I'll take a look."

He headed for the rear of the rover module. The fuel cells were the backup electrical system, to be used if the solar panels outside were unable to charge up the batteries that ran the rover's systems at night. The fuel cells on this old rover were powered by hydrogen and oxygen, which meant that their "waste" product was drinkable water. The fuel cells on the newer rovers ran on methane and oxygen generated from permafrost water and the Martian atmosphere.

Trumball drove on across the monotonous landscape. "Miles and miles of nothing but miles and miles," he murmured to himself. He knew he should be studying the land with a geologist's professional eye, categorizing the rock formations, watching how the sand dunes built up, checking the density of the rocks scattered everywhere, looking for craters. Instead he simply felt bored.

Precisely at the one-hour mark the timer on the panel chimed.

Dex called back to Craig, "Time to stop and plant a beacon, Wiley."

"Keep goin'," Craig said. "I'll suit up; gotta go outside anyway to check out the damned fuel cells."

Dex kept the rover trundling along while Craig struggled into his hard suit on his own. Once Craig announced he was ready, Dex stopped the vehicle and went back to check the older man's suit and backpack.

"Looks good, Wiley," he said.

"Okay," came Craig's voice, muffled by the sealed helmet. "Gimme one of the beacons."

Dex did that, and then started to tug on his own suit. Stupid flathead safety regs, he said to himself as Craig cycled through the airlock and went outside. I've gotta stand here in this tin can like some deadhead just because Wiley's outside. If anything goes wrong, he'll pop back into the airlock; he won't need me to come out and rescue him.

While Dex grumbled to himself he thought briefly about the safety regulation that required a second person to check out his suit. How the hell can you do that when the second man is already outside? he complained silently. He had no intention of going outside anyway, not unless Craig got into some unimaginable difficulty. The morphs who wrote these regulations must be the kind of guys who wear suspenders and a belt, he told himself. Old farts like Jamie.

Dex clomped back to the cockpit and sat awkwardly in the left seat. All the lights on the board were green, except the one for the fuel cells.

"How's it going, Wiley?" he called on the intercom.

"Checkin' these drat-damn fuel cells. Gimme a few minutes."

"Take your time," said Dex.

Sitting there idly, Dex scanned the horizon. Nothing. Dead as Beethoven. Deader. Nothing but rocks and sand and every shade of red the human eye could register. Not a thing moving out there—

He sat up bolt upright, not an easy thing to do in the hard suit. Something *was* moving out there! Just a flicker, off on the horizon, and then it was gone.

Dex went back to the equipment lockers beneath the bunks in the module's midsection. Bending over in the suit was awkward, he had to lower himself to his knees to reach the latches that opened the lockers. Cursing the suit and its gloves, he fumbled through the neatly ordered sets of tools until he found the electronically boosted binoculars. Then he hurried back to the cockpit, like some old movie monster trying to gallop.

His helmet visor was up, so Dex could put the binoculars against his eyes to scan the horizon. Nothing. Whatever it was had disappeared, gone away.

Wait! A flicker . . .

Dex adjusted the focus and it came into crisp view. A dust devil. A swirling little eddy of dust, red as a real devil. It would have been called a pillar of fire in the Old Testament, Dex thought, except that this one is on Mars, not Israel or Egypt. It occurred to him that there was a region on Mars called Sinai, south of the Grand Canyon.

"You oughtta be down there, pal," he murmured as he watched the minicyclone twist and dance across the distant horizon.

As he put the binoculars down Dex remembered that giant dust storms sometimes blanketed Mars almost from pole to pole. Usually during the spring season. He shook his head inside his helmet. It's too late in the season now; we timed the landing so the storms would be over. Besides, there weren't any this year.

Not yet, warned a tiny voice in his head. Spring lasts six months on Mars.

Jamie felt decidedly awkward at breakfast. Usually the team members took their morning meal when they chose to; there was no set time when everyone gathered at the galley each morning. It just happened that when Jamie came out of his quarters, Vijay, Dezhurova, and the English.biologist Trudy Hall were already sitting at the table, heads together, chatting busily.

When they saw Jamie approaching their chat stopped. He said "Good morning" to them and got a chorus of the same in return. Then watchful silence as he picked a breakfast package from the freezer. He could feel their eyes on him.

"The strawberries ought to be ready for picking in another few days," he announced to no one in particular.

"Yes, and the tomatoes, too," answered Trudy Hall.

Trudy and Fuchida were the gardeners, although everybody pitched in as needed. The hydroponic garden, in its own plastic dome, was intended not only to supply the bulk of the expedition's food; it also recycled their wastewater.

Jamie sat at the head of the table, with Trudy and Stacy on his left and Vijay at the other end, facing him. She smiled at him and he made a self-conscious smile back at her.

"Sleep well?" Trudy asked, her face the picture of innocent curiosity.

Jamie nodded and turned his attention to the bowl of instant cereal in front of him.

Conversation was a strain. No matter what Hall or Dezhurova said, it sounded to Jamie like arch references to sex. Vijay seemed perfectly relaxed, though. She's *enjoying* this banter, Jamie thought.

He went through his meal as quickly as he could and then headed for the comm center.

"I've got to check in with the others," he said to them.

"I already talked with both teams," Stacy called to his retreating back. "Possum has a cranky fuel cell, but otherwise everything is okay."

Jamie stopped and turned back toward her. "And Tómas?"

"They're heading off for the big caldera, on schedule."

"Good," said Jamie. Then he kept on walking toward the comm center.

A few minutes after he had spoken with Fuchida, Vijay slipped into the cubicle and sat beside him.

"It isn't a crime, you know," she said, a slight smile curving her lips.

"I know."

"Consenting adults and all that."

"I know," he repeated.

"Did you think the others'd be jealous?"

"Aw, come on, Vijay . . ."

She laughed lightly. "That's better. Lord, you were uptight back there!"

"Do they know?"

"I didn't say anything, but the way you were behaving they must have guessed it."

"Damn."

"It's nothing to be ashamed of."

"I know, but—"

"It happened, Jamie. Now forget about it. Get on with the program. I'm not trying to force a commitment out of you. I don't want that."

He felt relieved and disappointed at the same time. "Vijay, I . . . look, this kind of complicates everything."

She shook her head. "No worries, mate. No complications. It happened and it was very nice. Maybe it'll happen again, when the moon is right. Maybe not. Don't give it another thought."

"How the hell can I not give it another thought?"

Her smile returned. "That's what I wanted to hear from you, Jamie. That's all I wanted to hear."

"Hydrogen is the cussedest damned stuff in the universe," Craig was muttering as he drove the rover. That red warning light still glared from the control panel.

Sitting beside him, Dex said, "But the Lord must've loved hydrogen—"

"Because He made so much of it," Craig finished for him. "Yeah, I know."

"Ninety percent of the universe is hydrogen, Wiley. More."

"That's why the universe is so damned cantankerous."

"What've you got against hydrogen—beside the fact that it's leaked out of the fuel cells?"

"Stuff always leaks. It's sneaky-pete stuff, leaks through seals and gaskets that'd hold anything else."

"The seals on that fuel cell should've held the hydrogen," Trumball said, more seriously. "The manufacturer's going to pay a forfeiture fee because they didn't make the seals hydrogen-tight."

"Helluva lot of good that'll do us if we get ourselves killed out here."

"Hey, lighten up, Wiley! It's not that serious. We're okay."

"I don't like headin' away from the base with our backup power system dead."

"We can take on more hydrogen when we get to the fuel generator," Trumball said.

"Uh-uh. The generator produces methane and oxy. Not hydrogen."

"There's a water generator on board, isn't there?"

"Yeah."

"So," Trumball waved a hand in their air, "we take on extra water and electrolyze it into oxygen and hydrogen. *Voila!*"

Craig cast him a sour look. "Electrolyze the water."

"Right."

"And what do we drink, amigo?"

"Water from the fuel cells."

"Now wait a minute . . ."

"Naw, you listen to me, Wiley. Here's the thing of it: We take on the water, electrolyze it, and use the hydrogen to run the fuel cells."

"What about the oxygen?"

"Store it, dump it, whatever. We've got plenty of oxy anyway. You with me so far?"

"We pump the hydrogen into the goddamned leaky fuel cells, big deal."

"Yeah, but we run the fuel cells to provide our electricity at night, instead of the lithium batteries."

"Now, why the hell—"

"So it doesn't matter if the fuel cells leak; we'll work 'em and get power out of 'em before the hydrogen leaks away."

Both hands on the rover's steering wheel, his eyes fixed on the land ahead, Craig looked like a man waiting for a card shark to deal him a deuce.

"Now what else do the fuel cells produce besides electricity?" Trumball asked, grinning with all his teeth.

"Water."

"Which we drink a little of and electrolyze the rest into fresh hydrogen and oxygen to run the fuel cells!"

Craig shook his head. "Great. You've invented the perpetual motion machine."

"Yeah, sure. I'm not that dufo, Wiley. We'll lose hydrogen all the time, I know that. But the loss'll be slow enough so we can use the fuel cells for overnight power all the way out to Ares Vallis and back to the generator!"

"You done the math?"

"I did some rough numbers. I'll put it through the computer as soon as you give me an accurate fix for the fuel cells' normal efficiency rating."

Scratching his stubbly jaw, Craig said, "That data oughtta be in the computer files."

"Okay, go get it."

The older man hesitated. "We'll need approval. I'll have to tell Jamie what we're plannin' to do and he'll prob'ly buck it up to Tarawa."

Trumball grinned his widest. "Ask for all the approvals you want, Wiley, as long as we do it anyway."

"Now wait a minute—"

"What're they going to say?" Trumball interrupted. "If they say no, they're effectively cancelling the excursion. And we won't let them do that to us, will we?"

"You mean, even if they say no we go ahead anyway?"

"Sure! Why not? How're they going to stop us?"

"Use the fuel cells for overnight power?" Jamie asked, not certain he had heard Craig correctly.

"It's sorta like turnin' a lemon into lemonade," Possum replied.

Jamie stared at the display screen. Craig's unshaven face was dead serious. He appeared to be sitting in the cockpit, in his coveralls. Dex must be right beside him, driving. A glance at the data readouts on the displays beside the main screen showed that the rover was plowing ahead at a steady thirty kilometers per hour.

"It sounds risky to me," Jamie said, stalling for time to think.

"We been through the numbers," Craig replied. "It oughtta work."

"And if it doesn't?"

"Then we'll be ridin' along without a backup power system, the way we are now."

"I don't like it."

"The alternative," Trumball's voice interjected, "is to scrub this excursion and come home with our tails between our legs."

"That's what your father wants," Jamie said. He had intended to wait until evening and speak to Dex privately about the elder Trumball's ire. Dex's father had sent three replies to Jamie's last message within the past twelve hours, each one more furious than the one preceding it.

A hand engulfed the view of the rover's cockpit and swivelled the camera to focus on Dex.

"Dear old Dad's prone to displays of temper," he said easily, grinning. "Just relay his messages to me. I'll handle him."

"You just might be shooting down the funding for the next expedition, Dex," Jamie said.

Trumball shook his head vigorously. "No way. Once we bring back this Pathfinder hardware, investors will be running after us with money in their hands."

So that you can come back to Mars and loot it of anything else you can lay your hands on, Jamie thought. He pictured Trumball in a conquistador's steel cuirass and helmet.

A hand swivelled the camera again. "I ain't worried 'bout the next expedition," Craig said somberly. "I just want to get through with this excursion in one piece."

"I'll have to talk to Tarawa," Jamie said, hating himself for bucking the decision upstairs.

"Okay, fine," came Trumball's voice. "It'll take us at least another week to reach the generator."

Damn! thought Jamie as he went through the motions of continuing their discussion. Dex knows damned well that the farther out they are, the less chance of calling them back.

Once he signed off and cut the connection to the rover, though, a different thought wormed into his consciousness: The longer they're out on their excursion, the longer Dex is away from here. Away from Vijay.

He hated himself even more for that.

"Y'know, we shoulda flown out to the Pathfinder site," Wiley Craig mused as he drove the rover through the dry, cold morning across the Plains of the Moon.

"Tired of driving?" Dex Trumball asked, sitting in the cockpit's right seat.

"Kinda boring right now."

"I checked out the idea," Dex said. "The rocket plane doesn't have the range to make it out to Ares Vallis."

"Coulda hopped the fuel generator and gassed 'er up, just like we're doin' for this wagon."

"I suppose so. But we'd need a couple of fill-ups and that would mean flying the generator at least two different hops. And landing the plane twice more, too."

"Too risky, huh?"

"Oh, I wouldn't mind the risk," Dex said quickly. "But the rocket plane couldn't carry the hardware once we got there. Not with a full fuel load, at least."

Craig let out a long sigh that was almost a moan. "So we drive."

"We're getting there, Wiley."

"Awful slow."

"We're setting a record for a land traverse of an alien world. We'll be covering close to ten thousand klicks before we're back at the base."

"More'n those guys who circumnavigated Mare Imbrium back on th' Moon?"

"Oh, hell yes. They only covered twenty-five hundred kilometers."

"Huh."

"Pikers."

"Small-time stuff."

Trumball grinned at his partner. They were both unshaven, their chins and cheeks bristly with the beginnings of beards they had agreed not to cut off until they returned to the domed base.

"We're driving across what used to be the bottom of an ancient sea," Trumball said, gesturing at the undulating ground outside. "I bet if we stopped to do some digging we'd find plenty of fossils."

Craig cocked a brow at him. "And how d'you recognize what's a fossil and what's just a plain ol' rock? Think you'll find trilobites or a chambered nautilis that looks just like fossils on Earth?"

Dex took a deep breath, almost a sigh. "No, I guess not. They'd be different."

After a few moments of silence, Dex said, "Let me ask you something, Wiley."

"What?"

"I've been trying to convince Jamie we should move out base camp to the canyon, but he's too stubborn to even consider it. Whose side are you on? Mine or Jamie's?"

Jamie stared at the three-dimensional image of the cliff face, bending over the immersion table display and concentrating as if he could make the ancient village appear before his eyes by sheer willpower.

Stacy Dezhurova was at the comm console, as usual. Trudy and Vijay were tending the hydroponic garden. And Jamie was growing impatient.

I should never have let Dex go out on this crazy excursion of his, he told himself. Not only is it getting me in hot water with his father, it's screwing up the mission to the ancient village.

Jamie knew that he could not head out for the canyon while four of the expedition's people were in the field. He had to wait for them to come back to the dome. Fuchida and Rodriguez would return from Olympus Mons in a few days, unless they ran into trouble. But Dex and Possum won't be back for another four weeks, at least.

Don't let yourself get so worked up about it, he said silently. Be patient. If it's really an ancient village tucked in those cliffs, it's been there a long, long time. Another few weeks isn't going to make much difference.

Still he burned to get going, to get out of this dome, out in the field, away from the others.

Away from Vijay, he realized.

She's got me wound up like a spring. First no and then yes and now maybe. Is she doing it on purpose? Trying to drive me crazy? Is it her sense of humor?

Strangely, he found himself grinning at the thought. We're already crazy. We wouldn't be here otherwise. This just adds another dimension to the craziness.

Be calm, the Navaho side of his mind advised. Seek the balanced path. Only when you're in balance can you find beauty.

Sex. We tie ourselves into knots over it. Why? She can't get pregnant. Not here. Not unless she really wants to and she's too smart to want that. So what difference does a little roll in the hay make?

Then he thought of her admission that she had slept with Trumball, and Jamie knew that sex could be a fuse that kindles an explosion.

Take it one step at a time, he thought. One day at a time. Then he grinned again. One night at a time.

Dezhurova's voice cut into his awareness. "Jamie, you should take a look at this."

Jamie straightened up, felt his vertebrae pop, and turned toward the comm console, where Stacy was sitting with a headset clipped over her limp sandy-blond pageboy.

"What is it?"

"Latest met forecast from Tarawa."

Jamie saw a polar projection map of Mars's two hemispheres, side by side, on Dezhurova's main screen. Meteorological isobars and symbols for highs and lows were sprinkled across it.

Stacy tapped a fingernail on a red L deep in the southern hemisphere. Jamie noticed that her nails were manicured and lacquered a dark red.

"That is a dust storm," she said.

Bending over her shoulder to peer at the map, Jamie nodded. And noticed that Stacy was wearing a flowery perfume.

"Way down on the other side of Hellas," he muttered.

"But they're forecasting it to grow." She touched a key and the next day's map appeared on the screen. The storm was bigger, and moving westward.

"Still way below the equator," Jamie said.

"Even so."

"Can you get a real-time view of the area?"

"On two," she replied. The screen immediately to her right brightened to show a satellite view of the region.

"Dust storm, all right," Jamie said. "Big one."

"And growing."

He thought aloud, "Even if it grows to global size it'll take more than a week to bother us here. Fuchida and Rodriguez will be back well before then."

"But Dex and Possum . . ."

Jamie pictured Dex's reaction to being called back to base because of the possibility of a dust storm engulfing him. I'd have to order him to return, Jamie knew. And he might just ignore the order.

"Tell Tarawa I need to talk to the meteorology people right away," he said to Stacy.

"Right."

•   •   •

Dex Trumball frowned as he listened to Jamie on the rover's comm link.

"The meteorology people don't expect the storm to get across the equator, but they're keeping an eye on it."

"So what's the problem?" Trumball asked, glancing over at Craig, driving the rover.

The ground they were traversing was rising slightly, and rougher than the earlier going. A range of rugged hills rose on their left, and the last rays of the dying sun threw enormously elongated shadows across their path, turning even the smallest rocks into dark phantoms reaching out to block their way.

"It's a question of timing," Jamie replied. "Each day you get farther from the base. If we wait to recall you until the storm's a real threat, it might be too late."

"But you don't know that the storm's going to be a real threat, do you?"

"The prudent thing to do," Jamie said, "is to turn back and try this excursion again late in the summer, when the threat of storms is practically zero."

"I don't want to turn back because of some ding-dong threat that probably won't materialize."

"It's better than getting caught in a dust storm, Dex."

Trumball looked across at Craig again. The older man gave him a sidelong glance, then returned to staring straight ahead.

"You made it through a dust storm, didn't you?" he said. "On the first expedition."

It took several moments for Jamie to reply, "We had no choice. You do."

"Well, lemme tell you something, Jamie. I choose to keep on going. I'm not going to stop and turn back because of some cockamamie storm that's a couple thousand klicks away."

Sitting in front of the comm console, with Stacy beside him and Vijay at his back, Jamie kneaded his fists into his thighs.

If I order him to return and he refuses, then whatever authority I have over these people goes down the drain. But if I let him continue then they'll all know that Dex can do whatever he wants to and I have no way to control him.

He realized that it was Dex who was making the decisions. The idea of putting Craig in charge was a farce from the beginning. Possum was not raising his voice, not saying a word at all.

Which way? Which path? Jamie thought furiously for several silent moments. He drew up in his mind an image of Trumball's route across Lunae Planum and into Xanthe Terra.

"Hold on for a minute, Dex," he said, and cut off the transmission.

Turning to Dezhurova, he ordered, "Let me see their itinerary, Stacy."

She punched up the image on the screen before Jamie's chair. A black line snaked across the map, with pips marking the position expected at the end of each day. Jamie scanned it swiftly, then hit the transmit key again.

"Dex?"

"We're still here, chief."

"If the storm crosses the equator and threatens you, it won't happen for at least four or five more days. By then you'll be much closer to the fuel generator than to the base, here."

"Yeah?" Trumball's voice sounded wary.

"In two days from now you ought to be at the halfway point between here and the generator."

"Right."

"That's going to be our decision point. The point of no return. I'll decide then whether you can keep going or have to turn back."

"In two days."

"Yes. In the meantime we'll keep close track of the storm. Stay in touch with us hourly."

This time it was Trumball who hesitated for several moments before answering, "Okay. Sure."

"Good," said Jamie.

"We'll be bedding down for the night in another hour," Trumball said. "Call you then."

"Good," Jamie repeated.

He cut the transmission and leaned back in the little wheeled chair, feeling as if he had sparred ten rounds with a professional boxer.

Dex Trumball was driving slowly through the inky blackness of the Martian night.

"Supper's on the table," Craig called out. "Come on and eat it or I'll throw it to th' hawgs."

"Why don't we keep on going, Wiley?" Trumball asked over his shoulder.

" 'Cause we don't want to break our cotton-pickin' necks, that's why. Shut 'er down for the night, Dex."

"Aw, come on, Wiley. Just a few klicks more."

"Now," Craig said, with iron in his tone.

With a sigh, Trumball leaned on the brake pedals and brought the rover to a slow, smooth stop.

Once he had shut down the drive motors and come back to the table between the bunks, Dex sank down on the edge of his bunk and stared for a few moments at the tray of prepackaged dinner.

"I know what you're up to, y'know," Craig said, sitting on the edge of his own bunk, on the other side of the folding table.

Dex grinned at the older man. "Yeah? What?"

"You wanta get so close to the generator that when Jamie comes to his decision point we'll be closer to it than to th' base. Right?"

With a nod, Trumball answered, "Why not?"

"You're not scared of a dust storm?"

"Wiley, if Jamie weathered one of those storms during the first expedition, why can't we?"

"Be smarter to be back at the base when a storm hits, nice 'n' cozy."

"*If* a storm hits. How'd you feel if we turned tail and went back to the dome and then no storm materializes?"

"Alive," said Craig.

Trumball considered the older man for a moment. Then, as he dug a plastic fork into the unidentifiable stuff on the tray before him, he asked, "If Jamie orders us back, what'll you do?"

Craig stared back at him, sad, pouchy, ice-blue eyes unwavering. "Don't know yet," he answered. "But I'm turnin' over the possibilities in my mind."

Trumball grinned at him. "Yeah? Well, turn this over, too, Wiley. There'll be a finder's fee for picking up the Pathfinder hardware. A nice sizable wad of cash for the guys who bring it back. That'll be you and me, Wiley."

"How much?"

Trumball shrugged. "Six figures, I guess."

"H'mp."

Watching the older man's face carefully, Trumball added, "Of course, I don't need the money. I'd be willing to give my half to you, Wiley. If we keep on going no matter what Jamie says."

Craig's face was impassive. But he said, "Now that sounds purty interesting, ol' pal. Purty damn' interesting."

"How's the weather report?" Craig asked.

"About the same," Dex replied, from up in the rover's cockpit. He was driving while Craig cleaned up their breakfast crumbs and folded the table back down into the floor between the bunks.

Craig came up and sat in the right-hand seat. The sun was just clear of the increasingly rugged eastern horizon.

"Want me to drive?" he asked.

"No way, Wiley. I'm going to break the interplanetary speed record today and get this baby up to thirty-five klicks per hour."

Craig made a snorting laugh. "You'll need a helluva tailwind for that, buddy."

"Nope, just some downhill slope."

"Lotsa luck."

"I'm not kidding, Wiley. The plain slopes downhill all the way to Xanthe."

"Sure," said Craig. "And if we had a good breeze behind us we could really make time."

Trumball glanced at him, then said, "Check the incoming messages, huh?"

There were two messages in the file, both from Trudy Hall. The first one told them about Fuchida's accident in the caldera atop Olympus Mons and Rodriguez's rescue of him. And the biologist's discovery of the siderophiles. The two men listened to Hall's brief summary, then glanced at each other.

Craig let out a low whistle. "I wonder what Mitsuo's Jockey shorts look like."

Trumball laughed and shook his head. "I don't want to know."

Hall's second message was a weather report. The dust storm was spreading, but still confined below the equator.

"Long as it stays in the southern hemisphere we're free and clear," Trumball said happily.

Craig was less cheerful. As he stared at the weather map on their screen he muttered, "It's growin', though. If it crosses the equator we're gonna be in trouble."

"Don't be a dweeb, Wiley. This vehicle's been through a dust storm before, y'know."

"Yeah, and I've jumped off a burning oil platform into th' Gulf of Mexico, too. Doesn't mean I wanna do it again."

Trumball's answer was to lean harder on the accelerator. Craig watched the speedometer edge up past thirty-one kilometers per hour. With a grim smile, he remembered an old prizefighter's maxim: *You can run but you can't hide.*

"By golly, there she is!"

Wiley Craig pointed with his right hand while keeping his left on the steering wheel.

Dex Trumball squinted into the bright morning sun. Off on the rough, crimson horizon he saw a tall metal shape, gleaming and alien-looking in the Martian landscape.

The rover was plunging at top speed across a field of rocks, its spindly, springy wheels jouncing and rattling them so hard they had both strapped themselves into the cockpit seats.

"We've drifted too far north, Wiley," said Trumball. "It's going to cost us a half a day to get to her."

Craig's bristly, bearded face was split by a big, gap-toothed grin. "Don't care how far away she is; she shore looks purty, don't she?"

Dex nodded and admitted, "Yeah, she sure does."

The dust storm in the southern hemisphere had petered out at last, according to the previous night's weather report. Craig had expressed great relief. Trumball, equally grateful that the storm would not hit them, played it much cooler.

"Even if it had crossed the equator, we could've ridden it out."

"I don't know, Dex," Craig had said soberly. "Some of those storms last for weeks."

"Not this time of year."

"Uh-huh. And it never rains in California."

Trumball got up and headed back toward the equipment racks near the airlock while Craig steered the rover through the rock field and onto smoother, slightly higher ground. The generator took shape before his eyes, a tall polished aluminum cylinder catching the glint of the morning sun, resting on three slim-looking metal legs, the nozzles of three rocket engines hanging beneath the vehicle's end skirt.

"Come on," Dex called from the rear of the rover module, "goose her up a little more. Let's make as much time as we can."

"Let's not throw a wheel, either," Craig countered. "Another half hour ain't gonna kill us."

Trumball grumbled to himself as he checked out the video monitoring equipment. The outside cameras were recording everything; not only would the views be a bonanza for geologists studying Mars, they would be great background material for the virtual reality tours that Dex would beam Earthward.

By the time Craig pulled the rover to a stop next to the generator Dex was suited up and already stepping into the airlock.

"You just wait a minute there, buddy," Craig called to him. "You're not goin' outside without being checked out."

"Aw, come on, Wiley. I went through the checklist myself. Don't chickenshit me."

But Craig would not be put off. He checked Trumball's suit quickly but thoroughly, then pronounced him ready to go outside.

"I'll holler when I'm suited up and you come back in and check me over."

"Yeah, yeah."

The generator was chugging away, sucking up water from the line it had drilled down to the permafrost level under Craig's remote guidance, pulling in the thin Martian air and separating its components automatically.

By the time Craig came through the airlock hatch and stepped onto the rusty ground, Trumball had ascertained that the methane and water tanks were both filled almost to capacity.

"Okay, great," Wiley said. "Now we gotta fill our tanks."

It took more than an hour. While Craig handled the hoses and watched the gauges, Dex beamed a VR session back to Tarawa: The intrepid explorers hacking their way through the Martian wilderness have made their rendezvous with the refueling generator. On to Pathfinder!

Once they climbed back inside the rover, Dex scrambled quickly out of his suit and made his way to the cockpit. A brief scan of the control panel showed everything in the green, except for the glowering red light of the fuel cells. We'll get that into the green, too, he told himself. Soon as Wiley electrolyzes enough of our water to feed 'em.

By sundown they were well on their way toward Ares Vallis, the generator below their horizon and out of sight. Dex was still driving, Craig in back tinkering with the fuel cells.

"How're they holding?" Trumball called over his shoulder.

Craig's weary sigh was audible even from the rear of the module. "Leakproof welds my hairy butt," he groused.

"What's the matter?"

"These damn dewars are supposed to hold liquid hydrogen," Craig said, kicking a booted toe on the stainless steel cylinder on the rover floor.

"Yeah?"

"Well, the damned welds on 'em leak like a sieve that's been shotgunned."

"They're still leaking?"

"Does the pope eat spaghetti?"

"How bad?"

Craig clumped up toward the cockpit and slid into the right-hand seat. "I gotta do some calculations. It ain't good, though, I can tell you that without a computer."

Trumball saw that Craig was more disgruntled than worried. We can get along without the fuel cells, he thought. Hell, we've been getting along without 'em for days now. Still, it'd be good to get that damned red light off the board.

"The newest fuel cells back on Earth use nanotube filaments to store the hydrogen," Craig was muttering. "Nanotubes *work*, pardner. They soak up molecular hydrogen like a sponge and hold onto it like a vise. But all we got is these leaky damned dewars."

The sun was nearing the horizon, Dex saw. A thin patch of cloud high above was already reflecting brilliant red highlights.

"We're going to have a beautiful sunset, Wiley."

Craig looked up from the panel's computer display. "Yep. A purty one. Reminds me of Houston. We used to get some bee-yootiful sunsets there, thanks to all the industrial waste the refineries poured into the air."

Trumball laughed. "No factories out here."

"No, but . . ." Craig's voice petered off into thoughtful silence.

"What's the matter, Wiley?"

"Those clouds."

At that instant the communications chime sounded. Trumball tapped the ON button and Stacy Dezhurova's face appeared on the panel screen.

"Latest weather report," she said, looking worried. "New dust storm has started, this time in the northern hemisphere."

"Where?" Trumball asked.

"Exactly where you're heading," came her reply.

Jamie stared at the weather map on the screen. He had superimposed the position of Trumball and Craig's rover, and the route they had to follow to reach the Pathfinder.

The storm's going to roll right over them, he saw.

"What do you want to do?" Stacy Dezhurova asked from her chair at the comm console.

Jamie looked up at her. She looked concerned.

"They're more than halfway to the Pathfinder site," he said, thinking aloud. "If I tell them to turn around and head back to the generator the storm will overtake them anyway."

"So you think they should just keep on going?"

"The storm's heading east to west; they're going west to east. They could drive through it."

"Assuming they can drive when the storm hits them."

"If not, they'll have to sit still until it passes them."

Dezhurova nodded, her normally somber face positively morose.

"If only we could predict how big the storm's going to get," Jamie muttered. "We've been studying Martian weather for more than twenty years now and we still can't make a decent forecast."

Stacy made a weak grin. "They have been studying terrestrial weather for almost two centuries and the meteorologists still can't make a decent forecast on Earth, Jamie."

"It might not be as bad as it looks," he said, remembering the storm he had endured. "If they button up tight they'll be all right."

"But what if the storm grows? The big ones take weeks to clear up . . . months."

With a grimace, Jamie said, "This one doesn't look that bad. So far."

Dezhurova countered, "The one in the southern hemisphere hung in for a solid week."

"I know," he admitted, staring again at the weather map, as if he could force it to reveal its secrets if he scowled at it hard enough.

Dezhurova fell silent, letting Jamie work out his thoughts for himself. At last he got to his feet and said, "We'll thrash it out over dinner. Let everybody chip in their ideas."

With Fuchida and Rodriguez back from Olympus Mons, there were six of them at dinner. Even so, their ideas were almost nonexistent. They talked the situation through over dinner, mulling through one possibility after another. It all boiled down to a choice between letting Craig and Trumball continue into the storm or ordering them to turn back to the generator and allowing the storm to catch up with them.

"They're way too far out to get back here before the storm overtakes them," said Rodriguez. "They're gonna get caught in it, one way or the other."

"Dex won't want to turn around," Vijay said, with firm certainty. "He'll want to push ahead, no matter what."

"If only we knew how big the storm will grow," Trudy Hall said. "We're trying to make a decision rather in the blind, don't you think?"

"The storm will grow," Fuchida predicted. "It might even reach us here."

"Here?" Trudy looked suddenly alarmed.

"It's a strong possibility," said Fuchida. He was sitting with his bad leg propped on an empty chair. Vijay had X-rayed his ankle, injured on Mt. Olympus, and found no fracture. She had wrapped it tightly with an elastic bandage.

"Are you a meteorologist, too?" Stacy asked the Japanese biologist, straight-faced.

"Yes, I am," Fuchida replied with dignity. Then he added, "When I call up the meteorology program on my laptop."

Rodriguez pointed out, "The biggest problem is the solar cells. If the dust covers them, the rover loses its primary power source."

"So they go to the batteries," Hall said.

"For how long? Their fuel cells aren't working right, remember? Their backup power system isn't reliable."

Trudy looked surprised. "I had forgotten that."

"They can't sit in the dark for more than forty-eight hours—fifty, tops," Rodriguez said.

"They can stretch it if they power down," said Jamie.

"How far? They got to keep the heaters going, and that's what takes up most of the juice."

Stacy Dezhurova said, "If they go back to the generator that can refill the fuel cells as much as they need to."

"That's right," Jamie said, pushing himself up from the table. "But my instinct is to let them continue ahead; it's the shortest path out of the storm."

"Unless the storm grows much larger and stronger," Hall said.

"If it grows that much they're in trouble no matter what they do."

"And the dust might damage the solar cells," Rodriguez added gloomily. "Degrade them to the point where they can't provide enough power to run the rover."

"That's a cheerful thought," Hall said.

The others nodded glum agreement.

Jamie went to the comm center again and sat at the main console. All the others crowded in behind him. As he called to the rover, Jamie felt the heat and tension in the little cubicle. Too many bodies pressed together. Too many fears building up.

Mars is a gentle world, he reminded himself as he waited for the rover to reply. It doesn't want to harm us.

No, the other side of his mind replied. Not unless you do something stupid, like get caught in a dust storm three thousand klicks from home.

Craig's scruffy face filled the screen. From what Jamie could see, he was still driving the rover through the lengthening shadows of nightfall.

Jamie went through the situation and the two possible courses of action with Craig. Then he asked, "Possum, what do you think? Which way do you want to go?"

Before Craig could answer, Dex Trumball pivoted the camera to himself and said, "We're pushing on! No sense turning tail."

Patiently, Jamie said, "Dex, I asked Possum, not you. He's in charge."

"Wiley and I agree," Trumball insisted. "We want to keep on going and get the hell out of this storm. Turning back would be a waste of time."

"It might be the safer course to take," Jamie said. "You could make it back to the generator before the storm overtook you, and ride it out there, where you're assured of fuel, water, and oxygen."

"We're going forward," Trumball snapped.

"Possum, what do you have to say about it?" Jamie asked.

The camera view swivelled back to Craig's jowly face. "First off, I'd rather be called Wiley than Possum. Second, I agree with Dex: Let's push ahead and get through this blow."

Jamie sat digesting that for a few silent moments. He could feel the others stirring nervously behind him.

"You're sure?" he said, stalling for time to think.

"Yep," Craig replied.

It would be safer for them to camp by the generator, Jamie told himself. But if the storm lasts for a week or more they'll run out of food and have to start back. Without getting the Pathfinder hardware. Their whole trek would be for nothing. That's what's eating at Dex. To go all the way out there and return empty-handed. That's what's fueling his fire.

On the other hand, he thought, what if they get killed out there? Is the hardware so important that I should let them risk their lives over it?

Trumball swung the camera back to his own face. His ragged dark beard made him look truculent, belligerent, as if he were daring Jamie to contradict him.

"Well?" he demanded. "What are your orders, chief?" The sarcastic stress he laid on the word *orders* was obvious.

"Keep on going," Jamie heard himself say. "And good luck."

Trumball looked surprised.

Vijay followed Jamie into his cubicle when they all filed out of the comm center. What the hell, Jamie thought. If the others didn't realize we've been sleeping together, they know it now.

Later, cupped against one another in the narrow bunk, she whispered to him, "You did the right thing, Jamie."

"Did I?"

"Dex wouldn't have obeyed an order to turn around. He would have defied you openly."

Jamie sighed in the darkness. "Yes, I suppose he would have."

"It was smart to avoid an open conflict."

"Maybe."

"You don't think so?"

"It's not important," he said.

"But it is!" She propped herself on one elbow and looked down at him. "Your authority shouldn't be challenged."

"That doesn't worry me, Vijay."

"It doesn't? Then what does?"

He gazed up at her lovely face, outlined in the faint glow from the digital clock. So beautiful, so serious, so concerned about him.

"What bothers me is that I *want* Dex to be away from here. Away from you. Away from us."

"Wind's pickin' up," Wiley Craig said.

Trumball was driving the rover with single-minded concentration through a field of rocks big enough to stop army tanks, steering between the minivan-sized boulders while his geologist's mind begged to go outside and see what they were made of. No time for that, Dex told himself, glancing up at the darkening sky. We'll do the science on the way back.

Craig was peering at the readouts on the display screen. The wind was up to eighty-five knots: Hurricane speed on Earth yet only a zephyr in the rarified atmosphere of Mars. But the wind speed was increasing, and off on the horizon before them an ominous dark cloud hung low over the land.

"How're the fuel cells doing?" Trumball asked, without taking his eyes from his steering.

Craig tapped a few keys on the control panel. "Down to sixty-three percent."

"Might as well use them as soon as the solar cells crap out," Trumball said, through gritted teeth. "Save the batteries."

"Use 'em or lose 'em," Craig agreed. "Get some work outta them before they fade to zero."

It took a conscious effort for Dex to unlock his jaws. He had clamped his teeth together so hard it was giving him a headache. If it wasn't so scary it'd be funny, he told himself. I'm steering this buggy like a kid in a video game, trying to get through this frigging rock field and out into the open before the storm hits us.

"Any new data on the storm?" he asked.

Craig tapped more keys, stared at the display screen a moment, then sighed mightily. "She's gettin' bigger."

"Great."

We should have gone back to the generator, Dex admitted silently. Jamie should've *ordered* us to go back. Wiley should've insisted on it. This isn't a game; that storm could kill us, for chrissakes.

"Want me to drive?" Craig asked gently.

Trumball glanced at the older man. "Wiley, if I wasn't driving I'd be biting my fingernails up to the elbows."

Craig laughed. "Hell, this isn't all that bad, Dex. Lemme tell you about the time a hurricane hit us while we were tryin' to cap a big leak on an oil platform in the Gulf of Mexico. Right near Biloxi it was . . ."

Trumball listened with only half his attention, but he was grateful that Craig was trying to ease his tension. It wasn't working, of course, but he was grateful that Wiley was at least trying.

"It's definitely going to reach your base camp," said the meteorologist. "At its present rate of growth and forward speed, the storm will overrun your area in two days—er, that's two Martian days, sols."

Jamie and Stacy Dezhurova watched the report in the comm center. The meteorologist appeared to be in Florida, perhaps Miami. Jamie could see palm trees and high-rise condos through the man's office window, behind his youthful but intently serious face.

The young meteorologist went on to give all the data he could present: maximum wind speeds would be above two hundred knots; the storm's forward progress was a steady thirty-five knots; height of the clouds; dust burden; opacity. Many of the numbers were estimates or averages.

"We must make certain all the planes are tied down really tight," Stacy muttered as the meteorologist droned on.

Jamie nodded. "And the generator, too." He knew, in the calculating side of his brain, that even a two-hundred-knot wind on Mars did not have the momentum to knock down the tall cylinder that housed the fuel and water generator, especially when its tanks were full. The Martian atmosphere was so thin that there was little punch to its winds. Yet the other side of his mind pictured the generator toppling, blown over like a big tree in a hurricane.

Dezhurova nodded. "We must get on it right away."

"Tómas and I will do the outside work," Jamie said once the meteorologist finished his report. "You see that everything in here is buttoned up and everybody's ready for a blow."

He slid his wheeled chair to the screen where the meteorologist's frozen image stared out at them, face lined with concern, and punched the transmit key.

"Dr. Kaderly, thanks for your report. It helps a lot. Please keep us updated and let us know immediately if there's any change in the storm's progress."

Then he turned back to Stacy, sitting beside him. "Send Kaderly's report to Poss . . . I mean, to Wiley Craig and Dex. Then get the others started getting ready for the storm."

"Right, chief."

Jamie got up and headed for the airlock and the hard suits waiting by the lockers there. Somehow he didn't mind it when Stacy called him chief. There was no mockery in her tone.

As he began pulling on the rust-stained leggings of his hard suit, Jamie thought about Dex and Craig out there between Xanthe and Ares Vallis. They're going to be caught in the storm for two sols, at least. Without a backup electrical system. The batteries ought to see them through okay, if they power down to a minimum. That means they're going to have to stop and sit there until the storm blows past them.

They'll be okay. If they just keep their cool and wait it out, they'll get through the storm all right.

If the dust doesn't damage their solar panels.

"What do you think, Wiley?" asked Dex Trumball as soon as the meteorologist's detailed report ended.

Craig was driving the rover at a steady thirty klicks per hour. "How the hell fast is one knot? I always get confused."

Sitting in the right seat, staring out at the darkening horizon in front of them, Dex said, "It's one nautical mile per hour."

"What's that in real miles?"

"Does it make that much difference?"

Craig hunched his shoulders. "Naw, I guess not."

"It's about one point fifteen statute miles."

"Fifteen percent longer'n a regular mile?"

"That's right." Trumball was starting to feel exasperated. What difference did fifteen percent make? They were driving straight into a dust storm. A big one.

"So it'll take about two sols for the storm to pass over us."

"If we're sitting still, yes."

Craig glanced over at Dex, then turned back to his driving. "You want to keep mushing ahead?"

"Why not? As long as the solar cells are working, why not push ahead? Get the hell out of this mess as quick as we can."

"Hmm." Craig seemed to think it over carefully. "Hell of it is, we got some nice smooth territory here. Pretty easy driving."

The land outside was not entirely free of rocks, but it was much more open and flat than the broken and boulder-strewn region of Xanthe they had been through. The ground was sloping downward gently, generally trending toward the lowlands of the Ares Vallis region.

"We're going to turn this route into a regular excursion for the tourists, Wiley," Dex said, mainly to take his mind off the ominous cloud spreading across the horizon before them.

"Build a road? Out here?"

"Won't need a road. We'll put up a cable-car system, like they're doing on the Moon. Just put up poles every hundred meters or so and string a line between 'em. The cars hang from the line and zip along, whoosh!" Dex made a swooping motion with one hand.

Craig fell into the game. "The cable carries the electrical current to run the cars, huh?"

"Right," Dex said, trying not to look out at the horizon. "Cars can carry a couple dozen people. They're sealed like spacecraft, carry their own air, heat, just like this rover."

"Only they skim over th' ground," Craig said.

"They'll be able to go a lot faster that way. A hundred klicks an hour, maybe."

Without taking his eyes from his driving, Craig said softly, "Wish we had one of 'em now."

Dex stared out the windshield. It was starting to get dark out there. The mammoth cloud of dust was coming toward them like a vast Mongol horde of conquerors. Soon it would engulf them entirely and they would be lost in the dark.

He remembered an old adage about the weather: *Red sky at night, sailor's delight.*

Yeah, but that was back on Earth. Here on Mars the sky was always red. And there hadn't been any sailors here for hundreds of millions of years, at least.

As he stared at the approaching cloud he shivered involuntarily.

Jamie was outside with Rodriguez, adding extra tie-down lines to the planes, when the call came through from Pete Connors, mission controller at Tarawa.

Inside his hard suit, he could not see the former astronaut, only hear his caramel-rich baritone voice. Connors sounded concerned, worried.

"Old man Trumball's on the warpath, Jamie. I just heard about it from Dr. Li. He called Li and raised hell about you. He's calling everybody on the ICU board. God knows who else he's bitching to."

Jamie had asked that Connors's call be put on the personal frequency, so that he could listen to the man in privacy.

"I don't need this," he muttered as he tugged at the line that held the soarplane's wingtip to one of the bolts they had sunk into the ground.

Connors's voice went on, unhearing, more than a hundred million kilometers away. "I've talked to several of the board members myself. None of them really wants to remove you, but they're pretty scared of Trumball. He must be threatening to cut off funding for the next expedition."

Straightening in the hard suit was not an easy task. Jamie found himself puffing with exertion as he looked back toward the dome. Fuchida and Dezhurova were in the garden bubble, carefully checking its plastic skin for pinhole leaks or wrinkles where the wind might grab and tear the fabric apart.

Once the dust starts blowing, will the particles have enough force in them to penetrate the bubble's skin? he wondered. Not likely, but then the odds against the main dome being hit by meteoroids were a zillion to one and that had happened on the first expedition.

Connors was still talking. "I had a long talk with Fr. DiNardo about it. He's a damned good politician, that Jesuit, you know that? He says you should sit tight and ignore the whole thing. It'll probably blow over as soon as the storm dissipates and Trumball realizes nothing's happened to his son."

Jamie nodded inside his helmet as he walked over to the soarplane's other wingtip and started tightening the lines already fastened there.

"DiNardo said," Connors continued, "that you shouldn't even think about resigning unless Trumball keeps up the pressure even after the storm blows out and it becomes clear that a majority of the board's going to go along with him."

Resigning? Jamie thought, alarmed. He thinks I should resign?

Connors went on with his dolorous report, reminding Jamie several times more that he hated to bother him with this political maneuvering but he thought Jamie ought to know about it.

Finally he said, "Well, that's the whole story, up to now. I'll wait for your answer. Be sure you mark it personal to me; that way nobody else'll look at it. At least, nobody else *should* look at it. I don't know how many people around here are reporting to Trumball on the sly."

Wonderful news, Jamie groaned silently.

"Well, okay, that's it, pal. I'll wait for your answer. 'Bye for now."

Off on the eastern horizon, Jamie saw, the sky was darkening. Or is it just my imagination? he asked himself. I'll check the instrumentation when I get back into the dome.

How's that old rhyme go? Jamie asked himself. *Red sky at night, sailor's delight. Red sky at morning, sailor take warning.* What about when the sky turns black?

The storm's going to hit here, all right. No way around that. And now I've got another storm, a political squall, back on Earth.

He glanced down at the suit radio's keypad on his wrist, then said carefully, "Personal message to Pete Connors at Tarawa. Pete, I got your message. We're battening down for the storm right now, so I don't have time to reply. I want to think about this before I answer you, anyway. Thanks for the news, I guess. I'll get back to you."

Damn, he thought as he stared out at the eastern horizon. It sure looks like it's clouding up out there. Maybe the storm's picked up speed. That'd be good; it'll roll over Dex and Craig and get them out into the clear sooner.

Starting back toward the dome's airlock, Jamie said to himself, Why is Trumball so clanked up? Why is he out to remove me as mission director? Prejudice? Just plain malice? Or is he the type who's not happy unless he's forcing other people to jump through his hoops?

Then Jamie heard his grandfather whisper, Put yourself in his shoes. Find what's bothering him.

Okay, Grandfather, he replied silently. What's bothering the old man?

His son is in danger, came the immediate reply. He's worried about Dex's safety. That's natural. That's good.

But Trumball knew that exploring Mars carried its risks. Maybe he never considered that his own son would have to face those risks, just like the rest of us.

He was all in favor of going after the Pathfinder hardware. But he didn't think his son would be in any danger. Now he knows differently and he's scared. He's sitting in an office in Boston and his son is out in the middle of a dust storm a hundred million kilometers away and there's nothing he can do about it.

Except get angry and vent his fury on the most convenient target he can find: The mission director who allowed his son to go out into danger. Me. He's pissed at me because he can't do anything else about the situation. He's scared and frustrated and trying to solve his problem the way he's solved problems before: Fire the guy he's mad at.

Jamie took a deep breath and felt a calm warmth flow through him. He heard his grandfather's gentle laughter. "Never lose your temper with a customer," his grandfather had told him years ago, when Jamie had been a little boy angered by the pushy, demanding, loud-mouthed tourists who yelled at Al in his Santa Fe shop. "Let 'em whoop and holler, it don't matter. Once they calm down they're so ashamed of themselves that they'll buy twice what they started out to buy, just to show they're sorry."

Damn! Jamie said to himself as he trudged back to the airlock. It would be so satisfying to get sore at Trumball, to send him a blistering message telling him to mind his own damned business. So easy to taunt the old man from a hundred million kilometers' distance.

But I can't get angry at him, Jamie realized. I understand what he's going through. I understand him and you can't hate a man you understand.

As he stepped into the airlock and swung its outer hatch shut, he reminded himself, But just because you understand him doesn't mean he can't hurt you. You understand a rattlesnake, too, but you don't let him bite you. Not if you can avoid it.

•   •   •

"That's all she wrote," said Craig.

He touched the brakes and brought the rover to a gentle stop.

"It's not even six o'clock yet, Wiley," Dex protested. "We can get in another hour or more."

Craig got up from the driver's seat. "I got an idea."

The sky was a dismal gray above them, getting darker by the minute. Dex could hear the wind now, a thin screeching sound like the wail of a distant banshee.

"I'll drive," he offered.

"Nope," said Craig, heading back toward the bunks. "You gotta know when to hold 'em and know when to fold 'em. We sit still now and get ready for the storm."

"It's not that bad yet," Trumball insisted, turning in his seat to watch the older man. "We can push on a little more, at least."

Craig knelt down and pulled open the storage drawer beneath the bottom bunk. "The real danger from the storm's gonna be the damage the sand does to our solar panels, right?"

"Right," Dex answered, wondering what his partner was up to.

Craig pulled a set of sheets from the storage drawer. "So we cover the solar panels."

"Cover them? With bedsheets?"

"And anything else we got," Craig said. "Coveralls, plastic wrap, anything we got."

"But once they're covered they'll stop producing electricity for us. We'll have to go onto the batteries."

Craig was emptying the drawer beneath the other bunk now. "Take a look at the instruments, buddy. It's gettin' mighty dark mighty quick. Those solar cells are already down to less'n thirty percent nominal, right?"

Dex glanced at the panel instruments. The solar panels' output hovered just above twenty-five percent of their maximum output.

"Right," he replied dismally.

"So don't just sit there," Craig called, almost jovially. "Get up and find the duct tape, for cryin' out loud."

Dex thought, This is just busywork. We won't be able to keep the panels covered once the storm hits. Wind speeds are going to over two hundred knots, for chrissake. That'll rip off anything we try to cover the panels with.

But he pushed himself out of the chair, wormed his way past Craig, and started searching through the supplies locker, grateful for the chance to be doing something active instead of just sitting and watching the storm approach them.

Wiley Craig ran the beam from his hand lamp across the rover from nose to tail.

"Well . . . it ain't a thing of beauty," he said, "but it oughtta get the job done."

Standing beside him, Dex thought that the rover's top looked like a Christmas present wrapped by clumsy children. Bedsheets, plastic wrapping, a tarpaulin, and several sets of spare coveralls—sliced apart to cover more area—were spread over the solar panels and taped down heavily.

"Do you think they'll stay put once the wind starts up?" he asked.

Craig was silent for a moment, then said, "Oughtta. Wind must be purty near seventy knots already and they're not flappin'."

Dex could hear the wind keening outside his helmet, softly but steadily, becoming insistent. He thought he also heard something grating across his suit's outer skin, like fine grains of sand peppering him. He almost could feel the dust scratching against him.

It was fully dark now. Dex felt tired, physically weary, yet his insides were jumpy, jittery. In the light from Wiley's lamp he could see that the air was clear; no dust swirling. None that he could see. Yet there was that gritty rasping on the suit's hard shell.

"We could have driven another hour," he said to Craig.

"Maybe."

"Hell, Wiley, I've driven through snowstorms in New England." Despite his words, Dex's voice sounded quavery, even to himself.

"This ain't the Massachusetts Turnpike out here, buddy."

"So what do we do now? Just sit and bite our nails?"

"Nope. We're gonna collect all the data we can. Then we're gonna have dinner. Then we're gonna get a good night's sleep."

Dex stared at Craig's space-suited figure. *He doesn't sound worried at all. The goddamned fuel cells are leaking and the solar panels are shut down and we'll have to live off the batteries for god knows how long and he's as calm and unruffled as a guy riding out a blizzard in a first-class ski lodge.*

"Okay, boss," Dex asked, trying to sound nonchalant, "what do you want me to do now?"

"You go inside and check the fuel cells, make sure all the comm systems are workin', and call back to the base, let 'em know we're buttoned up for the night."

Dex nodded. The commsats in orbit will pinpoint our location. If anything happens to us, he thought, at least they'll know where to find the bodies.

Craig whistled tunelessly as he trudged back to the airlock for a met/geo beacon to plant outside the rover. Dex went back inside and started to take off his hard suit. He knew that he should stay suited up and be prepared to go outside in case Craig got into trouble. But he was too tired, too drained, too plain frightened even to think about that.

His eyes smarted briefly as he painstakingly vacuumed the dust off his suit. Ozone, from the superoxides in the soil, he knew. We could keep ourselves supplied with oxygen just by dumping some of the red dirt in here, he told himself.

Once out of the suit, he went up to the cockpit and stared out at the darkening landscape, feeling his insides fluttering. I'm scared, Dex said to himself. Like a kid afraid of the dark. Scared. Wiley's as calm as can be and I'm falling apart. Shit!

With nothing better to do, he checked the communications file for incoming messages. The usual garbage from the base, plenty of satellite data about the approaching storm. And a message marked personal for him.

Only one person in the solar system would be sending me a personal message, Dex thought. With a mixture of anger and relief he tapped the proper keys and saw his father's glowering skull-like face appear on the rover's control panel screen.

Just what I need, he thought. Comic relief from dear old Dad.

"Well," Jamie said to the five of them, "we're as ready for the storm as we can be."

"So are Possum and Dex," said Stacy Dezhurova.

"He wants to be called Wiley," Jamie reminded her.

Dezhurova sighed dramatically. "The male ego. Perhaps I should change my name, too."

They were sitting around the galley table, picking at their dinner trays. No one seemed to have much of an appetite, despite the hard labor they had put in getting ready for the storm.

Vijay asked lightly, "What name would you choose for yourself, Stacy?"

"Not Anastasia," Dezhurova answered quickly. "And not Nastasia, either. It's too . . . complicated."

"I think Anastasia's a pretty name," Rodriguez said. "I like it."

"Then you can have it," Dezhurova said.

They all laughed. Nervously.

Jamie wondered if he should tell them about Trumball's move to replace him as mission director. It affects them as much as it does me. More, in fact.

Yet he remained silent, unready to burden them with the political maneuverings going on back on Earth. That's a different world, Jamie said to himself. We've got our own problems to face here, our own realities.

It all seemed so unreal to him, so remote and intangible. Like the ghost stories his grandfather would make up for him when he was a child. Like the legends of First Man and First Woman when the world was new.

This is the new world, he realized. Mars. New and clean and full of mysteries. I can't let Dex and his father turn it into a tourist center. I can't let them start to ruin this world the way they destroyed the world of the People. That's why I've got to fight them.

A new understanding flooded through him. It was as if he'd been lost in a trackless wilderness and suddenly a path opened up before his eyes, the path to harmony and beauty and safety.

I can't let them bring tourists here. I can't let them start to tear up the natural environment so they can build cities and hotels. Bring climbers to Olympus Mons. Build ski runs. I've got to fight them. But how?

"Listen to that!"

Jamie's attention snapped back to the galley, the dome, and his five fellow explorers. The wind had keyed up to a higher pitch. He watched their five faces as they stared up into the shadows of the dome. Something creaked ominously.

"The dome is perfectly safe," Fuchida said to no one in particular. "It was designed to withstand the highest winds ever recorded on Mars, with a huge safety factor added in."

"Then what made that noise?" Trudy Hall asked, her voice small and hollow.

"The dome will flex a little," Jamie told them. "Nothing to worry about."

"Really?" Trudy seemed utterly unconvinced.

Jamie made a smile for her. "Really. In fact, if it didn't flex, if it was built to remain totally rigid, it might crack under a high-enough wind load."

"Like the mighty oak and the little sapling," Vijay said.

"Oh, yes, I know that one," Hall said, looking slightly relieved. "The oak stands firm against the hurricane and gets knocked down, while the sapling bends with the wind and survives."

"Exactly."

Dezhurova pushed up from the table. "I'm going to check the outside camera views and see if the dust is obscuring them yet."

"Good idea," said Jamie. He got to his feet, too. "I'll put in a call to Wiley and Dex, check on how they're doing."

Vijay turned to Fuchida. "How does your ankle feel?"

"Not bad," the biologist replied. "I can walk on it without much pain."

"Then let's check out the garden one more time before going to bed."

Jamie thought Stacy suppressed a smirk at Vijay's mention of bed.

Rodriguez got up from the table. "Come on, Trudy. I'll play you a round of Space Battle."

"Not with you, Tommy. You're a shark. Besides, I won't be able to concentrate on the game with this storm on top of us."

Rodriguez went around to her chair. "Come on, I'll give you a ten-thousand-point handicap. It'll be fun. Take your mind off the storm."

She got up. Reluctantly, Jamie thought.

Jamie felt glad that their electrical power came from the nuclear generator, which would not be affected by the storm. He followed Stacy to the comm center, forcing himself not to turn back to look at Vijay.

As Dex stared at the blank screen on the rover's control panel, he could still see his father's image, like the retinal glow of a flashbulb or the lingering presence of a powerful genie.

He wants to dump Jamie, Dex said to himself. He wants to dump Jamie, but he didn't say a word about who he wants to take Jamie's place.

Dex sank back in the cushioned chair, his mind spinning. Could I do it? The answer came to him immediately. Certainly I could do it. I could head this operation without any trouble. But would the others listen to me? Especially if they think I pulled strings with my father to knock Jamie off.

This is tricky, he realized. The thought of being named mission director filled Dex with a warm flush of pride. They'd listen to me. They'd have to. After all, it won't be just my father who picks me; the whole ICU board would have to vote on it. Probably they'd want a unanimous vote.

But would Dad put me in charge? Does he trust me that much? Or would it be just another one of his ways to keep me under his thumb?

Jesus H. Christ, he swore. I'm on friggin' Mars and he's still got me jumping through his goddamned hoops!

Craig came stomping in through the airlock hatch.

"Gettin' dusty out there," he said, once he lifted the visor of his helmet.

Dex started to get up from his seat, but Craig called back, "I'm okay. It'll just take me a little time to vacuum all this crud off th' suit."

Dex went back anyway and helped him out of the backpack. It too was covered with a thin sheen of pinkish powder. Even Craig's helmet was tainted.

"We're going to get buried in this stuff," he heard himself say. He wished his voice didn't sound so shaky.

"Looks that way," Craig said easily. "Th' covers on the solar panels are holdin' down good, though. Wind might be makin' a lotta noise, but there's not much punch in her."

"That's good."

They were just starting to eat their dinners when the comm unit buzzed. Dex got up and went to the cockpit. He slid into the driver's seat and tapped the ON key.

Jamie Waterman's coppery-red serious face filled the panel screen. "Hello, Dex. How are you two doing?"

"Just having dinner, chief."

Jamie said, "It's starting to blow here. According to the latest met report, you'll be in the storm at least through tomorrow."

Dex nodded. He had seen the meteorology report; studied it hard.

"How are the batteries performing?" Jamie asked.

"We're still on the fuel cells. Wiley decided to run them to exhaustion before we go to the batteries."

"Smart move."

"What's happening there?"

Jamie seemed to think it over for a few moments. "We're in good shape. We've got everything battened down. It's going to be a noisy night, though."

Despite himself, Dex gave a snorting, derisive laugh. "Tell me about it."

"Your telemetry is coming through all right," Jamie said. "We're getting good data from you."

"Fine."

"The transmission will probably degrade as dust piles up on your antennas, though."

"I know." Dex started to feel a tendril of exasperation. Jamie's just talking to hear himself talk, he thought.

"I can't think of anything else we can do for you," he said. "I wish I'd ordered you to stay at the generator."

Dex suppressed an urge to say, *Me, too.* Instead, he leaned closer to Jamie's image on the display screen and said as cheerfully as he could, "We're doing fine out here. And when the storm clears up we'll be that much closer to the Pathfinder site."

Again Jamie was silent for several maddening moments. At last he said, "It's too late to worry about what might have been. Good luck, Dex. Give Wiley my best wishes."

"Right. We'll call you in the morning."

"If the antennas are still functioning," Jamie said.

"We'll clean them off if they're covered with dust," Dex replied, sharply.

"Good. Okay. Good night."

"Good night." Dex punched the OFF key. *Christ, he looks like he doesn't expect to see us again.*

Then he thought, *Maybe that's what Jamie wants. Get me out of his hair. No, he's not like that. But it's exactly how I'd feel if our situation was reversed.*

To his surprise, it was Rodriguez who could not keep his mind on the Space Battle game. Time and again he focused his concentration on the computer screen, but his attention wandered with every shriek of the wind outside. The dome seemed to creak and groan like an old wooden sailing ship in a gale; Rodriguez almost thought he could feel the floor shuddering and pitching.

He and Trudy Hall sat side by side in her bio lab, with two high-speed joysticks plugged into the beeping, chattering computer. The screen showed sleek space battle-craft maneuvering wildly against a background of stars and planets while they zapped at each other with laser beams. Ships exploded with great roars of sound.

Finally, when he had lost the third round of the computer game, Rodriguez pushed his chair back and said, "That's enough. I quit."

"You let me win," Trudy said. There was more delight in her smiling expression than accusation.

He shook his head vehemently. "Naw. I was trying. I just couldn't concentrate."

"Really?"

Rodriguez's shoulders drooped. "Really."

"Worried about the storm?"

"It's kinda silly, I know. But yeah, it's got me spooked . . . a little."

"Me, too," Hall admitted.

"You sure don't look it," he said, surprised. "You look calm as a cucumber."

"On the outside. Inside I'm as jumpy as . . . as . . ."

"As a flea on a hot griddle?"

She laughed. "What a ghastly idea."

He got to his feet. "Come on, I'll buy you a cup of coffee. Or maybe you prefer tea."

She stood up beside him, slim and spare next to his solid, chunky build. They were almost the same height, though, and her dark brown hair was only a shade lighter than his.

"Actually, I still have a drop or two of good brown sherry in my quarters."

Rodriguez's brows rose. "We're not supposed to take any liquor—"

"It's left over from our landing party. Should have finished it then, I suppose, but I saved a bit for a possible emergency."

"Yeah, but . . ."

"This counts as an emergency, don't you think?"

Inadvertently, Rodriguez glanced up into the shadowy height of the darkened dome. The wind moaned outside.

"There's not enough to make anyone drunk, you realize," Hall said. "Just a bit to take the edge off, you know."

He looked back at her and saw the fear and helplessness in her eyes. She's just as scared as I am, he told himself. She feels just the way I do.

"Okay," he said.

"Come on, then," Trudy said, holding her hand out to him. "Walk me home."

He took her hand. Then as they walked through the empty shadows of the dome, with the wind howling now and the structure making deeper, stranger noises of its own, he slid his arm around her waist. She leaned her head against his shoulder and they walked together toward her cubicle and a night when neither of them wanted to be alone.

Stacy Dezhurova was staring hard at the display screens, watching how the wind was fluttering the tied-down wings of the soarplanes. The wings of the bigger, heavier rocket plane were also undulating noticeably, straining against the tie-downs fastened to the ground.

"We've done all we can, Stacy," said Jamie, behind her. "You ought to get some sleep now."

"But if one of the planes breaks loose . . ."

"What can we do about it?" he asked gently. "We parked them downwind of the dome. If they break loose, at least they won't come crashing in here."

She nodded, but kept her eyes glued to the screens.

"Stacy, do I have to *order* you to your quarters?"

Dezhurova turned and looked up at him. "Someone ought to stay on duty. Just in case."

"Okay," Jamie said. "I will. Go get some sleep."

"No. I couldn't sleep anyway. I'll stay."

Jamie pulled up the other wheeled chair and sat next to her. "Stacy . . . we're going to need you tomorrow, bright-eyed and bushy-tailed, rested and able to perform at your best."

She looked away from him briefly. Then, jabbing a finger at the digital clock next to the main display screen, she said, "It's twenty-one-fifteen, almost. I'll stay here until oh-two hundred. Then you can come on until six. That will give each of us four hours' sleep. Okay?"

"One A.M.," Jamie said.

Her serious expression did not change at all as she asked, "Will that give you and Vijay enough time?"

Jamie felt his jaw drop open.

Dezhurova laughed. "Go on. Set your alarm for one. Then you can relieve me."

Jamie got up from the chair thinking, Stacy could take the director's job. She'd be good at it.

Vijay was sitting at the galley table when Jamie left the comm center. He walked straight to her and she looked up at him with her big, soulful eyes filled with—what? he wondered. Anxiety? Loneliness? Fear?

And what's in my eyes? Jamie wondered as he extended his hand toward her. She took it in hers, rose from her chair, and walked wordlessly with him toward his quarters. What am I doing? Jamie asked himself. This isn't love. This isn't the kind of romantic moment that poets write about. It's need; we need each other. We're scared of this storm, of being so far from home, so far from safety. We need the comfort of another person, someone to hold on to, someone to hold me.

They said hardly a word to each other as they stripped and got into Jamie's narrow bunk. Their lovemaking was torrid, as if all the rage and power of the storm had possessed them both. The first time, ten nights ago, they had taken pains to be as quiet as possible. Not this night. Not with the wind wailing outside. Now they lay, languid, spent, thoughts drifting idly, all barriers down, all furies calmed.

Should I tell her about Trumball? he asked himself. There was no urgency in the thought. It simply rose to his consciousness dreamily, like a whisper struggling through a drug-induced haze.

Jamie kissed Vijay's bare shoulder; she muttered something sleepily and snuggled closer to him. As he drifted toward sleep with Vijay's body warm and softly cupped next to him, he knew he would feel empty and alone without her. And afraid.

Sharp, cold reality stabbed through him. You can't talk about love. You can't even think about it. Not here. Not under these conditions. You made that mistake last time and it brought nothing but pain to you and her. You can't expect Vijay to commit her life to you on the basis of what we're doing here.

Which means, he heard himself reason, that you can't burden her with your problem about Trumball. It's your problem, not hers. You've got to find the right path for yourself, alone.

Jamie turned slightly in the bunk and looked over at the glowing red numerals of the digital clock. Get some sleep. It's going to be one A.M. damned soon.

It was nearly midnight as Stacy returned to her chair in the comm center and set a plastic cup of hot tea on the console beside the main display screen. The wind was screeching outside, a thin tortured wail like the distant howl of souls in hell. Wearily she started checking all the dome's environmental systems again.

With deliberate calm, Dezhurova tapped into the environmental monitoring display. Everything was normal in the dome, except for one of the air-circulation fans, which had gone off-line earlier in the day. She would attend to that in the morning, she told herself.

She opened the program for the sensors that monitored environmental conditions in the garden bubble. Before she could check them, though, the yellow light on the main communications console began blinking and her screen showed: INCOMING MESSAGE.

She grumbled to herself as she tapped at the keyboard. What does Tarawa want now?

To her surprise, it wasn't mission control at Tarawa. Her comm screen showed a bleary-eyed, tousle-haired Dex Trumball.

Dex could not sleep.

He lay in his bunk listening to the wind shrieking just inches away, hearing the iron-rich sand scratching at the rover's thin metal skin, *feeling* the storm clawing at the rover, trying to find a way inside, a loose latch, a slight seam, the tiniest of openings in the welds that held the rover's skin together.

We could be dead in a minute, he knew. Or worse, buried alive under the sand with the electrical power gone. Suffocate to death when the air gives out.

And we can't do anything about it! Just lay here and take it. Let the friggin' storm pound us and batter at us until it finds a way to kill us.

He sat up abruptly, heart racing, chest heaving. He felt sweaty and cold at the same time. He had to urinate again.

Peering through the darkness, he could make out in the faint glow from the instrument panel up in the cockpit the lumpy form of Craig, sleeping in the bunk on the other side of the module. Craig lay on his back, mouth slightly open, snoring gently.

Christ, he's as relaxed as a baby in its cradle, Trumball thought as he slipped quietly out of his bunk.

He padded barefoot to the lavatory, opposite the racks where the hard suits stood like ghosts in armor. Fear fills the bladder, Dex told himself as he urinated into the stainless steel toilet bowl. This motherfucking storm's scaring the piss out of me. It was his fourth trip to the toilet since he had gone to bed.

"You all right, buddy?" Craig asked softly as he crawled back into his bunk.

"Yeah," Dex snapped. "I'm fine."

"Kinda noisy out there, ain't it?"

"It sure is."

"Don't let it spook you, kid. We're safe as can be inside here."

Dex knew Craig was trying to reassure him, calm him. He knew he should be grateful to Wiley. Instead he felt angry that the older man had called him "kid." And ashamed to be caught in his terror.

The wind quieted a bit. The shrieking softened. Maybe it's over, Dex thought. Maybe it's winding down.

He lay back on his sweat-soaked pillow and closed his eyes again. But the instant he did, the wind gusted again with a furious scream. Dex felt the rover rock.

He bolted up to a sitting position and pounded the mattress with both fists, almost sobbing. Leave me alone! Leave me alone! Go away and leave me alone, please, please, please.

The wind continued to howl, though. If anything, it got louder.

Blearily, he shuffled up to the rover's cockpit and slumped into the right-hand seat. Let's see what's happening at the dome. Talk to somebody. Anybody. Take your mind off this mother-humpin' storm.

Stacy's stolid, fleshy face filled the tiny screen on the control panel. The picture was streaked, grainy, but she looked surprised.

"Dex?"

"Yeah," he said softly, not wanting to wake Craig again. "Too noisy out here to sleep. How's everything there?"

•   •   •

Dezhurova spoke with Dex for a few seconds, then realized that Trumball merely wanted to chat because he could not sleep in the midst of the storm. Reception was weak; his video kept breaking up. Probably dust is piling up on his antennas, she thought. She kept on talking with him, but turned her real attention to the monitoring screens and continued checking the environmental conditions in the garden bubble.

Temperature below nominal, she saw. That should not be. Air pressure was falling, too.

Her breath caught in her throat. Without even thinking about Dex, still jabbering on the main comm screen, Stacy grabbed the loudspeaker mike and bellowed: "Emergency! The garden dome is ripping apart!"

Dex gaped at the tiny comm screen.

"Jamie, everyone—the garden dome is ripping apart!" Dezhurova repeated, roaring like the crack of doom. "We need everyone, right now!"

Then the comm screen went dark.

Dex sat in the rover's cockpit, icy sweat trickling down his ribs, staring at the dead comm screen.

My god almighty, he thought, panting with mounting terror as he sat in the shadows. If the garden bubble goes, the main dome could go, too. Then we'd all be dead.

Mitsuo Fuchida lay in his bunk, staring up into the darkness, listening to the wind and the accompanying creaks and groans of the dome.

It's like being on a ship at sea, he said to himself, except that it doesn't rock.

He had considered taking a tranquilizer before going to bed, but decided that he would not need one. He had looked death in the face, back at the lava tube on Olympus Mons. This windstorm held no more terrors for him. Death will come or not, he thought. What cannot be controlled must be accepted.

Still, he lay awake listening to the storm until he heard Stacy's shout: "Emergency! The garden dome is ripping apart! We need everyone, right now!"

Automatically he leaped out of bed, a stab of pain from his injured ankle shooting through his leg. Awkward with the bandaged ankle, Fuchida limped to the comm center. Jamie, Vijay, Rodriguez, and Trudy

Hall were also hurrying there, each of them hastily pulling on rumpled coveralls as they ran.

"The garden dome has been punctured," Stacy said, jabbing a thick finger at the monitor screen.

"Camera view," Jamie snapped, slipping into the wheeled chair beside her.

He peered at the screen. "Can't see anything—wait, the dome fabric is rippling."

"Pressure and temperature both falling rapidly," Dezhurova said, an unaccustomed edge of fear in her voice.

"The plants will die!" Trudy was saying, her voice pitched high, frightened. "The nighttime temperature—"

"I know, I know," Jamie snapped. Turning toward Rodriguez, he said, "We have spare cans of epoxy, don't we? Where are they?"

Rodriguez bent over one of the unused consoles and punched at its keyboard, then started scrolling through a list so fast it looked like a blur.

He saw what he wanted and froze the display. "Repair epoxy," he said, pointing to the screen. "It's stored in locker seventeen, A shelf."

"Go get it," Jamie commanded. "As much as you can carry."

Rodriguez brushed past Fuchida as he raced out of the comm center, staggering the limping biologist. Vijay headed out, too. "I'll help Tommy," she called over her shoulder.

Jamie jumped up from his chair. "Stacy, get suited up. Trudy, you help her. Mitsuo, take over the comm chair."

"Where are you going?" Stacy demanded.

As he rushed out into the dome's dimly lit central area, Jamie said, "We've got to slap some temporary patches on the holes in the dome, if they're not already too bad."

"You can't go in there!" Trudy yelped.

"Somebody's got to stop the leak before it gets worse."

"Wait for Tómas," Dezhurova said. "The epoxy—"

"No time!" Jamie snapped, sprinting away from them. He headed for the airlock as they yelled after him.

"Get Stacy suited up!" he yelled back. "Mitsuo! Turn on all the lights in there!"

The dome flared into daytime brightness as Jamie reached the airlock that connected to the garden. Not in here, Mitsuo, Jamie corrected silently. In the garden, for the sake of Christ!

The pressure on the other side of the airlock had not fallen so low that the lock automatically sealed, Jamie realized as he pushed through the double hatches. Not yet, he told himself.

It was cold inside the garden. Jamie shivered involuntarily as he stepped in. The wind shrieked louder and the dome fabric was flapping noisily, like a sail luffing in the breeze. At least the full-spectrum sunlamps were on. Mitsuo heard me after all.

The emergency patches were stored in a closed box next to the airlock hatch. Tearing it open and grabbing a double handful of the thin plastic sheets, Jamie thought that they should have learned their lesson from the first expedition and scattered the sheets on the floor around the dome's perimeter.

Now he released them and saw them flutter in the air currents, then slap themselves against a pair of puncture holes on the far side of the dome.

Rodriguez boiled through the hatch, a big spray can of epoxy in each hand. He looked like a two-gun frontier sheriff, grim and determined.

"I'll take them," Jamie said over the shrieking wind. "No sense both of us risking—"

"You're not gonna be the only hero tonight," Rodriguez said, pushing past Jamie and heading for the spots where the temporary patches were fluttering against the side of the dome.

Vijay stepped through with more cans. Jamie grabbed one from her and they both ran after Rodriguez.

The plants didn't look too bad, Jamie thought, glancing at the rows of hydroponics trays. But what the hell do I know? Green leaves, mostly curled tight. Are the ones closest to the rips drooping more than the others? Christ, some of them look gray!

"I think we got it sealed," Rodriguez said, after a furious few minutes of spraying.

Jamie looked around. The dome had stopped flapping. Fuchida must be pumping more air in here, keeping the pressure up. The wind outside sounded just as loud, maybe even louder, but now the dome's plastic structure seemed rigid, safe.

"Maybe you're right," he said cautiously.

"It's cold in here," Vijay said, hugging herself.

"Go and tell Mitsuo to goose up the heaters," Jamie instructed. "Tómas, let's spray the whole perimeter of the bubble, down here where the fabric joins with the flooring. If there's going to be any more problems, that's where they'll happen."

"Right," said Rodriguez.

Just then Dezhurova clomped in, buttoned up in her hard suit.

"We got it under control," Rodriguez shouted happily at her.

She raised her visor and glowered at him. Rodriguez laughed.

"Stacy," Jamie said, "I want you and Tómas to check the integrity of the dome. Spray anything that looks like a potential leak."

"The epoxy is not transparent. It will cut down on the sunshine the plants receive."

"That's okay. The lamps can make up for lack of sunlight, temporarily. The important thing is to ensure the dome's integrity."

Trudy Hall stepped through the airlock hatch. "Oh, my lord! The tomatoes are *ruined!*"

Jamie grabbed her by the arm. "Trudy, you and Mitsuo should check out all the plants, see how much damage has been done. I'll take over at the comm center."

"All right, certainly." She rushed to the trays of plants at the far side of the dome.

Jamie was still at the comm console when the sun finally came up and the others began to stir. The wind was still yowling outside, but with the sunrise the visibility outside improved somewhat. In the screens that showed the outside camera views Jamie could see that the planes were all still there, although one of the soarplane's wings seemed bent oddly. One of the cameras had ceased functioning, but otherwise everything seemed to be in reasonably good shape.

Red sky at morning, he thought.

"Want some coffee?"

It was Vijay, standing at the comm center doorway with a steaming mug in her hands.

"Good idea," said Jamie, reaching for it.

"How is everything?" she asked, sliding into the chair next to his.

"We're in reasonably good shape."

"How much damage to the garden was there?"

"Trudy was almost in tears over the tomatoes and some of the soybeans, but most of the plants are all right. We caught the leak in time."

"We won't have to pack up and go home, then?"

He shook his head slowly. "No. We might have to go without soy-burgers for a while, but the garden will still feed us."

"That was a very brave thing you did, dashing in there like that."

Jamie felt his brows hike up. He didn t feel very brave. With a shrug he replied, "Seemed like the right thing to do. We had to get those patches in place."

"You could have been killed."

"I never even thought of that," he confessed. "It all happened so fast . . ."

"You're a bloody hero, Jamie." She wasn't joking, he saw. She was in dead earnest.

Feeling suddenly uncomfortable, Jamie changed the subject. "I haven't been able to raise Dex and Wiley yet."

"You expected that, di'n't you?"

He nodded. "Probably a lot of dust on their antennas by now. We'll just have to be patient."

"You're good at that," she said, with a smile.

He caught her implication. "It's a lot more fun being patient with you than with them," he said, low and swift, afraid of being over-heard.

Before she could reply, Rodriguez burst in, white teeth gleaming in a huge grin. "Well, we made it through the night," he said, then burst into hearty laughter.

Jamie threw a perplexed glance at Vijay, who shrugged her shoulders.

"You were terrific, boss," the astronaut said, beaming at Jamie. "Saved our necks, man."

Jamie shook his head, but Vijay nodded agreement. "If the garden had gone, we'd have to pack up and leave, wouldn't we?"

"Maybe," Jamie conceded. "Anyway, the garden's going to be all right. So let's get on with the program, okay?"

"Right!" Rodriguez said. "You had breakfast yet, boss? I'm hungry enough to eat a Martian buffalo."

From the doorway, Stacy Dezhurova snapped, "You'll have to find one first, Tómas."

"Lemme grab some juice," Rodriguez said, still grinning buoyantly, "then I'll spell you at the console while you guys grab breakfast."

"I thought you were starving," Jamie said, getting up from the chair.

"Yeah, I know, but I can wait. You guys go eat. I'll hold the fort here."

Jamie looked to Dezhurova, who said, "I'll get your juice, Tómas."

"Okay, thanks."

Jamie said. "Well, if you're going to take over, see if you can raise Craig and Dex."

"Right." Rodriguez sat heavily on the little chair, making it roll away from the console a few feet.

As he went to the galley with Vijay and Dezhurova, Jamie wondered aloud, "Tómas sure is chipper this morning. He must have had a good restful sleep."

Dezhurova sputtered into laughter. "Not exactly."

"What do you mean?"

Stacy looked up into Jamie's face. "Didn't you hear them? Him and Trudy? They were at it all night long."

Inadvertently, Jamie glanced at Vijay, who was trying to suppress a smirk.

"At least you two are quiet about it," Stacy went on, matter-of-factly. "My cubicle is next to Trudy's. Tom was snorting all night like Ferdinand the Bull. He even drowned out the storm."

Vijay broke out in laughter.

They had just started to eat breakfast when Fuchida limped up to the table, looking distressed.

"What's wrong, Mitsuo?" Jamie asked.

"Am I the only one who wonders why the garden dome began to rip apart?" he asked.

"What do you mean?"

The biologist sat across from Jamie and Vijay and propped his bandaged ankle on an empty chair.

"How can the dust rip the bubble fabric?" he asked, like a professor posing a problem for his class.

Dezhurova got up from the table. "I promised Tómas I would bring him juice," she remembered. "He probably needs it."

Fuchida did not catch her insinuation. "The bubble's plastic cannot be punctured by dust particles," he said quietly, firmly. "Yet the fabric was punctured."

"I thought it ripped along the base where it connects with the flooring," Jamie said.

"No," Fuchida replied, raising one finger for emphasis. "There are two small punctures. If not repaired so quickly, they would have grown into a rip that would have torn the entire dome off its foundation."

"But we did catch it in time," Vijay said. "Jamie did, that is."

Fuchida acknowledged the fact with a small dip of his chin. "Still, we must ask how the dome was punctured."

Jamie suggested, "Small rocks blown by the wind?"

"I doubt it," the biologist said.

"Then how?"

"I don't know. But it troubles me. The dome should not have failed. That plastic fabric has been tested under much more severe conditions in laboratory simulations. It should not have failed."

"Yet it did," Vijay said, almost in a whisper.

"It did indeed." Fuchida looked like a prosecuting attorney to Jamie. Suspicious, almost angry.

"Well," Jamie said, "I don't know how it failed, but we ought to figure out some way of making certain it doesn't happen again."

"Hey buddy," Craig said cheerfully, "we made it through the night."

From across the narrow table between their bunks, Dex nodded glumly. He felt exhausted, sleepless eyes gummy, coveralls rumpled and stinking of fear.

The wind was still screeching outside. Particles of iron-cored grit were still grinding against the rover's thin skin, like an endless army of soldier ants working tirelessly to break through their defenses and come in and devour them.

"Communications're out, of course," Craig added.

"Of course," said Dex blearily.

"Soon's the wind dies down to less'n a hundred knots we'll go outside and dust off the antennas. Squirt a signal back to base, let 'em know we're okay."

"If they're okay," Dex replied gloomily.

"They'll be all right," said Craig. "That big dome's built like the Rock of Gibraltar. Been through dust storms before, y'know. Been settin' out there more'n six years, after all."

"I suppose so," Dex admitted.

Unbidden, his mind was cataloguing all the things that might not be okay. If the covers had ripped off during the night, the solar cells could be scratched and pitted so badly they'd be useless. The fuel cells were already down to zero; they were living off the batteries. The gritty dust could have worked its way into the wheel bearings, immobilizing them completely. Then we'll have a choice of starving or suffocating, Dex thought. Or the dust could have scoured the antennas so badly their comm systems would be completely shot. Then we couldn't navigate, couldn't get positioning data from the satellites; we'd be lost out here forever.

Or the whole frigging base dome might have blown down during the night, he added.

"Hey!" Craig snapped. "You listenin'?"

"Sorry," Dex said, trying to sit up a little straighter.

"I said we'd better stick to a cold breakfast. No sense drainin' the batteries by usin' the microwave."

"I'll get breakfast," Dex said, pushing himself up from his bunk. "You can do the systems check."

"Already did that. After breakfast we power down. Shut off the freezer, let it coast; food'll keep cold inside okay. Air fans on low. Lights to minimum. Until we get the solar panels uncovered and workin' again."

"If they'll work again," Dex muttered as he went back to the compact stand of racks that served as the rover's galley.

"Didn't get much sleep last night, huh?"

"How'd you guess?" Dex pulled out the first two cereal packages he could reach.

"Listen, kid, the worst is over. Storm's peterin' out now. In another couple hours—"

Dex whirled on him. "You listen, pal! You don't like being called Possum? Well I don't like being called kid. Got that?"

"Then stop behavin' like a kid," Craig shot back, scowling.

Dex started to reply, but found he had no answer for the older man.

"You're scared, okay. I am, too. What th' hell, we're stranded out here in the middle of downtown Mars. For all I know we're covered with sand twelve feet deep and ever'body in the base is dead. Okay! We'll have to deal with that. You do what you can do. You don't sit around mopin' and grumblin' like some teenager with an acne problem."

Despite himself, Dex laughed. "Is that what I've been doing?"

Still sitting on his bunk, Craig's leathery face rearranged itself into a small smile. He nodded. "Sort of," he said.

"I'm scared, Wiley," he admitted. "I don't want to die out here."

"Shit, buddy, I don't want to die *at all*."

As he put both cereal packages on the table, Dex said, "Maybe we ought to go outside and see how bad the damage is."

"Still blowin' pretty strong out there. Be better to wait a couple hours."

"I'll go nuts sitting in here with nothing to do but listen to that wind."

Craig nodded. "Hmm. Yeah, me, too."

"So?"

"So let's have us a nice leisurely breakfast and then take our time suitin' up."

"Good," said Dex, feeling some of the fear ease away. Not all of it. But he felt better than he had during the night.

"Not as bad as it could've been," Craig pronounced. But his voice sounded heavy, unhappy, in Dex's earphones.

The sky was still gray, sullen. The wind was still keening, although nowhere near as loud as it had been. Dex was surprised that inside the hard suit he felt no push from the wind at all. He had expected to have to lean over hard and force himself forward, like a man struggling through a gale. Instead, the thin Martian air might just as well have been totally calm.

On one side the rover was half buried in rust-red sand. From the nose of the cockpit to the tail of the jointed vehicle's third segment, the sand had piled up as high as the roof on the windward side.

"Good thing the hatch was on the leeward side," Dex said. "We might've had trouble getting it open if it was buried in this stuff."

"Naw, I don't think so," Craig answered, kicking at the pile. Dust flew like ashes, or like dry autumn leaves when a child scuffs at them.

"Maybe."

"Besides," Craig added, "I turned her so the hatch'd be on the sheltered side when we stopped for the night."

Dex blinked inside his helmet, trying to remember if he was driving then or Craig. Wiley's not above taking credit for good luck, he thought.

"Come on, let's see what's happened topside."

As they trudged around the rover, back to the side that was almost free of the dust, Dex could see that at least part of the makeshift coverings they had taped down over the solar panels had been blown loose. One sheet was flapping fitfully in the wind.

As Craig climbed up the ladder next to the airlock hatch to inspect the solar panels, Dex caught sight of the most beautiful apparition he had seen on Mars: The dull gray dust-laden clouds thinned enough, for a few moments, for him to see the bright pink sky overhead. His heart leaped inside him. The storm's breaking up! It's breaking up at last.

"Worse than I hoped for," Craig's voice grated in his earphones, "but better'n I was scared of."

Craig came down from the ladder. "We got some scratches and pittin' up there where the tarp came loose. The rest of the panels look okay, though."

"Good," said Dex, suddenly enthusiastic. "Listen, Wiley, I'm going to duck back inside and put on the VR rig. Nobody's ever recorded a Martian dust storm before. This'll make great viewing back home!"

He heard Craig chuckling inside his helmet. Then the older man said, "Startin' to get some of your spirit back on-line, huh?"

"I . . ." Dex stopped, perplexed for a moment. Then he put a gloved hand on the shoulder of Craig's suit. "Wiley, you really helped me. I was scared shitless back there, and you pulled me through it."

"You did it for yourself," Craig said, "but I'll be glad to take the credit for it."

Dex felt his insides go hollow.

As if he sensed it, Craig said, "Don't worry, son. What happened here is between you and me, nobody else."

"Thanks, Wiley." The words sounded pitifully weak to Dex, compared to the enormous rush of gratitude and respect that he felt.

"Okay," Craig said gruffly. "Now before you start doin' your VR stuff, let's get the antennas cleaned off so we can tell Jamie and the gang that we're okay."

Rodriguez gave a sudden whoop from the comm center.

"Wiley's calling in!"

Jamie bolted up from the galley table while Vijay stayed to help the limping Fuchida. In the comm center Jamie saw Craig's scruffy-bearded face on the main screen.

". . . solar panel output's degraded by four-five percent," Craig was reporting. "Coulda been a lot worse."

"What about the fuel cells?" Rodriguez asked.

"Dex's electrolyzing our extra water; gonna feed the hydrogen and oxy to 'em. That way we can rest the batteries."

Poking his head into the comm camera's view, Jamie asked, "Do you have to dig yourselves out?"

Craig looked very pleased. "Nope. The wheels and drive motors are all okay. We just put 'er in gear and pulled ourselves loose. We're movin' now."

"Wow!" Rodriguez exclaimed.

"That's great," said Jamie, feeling genuinely pleased and relieved. "That's just great, Wiley."

"Oughtta be at Ares Vallis in another three–four days," Craig said. Then he added, "If the weather holds up."

Rodriguez laughed. "There's not another storm in sight."

"Good."

When Craig signed off, Rodriguez began checking the telemetry from the rover and Jamie went back to the inventory list. The wind was still yowling outside like dead spirits begging to come in out of the cold.

Jamie was tired, physically and emotionally drained, as he made his way back to the comm center for what must have been the hundredth time that day.

As the storm wound down, he had spent most of the day in the greenhouse bubble, checking and rechecking the area that had been damaged. He had even suited up and gone outside to inspect the damaged areas without the emergency patches and epoxy covering them. It was hard to say, but the areas seemed to have been punctured, not torn. Of course, once punctured the plastic fabric began to rip along the seam where it connected to the foundation of the dome.

What we need here is a forensic structural engineer, Jamie told himself. If there is such a person. Maybe Wiley could make some sense of it.

He took dozens of photographs of the damaged areas and transmitted them back to Tarawa for their analysis. There was nothing more he could think to do, but he kept feeling that he was missing something. Something important.

What is it, Grandfather? he asked silently. What have I overlooked?

Once in the comm center he slumped down on the little chair and put through another message to Tarawa.

"Pete: The greenhouse dome looks okay now, but I'm worried about what might happen in the next storm. Maybe that won't be for another year, but it's a problem we ought to think about now, not when the dust starts blowing again. It's obvious that we overlooked this problem, but with twenty-twenty hindsight I think we ought to pay attention to it.

"Can you get the world's assembled experts to figure out how we can protect the greenhouse bubble with the materials we have on hand? That includes native Martian materials, of course. What I'm wondering is, can we make glass bricks out of the Martian sand? Build an igloo that's transparent? Look into it for me, will you?"

The wind died down almost completely after sunset. Jamie was tempted to put on a suit and go out to see if the stars were still in their places, but he felt too tired. The outside cameras showed that the planes were still there, although what condition their solar panels might be in would have to wait for a closer inspection.

The dome was quiet, back to normal, when Jamie finally went to his quarters. Vijay was already there, in the bunk. He blinked with surprise.

"Tómas is bunking with Trudy," she said, matter-of-factly.

Nodding, Jamie muttered, "I wonder if Mitsuo and Stacy are going to get it on?"

Vijay giggled softly. "Not bloody likely."

"Why not?"

"Stacy's gay."

Jamie's eyes popped open. "What?"

"Stacy's a lesbian."

There's nothing wrong with that, Jamie told himself. Still, he felt shocked.

"Poor Mitsuo," he heard himself whisper as he got under the covers beside her.

Vijay moved over to make room for him on the narrow bunk. "I don't know about him. He hasn't come on to any of the women."

"Maybe he's gay, too?"

"I doubt it. I think he's just got more self-control than you western ape-men."

Jamie wanted to debate the point, but instead he closed his eyes and fell instantly asleep.

Meanwhile, back on Earth . . . [2]

What would drive the sons and daughters of Earth out into the cold and dangerous depths of interplanetary space? The lure of profit or power or just plain adventure might be enough to draw some daring souls, but for a significant expansion of the human race across the space frontier, there must be some powerful force (or forces) driving people off-planet.

Shortly after I finished Mars I began work on a novel that featured Dan Randolph, the hard-driving visionary founder of Astro Manufacturing, Inc., a corporation involved in space transportation and manufacturing. In this novel, Empire Builders, I postulated a looming global ecological disaster: the greenhouse cliff.

Most scientists around the world are convinced that the Earth's climate is heating up, and that the human race's outpouring of greenhouse-enhancing gases such as carbon dioxide are a significant factor in the global warming. A small but insistent minority of scientists protest that global warming is largely illusory, or at least its impact has been grossly exaggerated.

For my Grand Tour novels, I speculated that global warming is not only real, but that its impact will hit suddenly, over a matter of a decade or so, not the gradual, centuries-long effect that most people expect. A greenhouse cliff, with a sudden, drastic rise in sea levels that floods coastal cities worldwide, leading to a collapse of the electrical power grid that is the cornerstone of our industrial society. Together with shifts of climate that wipe out large swaths of farmlands, the greenhouse cliff causes a global catastrophe of unparalleled proportion.

---

2. Homer invented that technique, in the *Odyssey,* when he switched from Odysseus's adventures to the plight of his wife, Penelope, by using the phrase, "Meanwhile, back in Ithaca . . .."

Visionaries such as Dan Randolph try to develop the resources of energy and raw materials that exist in space to help rebuild the Earth's shattered society. Others, such as Martin Humphries, want to use those resources to further their own schemes of power and profit.

But what is happening on Earth? We get a glimpse of this in "Greenhouse Chill." Incidentally, the possibility that a greenhouse warming can lead to a new ice age is now an accepted concept among many scientists; see William H. Calvin's A Brain for All Seasons (University of Chicago Press, 2002).

But I published first!

GREENHOUSE CHILL

et's face it, Hawk, we're lost."

Hawk frowned in disappointment at his friend. "You're lost, maybe. I know right where I am."

Squinting in the bright sunshine, Tim turned his head this way and that, searching the horizon. Nothing. Not another sail, not another boat anywhere in sight. Not even a bird. The only sounds he could hear were the soft gusting of the hot breeze and the splash of the gentle waves lapping against their stolen sailboat. The brilliant sky was cloudless, the sea stretched out all around them, and they were alone. Two teenaged runaways out in the middle of the empty sea.

"Yeah?" Tim challenged. "Then where are we?"

"Comin' up to the Ozarks, just about," said Hawk.

"How d'you know that?"

Hawk's frown evolved into a serious, superior, *knowing* expression. He was almost a year older than Tim, lean and hard-muscled from back-breaking farm labor. But his round face was animated, with sparkling blue eyes that could convince his younger friend to join him on this wild adventure to escape from their parents, their village, their lives of endless drudgery.

Tim was almost as tall as Hawk, but pudgier, softer. His father was the village rememberer, and Tim was being groomed to take his place in the due course of time. The work he did was mostly mental, instead of physical, but it was pure drudgery just the same, remembering all the family lines and the history of the village all the way back to the Flood.

"So," Tim repeated, "how d'you know where we're at? I don't see any signposts stickin' up outta the water."

"How long we been out?" Hawk asked sternly.

With a glance at the dwindling supply of salt beef and apples in the crate by the mast, Tim replied, "This is the fifth mornin'."

"Uh-huh. And where's the sun?"

Tim didn't bother to answer, it was so obvious.

"So the sun's behind your left shoulder, same's it's been every mornin'. Wind's still comin' up from the south, hot and strong. We're near the Ozarks."

"I still don't see how you figure that."

"My dad and my uncle been fishin' in these waters all their lives," Hawk said, matter-of-factly. "I learned from them."

Tim thought that over for a moment, then asked, "So how long before we get to Colorado?"

"Oh, that's *weeks* away," Hawk answered.

"Weeks? We ain't got enough food for weeks!"

"I know that. We'll put in at the Ozark Islands and get us some more grub there."

"How?"

"Huntin'," said Hawk. "Or trappin'. Or stealin', if we hafta."

Tim's dark eyes lit up. The thought of becoming robbers excited him.

The long lazy day wore on. Tim listened to the creak of the ropes and the flap of the heavy gray sail as he lay back in the boat's prow. He dozed, and when he woke again the sun had crawled halfway down toward the western edge of the sea. Off to the north, though, ominous clouds were building up, gray and threatening.

"Think it'll storm?" he asked Hawk.

"For sure," Hawk replied.

They had gone through a thunderstorm their first afternoon out. The booming thunder had scared Tim halfway out of his wits. That and the waves that rose up like mountains, making his stomach turn itself inside out as the boat tossed up and down and sideways and all. And the lightning! Tim had no desire to go through that again.

"Don't look so scared," Hawk said, with a tight smile on his face.

"I ain't scared!"

"Are too."

Tim admitted it with a nod. "Ain't you?"

"Not anymore."

"How come?"

Hawk pointed off to the left. Turning, Tim saw a smudge on the horizon, something low and dark, with more clouds over it. But these clouds were white and soft-looking.

"Island," Hawk said, pulling on the tiller and looping the rope around it to hold it in place. The boat swung around and the sail began flapping noisily.

Tim got up and helped Hawk swing the boom. The sail bellied out again, neat and taut. They skimmed toward the island while the storm clouds built up higher and darker every second, heading their way.

They won the race, barely, and pulled the boat up on a stony beach just as the first drops of rain began to spatter down on them, fat and heavy.

"Get the mast down, quick!" Hawk commanded. It was pouring rain by the time they got that done. Tim wanted to run for the shelter of the big trees, but Hawk said no, they'd use the boat's hull for protection.

"Trees attract lightnin', just like the mast would if we left it up," said Hawk.

Even on dry land the storm was scarifying. And the land didn't stay dry for long. Tim lay on the ground beneath the curve of the boat's hull as lightning sizzled all around them and the thunder blasted so loud it hurt his ears. Hawk sprawled beside Tim and both boys pressed themselves flat against the puddled stony ground.

The world seemed to explode into a white-hot flash and Tim heard a crunching, crashing sound. Peeping over Hawk's shoulder he saw one of the big trees slowly toppling over, split in half and smoking from a lightning bolt. For a moment he thought the tree would smash down on them, but it hit the ground a fair distance away with an enormous shattering smash.

At last the storm ended. The boys were soaking wet and Tim's legs felt too weak to hold him up, but he got to his feet anyway, trembling with cold and the memory of fear.

Slowly they explored the rocky, pebbly beach and poked in among the trees. Squirrels and birds chattered and scolded at them. Tim saw a snake, a beautiful blue racer, slither through the brush. Without a word between them, the boys went back to the boat. Hawk pulled his bow and a handful of arrows from the box where he had stored them while Tim collected a couple of pocketfuls of throwing stones.

By the time the sun was setting they were roasting a young rabbit over their campfire.

Burping contentedly, Hawk leaned back on one elbow as he wiped his greasy chin. "Now this is the way to live, ain't it?"

"You bet," Tim agreed. He had seen some blackberry bushes back among the trees and decided that in the morning he'd pick as many as he could carry before they started out again. No sense leaving them to the birds.

"Hello there!"

The deep voice froze both boys for an instant. Then Hawk dived for his bow while Tim scrambled to his feet.

"Don't be frightened," called the voice. It came from the shadowy bushes in among the trees, sounding ragged and scratchy, like it was going to cough any minute.

On one knee, Hawk fitted an arrow into his hunter's bow. Tim suddenly felt very exposed, standing there beside the campfire, both hands empty.

Out of the shadows of the trees stepped a figure. A man. An old, shaggy, squat barrel of a man in a patchwork vest that hung open across his white-fuzzed chest and heavy belly, his head bare and balding but his brows and beard and what was left of his hair bushy and white. His arms were short, but thick with muscle. And he carried a strange-looking bow, black and powerful-looking, with all kinds of weird attachments on it.

"No need for weapons," he said, in his gravelly voice.

"Yeah?" Hawk challenged, his voice shaking only a little. "Then what's that in your hand?"

"Oh, this?" The stranger bent down and laid his bow gently on the ground. "I've been carrying it around with me for so many years it's like an extension of my arm."

He straightened up slowly, Tim saw, as if the effort caused him pain. There was a big, thick-bladed knife tucked in his belt. His feet were shod in what looked like strips of leather.

"Who are you?" Hawk demanded, his bow still in his hands. "What do you want?"

The stranger smiled from inside his bushy white beard. "Since you've just arrived on my island, I think it's more proper for you to identify yourselves first."

Tim saw that Hawk was a little puzzled by that.

"Whaddaya mean, your island?" Hawk asked.

The old man spread his arms wide. "This is my island. I live here. I've lived her for damned near two hundred years."

"That's bull-dingy," Hawk snapped. Back home he never would have spoken so disrespectfully to an adult, but things were different out here.

The shaggy old man laughed. "Yes, I suppose it does sound fantastic. But it's true. I'm two hundred and fifty-six years old, assuming I've been keeping my calendar correctly."

"Who are you?" Hawk demanded. "Whatcha want?"

Placing a stubby-fingered hand on his chest, the man replied, "My name is Julius Schwarzkopf, once a professor of meteorology at the University of Washington, in St. Louis, Missouri, U. S. of A."

"I heard of St. Louie," Tim blurted.

"Fairy tales," Hawk snapped.

"No, it was real," said Professor Julius Schwarzkopf. "It was a fine city, back when I was a teacher."

Little by little, the white-bearded stranger eased their suspicions. He came up to the fire and sat down with them, leaving his bow where he'd laid it. He kept the knife in his belt, though. Tim sat a little bit away from him, where there were plenty of fist-sized rocks within easy reach.

The Prof, as he insisted they call him, opened a little sack on his belt and offered the boys a taste of dried figs.

As the last embers of daylight faded and the stars began to come out, he suggested, "Why don't you come to my place for the night? It's better than sleeping out in the open."

Hawk didn't reply, thinking it over.

"There's wild boars in the woods, you know," said the Prof. "Mean beasts. And the cats hunt at night, too. Coyotes, of course. No wolves, though; for some reason they haven't made it to this island."

"Where's your cabin?" Hawk asked. "Who else lives there?"

"Ten minutes' walk," the Prof answered, pointing with an out-stretched arm. "And I live alone. There's nobody but me on this island—except you, of course."

The old man led the way through the trees, guiding the boys with a small greenish lamp that he claimed was made from fireflies' innards. It was fully dark by the time they reached the Prof's cabin. To Tim, what little he could make out of it looked more like a bare little hump of dirt than a regular cabin.

The Prof stepped down into a sort of hollow and pushed open a creaking door. In the ghostly green light from his little lamp, the boys stepped inside. The door groaned and closed again.

And suddenly the room was brightly lit, so bright it made Tim squeeze his eyes shut for a moment. He heard Hawk gasp with surprise.

"Ah, I forgot," the Prof said. "You're not accustomed to electricity."

The place was a wonder. It was mostly underground, but there were lights that made everything look like it was daytime. And there were lots of rooms; the place just seemed to go on and on.

"Nothing much else to do for the past two centuries," the Prof said. "Home improvement was always a hobby of mine, even back before the Flood."

"You remember before the Flood?" Tim asked, awed.

The Prof sank his chunky body onto a sagging, tatty sofa and gestured to chairs for the boys to sit on.

"I was going to be one of the Immortals," he said, his rasping voice somewhere between sad and sore. "Got my telomerase shots. I'd never age—so long as I took the booster shots every fifty years."

Tim glanced at Hawk, who looked just as puzzled as he himself felt.

"But then the Flood wiped all that out. I'm aging again . . . slowly, I grant you, but just take a look at me! Hardly immortal, right?"

Hawk pointed to the thickly stacked shelves lining the room's walls. "Are all those things books?"

The Prof nodded. "My other hobby was looting libraries—while they were still on dry land."

He babbled on about solar panels and superconducting batteries and thermoionic generators and all kinds of other weird stuff that started to make Tim's head spin. It was like the Prof was so glad to have somebody to talk to he didn't know when to stop.

Tim had always been taught to be respectful of his elders; sometimes the lessons had included a sound thrashing. But no matter how respectfully he tried to pay attention to the Prof's rambling, barely understandable monologue, he kept drifting toward sleep. Back home everybody was abed shortly after nightfall, but now this Prof was yakking on and on. It must be pretty near midnight, Tim thought. He could hardly keep his eyes open. He nodded off, woke himself with a start, and tried as hard as he could to stay awake.

"But look at me," the Prof said at last. "I'm keeping you two from a good night's sleep, talking away like this."

He led the boys to another room that had real beds in it. "Be careful how you get on them," he warned. "Nobody's slept in those antiques in fifty years or more, not since a family of pilgrims got blown off their course for New Nashville. Stayed for damned near a month. Ate me out of house and home, just about, but I was still sad to see them go. I . . ."

Hawk yawned noisily and the Prof's monologue petered out. "I'll see you in the morning. Have a good sleep."

Tim didn't care about the Prof's warning. He was so sleepy he threw himself on the bare mattress of the nearer bed. He raised a cloud of dust, but after one cough he fell sound asleep.

Because the Prof's home was mostly underground it stayed dark long after sunrise. Tim and Hawk slept longer than they ever had at home. Only the sound of the Prof knocking hard on their bedroom door woke them.

The boys washed and relieved themselves in a privy that was built right into the house, in a separate little room of its own, with running water at the turn of a handle.

"Gravity feed," the Prof told them over a hearty breakfast of eggs and ham and waffles and muffins and fruit preserves. "Got a cistern for rainwater up in the hills and pipes carry the water here. I boil all the drinking and cooking water, of course."

"Of course," Hawk mumbled, his mouth full of blueberry muffin.

"We've got to haul your boat farther up out of the water," the Prof said, "and tie it down good and tight. Big blow likely soon."

Tim glanced out the narrow slit of the kitchen's only window and saw that it was dull gray outside, cloudy.

Once they finished breakfast, the Prof took them to still another room. This one had desks and strange-looking boxes sitting on them, with windows in them.

The Prof slipped into a little chair that creaked under his weight and started pecking with his fingers on a board full of buttons. The window on the box atop the desk lit up and suddenly showed a picture.

Tim jerked back a step, surprised. Even Hawk looked wide-eyed, his mouth hanging open.

"Not many weather satellites still functioning," the Prof muttered, as much to himself as the boys. "Only the old military birds left; rugged little buggers. Hardened, you know. But even with solar power and gyro stabilization, after two hundred years they're crapping out, one by one."

"What is that?" Hawk asked, his voice strangely small and hollow. Tim knew what was going through his friend's mind: *This is witchcraft!*

The Prof launched into an explanation that meant practically nothing to the boys. Near as Tim could figure it, the old man was saying there was a machine hanging in the air like a circling hawk or buzzard, but miles and miles and higher, so high they couldn't see it. And the machine had some sort of eyes on it and this box on the Prof's desk was showing what those eyes saw.

It didn't sound like witchcraft, the way the Prof explained it. He made it sound just as natural as chopping wood.

"That's the United States," the Prof said, tapping the glass that covered the picture. "Or what's left of it."

Tim saw mostly wide stretches of blue stuff that sort of looked like water, with plenty of smears of white and gray. Clouds?

"Florida's gone, of course," the Prof muttered. "Most of the Midwest has been inundated. New England . . . Maryland and the whole Chesapeake region . . . all flooded."

His voice had gone low and soft, as if he was about to cry. Tim even thought he saw a tear glint in one of the old man's eyes, though it was hard to tell, under those shaggy white brows of his.

"Here's where we are," the Prof said, pointing to one of the gray smudges. "Can't see the island, of course; we're beneath the cloud cover."

Tim looked at Hawk, who shrugged. Couldn't figure out if the Prof was crazy or a witch or what.

The Prof tapped at the buttons on the oblong board in front of him and the picture on the box changed. Now it showed something that was mostly white. Lots of clouds, still, but they were almost all white and if that was supposed to be ground underneath them the ground was all white, too.

"Canada," said the Prof, grimly. "The ice cap is advancing fast."

"What's that mean?" Hawk asked.

The Prof sucked in a big sigh and looked up at the boys. "It's going to get colder. A lot colder."

"Winter's comin' already?" Tim asked. It was still springtime, he knew. Summer was coming, not winter.

But the Prof answered, "A long winter, son. A winter that lasts thousands of years. An ice age."

Hawk asked, "What's an ice age?"

"It's what follows a greenhouse warming. This greenhouse was an anomaly, caused by anthropogenic factors. Now the CO_2's being leached out of the atmosphere and the global climate will bounce back to a Pleistocene condition."

He might as well have been talking Cherokee or some other redskin language, Tim thought. Hawk looked just as baffled.

Seeing the confusion on the boys' faces, the Prof went to great pains to try to explain. Tim got the idea that he was saying the weather was going to turn colder, a lot colder, and stay that way for a *really* long time.

"Glaciers a mile thick!" the Prof said, nearly raving in his earnestness. "Minnesota, Michigan, the whole Great Lakes region was covered with ice a mile thick!"

"It was?"

"When?"

Shaking his head impatiently, the Prof said, "It doesn't matter when. The important thing is that it's going to happen all over again!"

"Here?" Tim asked. "Where our folks live?"

"Yes!"

"How soon?" asked Hawk.

The Prof hesitated. He drummed his fingers on the desktop for a minute, looking lost in thought.

"By the time you're a grandfather," he said at last. "Maybe sooner, maybe later. But it's going to happen."

Hawk let a giggle out of him. "That's a long time from now."

"But you've got to get ready for it," the Prof said, frowning. "It will take a long time to prepare, to learn how to make warm clothing, to grow different crops or migrate south."

Hawk shook his head.

"You ought to at least warn your people, let them know it's going to happen," the Prof insisted.

"But we're headin' for Colorado," Tim confessed. "We're not goin' back home."

The Prof's bushy brows knit together. "This climate shift could be just as abrupt as the greenhouse cliff was. People who aren't prepared for it will die—starve to death or freeze."

"How do you know it's gonna happen like that?" Hawk demanded.

"You saw the satellite imagery of Canada, didn't you?"

"We saw some picture of something, I don't know what it really was," Hawk said. "How do you know what it is? How do you know it's gonna get so cold?"

The Prof thought a moment, then admitted, "I don't *know*. But all the evidence points that way. I'm sure of it, but I don't have conclusive proof."

"You don't really know," Hawk said.

For a long moment the old man glared at Hawk angrily. Then he took another deep breath and his anger seemed to fade away.

"Listen, son. Many years ago people like me tried to warn the rest of the world that the greenhouse warming was going to drastically change the global climate. All the available evidence pointed to it, but the evidence was not conclusive. We couldn't convince the political leaders of the world that they were facing a disaster."

"What happened?" Tim asked.

Spreading his arms out wide, the Prof shouted, "This happened! The world's breadbaskets flooded! Electrical power distribution systems totally wiped out. The global nets, the information and knowledge of centuries—all drowned. Food distribution gone. Cities abandoned. Billions died! Billions! Civilization sank back to subsistence agriculture."

Tim looked at Hawk and Hawk looked back at Tim. Maybe the old man isn't a witch, Tim thought. Maybe he's just crazy.

The Prof sighed. "It doesn't mean a thing to you, does it? You just don't have the understanding, the education or . . ."

Muttering to himself, the old man turned back to his magic box and pecked at the buttons again. The picture went back to the first one the boys had seen.

Abruptly the Prof jabbed a button and the picture winked off. Pushing himself up from his chair, he said, "Come on, we've got to get your boat farther up out of the water and tied down good and strong."

"What for?" Hawk demanded, suddenly suspicious.

With a frown, the Prof said, "This area used to be called Tornado Alley. Just because it's covered by water doesn't change that. In fact, it makes the twisters even worse."

The boys had heard of twisters. One had levelled a village not more than a day's travel from their own, only a couple of springtimes ago.

When it came, the twister was a monster.

The boys spent most of the day hauling their boat up close to the trees and then tying it down as firmly as they could. The Prof provided ropes and plenty of advice and even some muscle power. All the time they worked the clouds got thicker and darker and lower. Tim expected a thunderstorm any minute as they headed back for the Prof's house, bone tired.

They were halfway back when the trees began tossing back and forth and rain started spattering down. Leaves went flying through the air, torn off the trees. A whole bough whipped by, nearly smacking Hawk on the head. Tim heard a weird sound, a low dull roaring, like the distant howl of some giant beast.

"Run!" the Prof shouted over the howling wind. "You don't want to get caught here amidst the trees!"

Despite their aching muscles they ran. Tim glanced over his shoulder and through the bending, swaying trees he saw a mammoth pillar of pure terror marching across the open water, heading right for him, sucking up water and twigs and anything in its path, weaving slowly back and forth, high as the sky, bearing down on them, coming to get him.

It roared and shouted and moved up onto the land. Whole trees were ripped up by their roots. Tim tripped and sprawled face-first into the dirt. Somebody grabbed him by the scruff of his neck and yanked him to his feet. The rain was so thick and hard he couldn't see an arm's length in front of him but suddenly the low earthen hump of the Prof's house was in sight and the old man, despite his years, was half a dozen strides ahead of them, already fumbling with the front door.

They staggered inside, the wind-driven rain pouring in with them. It took all three of them to get the door closed again and firmly latched. The Prof pushed a heavy cabinet against the door, then slumped to the floor, soaking wet, chest heaving.

"Check . . . the windows," he gasped. "Shutters . . ."

Hawk nodded and scrambled to his feet. Tim hesitated only a moment, then did the same. He saw there were thick wooden shutters folded back along the edges of each window. He pulled them across the glass and locked them tight.

The twister roared and raged outside but the Prof's house, largely underground, held firm. Tim thought the ground was shaking, but maybe it was just him shaking, he was so scared. The storm yowled and battered at the house. Things pounded on the roof. The rain drummed so hard it sounded like all the redskins in the world doing a war dance.

The Prof lay sprawled in the puddle by the door until Hawk gestured for Tim to help him get the old man to his feet.

"Bedroom . . ." the Prof said. "Let me . . . lay down . . . for a while." His chest was heaving, his face looked gray.

They put him down gently on his bed. His wet clothes made a squishy sound on the covers. He closed his eyes and seemed to go to sleep. Tim stared at the old man's bare, white-fuzzed chest. It was pumping up and down, fast.

Something crashed against the roof so hard that books tumbled out of their shelves and dust sifted down from the ceiling. The lights blinked, then went out altogether. A dim lamp came on and cast scary shadows on the wall.

Tim and Hawk sat on the floor, next to each other, knees drawn up tight. Every muscle in Tim's body ached, every nerve was pulled tight as a bowstring. And the twister kept howling outside, as if demanding to be allowed in.

At last the roaring diminished, the drumming rain on the roof slackened off. Neither Tim nor Hawk budged an inch, though. Not until it became completely quiet out there.

"Do you think it's over?" Tim whispered.

Hawk shook his head. "Maybe."

They heard a bird chirping outside. Hawk scrambled to his feet and went to the window on the other side of the Prof's bed. He eased the shutter open a crack, then flung it all the way back. Bright sunshine streamed into the room. Tim noticed a trickle of water that had leaked through the window and its shutter, dripping down the wall to make a puddle on the bare wooden floor.

The Prof seemed to be sleeping soundly, but as they tiptoed out of the bedroom, he opened one eye and said, "Check outside. See what damage it's done."

A big pine had fallen across the house's low roof; that had been the crash they'd heard. The water pipe from the cistern was broken, but the cistern itself—dug into the ground—was unharmed except for a lot of leaves and debris that had been blown into it.

The next morning the Prof felt strong enough to get up, and he led the boys on a more detailed inspection tour. The solar panels were caked with dirt and leaves, but otherwise unhurt. The boys set to cleaning them while the Prof mended the broken water pipe.

By nightfall the damage had been repaired and the house was back to normal. But not the Prof. He moved slowly, painfully, his breathing was labored. He was sick, even Tim could see that.

"Back in the old days," he said in a rasping whisper over the dinner table, "I'd go to the local clinic and get some pills to lower my blood pressure. Or an EGF injection to grow new arteries." He shook his head sadly. "Now I can only sit around like an old man waiting to die."

The boys couldn't leave him, not in his weakened condition. Besides, the Prof said they'd be better off waiting until the spring tornado season was over.

"No guarantee you won't run into a twister during the summer, of course," he told them. "But it's safer if you wait a bit."

He taught them as much as he could about his computers and the electrical systems he'd rigged to power the house. Tim knew how to read some, so the Prof gave him books while he began to teach Hawk about reading and writing.

"The memory of the human race is in these books," he said, almost every day. "What's left of it, that is."

The boys worked his little vegetable patch and picked berries and hunted down game while the Prof stayed at home, too weak to exert himself. He showed the boys how to use his high-powered bow and Tim bagged a young boar all by himself.

One morning well into the summertime, the Prof couldn't get out of his bed. Tim saw that his face was gray and soaked in sweat, his breathing rapid and shallow. He seemed to be in great pain.

He looked up at the boys and tried to smile. "I guess I'm . . . going to become immortal . . . the old-fashioned way."

Hawk swallowed hard and Tim could see he was fighting to hold back tears.

"Nothing you can do . . . for me," the Prof said, his voice so weak that Tim had to bend over him to hear it.

"Just rest," Tim said. "You rest up and you'll get better."

"Not likely."

Neither boy knew what else to say, what else to do.

"I bequeath my island to you two," the Prof whispered. "It's all yours, boys."

Hawk nodded.

"But you . . . you really ought to warn . . . your people," he gasped, "about the ice . . ."

He closed his eyes. His labored breathing stopped.

That evening, after they had buried the Prof, Tim asked Hawk, "Do you think we oughtta go back and tell our folks?"

Hawk snapped, "No."

"But the Prof said—"

"He was a crazy old man. We go back home and all we'll get is a whippin' for runnin' away."

"But we oughtta tell them," Tim insisted. "Warn them."

"About something that ain't gonna happen until we're grandfathers? Something that probably won't happen at all?"

"But—"

"We got a good place here. The crazy old coot left it to us and we'd be fools to leave it."

"What about Colorado?"

"We'll get there next year. Or maybe the year after. And if we don't like it there we can always come back here."

For the first time in his life, Tim not only felt that Hawk was wrong, but he decided to do something about it.

"Okay," he said. "You stay. I'm goin' back."

"You're as crazy as he was!"

"I'll come back here. I'm just goin' to warn them and then I'll come back."

Hawk made a snorting noise. "If they leave any skin on your hide."

For a week Tim patched up their boat and its ragged sail and filled it with provisions. The morning he was set to cast off, Hawk came to the pebbly beach with him.

"I guess this is good-bye for a while," Tim said.

"Don't be a dumbbell," Hawk groused. "I'm goin' with you."

Tim felt a rush of joy. "You are?"

"You'd get yourself lost out there. Some sea monster would have you for lunch."

"We can always come back here again," Tim said, grunting, as they pushed the boat into the water.

"Yeah, sure."

"We hafta warn them, Hawk. We just hafta."

"Shut up and haul out the sail."

For several days they sailed north and east, back along the way they had come. The weather was sultry, the sun blazing like molten iron out of a cloudless sky.

"Ice age," Hawk grumbled. "Craziest thing I ever heard."

"I saw pictures of it in the books the Prof had," said Tim. "Big sheets of ice covering everything."

Hawk just shook his head and spit over the side.

"It really happened, Hawk."

"The weather don't change," Hawk snapped. "It's the same every year. Hot in the summer, cool in the winter. You ever known anything else?"

"No," Tim admitted.

"You ever seen ice, except in the Prof's pictures?"

"No."

"Or that stuff he called snow?"

"Never."

"We oughtta turn this boat around and head back to the island."

Tim almost agreed. But he saw that Hawk made no motion to change their course. He was talking one way but acting the other.

They fell silent. Tim understood Hawk's resentment. Probably nobody would listen to them when they got home. The elders would be pretty mad about the two of them running off and they wouldn't listen to a word the boys had to say.

For hours they skimmed along, the only sound the gusting of the hot southerly wind and the hiss of the boat cutting through the placid water.

"It's all fairy tales," Hawk grumbled, as much to himself as to Tim. "Stories they make up to scare the kids. What do they call 'em?"

"Myths," said Tim.

"Myths, that's right. Myths." But suddenly he jerked to attention. "Hey, what's that?"

Tim saw he was looking down into the water. He came over to Hawk's side of the boat.

Something was glittering down below the surface. Something big.

Tim's heart started racing. "A sea monster?"

Hawk shook his head impatiently. "I don't think it's moving. Leastways it's not following after us. Look, it's falling behind."

They lapsed into silence again. Tim felt uncomfortable. He didn't like it when Hawk was sore at him.

Apologetically, he said, "Maybe you're right. The old man was most likely a little crazy."

"A *lot* crazy," Hawk said. "And we're just as crazy as he was. The weather don't change like that. It's just not possible. There never was a Flood. The world's always been like this. Always."

Tim was shocked. "No Flood?"

"It's one of them myths," Hawk insisted. "Like sea monsters. Ain't no such thing."

"Then what did we see back there?"

"I dunno. But it wasn't no sea monster. And the weather don't change the way the Prof said it's goin' to. There wasn't any Flood and there sure ain't goin' to be any ice age."

Tim wondered if Hawk was right, as their boat sailed on and the glittering stainless steel stump of the St. Louis Gateway Arch fell farther and farther behind them.

When the human race begins to expand its habitat through the solar system, it won't be only scientists and engineers who go to other worlds. There will be entrepreneurs like Sam Gunn and Dan Randolph, visionaries like Chet Kinsman and Jamie Waterman, saints, sinners, pilgrims, adventurers . . .

Adventurers. Some people make adventure their business. And what a business opportunity the hellishly hot surface of the planet Venus will be!

HIGH JUMP

The things a man will do for love.

I had been Hal Prince's stunt double for more than five years. To the general public he was the greatest daredevil that ever lived, the handsome star of the most exciting adventure videos ever recorded, the tall sandy-haired guy with the flashing smile and twinkling eyes who always did his own stunts.

Well, I had known him when he was Aloysius Prizanski, back before he got his nose fixed, when he'd been a wannabe actor hungry enough to jump into a pool of blazing petrol from the bridge of an ocean liner.

Back then he did his own stunts, sure enough, but once he got so popular that he could command half a bill just for signing a contract, the insurance people insisted that he was just too goddamned valuable to risk.

So I did his stunts. His old pal. His asshole buddy. Ugly old me. It was no big secret in the industry, but as far as the general public was concerned, it was Handsome Hal himself who'd risked his own neck riding the hundred-gee catapult at Moonbase into lunar orbit and sledding down the dry-ice-coated flank of Olympus Mons in nothing more than a Buckyball suit.

To say nothing of skydiving into Vesuvius while it was boiling out steam and the occasional blurp of hot lava. That one cost me three months in a burn recovery center, although I never let Hal know it. He thought I'd just gotten miffed at him and taken off to sulk.

Now I was going to do the high jump for him. On Venus, yet. Pop myself out of an orbiting spacecraft and drop all the way down to the planet's red-hot surface.

And I mean red-hot. The ground temperature down there is hot enough to melt aluminum. The air pressure is almost a hundred times what it is at sea level on Earth; like the pressure in the ocean, more than a kilometer down.

And by the way, Venus's air is almost all choking carbon dioxide. The clouds that cover the planet from pole to pole are made of sulfuric acid. And they're filled with bugs that eat metal, too.

The stunt was to jump from orbit and go all the way down to the ground. I had just come back from the patch-up job after the Vesuvius barbecue. Truth to tell, I was scared into constipation over this stunt.

But I didn't tell Hal. Or anybody else.

We all have our little secrets. My doubling for him was Hotshot Hal's secret. But I had a few of my own, too.

Angel Santos doubled for Hal's female co-stars; if it weren't for her toughness and quick thinking I'd have been fried inside old Vesuvius.

Angel was really beautiful: a face to die for, with big wide-set corn-flower blue eyes, full bust, narrow waist, long legs—the works. Don't strain your eyes looking for her in any of Hal's videos, though; like me, she was strictly a stunt double, wearing whatever wigs and rigs that were necessary to make her look like Hal's female co-star—whoever she happened to be.

Angel could've been a star in her own right, but she had absolutely no interest in acting. She was hooked on the challenges of danger, just like me. We got along together great, two of a kind. She made me feel really good about myself, too. People looked up from their dinners when I walked into a restaurant with Angel on my arm. I mean people *never* looked at me. Especially when Heroic Hal was anywhere in sight. Okay, I knew they were looking at Angel, not me, but I got respect for having her on my arm, at least. Boosted my machismo rating with the dumbshit ordinary folks.

But once Angel met with Hedonistic Hal she got hooked on him. I didn't realize it at first. We'd all go out together, the three of us. It didn't take long, though, before they started going out without me, just the two of them. I was left out in the cold.

Then came the Venus jump.

I was thinking about packing it in. Let Hal the Heartbreaker get somebody else. He wasn't thinking about me at all anymore; he only had eyes for Angel. And she clung on him like he was the last lifeboat on the *Titanic*. She wasn't even involved in this Venus stunt, it was my trick alone. But she came along for the ride, all the way out to Venus—with Hal the Hunk.

But then I decided I'd do the stunt, after all. I wanted to be noticed; I wanted to break the lock the two of them had on each other, and the only way I knew to do that was to go through with the toughest, most daring and dangerous stunt that'd ever been tried. Admiration, that's what I was after. I wanted to make their eyes shine—for me.

The High Jump: from Venus orbit all the way to the ground. And back, of course. None of the publicity flaks even mentioned the return trip, but I thought about that part of it *a lot*.

Okay, so we're in orbit around Venus—Hal, Angel, me, our crew of technicians and our tech directors, plus the ship's crew. We had decided to keep the ship's crew in the dark about me doubling for Hal. As far as they were concerned I was just another techie. The fewer people outside the industry who knew about my doubling for him, the better.

So Hal's doing the mandatory media interview, all dolled up in a space suit, no less, with the helmet tucked under one arm. Standing there by the airlock hatch, he looks like a freaking Adonis, so help me, a Galahad, literally a knight in shining armor. And Angel's right there beside him, hanging on his arm, gazing up into his sparkling green eyes as if she's about to have an orgasm just looking at him.

The media people were all back on Earth, of course. We didn't want them on the ship with us, too much of a chance of them finding out about Hal's little secret. Since it took messages more than eight minutes to travel from them to us (and vice-versa) they had prerecorded their questions and squirted them to us a couple of hours earlier.

Now Homeric Hal stood there like a young Lancelot and spoke foursquare into the camera, replying to each of their questions after only an hour or so to study the lines his publicity flaks had written for him.

"Yes," he said, with his patented careless grin, "I suppose we could use computer graphics for these stunts instead of doing them live. But I don't think the public would be so interested in a computer simulation. My fans want to see the real thing! It's the unexpected, the element of danger and risk, that excites the viewers."

The next questioner asked why Hal was so eager to risk his beautiful butt on these stunts.

He did his bashful routine, shrugging and scratching his head. "I don't really know. I guess I got hooked on the excitement of it all, and . . . and . . ."

He hesitated, as the script required. I thought sourly that what he's really hooked on is the money. Mucho bucks in this game. He let me take over the dangerous part of it easily enough.

"... and ... well I guess it's the thrill of taking enormous risks and coming out alive. It makes your heart beat faster, that's for sure. Gets the old adrenaline pumping!"

His adrenaline was pumping, all right. But it wasn't about the risks of the Venus jump. It was Angel, draped over him and drinking in every syllable he uttered.

The media interview ended at last. Hal's smile winked off. "Okay," he said, starting to peel off his suit. "Let's get to work."

To his credit, Hal gave me a farewell hug just before I stepped into the airlock. It was an awkward hug, with me in the bulky thermally insulated space suit that we'd had specially built for this stunt.

"Take care of yourself, pal," he said, his voice gone husky.

"Don't I always?" I said back to him.

I stepped into the airlock and turned around to face him again. And there was Angel, right beside him. I blew a kiss as the hatch closed and sealed me in—not an easy thing to do from inside my heat-proofed helmet.

There were two technicians already outside, in space suits of course, to help click me into the aeroshell. It wasn't a spacecraft, just a heat shield that carried the bare minimum of equipment I'd need to make it down to the surface. I mean, that Humphries kid had reached Venus's surface a couple of years earlier, but he'd never walked on the planet's rocky ground, as I was going to do. He'd been inside a specially designed submersible; *it* touched down on the surface, not him on his own two feet. And he was supported by an even bigger ship that cruised a few kilometers above him, at that.

Plus, he'd landed in the highland mountains of Aphrodite. It's only four hundred degrees Celsius up there. Big deal. I was going down to the lowlands, where it's four-fifty, minimum, and doing it without a ship. Just me in a thermal suit and a handful of equipment.

Plus the heat shield, yeah, but that was just to get me through the entry phase. I mean, we were orbiting Venus at just about seven kilometers per second. You can't dip into the atmosphere in nothing but your high-tech long johns at that speed—not unless you want to make yourself into a shooting star.

I had no intention of becoming a cinder. The heat shield was flimsy enough, nothing more than a shallow bathtub coated on one side with a heat-absorbing plastic that boils off when it reaches fifteen hundred degrees. The boiled-off goop carries the heat away with it, leaving me safe on the other side of the shield. At least, that's the way it's supposed to work.

Believe me, the heat shield looked damned flimsy as I climbed into it. The techs checked out all my suit's systems and the connections, then clamped me into the shield's shallow protection. None of us said much while they got me properly clicked in.

Finally, they each patted my thick helmet and wished me luck. I thanked them, and they clambered through the airlock and shut the hatch. I was alone now, with nothing to keep me company but the automated voice of the computer ticking off the last three minutes of the countdown.

Three minutes can be a long time, when you're alone hanging outside an orbiting spacecraft, a hundred million kilometers from blue skies and sunny beaches. I was locked into the heat shield, arms and legs stretched out like a guy in a B&D video, with nothing to do but worry about what was coming next.

To keep my nerves from twitching, I looked out through one corner of my faceplate at what little I could see of Venus.

She was gorgeous! The massive, curving bulk of the planet gleamed like a gigantic golden lamp, a brilliant saffron-yellow expanse against the cold blackness of space. She glowed like a thing alive. Goddess of beauty, sure enough. At first I thought the cloud deck was as solid and unvarying as a sphere of solid gold. Then I saw that I could make out streamers among the clouds, slightly darker stretches, patches where the amber yellowish clouds billowed up slightly. I stared fascinated at those fantastically incredible clouds. They shifted and changed as I watched. It was almost like staring into a fire, endlessly fascinating, hypnotic.

A human voice broke into my enchantment. "You okay out there?"

"Sure," I snapped. "I'm fine."

"Separation in thirty seconds." It was the voice of our tech controller in my helmet earphones. "Speak now or forever hold your jockstrap."

"Let 'er rip," I said, in time-honored, devil-may-care fashion. Just in case some wiseass was eavesdropping with a recorder.

"Five . . . four . . ." Well, you know the rest. I felt a quiver and then a not-too-gentle push against the small of my back: the latches releasing and then the spring-loaded actuator that pushed my aeroshell away from the orbiting spacecraft.

And there I was, as the flyguys say, watching our orbiter dwindle away from me. Before I had time to grit my teeth the retrorockets kicked in, and I mean *kicked*. I couldn't hear anything in the vacuum of space, naturally, but I sure felt it. The whole goddamned aeroshell rattled like a studio set in an earthquake. I heard a kind of a roar inside my head; not sound, really, so much as my bones picking up the vibrations as the rockets tried to shake me to death.

I hung on—nothing else I could do—for the forty-five seconds of retro burn, knowing the cameras from the ship were getting every picosecond of it in glorious full color. Every bone in my body was quivering like a struck gong. I wondered if I'd get out of this with any teeth unchipped.

Then suddenly it all stopped. I was either dead or the rockets had burned out.

"Retro burn complete," said the controller calmly. "You are go for entry into Venus's atmosphere."

Stretched out inside this shallow soap dish of an aeroshell, I nodded inside my helmet. Now comes the fun part, I said to myself.

The first thing I noticed was streaks of bright light flicking past me. Hitting the top of the atmosphere at seven klicks per second heated up the gases to incandescence. Pretty soon I was surrounded with white-hot plasma boiling off the heat shield and billowing out past me. I lay there on my back, helpless as a newborn rat, with white-hot gas streaming past the edges of my shell. I could hear noise now, a high-pitched whining sound that deepened into the kind of roar you hear when you open a blast furnace.

And the shell was shaking again, worse than before. If I hadn't been latched down, and if my protective suit hadn't been well padded, I'd have been pummeled to jelly. Mouth protector, I thought as I tasted blood. I should've brought a mouth protector. I tried to keep my mouth open so I wouldn't chew off my tongue or bite a hole through my cheek and cursed myself for the oversight.

The controller tried to tell me something, but the plasma sheath around the rapidly descending aeroshell broke up his radio message into garbled little hashes of static. I tried to focus my eyes on the data screen inside my helmet, next to the faceplate, but everything was jouncing around so bad I couldn't see anything but a multicolored blur.

Must be close to breakup, I thought.

And *bang!* The aeroshell clamps unlatched and the shell itself snapped into a dozen separate pieces, just the way it was designed to. Gave me a jolt, let me tell you.

So now I was in free-fall, dropping like a stone toward the top layer of clouds. The shaking eased off enough so I could read the altimeter inside my helmet. I passed eighty kilometers like a doomed soul falling into hell.

My biggest worry was the superrotation winds. They could blow me halfway around the planet and I'd miss my landing spot. That's where the return rocket vehicle was sitting on the surface, waiting for me in that baking heat and corrosive sulfur-laced atmosphere.

Venus turns very slowly, its "day" is 243 Earth days long—that's how long it takes the planet to make one complete turn around its axis. So the Sun blazes down on the subsolar point, the spot where the Sun is directly overhead, like a freaking blowtorch. The upper atmosphere, blast-heated like that, develops winds of four hundred kilometers per hour and more that rush around the entire planet in a few days. In a way, they're like the jet streams on Earth, only bigger and more powerful.

If I got caught in one of those superpowerful jet streams I'd be blown so far away from my landing point that I'd never make it back to the return vehicle. Then I'd have a choice of whether I wanted to be baked to death or suffocate.

So the plan was to cannonball through the superrotation's jet streams as fast as possible, get down into the lower altitudes where the air pressure thickens into soup and the winds are smothered into sluggish little nothings.

That was the plan.

I was dropping like a brick, headfirst, the wind screeching past me and the billowing sickly yellow-gray clouds rushing up.

"How'm I doing?" I yelled into my helmet mike.

"Drifting off course," came the director's voice, calm as a guy ordering a margarita back in L.A.

I looked to the left of my faceplate, at the miniscreen that showed my position. I was a red dot, the return vehicle was a green dot. There were concentric circles around the green dot. If I was within two circles of the center I'd be okay. That red dot was already close to the edge of the second circle.

"Better do some maneuvering," the director suggested, flat as Kansas.

"Too soon," I said. The maneuvering jets on the back of my suit only carried so much fuel. Use 'em up now and I'd be helpless later.

But that red dot that was me was drifting past the second circle. I was in trouble.

"Maneuver!" the director snapped. I had to smile; at least I got his blood pressure up a little.

"No sense shovelling shit against the tide," I said. "I'll wait until I'm under the jet stream."

"You'll be too far!" He was getting really clanked up now.

My eyes flicked back and forth. The miniscreen on my right showed I was passing seventy klicks, almost into the top cloud deck. The super-rotation winds should be dying down. But the radar plot on the left of my faceplate showed my red dot almost off the chart completely.

"Check pressure," I called out. The altimeter readout was replaced by a rapidly changing set of numbers. According to the probe sampling the air I was falling through, the pressure was rising steeply.

I nodded inside the helmet. Yes, the radar plot showed I wasn't drifting any farther from the landing spot.

"Cranking up the jets," I said, wriggling my right arm out of the suit's sleeve to press the actuator stud on the control board built inside the suit's chest cavity. We had decided to keep all the controls inside the suit, safe from the corrosive oven-hot atmosphere outside.

"About time," groused the director.

"No sweat," I told the him. Which, I realized, wasn't exactly true. I was perspiring enough to notice it. I wiped my brow before sliding my arm back into its sleeve.

The jets came on, gently at first and then accelerating slowly. I twisted my body around and spread my arms out. That unfolded the air-foils that ordinarily wrapped around my sleeves. Like a jet-propelled bat, I dove into the sulfuric-acid clouds, watching the radar plot as my little green dot started edging closer to the red dot.

My suit's exterior was all ceramicized plastic, for three reasons. One, the material was a good heat insulator, and I was going to need all the protection from Venus's fiery hell that I could get. Two, the stuff was impervious to sulfuric acid—of which the cloud droplets had plenty. Three, it would not be attacked by the bugs that lived in those sulfuric-acid clouds.

The aerobacteria had destroyed the first two ships that had entered Venus's clouds. They feast on metals, gobble 'em up the way a macrovitamin faddist gulps pills. The exobiologists had assured us that those bugs would not even nibble at the plastic exterior of my suit.

There was plenty of metal in the suit, a whole candy store's worth, as far as the bugs were concerned. But it was all covered by thick layers of plastic. I hoped.

Once in the clouds my vision was reduced to zero. From the outside mikes I could hear wind whistling past, but the altimeter showed that my rate of fall was slowing. The atmosphere was getting thicker, making it harder to gain headway.

The jets burped once, twice, then gave out. Fuel exhausted. And I was only between the first and second circles on the radar plot. I was sailing through the heavier layers of cloud, heading for the rendezvous spot like a soaring bird now.

"Looking good," the director said encouragingly.

I shook my head inside the helmet. "I'm not going to make the rendezvous."

Silence for a few heartbeats. Then, "So you'll have to walk a bit."

"Yeah. Right."

The thermal suit would hold up for maybe an hour on the surface. Not much more. The problem was heat rejection.

Down there on the surface, where the freaking rocks are red hot and the air is thicker than seawater, it's four hundred and fifty degrees Celsius. More, in some places. No matter how well the suit is built, that heat seeps in on you, sooner or later. So the engineers had built a heat-rejection system into my suit: slugs of special alloy that melted at four hundred Celsius. The alloy absorbed heat, melted, and was squirted out of the suit, taking the heat with it.

It was pretty crude, but it worked. It would keep my suit's interior reasonably cool, or so the engineers promised. After about one hour, though, the suit would run out of alloy and I'd start to bake; my protective suit would turn into a pretty efficient steam cooker.

That's what I had to look forward to. That's why I was trying my damnedest to land as close to that return ship as possible.

I broke out of the top cloud deck at last and for a few minutes I was in relatively clear air. Clouds above me, more clouds below. I was still gliding, but slower and slower as the air pressure built up steeply. At least

I was past the bugs. The temperature outside was approaching a hundred degrees, the boiling point of water. The bugs couldn't survive in that heat.

Could I?

Lightning flashed in my eyes, scaring the bejeesus out of me. Then came a slow, rolling grumble of thunder. The lightning must have been pretty damned close.

That second cloud deck was alive with lightning. It crackled all around me, thunder booming so loud and continuous that I shut off the outside mikes. Still the noise rattled me like an artillery barrage. Had I come down in the middle of a thunderstorm? Was I somehow *attracting* the lightning? You get all kinds of scary thoughts. As I dropped deeper and deeper into Venus's hot, heavy air, my mind filled with what-ifs and should'ves.

The lightning seemed to be only in the second cloud deck. I watched its flickering all across the sky as I fell through the brief clear space between it and the third deck. It was almost pretty, at this distance.

The third and last of the cloud decks was also the thinnest. At just a smidge above fifty kilometers' altitude I glided through its underbelly and saw the landscape of Venus with my own eyes.

I stared down at a distant landscape of barren rock, utter desolation, nothing but bare, hard, stony ground as far as the eye could see, naked rock in shades of gray and darker gray, with faint streaks here and there of lighter stuff, almost like talc or pumice.

I saw a series of domes, and farther in the distance the bare rocky ground seemed wrinkled, as if something had squeezed it hard. There were mountains out near the horizon, although that might have been a distortion caused by the density of the thick atmosphere, like trying to judge shapes deep underwater.

Below me was an immense crater, maybe fifty klicks across. It looked sharp-edged, new. But they'd told me there wasn't much erosion going on down there, despite the heat and corrosive atmosphere. It took a *long* time for craters to be erased on Venus; half a billion years or more.

The air was so thick now that I was scuba diving, rather than gliding. The bat wings were still useful, but now I had to flap my arms to push through the mushy atmosphere. The servomotors in my shoulder joints buzzed and whined; without them I wouldn't have the muscular strength to swim for very long.

I was still a long way from the rendezvous point, I saw. Inching closer, but only inching.

Then I got an idea. If Mohammed can't make it to the mountain, why not get the mountain to come to Mohammed?

"Can you hop the ship toward me?" I asked.

Nothing but static in my earphones.

I yelled and changed frequencies and hollered some more. Nothing. Must've been the electrical storm in the second cloud deck was screwing up my radio link. I was on my own, just me and the planet Venus.

She looks so beautiful from a distance, I thought. She glows so bright and lovely in the night sky that just about every culture on Earth has named her after their goddess of beauty and love: Aphrodite, Inanna, Ishtar, Astarte, Venus. I've watched her when she's the dazzling Evening Star, brighter than anything in the sky except the Sun and Moon. I've seen her when she's the beckoning Morning Star, harbinger of the new day. Always she shines like a precious jewel.

Even when we were in orbit around her, she glowed like an incredible golden sphere. But once you see her really close up, especially when you've gone through the clouds to look at her unadorned face, she isn't beautiful anymore. She looks like hell.

And that's where I was going, down into that inferno. The air was so thick now that I was really pushing myself through it, slowly sinking, struggling to get as close as possible to the spot where the return vehicle was waiting for me. If I hadn't been encased in the heavy thermal suit I guess I would've hovered in the atmosphere, floating like a chunk of meat in a big stewpot, slowly cooking.

I was passing over a big, pancake-shaped area, a circular mass of what must have once been molten lava. It was frozen into solid stone now, if "frozen" is a word you can use for ground that's more than four times hotter than boiling water. I caught a glimpse of mountains off to my left, but I was still so high they looked like wrinkles.

My radar tracking plot had gone blank. The link from the ship up in orbit was shot, together with my voice channels. Pulling my arm out of its sleeve again I poked on the control panel until my radio receiver picked up the signal from the return vehicle's radar beacon. I displayed it on my miniscreen. Now my position was in the center of the display; the ship was more than sixty kilometers off to my left.

Sixty klicks! I'd never make that distance on foot. Could I sail that far before hitting the ground?

We had picked the rendezvous site for two reasons. One, it was about as low—and therefore as hot—as you could get in Venus's equatorial region. Second, it was the area where the old Russian spacecraft, *Venera 5*, had landed more than a century ago. The video's producers thought it'd be a neat extra if we could bring back imagery of whatever's left of the old clunker.

Down I swam. I really was swimming now, thrashing my arms and legs, making the suit's servomotors wheeze and grind with the effort. I was sweating a lot now, blinking at the stinging salty drops that leaked down into my eyes, asking myself over and over again if Hal was worth all this. A guy could get killed!

The ground came up ever so slowly. I felt like an old wooden sailing ship sunk in battle, sinking gently, gently to the bottom of the ocean. On a world that had never seen wood, or liquid water, or felt a foot on its baking stony surface.

At last I touched the ground. Like a skin diver reaching the bottom of the ocean, I eased down the final few meters and let my heavily booted feet make contact with the red-hot rock.

"I'm down," I said, for the record. I didn't know if they could hear me, up in orbit, but the suit's recorders in their "black box" safety capsules would store my words even if I didn't make it back up.

I glanced at the radar plot. My antennas were picking up the return vehicle's beacon loud and clear. It was only seven kilometers from where I stood.

Seven klicks. In four hundred fifty degrees. Just a nice summer stroll on the surface of Venus.

Despite the triple layer of clouds that completely smothered the whole planet, there was plenty of light down at the surface. Sort of like an overcast day in Seattle or Dublin. I could see all the way out to the horizon. The air was so thick, though, that it was sort of like looking through water. The horizon warped up around the edges of my vision, like the way water dimples in a slim glass tube.

The suit felt damned heavy; it weighed more than eighty kilos on Earth, and just about 90 percent of that here on Venus. Call it seventy-some kilos. If it hadn't been for the servomotors on the suit's legs I wouldn't have been able to go more than a few meters.

So I started plodding in the direction my radar screen indicated. Clump with one boot, squeak, groan, click go the servomotors, thump goes the other boot. Over and over again.

I kept up a running commentary, for the record. If and when I got back to Hal and the others, they would morph his voice for mine and have a fine step-by-step narration of the first stroll on Venus. Ought to get a nice bonus out of it, even if it went to my heirs because I got fried to a crisp walking that walk.

Come to think of it, I didn't have any heirs. No family at all. Orphan me. My family had been Hal and the guys we worked with. Including Angel, of course. Our crew was fully integrated. No biases allowed, none whatsoever.

It was *hot*. And getting hotter. After a while I started to feel a little dizzy, weak in the knees. Dehydration. At least I wasn't sweating so much. But I knew if I didn't drink some water and swallow a salt pill I'd be dead before long. Trouble was, every sip of water I drank meant less water for the suit's cooling system. And there wasn't a recycler in the suit; no room for it. Besides, I was only supposed to be on the surface for an hour or less.

"Anyway," thoughtful Hal had told the safety engineers, "who wants to drink his own recycled piss and sweat?"

I wouldn't mind, I thought. Not here and now.

On I walked, creeping closer to the return vehicle. I tried to go into a meditative state while I was walking, letting the servomotors' wheezing and groaning lull me into a blankness so I could keep on moving automatically and let all this pain and discomfort slip out of my thoughts.

Didn't work. The suit's left leg was chafing against my crotch. Both my legs were tiring fast. My back itched. The air seemed to be getting stale; I started coughing. My vision was blurring, too.

And then the snake made a grab for me.

Venusian snakes have nothing to do with the kinds of snakes we have on Earth. They are feeding arms of underground creatures, big bulbous ugly sluglike things that live under the red-hot surface rocks. Don't ask me how anything can live in temperatures four or five times hotter than boiling water. The scientists say they're made of silicones and have molten sulfur for blood. All I saw was a set of their damned feeding arms—snakes.

There's a basic human reaction to the sudden sight of a snake. Run away!

The snake suddenly popped up in front of me, slithering out of its hole. I hopped a meter and a half, even with the weight of the suit, stumbled, and fell flat on my back. Well, not *flat* on my back, there was too much equipment strapped onto me for that. But I hit the ground and all the air whooshed out of my lungs.

Faster than an eye blink three snakes wrapped themselves around me. I saw another two wavering in the air, standing up like quivering antennas.

"No metal!" I screamed, as if they could hear or understand. "No metal!"

That didn't seem to bother them at all. They had latched onto me and they weren't going to let go. Could they sense the metal beneath my suit's plastic exterior? Could they burn their way through to it? Liquid sulfur would do the job pretty damned quick.

I couldn't sit up, not with their greedy arms wrapped all over me. I grabbed one of the snakes and pried it off me. It took both hands and all the strength of my servo-aided muscles. The underside of the thing had long, narrow mouths, twitching open and closed constantly. Disgusting. There were some kind of filaments around the lips, too. Really loathsome.

Fighting an urge to barf, I bent the snake over backwards, trying to break it. No go. It was rubbery and flexible as a garden hose. Blazing hot anger boiled up in me, real fury. These brainless sonsofbitches were trying to kill me! I twisted it, pounded its end on the red-hot rock, fought one leg loose, and stomped on it with my boot.

It must have decided I wasn't edible. Or maybe I was giving it more pain than it wanted. All of a sudden all the snakes let loose of me and snapped back into their holes as if they had springs attached to their other ends. *Zip!* and they were gone.

Shaking inside, I slowly got to my feet again. Some scientists have a theory that the snakes are all connected to one big, huge, underground organism. Or maybe there's more than one, but they communicate with each other. Either way, once it—or they—decided I was too much trouble to deal with, I wasn't bothered with 'em again.

But I didn't know that. I staggered on toward the return vehicle, scared, battered, bone weary, and very, *very* hot.

And there was the old Russian craft, up ahead. At first I thought it was a mirage, but sure enough it was the spacecraft, sitting on a little rise in the ground like a forgotten old monument to past glory.

Maybe I was just too tired to care, but it looked very unimpressive to me. Not much more than a small round disc that had sagged and half-collapsed on one side to reveal the crumpled remains of a dull metal ball beneath it, sitting on those baking, red-hot rocks. It reminded me of an old-fashioned can of soda pop that had been crushed by some powerful hand.

I staggered over to it and touched the collapsed metal sphere. It crumbled into powder. Sitting there for more than a century in this heat, in an atmosphere loaded with corrosive sulfur and chlorine compounds, the metal had just turned to dust. Like the mummies in old horror shows. Nothing left but dust.

I walked slowly around it anyway, letting my helmet camera record a full three-sixty view. History. The first man-made object to make it to the surface of another planet.

Just like me. I was going to be history, too. I was baking inside my suit. The temperature readout was hitting fifty; damned near two hundred in the old Fahrenheit scale, and that was *inside* the suit. I was being broiled alive. If it weren't for my monomolecular long johns my skin would've been blistering.

Plodding along. I left old *Venera 5* behind me, following the beep-beep of the return ship's beacon, hoping it was working okay and I was heading in the right direction. Can there be an electronic mirage? I mean, could I be wandering off into the oven-hot wilderness, chasing a signal that got warped somehow and is leading me away from the return vehicle?

Is there a return vehicle at all? I started to wonder. Maybe this is Hal's way of getting rid of me. Get the competition out of the way. Then it's him and Angel without any complications. No, that doesn't make any sense, I told myself. You're getting paranoid in this heat, going crazy.

I pushed on, one booted foot in front of the other. Wasn't making footprints, though; hot though it may be, the surface of Venus is solid rock. At least it is here. Solid and scorching hot. Over on the nightside, from what I'd heard, you can see the ground glowing red-hot.

". . . get through?" crackled in my earphones. "Do you copy?"

"I hear you!" I shouted, my throat so dry that my voice cracked. The storm, the electrical interference, must have ended. Or moved off.

Nothing but hissing static came through. Then the director's voice,

". . . signal's weak . . . up gain?" His message was breaking up. There was still a lot of interference between the orbiter and me.

"Am I on the right track?" I asked. "According to my radar plot I'm still five klicks from the ship. Please confirm."

Hal's voice crackled in my earphones, ". . . *enera five!* Great video, pal!"

Terrific. The video got through but our voice link is chopped up all to hell and back.

Then it hit me. If the video link is working, switch the voice communications to that channel. I told them what I was doing while I made the change on the comm panel.

"Can you hear me better now?" I asked, my voice still cracked and dry as dehydrated dust.

No answer. Crap, I thought, it isn't working.

Then, "We hear you. Weak but clear. Are you okay?"

I can't tell you how much better I felt with a solid link back to the orbiter. It didn't really change things. I was just as tired and hot and far from safety as before. But I wasn't alone anymore.

"According to the signals from your beacon and the return vehicle's," the director said, as calmly professional as ever, "you are less than five klicks from the ship."

"Five klicks, copy."

"That distance holds good if there's no atmospheric distortions warping the signals," he added.

"Thanks a lot," I groused.

Hal came on again and talked to me nonstop, trying to buck me up, keep me going. At first I wondered why he was doing the pep-talk routine, then I realized that I must be dragging along pretty damned slowly. I put my life-support graph on the helmet screen. Yeah, air was low, water lower, and I was almost out of the heat-absorbing alloy.

I turned around three-sixty degrees and saw the ragged trail of molten alloy I was leaving behind me, like a robot with diarrhea. The alloy was shiny, new-looking against the cracked, worn, old rocks. And there were lines curving along the ground, converging on the trail every few meters.

Snakes! I realized. They like metals. I turned back toward the distant rescue vehicle and made tracks as fast as I could.

Which wasn't all that fast. Inside the cumbersome suit I felt like

Frankenstein's monster trying to play basketball, lumbering along, painfully slow.

I must have been describing all this into my helmet mike, talking nonstop. Hal kept talking, too.

And then the servo on my right knee seized up. The knee just froze, half bent, and I toppled over on my face with a thump that whacked my nose against the helmet's faceplate. Good thing, in a way. The pain kept me from blacking out. Blood spattered over my readout screens and the lower half of the faceplate. I must've screamed every obscenity I'd ever heard.

Hal and the controller were both yelling at me at once. "What happened? What's wrong?"

Through the pain of my broken nose I told them while I tried to get back on my feet. No go. My right leg was frozen in the half-bent position; there was no way I could walk. Blood was gushing down my throat.

So I crawled. Coughing, choking on my own blood, I crawled on my hands and knees, scraping along the blazing hot rocks with those damned snakes slithering behind me, feasting on the metal alloy trail I was leaving.

The radio crapped out again. Nothing but mumbles and hisses, with an occasional crackle so loud that I figured it must be from lightning. I couldn't look up to see if the clouds were flickering with light, but I saw a strange, sullen glow off on the horizon to my left.

". . . volcano . . ." came through the earphones.

Just what I needed. A volcanic eruption. It was too far away to be a direct threat, but in that undersea-thick atmosphere down on Venus's surface, volcanic eruptions can cause something like tidal waves, huge pressure waves that can push giant boulders for hundreds of kilometers.

Or knock over a flimsy rocket vehicle that's sitting on the plain waiting for me to reach it.

I'm not going to make it, I told myself.

"The hell you're not!" Hal snapped. I hadn't realized I'd spoken the words out loud.

"I can't go much farther," I said, glad that at least the radio link was back. "Running out of air, water, everything . . ."

"Hang tight, pal," he insisted. "Don't give up."

I muttered something about snake food. I rolled over on my side, completely exhausted, and saw that the snakes were gobbling up my alloy trail, getting closer to the source of the metal—me—all the time.

And then suddenly they all disappeared, reeled back into their holes so fast my eyes couldn't follow it.

Why? What would make them—

I heard a roar. A high-pitched banshee wail, really. Looking up as far as I could through the bloodied faceplate, I saw the sweetest sight of my life. A squat, bullet-shaped chunk of metal with a cluster of jet pods hanging off its ass end and three spindly, awkward legs unfolding out of its sides.

The return vehicle settled gently on the rocks half a dozen meters in front of me and released its jet pods with an ungainly thump. I crawled over to it with the last bit of my strength. The airlock hatch popped open and I hauled myself up into it.

The airlock was about as big as a shoe box but I tucked myself inside and leaned on the stud that closed the hatch and sealed it. I just sat there in that tight little metal cubbyhole and gasped into my helmet mike, "Take me up."

The acceleration from the booster rockets knocked me unconscious.

When I came to, I was on an air-cushion mattress in the orbiter's tiny infirmary. My face was completely bandaged except for holes for my eyes and mouth. They must have pumped enough painkillers in me to pacify the whole subcontinent of India. I felt somewhere between numb and floating.

Hal was there at my beside. And Angel.

They had flown the return vehicle to me, of course, once they got a good fix on my position. The little ship's cameras even got a good shot of the erupting volcano as it lifted up through the atmosphere— ahead of the pressure wave, thank goodness—and carried me safely to orbit.

"You did a great job, pal," Hunky Hal said, smiling his megawatt smile at me.

"We were so frightened," Angel said. "When the radio link went dead we thought . . ."

"Me, too," I whispered. My voice wasn't up to anything more.

"We'll get an Oscar for this one," Hal said. "For sure."

For sure.

"Get some rest now," he went on. "I've gotta get over to the processing guys and see how they're morphing your video imagery."

I nodded. Angel looked down at me, sweet as her namesake, then turned to Hal. He slid an arm around her waist and together they left me lying there in the infirmary.

Lovers. I felt my heart break. Everything I'd done, all that I'd gone through, and it didn't help at all. He wanted her now.

And I still loved him so.

Lars Fuchs, the pivotal character in the Asteroid Wars, first appeared in the novel Venus. In a sense, I've been writing his biography backward, starting at the end in Venus and then going to the beginning in The Precipice and the following novels of the Asteroid Wars.

When I began to think about doing a novel set on the planet Venus, the first question that had to be answered was: Who would be foolish enough to want to go to the surface of Venus? Certainly scientists are interested in the planet, but they can study it with robotic orbiting spacecraft and landers. They could even establish research stations in orbit around Venus, if they so desired. (And they will, eventually.) But send people to the surface? You'd have to be insane!

Well, the most interesting characters in fiction are pretty close to being insane, one way or another. I thought that perhaps a few danger freaks would get excited by the prospect of being the first human being to reach the hell-hot surface of Venus. And then a different thought struck me. Not a danger freak, but a coward. A weakling. A young man who must find his inner strength in the inhuman crucible of fire that is Earth's "sister planet." Or die.

Thus was born Van Humphries. In this story, adapted from the novel Venus, Van faces the first terrifying tests that Venus throws at him. But they are certainly not the last challenges he must face.

Incidentally, you will notice that Tómas Rodriguez, the astronaut we first met in "Red Sky at Morning," appears in this story, too. As I write the interconnected novels of the Grand Tour, I find some characters appearing again and again. Lars Fuchs is a good example. Jamie Waterman, too. For minor characters such as Rodriguez, their appearances are usually not pre-planned; when they show up it's a surprise to me, a pleasant surprise, like meeting an old friend.

DEATH ON VENUS

y name is Van Humphries. I will be the first human being to reach the hell-hot surface of the planet Venus, or I will die in the attempt.

My father gave me no other choice.

All my life my father had looked down on me; despised me and my illness, sneeringly called me Runt. Sick from birth, I'd been born with a form of pernicious anemia because of my mother's drug addiction. She had died giving birth to me, and my father blamed me for her death. He claimed she was the only woman he had ever truly loved, and I had killed her.

Father—Martin Humphries—lived in Selene City, on the Moon, where he played his chosen role of interplanetary tycoon, megabillionaire, hell-raising, womanizing, ruthless corrupt giant of industry, founder and head of Humphries Space Systems, Inc.

My older brother, Alex, was the apple of Father's eye. But three years ago, Alex was killed on the first human mission to Venus. His ship entered the clouds that totally cover our sister planet, but never came out again.

"It should've been you, Runt!" Father howled when we got the news. "It should've been you who died, not Alex."

Father stewed in helpless fury for months, then suddenly announced that he would give a ten-billion-dollar prize to whoever returned Alex's remains to him.

Ten billion dollars! I would have thought that half the world would leap at the chance to claim the prize. But then I realized that no one in his right mind would dare to try.

As beautiful as Venus appears in our skies, the planet itself is the most hellish place in the solar system. The ground is hot enough to melt aluminum. The air pressure is so high it has crushed spacecraft landers as if they were flimsy cardboard cartons. The sky is perpetually covered from pole to pole with clouds of sulfuric acid. The atmosphere is a choking mixture of carbon dioxide and sulfurous gases.

But Martin Humphries wanted his son's remains returned to him. So he offered his ten-billion-dollar prize.

And he did one other thing. He cut off my stipend, as of my twenty-fifth birthday. On that date I became penniless.

I had loved Alex, the big brother who'd protected me as best as he could from Father's cruel disdain. I decided that *I* would go to Venus and find his remains.

If I was successful, I would be financially secure and independent of Father for the rest of my life.

If I failed, I would join Alex on the red-hot surface of Venus.

I was not the only desperate one aiming for the prize money, I discovered. Lars Fuchs, a "rock rat" from the Asteroid Belt, was also on his way to Venus. From what Father told me, Fuchs was a monster. I had never seen my father look so disturbed about anyone. My father hated Lars Fuchs, that was apparent. He was also quite clearly afraid of him.

We travelled from Earth orbit to Venus orbit in a converted freighter named *Truax*. Tethered to the shabby old bucket was *Hesperos*, the craft that we would ride into the clouds of Venus and down to the planet's surface. *Hesperos* was small but efficient, a cross between a dirigible and submarine that would glide through Venus's thick clouds and carry us all the way down to the ground, where the atmospheric pressure was about the same as the pressure of ocean water more than a kilometer below the surface.

I had wanted Tómas Rodriguez to captain *Hesperos*, but Father had insisted on putting one of his former mistresses in charge, Desiree Duchamp. Tómas reluctantly accepted being bumped to second-in-command. Captain Duchamp, in turn, brought her daughter along. Marguerite was a biologist, of all things. Who needed a biologist on a planet as dead and devastated as Venus?

I soon found out two things: Captain Duchamp wanted her daughter with her because my lecherous father had his eye on her. And Marguerite Duchamp was a clone of her mother.

As Marguerite explained to me, "Mother's always said she's never met a man she'd trust to father a child with her. So she cloned herself and had the embryo implanted inside her. Eight and a half months later I was born."

It was a tense two months, going from Earth to Venus. At last the day arrived when we were to transfer from *Truax* to *Hesperos*, leaving the old freighter in orbit with a skeleton crew aboard her.

I took one last look at my stateroom. When we had boarded *Truax* the single room had seemed rather cramped and decidedly shabby to me. Over the nine weeks of our flight to Venus, though, I'd grown accustomed to having my office and living quarters all contained within the same four walls—or bulkheads, as they're called aboard ship. At least the smart wall screens had made the compartment seem larger than it actually was.

Now we were ready to transfer to the much smaller *Hesperos*. At least, the crew was. I dreaded the move. If *Truax* was like a tatty old freighter, *Hesperos* would be more like a cramped, claustrophobic submarine.

To make matters worse, in order to get to the dirigible-like *Hesperos* we were going to have to perform a space walk. I was actually going to have to seal myself into a space suit and go outside into that yawning vacuum and trolley down the cable that linked the two vessels, with nothing between me and instant death but the monomolecular layers of my suit. I could already feel my insides fluttering with near panic.

For about the twelve-thousandth time I told myself I should have insisted on a tugboat. Rodriguez had talked me out of it when we'd first started planning the mission.

"A pressurized tug, just so we can make the transfer without getting into our suits?" he had jeered at me. "That's an expense we can do without. It's a waste of money."

"It would be much safer, wouldn't it?" I had persisted.

Tómas Rodriguez had been an astronaut; he'd gone to Mars four times before retiring upward to become a consultant to aerospace companies and universities doing planetary explorations. Yet what he really wanted was to fly again.

He was a solidly built man with an olive complexion and thickly curled hair that he kept clipped very short, almost a military crew cut. He looked morose most of the time, pensive, almost unapproachable. But that was just a mask. He smiled easily, and when he did it lit up his whole face to show the truly gentle man beneath the surface.

But he was not smiling; he looked disgusted. "You want safety? Use the mass and volume we'd need for the tug to carry extra water. That'll give us an edge in case the recycler breaks down."

"We have a backup recycler."

"Water's more important than a tug that we'll only use for five minutes during the whole mission. That's one piece of equipment that we definitely don't need to carry along."

So I had let Rodriguez talk me out of the tug. Now I was going to have to perform an EVA, a space walk, something that definitely gave me the shakes.

My jitters got even worse whenever I thought about Lars Fuchs.

Once my father told me that Fuchs actually was racing for the prize money, I spent long hours digging every byte of information I could glean about him. What I found was hardly encouraging. Fuchs had a reputation for ruthlessness and achievement. According to the media biographies, he was a merciless taskmaster, a driven and hard-driving tyrant who ran roughshod over anyone who stood in his way. Except my father.

The media had barely covered Fuchs's launch into a high-velocity transit to Venus. He had built his ship in secrecy out in the Belt—adapted an existing vessel, apparently, to his needs. Unlike all the hoopla surrounding my own launch from Tarawa, there was only one brief interview with Fuchs on the nets, grainy and stiff because of the hour-long delay between the team of questioners on Earth and Fuchs, out there among the asteroids.

I pored over that single interview, studying the face of my adversary on my stateroom wall screen, in part to get my mind off the impending space walk. Fuchs was a thickset man, probably not much taller than I, but with a barrel chest and powerful-looking shoulders beneath his deep blue jacket. His face was broad, jowly, his mouth a downcast slash that seemed always to be sneering. His eyes were small and set so deep in his sockets that I couldn't make out what color they might be.

He made a grisly imitation of a smile to the interviewers' opening question and replied, "Yes, I am going to Venus. It seems only fair that I should take this very generous prize money from Martin Humphries—the man who destroyed my business and took my wife from me, more than thirty years ago."

That brought a barrage of questions from the reporters. I froze the image and delved into the hypertext records.

Fuchs had an impressive background. He had been born poor, but built a sizable fortune for himself out in the Asteroid Belt, as a prospector. Then he started his own asteroidal mining company and became one of the major operators in the Belt, until Humphries Space Systems undercut his prices so severely that Fuchs was forced into bankruptcy. HSS then bought out the company for a fraction of its true worth. My father had personally taken control and fired Fuchs from the firm that the man had founded and developed over two decades.

While Fuchs stayed out in the Asteroid Belt, penniless and furious with helpless rage, his wife left him and married Martin Humphries. She became my father's fourth and last wife.

I gasped with sudden understanding. She was my mother! The mother I had never known. The mother who had died giving birth to me six years afterward. The mother whose drug addiction had saddled me with chronic anemia from birth. I stared at her image on the screen: young, with the flaxen hair and pale blue eyes of the icy northlands. She was very beautiful, yet she looked fragile, delicate, like a flower that blooms on a glacier for only a day and then withers.

It took an effort to erase her image and go back to the news file. Fuchs had taken off for Venus in a specially modified ship he had named *Lucifer*. The Latin name for Venus as the morning star was Lucifer. It was also the name used by the Hebrew prophet Isaiah as a synonym for Satan.

Lucifer. And Fuchs. After a high-gee flight, he was already in orbit around Venus, more than a week ahead of me. Sitting there in my stateroom, staring at Fuchs's sardonic, sneering face on the wall screen, I remembered that the time had come to transfer to *Hesperos*. There was no way to get out of it. I still wished I was home and safe, but now I knew that I had to go through with this mission no matter what the dangers.

But my thoughts went back to my mother. I had never known that she was once Fuchs's wife. My father hardly ever spoke of her, except to blame me for her death. Alex had told me that it wasn't my fault, that women didn't die in childbirth unless there was something terribly wrong. It was Alex who told me about her drug dependency; as far as my father was concerned she was faultless.

"She was the only woman I ever really loved," he said, many a time. I almost believed him. Then he would add, cold as liquid helium, "And you killed her, Runt."

A single rap on my door startled me. Before I could respond, Desiree Duchamp slid the door open and gave me a hard stare.

She wore the same dun-colored flight coveralls as everyone else aboard ship, but on her they looked crisper, sharper, almost like a military uniform. Her eyes were large and luminous. She might have been beautiful if she would smile, but the expression on her face was severe, bitter, almost angry.

"Are you coming or not?" she demanded.

I drew myself up to my full height—not quite eye to eye with my captain—and forced my voice to be steady and calm as I answered, "Yes. I'm ready."

When she turned and headed down the passageway I squeezed my eyes shut and tried to conjure up a picture of my brother. I'm doing this for you, Alex, I said to myself. I'm going to find out why you died—and who's responsible for your death.

But as I headed down the passageway after Duchamp, the image in my mind was of my mother, so young and lovely and vulnerable.

We had done simulations of the EVA procedure a dozen times, and I had suited up each time. I thought it was silly, like children playing dress-up, but Duchamp had insisted that we pull on the cumbersome suits and boots and helmets and backpacks even though we were only going to play-act in *Truax*'s virtual reality chamber.

Now the crew was gathered at the main airlock, busily getting into their space suits. It looked to me like the changing room in some athletic team's locker, or a beachside cabana. I paid intense attention to every detail of the procedure, though. This time it would be for real. A mistake here could be fatal. Leggings first, then the thickly lined boots. Slide into the torso and wiggle your arms through the sleeves. Pull the bubble helmet over your head, seal it to the neck ring. Then work the gloves over your fingers. The gloves had a bony exoskeleton on their backs, powered by tiny servomotors that amplified one's muscle power tenfold. There were also servos built into the suit's joints: shoulders, elbows, knees.

Duchamp herself hung the life-support rig on my back and connected the air hose and power lines. The backpack felt like a ton weighing on my shoulders.

I heard the suit's air fans whine into life, like distant gnats, and felt cool air flowing softly across my face. The suit was actually roomy inside, although the leggings chafed a little against my thighs.

Marguerite, Rodriguez, and the four other crew members were all fully suited. Even Dr. Waller, our rotund dark-skinned Jamaican physician with the sunny disposition, was frowning slightly with impatience as they waited for me to finish up.

"Sorry I'm so slow," I muttered.

They nodded from inside their fishbowl helmets. Marguerite even managed a little smile.

"All right," Duchamp said at last, once she was convinced my suit was properly sealed. "Radio check." Her voice was muffled slightly by the helmet.

One by one the crew members called to the EVA controller up on the bridge. I heard each of them in my helmet earphones.

"Mr. Humphries?" the controller called.

"I hear you," I said.

"Radio check complete. Captain Duchamp, you and your crew are go for transfer."

With Duchamp directing us, they went through the airlock hatch, starting with Rodriguez. Then the doctor and, one by one, the three technicians. I followed Marguerite. Captain Duchamp grasped my arm as I stepped carefully over the sill of the hatch into the blank metal womb of the airlock.

Once she swung the inner hatch shut I felt as if I were in a bare metal coffin. I started to breathe faster, felt my heart pumping harder. Stop it! I commanded myself. Calm down before you hyperventilate.

But when the outer hatch started to slide open I almost panicked.

There was nothing out there! They expected me to step out into total emptiness. I tried to find some stars in that black infinity, something, anything to reassure me, but through the deep tinting of my helmet I could not see any.

"Hold one." Rodriguez's familiar voice calmed me a little. But only a little. Then I saw the former astronaut—now an astronaut once again—slide into view, framed by the outline of the open hatch.

"Gimme your tether," Rodriguez said, extending a gloved hand toward me. It looked like a robot reaching for me. I couldn't see his face at all. Even though the bubble helmets gave us fine visibility from inside them, their protective sun-shield tinting made them look like mirrors from the outside. All I could see in Rodriguez's helmet was the blank fishbowl reflection of my own helmet.

"C'mon, Mr. Humphries. Gimme your tether. I'll attach it to the trolley. Otherwise you'll swing away."

I remembered the drill from the simulations we had gone through. I unclipped one end of my safety tether from its hook at the waist of my suit and handed it mutely to Rodriguez. He disappeared from my view. There was nothing beyond the airlock hatch that I could see, nothing but a gaping, all-encompassing emptiness.

"Step out now, come on," Rodriguez's voice coaxed in my earphones. "You're okay now. Your tether's connected to the trolley and I'm right here."

His space-suited form floated into view again, like a pale white ghost hovering before me. Then I saw the others, a scattering of bodies floating in the void, each connected to the trolley by thin tethers that seemed to be stretched to their limit.

"It's really fun," Marguerite's voice called.

We were not in zero gravity. The two spacecraft were still swinging around their common center of gravity, still connected by the Buckyball cable. But there was nothing out there! Nothing but an emptiness that stretched to the ends of the universe.

Shaking inside, my heart thundering so loudly that I knew they could all hear it over my suit radio, I grasped the edge of the outer hatchway in my gloved hands and, closing my eyes, stepped off into infinity.

My stomach dropped away. I felt bile burning up into my throat. My mind raced. He missed me! Rodriguez missed me and I'm falling away from the ship. I'll fall into the Sun or go drifting out and away forever and ever.

Then something tugged at me. Hard. My eyes popped open and I saw that my tether was as taut as a steel rod, holding me securely. But the trolley seemed to be miles away. And I couldn't see any of the others even when I twisted my head to look for them.

"He's secured," Rodriguez's voice said in my earphones.

"Very well," Duchamp replied. "I'm coming out."

I was twisting around, literally at the end of my tether, trying to find the rest of us.

Then the massive bulk of Venus slid into my view. The planet was huge! Its tremendous mass curved gracefully, so bright that it was hard to look at it even through the heavy tinting of my helmet. For a dizzying moment I felt as if its enormous expanse was above me, over my head, and it was going to come down and crush me like a ponderous boulder squashing some insignificant bug.

But only for a moment. The fear passed quickly and I gasped as I stared at the overpowering awesome immensity of the planet. Tears sprang to my eyes, not from its brightness, from its beauty.

I felt someone tugging at my shoulder. "Hey, you okay, boss?" Rodriguez asked.

"Wha . . . yes. Yes, I'm all right."

"Don't freeze up on us now," the astronaut said. "We'll be ready to move soon's Duchamp gets herself connected to the trolley."

I couldn't take my eyes off Venus. She was a brilliant saffron-yellow expanse, glowing like a thing alive. Goddess of beauty, sure enough. At first I thought the cloud deck was as firm and unvarying as a sphere of solid gold. Then I saw that I could make out streamers among the clouds, slightly darker stretches, patches where the amber yellowish clouds billowed up slightly.

I was falling in love with a world.

"I'm secured. Let's get moving." Duchamp's terse order broke my hypnotic staring.

Turning my entire body slightly I saw the seven other figures bobbing slightly around the trolley, which was nothing more than a motorized framework of metal struts that could crawl along the Buckyball cable.

I looked down the length of the cable toward *Hesperos*, which seemed to be kilometers away. Which it was: three kilometers, to be exact. At that distance the fat dirigible that was our spacecraft looked like a toy model or a holographic image of the real thing. At its nose the broad cone of the heat shield stood in place like a giant parasol, looking faintly ludicrous and totally inadequate to protect the vessel from the burning heat of entry into those thick yellow clouds.

"All right, by the numbers, check in," Duchamp commanded.

As the crew members called in I thought again of what a farce Marguerite's "official" title of mission scientist was. But I was glad she was with us. I could talk to her. She didn't lord it over me as her mother did; even Rodriguez made it clear, without realizing he was doing it, that he regarded me as little more than a rich kid playing at being a scientist.

"All right, then," Duchamp said. "Captain to *Truax*. We are ready for transfer."

"Copy you ready for transfer, Captain. *Hesperos* main airlock is cycled, outer hatch open and waiting for your arrival."

"Activate trolley," she commanded.

"Activating."

I felt a very slight tug on my tether, and then all of us were moving toward the distant *Hesperos*, accelerating now, sliding down the long Buckyball cable like a small school of minnows flashing across a pond. *Hesperos* seemed to be coming up at us awfully fast; I thought we'd crash into her, but I kept silent. Sometimes you'd rather die than make an ass of yourself.

Sure enough, the trolley smoothly decelerated, slowly coming to a stop as the seven of us swung on our tethers like a trained team of acrobats in a silent ballet until we were facing down toward *Hesperos*. I marvelled that we went through the maneuver without bumping one another, but Rodriguez later told me it was simple Newtonian mechanics at work. My respects to Sir Isaac.

The trolley stopped about ten meters from the open airlock hatch, with us hanging by our tethers with our boots a mere meter or so from *Hesperos*'s hull. As we had done in the virtual-reality simulations, Duchamp unhooked her tether and dropped to the hatch, her knees bending as her boots hit the hull soundlessly.

She stepped into the airlock, disappearing into its shadowed depth for a moment. Then her bubble helmet and shoulders emerged from the hatch and she beckoned to me.

"Welcome aboard, Mr. Humphries," she said. "As owner, you should be the first to board *Hesperos*. After me, of course."

"I've tried to contact him a dozen times, Mr. Humphries," said the communications technician. "He simply doesn't answer."

It was the longest sentence the comm tech had spoken to me since I'd first met her. Her name was Riza Kolodny. She was a plain-looking young woman with a round face and mousey brown hair that she kept short, in the chopped-up look that had been fashionable a couple of years earlier.

I was bending over her shoulder, staring at the hash-streaked communications screen. Riza was chewing something that smelled vaguely of cinnamon, or perhaps it was clove. She seemed apprehensive, perhaps afraid that she was displeasing me.

"I've tried all the comm freaks," she said, lapsing into jargon in her nervousness, "starting with the frequency Captain Fuchs registered with the IAA. He just doesn't answer."

Hesperos was not built for creature comforts. The tubular gondola that hung beneath the vessel's bulbous gas envelope housed a spare and spartan set of compartments that included the bridge, galley, a single lavatory for all eight of us, work spaces, infirmary, supply lockers, and our so-called living quarters—which were nothing more than slim, coffin-sized berths partitioned off for a modicum of privacy. There was no room aboard *Hesperos* for anything but utilitarian efficiency. We all felt crowded, cramped. I had to fight off incipient claustrophobia whenever I slid into my berth; I felt like Dracula coming home for a good day's sleep.

The bridge was especially cramped. The comm center was nothing more than a console shoehorned in a bare few centimeters from the captain's command chair. I had to twist myself into a pretzel shape to get close enough to Riza's chair to see her screen. I could feel Duchamp's breath on the back of my neck; she was ignoring me, her dark eyes intently focused on the EVA displayed on the main screen before her. Rodriguez and the two other techs were outside in their space suits, clambering over the heat shield, checking every square centimeter of it.

"Maybe Fuchs's ship has broken down," I thought aloud. Wishful thinking, actually. "Maybe he's in trouble."

Riza shook her head, fluttering her butchered hairdo. "*Lucifer* is telemetering its systems status back to IAA headquarters on the regular data channel, same as we are. The ship's still in orbit with all systems functional."

"Then why doesn't he answer our call?" I wondered.

"He doesn't want to," said Duchamp.

I turned to face her, not exactly an easy thing to do in the jammed confines of the bridge.

"Why not?"

She gave me a frosty smile. "Ask him."

I glared at her. She was making a joke of my effort to contact Lars Fuchs. There were only the three of us on the bridge; Rodriguez's chair was empty.

"I could relay our call through IAA headquarters," Riza suggested. "He might reply to us if the request came through them."

"He won't," Duchamp said flatly. "I know Fuchs. He's not talking to us because he doesn't want to. And that's that."

Reluctantly, I accepted her assessment of the situation. Fuchs was going to remain silent. The only way we would learn of what he was doing would be to access whatever data he was sending back to the International Astronautical Authority in Geneva.

"Very well," I said, squeezing between Duchamp and the display screen she was watching. "I'm going to the observation port to do my news broadcast."

"Stay clear of the airlock," Duchamp warned. "Tommy and the others will be coming back in less than ten minutes."

"Right," I said as I ducked through the hatch. The main passageway ran the length of the gondola; it was so narrow that Rodriguez joked that a man could fall in love squeezing past someone there.

Before we left Earth the question of news coverage had come up. Should we bring a reporter along with us? Back when I thought I'd be bringing some of my friends along on the journey, I had been all in favor of the idea. I thought the nets would *love* to send a reporter to Venus, and I had several friends who could qualify for the role. Live broadcasts from the mission couldn't fail to get top ratings, I figured. Unfortunately, the net executives saw it differently. They pointed out to me that newscasts from *Hesperos* would be interesting the first day or two, but they'd quickly become boring on the long voyage out to Venus. They admitted that once we got there, live reports from Venus would be a sensational story—again, for a day or two. But afterward the story would lose its glamour and become nothing but colorless, tedious routine.

"It's science stuff," one of the junior executives—a sometime friend of mine, in fact—told me. "Science stuff is boring."

They certainly were not willing to pay a reporter's expenses, and insurance. It was Duchamp who suggested that I serve as the expedition's reporter, the face and voice of the *Hesperos*'s mission. "Who better?" she asked rhetorically. I liked the idea. It eliminated the need to carry an extra person along with us. I would file a personal report on the expedition's progress every day. I would become a household figure all around the Earth/Moon system. I really thought that would be terrific. Even if the nets wouldn't feature my broadcasts every day, people could access them whenever they wanted. I often wondered, as I went through my daily report, if my father ever watched me.

Duchamp was no fool. Removing the need to bring a reporter with us she also removed any possible objections I could raise about her replacing our astronomer with a biologist. Her daughter. Fait accompli. She had manipulated me beautifully and I hardly even minded it, although we both knew we didn't need a biologist aboard. Duchamp did it for personal reasons.

Yet I didn't mind. I was actually pleased that Marguerite was with us. Except for my daily news report I had no real duties aboard *Hesperos*. Time hung heavily as we coasted out to Venus and then established orbit around the planet. Marguerite had little to do, also, as far as ship's duties were concerned, although she usually seemed busy enough when I went looking for her.

Often she was in the little cubbyhole that had been converted into her laboratory. After leaving the bridge and heading for the observation port in the nose of the gondola, I naturally passed by her lab. It was smaller than a phone booth, of course.

The accordion-fold door was slid back, so I stopped and asked her, "Are you busy?"

"Yes," said Marguerite. It was a silly question. She was pecking at the keyboard of a laptop, one of several she had propped along the compartment's chest-high shelf. There was no room in her lab for a chair or even a stool; Marguerite worked standing up.

"Oh. I was on my way to do my news report and I thought I'd stop in the galley for a few minutes . . ." My voice trailed off; she was paying no attention to me, tapping at the keyboard of one laptop with a finger while she clicked away on a remote controller with her other hand, changing the images on one of her other screens. The images looked like photomicrographs of bacteria or something equally distasteful. Either that or really bad primitive art.

I shrugged, conceding defeat, and continued down the narrow passageway to the galley. It was nothing more than a set of food freezers and microwave ovens lining one side of the passageway, with a single stark bench on the other side, where one of the gondola's oblong windows showed the massive, curving bulk of the planet below, gleaming like a gigantic golden lamp.

I slumped down on the bench and gazed out at Venus's yellowish clouds. They shifted and changed as I watched. It was almost like staring into a fire, endlessly fascinating, hypnotic. The clouds' hue seemed to be slightly different from one orbit to another. At the moment they looked almost sickly, bilious. Maybe it's just me, I reasoned. I felt like that, sad and sick and alone.

"Mind if I join you?"

I looked up and there was Marguerite standing over me. I shot to my feet.

"Pull up a section of bench," I said brightly.

Marguerite was a physical duplicate of her mother. Younger, of course, not so taut or intimidating, yet the same tall, slim figure. The same sculptured cheekbones and strong jaw. The same jet black eyes and raven hair.

Where her mother was demanding and dominating, though, Marguerite seemed troubled, uncertain of herself. The mother wore her shoulder-length hair severely pulled back; the daughter's flowed softly, and was considerably longer.

Marguerite sat next to me and I caught a scent of perfume, very delicate, but a wonderful contrast to the metallic starkness of the ship.

"I'm sorry I was short with you back there," she said. "I was running the latest UV scans of the atmosphere. Sometimes it gets pretty intense."

"Oh, sure. I understand."

She was still wrapped up in her work. "*Something* down in those clouds absorbs ultraviolet light," she said.

"You think it's biological? A life form in the clouds?"

She started to nod, then thought better of it. As if she were a long-experienced scientist she buried her enthusiasm and answered noncommittally, "I don't know. Perhaps. We won't know for certain until we get down into the clouds and take samples."

Without thinking, I argued, "What about all the sampling the unmanned probes did, years ago? They didn't find any evidence of living organisms."

Suddenly Marguerite's dark eyes snapped with annoyance. "They weren't equipped to. They all carried nephelometers to measure droplet size, but not one of them carried a single instrument that could have detected any biological activity. A Shetland pony could've flown by and those dumbass robots would never have noticed."

"There weren't any biological sensors on any of the probes?"

"Not one," she said. "Venus is a dead planet. That's the official word."

"But you don't believe it."

"Not yet. Not until I've looked for myself."

I felt a new respect for Marguerite. She could be just as much a tigress as her mother in matters that she cared about.

"How much longer will we stay in orbit?" she asked.

I hunched my shoulders. "We're scanning the equatorial region with radar, looking for any sign of the wreckage of my brother's ship."

"Wouldn't it be all smashed into small pieces?"

"Probably not," I answered. "The atmosphere's so thick that his ship would've gone to the bottom like a ship sinking in the ocean, back home. I mean, the pressure down at the surface is like our oceans, a kilometer or more below sea level."

She thought about that for a moment. "So it wouldn't be like a plane falling out of the sky on Earth."

"Or like a missile hitting the ground. No. More like the *Titanic* settling on the bottom of the Atlantic."

"You haven't found anything yet?"

"Not yet," I admitted. *Hesperos* was in a two-hour equatorial orbit; we had circled the planet thirty times, so far.

"How much of a chance is there that you'll spot something?"

"Well, we know where he first entered the atmosphere, the latitude and longitude. But we can only guess where he might have drifted while he was in the clouds."

"He didn't have a tracking beacon?"

"Its signal broke up a lot once he went into the cloud deck, so we've got to scan a pretty wide swath along the equator."

Marguerite looked past me, out at the clouds swirling across the face of Venus. She stared at them as if she could get them to part by sheer willpower. I watched the profile of her face. How much she looked like her mother! The same face, yet somehow softer, kinder. It made me think about how little I looked like my father. Alex resembled Father. People had often exclaimed that Alex looked like a younger replica of Martin Humphries. But I resembled my mother, they said. The mother I never knew.

Marguerite turned back to me. "Are you really a planetary scientist?"

The question surprised me. "I try to be," I said.

"Then why aren't you working at it? There's your planet, right out there, and yet you spend your time wandering around the ship like a little lost boy."

"I've got a complete set of instruments taking data," I said. It sounded weak and defensive, even to me.

"But you're not doing anything with the data. You're not analyzing it or using it to change the sensors' operating parameters. You're just letting everything chug along on their preset programs."

"The data goes back to Professor Cochrane at Caltech. If she wants the instruments changed, she tells me and I make the changes."

"Like a graduate student," Marguerite said. "A trained chimpanzee."

That stung. "Well . . . I've got other things to do, you know."

"Like what?"

"I send in my news reports every day."

Her lips pulled down disapprovingly. "That must take all of ten minutes."

Strangely, I felt laughter bubbling up in me. I normally don't take kindly to criticism, but Marguerite had hit me fairly and squarely.

"Oh no," I answered her, chuckling. "It takes more like half an hour."

Her expression softened, but only a little. "Well then, let's see. I'll give you eight hours for sleeping and an hour and a half for meals . . . that leaves fourteen empty hours every day! If I had fourteen hours on my hands I'd build a whole new set of biosensors for when we dip into the clouds."

"I could help you," I said.

She pretended to consider the offer. "Uh-huh. Do you have any background in cellular biology?"

"I'm afraid not."

"Spectroscopy? Can you take apart one of the mass spectrometers and realign it to be sensitive to organic molecules?"

I must have been grinning like a fool. "Um, do you have a manual for that? I can follow instruction manuals pretty well."

She was smiling now, too. "I think you'd better stick to your own specialty."

"Planetary physics."

"Yes. But get active about it! There's more to science than watching the readouts of your instruments."

"I suppose so. But so far the sensors aren't showing anything that the old probes didn't get, years ago."

"Are you certain? Have you gone through the data thoroughly? You mean to tell me there's *nothing* different? No anomalies, no unexplained blips in the incoming data?"

Before I could think of an answer, Duchamp's voice came through the intercom speaker built into the overhead. "Mr. Humphries, radar scan has picked up a glint that might be wreckage. Could you come to the bridge, please?"

•   •   •

Rodriguez was back on the bridge when we got there, and with all three chairs occupied, the bridge was simply too small for both me and Marguerite to squeeze in. I ducked halfway through the hatch and stopped there. Marguerite stayed behind me, in the passageway, and looked in over my shoulder.

The main screen, in front of Duchamp's command chair, showed a frozen radar image: dark shadows and jumbled shapes of land forms with a single bright glint at its center. Rodriguez was leaning forward in his chair, studying the image, perspiration beading his brow.

"That could be it," he said, pointing to me. "It's definitely metal; the computer analysis leaves no doubt."

I stared hard at the blob of light. "Can we get better resolution? You can't tell what it is from this image."

Before Riza could reply from the comm console, Duchamp snapped, "We've amplified it as much as we can. That's the best we can get."

Rodriguez said, "It's within the footprint that your brother's craft would be expected to have, knowing what we know about when and where he went down. Nothing else metallic has shown up in the region."

"We'll have to go lower for better resolution," Duchamp said. "Get under the cloud deck and use the telescopes."

"What region is that?" Marguerite asked, from behind me.

"Aphrodite," said her mother.

"It's a highland region, more than two kilometers higher than the surrounding plains," Rodriguez said.

"Then it must be cooler," I said.

Duchamp smiled humorlessly. "Cooler, yes. The ground temperature is down to a pleasant four hundred degrees Celsius."

The lowland surface temperature averages above four hundred fifty degrees, I knew.

"Are we set for atmosphere entry?" I asked.

"The heat shield's been checked out," Duchamp replied. "Propulsion is ready."

"And still no word from Fuchs?"

Riza answered from the comm console, "He entered the cloud deck two hours ago, halfway around the planet. I got his entry position from the IAA."

"Then he hasn't seen the wreckage?"

Duchamp shook her head. "If we've seen that glint, he has, too."

"The plane of his entry was almost exactly equatorial," Riza said, almost apologetically. "He'll most likely come out of the clouds in the same region as the glint."

I felt a dull throb in my jaw and realized that my teeth were clenched tight. "Very well then," I said. "We'd better get under the clouds, too."

Duchamp nodded, then touched a stud on her chair's left armrest. "Captain to crew: Take your entry stations. Stand by for atmospheric entry in ten minutes." She lifted her hand and looked directly at me. "Clear the bridge of all nonessential personnel."

I took her unsubtle hint and backed out into the passageway. Marguerite was already striding away.

"Where are you going?" I called after her.

"To my lab. I want to record the entry."

"The automatic sensors—"

"They're not programmed to look for organic molecules or other exotic species. Besides, I want to get the entry process on video. It'll look good for your news report."

I started to reply, then sensed Rodriguez standing behind me.

"She threw you off the bridge, too?"

He grinned at me. "My entry station is up forward with the life-support technician." He squeezed past me and started along the passageway.

The trouble was, I had no official entry station. If we went strictly by the rules I should've slid into my berth and stayed strapped in there until we jettisoned the heat shield. But I had no intention of doing that.

"Is there room for a third person up there?" I asked, trailing after Rodriguez.

"If you don't mind the body odors," he said over his shoulder.

"I showered this morning," I said, hurrying to catch up with him.

"Yeah, well, it's gonna get a little warm up there, you know. You'd be more comfortable in your berth."

I lifted my chin a notch. "You don't have to pamper me."

Rodriguez glanced over his shoulder at me. "Okay, you're the boss. You wanta be in the hot seat, come on along."

Striding down the passageway behind him, I asked, "How are you and Duchamp getting along?"

"Fine," he said, without slowing down or looking back toward me. "No problems."

Something in his voice sounded odd to me. "Are you sure?"

"We've worked things out. We're okay."

He sounded strange . . . cheerful, almost. As if he was in on a joke and I wasn't.

We passed Marguerite's tiny lab. The accordion-pleat door was folded open and I could see her standing in the cubicle, her head bent over a palm-sized video camera.

"You'll have to strap down for the entry," Rodriguez told her. "It's gonna get bumpy for a while."

"I'll help her," I said. "You go ahead and I'll catch up with you." Mr. Gallant, that's me.

Rodriguez looked uncertain for a moment, but then he nodded acceptance. "The two of you have got to be belted in for the entry. I don't care where, but you've got to be in safety harnesses. Understood?"

"Understood," I assured him. Duchamp had made us practice the entry procedures at least once a day for the past two weeks.

"ENTRY BEGINS IN EIGHT MINUTES," the countdown computer announced.

Marguerite looked up from her work. "There. The vidcam's ready."

She pushed past me and started down the passageway to the observation blister, the camera in her hand.

"Aren't you going with Tom?" she asked.

"I was," I said, "but if you don't mind I'd rather stay with you."

"I don't mind."

"Rodriguez gave me the feeling I'd just be in his way up there."

"I'm sure he didn't mean it that way."

"I know when I'm being condescended to," I insisted.

"Tom's not like that."

We reached the blister, a metal bubble that extended outward from the gondola's main body. Three small observation ports studded its side, each window made of thick tinted quartz. Four padded swivel chairs were firmly bolted to the deck.

"You won't see much through the tinting," I said.

Marguerite smiled at me, and went to a small panel beneath the port that slanted forward. Opening it, she snapped her camera into the recess.

Then she shut the panel again. Three tiny lights winked on: two green, one amber. As I watched, the amber light turned red.

"What's that?" I asked, puzzled. "I thought I knew every square centimeter of this bucket."

"God is in the details," Marguerite said. "I got Tom and my mother to allow me to build this special niche here. It's like an airlock, with an inner hatch and an outer one."

"They allowed you to break the hull's integrity?" I felt shocked.

"It was all done within the standard operating procedures. Tom and Aki both checked it out."

Akira Sakamoto was our life-support technician: young, chubby, introspective to the point of surliness, so quiet he was almost invisible aboard the ship.

I was still stunned. "And the camera's exposed to vacuum?"

She nodded, obviously pleased with herself. "The outer hatch opened when the inner one sealed. That's why the third light is red."

"Why didn't anybody tell me about this?" I wasn't angry, really. Just surprised that they'd do this without at least telling me.

"It was in the daily logs. Didn't you see them?" Marguerite turned the nearest swivel chair to face the port and sat in it.

I took the chair next to her. "Who reads the daily reports? They're usually nothing but boring details."

"Tom highlighted it."

"When? When was this done?"

She thought a moment. "The second week out. No, it was the beginning of the third week." With an impatient shake of her head, she said, "Whenever it was, you can look it up in the log if you want the exact date."

I stared at her. She was smiling impishly. She was enjoying this.

"I'll fry Rodriguez's butt for this," I muttered. It was a phrase I had often heard my father growl. I never thought I'd say it myself.

"Don't blame Tom!" Marguerite was suddenly distraught, concerned. "My mother okayed it. Tom was only doing what I asked and the captain approved."

"ENTRY IN SIX MINUTES," came the automated announcement.

"So you asked, your mother approved, and Rodriguez did the work without telling me."

"It's only a minor modification."

"He should have told me," I insisted. "Breaching the hull is not minor. He should have pointed it out to me specifically."

Her roguish smile returned. "Don't take it so seriously. If Tom and my mother okayed it, there's nothing to worry about."

I knew she was right. But dammit, Rodriguez should have informed me. I'm the owner of this vessel. He should have made certain that I knew and approved.

Marguerite leaned over toward me and tapped a forefinger against my chin. "Lighten up, Van. Enjoy the ride."

I looked into her eyes. They were shining like polished onyx. Suddenly I leaned toward her and, reaching a hand behind the nape of her neck, I pulled her to me and kissed her firmly on the lips.

She pushed away, her eyes flashing now, startled, almost angry.

"Now wait a minute," she said.

I slid back in my chair. "I . . . you're awfully attractive, you know."

She glared at me. "Just because my mother's letting Tom sleep with her is no reason for you to think you can get me into your bed."

I felt as if someone had whacked me with a hammer. "What? What did you say?"

"You heard me."

"Rodriguez and your mother?"

The indignation in her eyes cooled a bit. "You mean you didn't know about them?"

"No!"

"They're sleeping together. I thought everyone on board knew it."

"I didn't!" My voice sounded like a little boy's squeak, even to myself.

Marguerite nodded, and I saw in her expression some of the bitterness her mother exuded constantly.

"Ever since we left Earth orbit. It's my mother's way of solving personnel problems."

"ENTRY IN FIVE MINUTES."

"We'd better strap in," Marguerite said.

"Wait," I said. "You're telling me that your mother is sleeping with Rodriguez to smooth over the fact that she's captain and he's only second-in-command?"

Marguerite did not reply. She concentrated on buckling the seat harness over her shoulders.

"Well?" I demanded. "Is that what you're saying?"

"I shouldn't have mentioned it," she said. "I've shocked you."

"I'm not shocked!"

She looked at me for a long moment, her expression unfathomable. At last she said, "No, I can see that you're not shocked."

"I'm accustomed to men and women enjoying sex together," I told her.

"Yes, of course you are."

Then a new thought struck me. "You're angry at your mother, is that it?"

"I'm not angry. I'm not shocked. I'm not even surprised. The only thing that amazes me is that you can live in this crowded little sardine can for week after week and not have the faintest inkling of what's going on."

I had to admit to myself that she was right. I'd been like a sleep-walker. Or rather, like a clown. Going through the motions of being the owner, the man in charge. All these things happening and I hadn't the slightest clue.

I sagged back in my padded chair, feeling numb and stupid. I started fumbling with my safety harness; my fingers felt thick, clumsy. I couldn't take my eyes off Marguerite, wondering, wondering.

She looked back at me, straight into my eyes. "I'm not like my mother, Van. I may be her clone, but I'm nothing like her. Don't ever forget that."

"ENTRY IN FOUR MINUTES."

Orbiting Venus's hot, thick atmosphere at slightly more than seven kilometers per second, *Hesperos* fired its retrorockets at precisely the millisecond called for in the entry program.

Strapped into the chair in the observation blister, I felt the ship flinch, like a speeding car when the driver taps the brake slightly.

I leaned forward as far as the safety harness would allow. Through the forward-angled port I could see the rim of the big heat shield and, beyond it, the smooth saffron clouds that completely shrouded the planet.

Except the clouds were no longer smooth. There were rifts here and there, long streamers floating above the main cloud deck, patterns of billows like waves rolling across a deep, deep sea.

Marguerite was turned toward the port also, so I could not see her full face, only a three-quarter profile. She seemed intent, her hands gripping the arms of her chair. Not white-knuckled, not frightened, but certainly not relaxed, either.

Me, I was clutching the arms of my chair so hard my nails were going to leave permanent indentations in the plastic. Was I frightened? I don't know. I was excited, taut as the Buckyball cable that had connected us to the old *Truax*. I was breathing hard, I remember, but I don't recall any snakes twisting in my gut.

Something bright flared across the rim of the heat shield and I suddenly wished I were up on the bridge, where I could see the instruments and understand what was happening. There was an empty chair up there; I should have demanded that I sit in it through the entry flight.

The ship shuddered. Not violently, but enough to notice. More than enough. The entire rim of the heat shield was glowing now and streamers of hot gas flashed past. The ride started to get bumpy.

"Approaching maximum gee forces," Duchamp's voice called out over the intercom speaker in the overhead.

"Max gee, check," Rodriguez replied, from his position up in the nose.

It was *really* bumpy now. I was being rattled back and forth in my chair, happy to have the harness holding me firmly.

"Maximum aerodynamic pressure," Duchamp said.

"Temperature in the forward section exceeding max calculated." Rodriguez's voice was calm, but his words sent a current of electricity through me.

The calculations have an enormous safety factor in them, I tried to reassure myself. It would have been easier if the ship didn't feel as if it were trying to shake itself apart.

I couldn't see a thing through the port now. Just a solid sheet of blazing hot gases, like looking into a furnace. I squeezed my eyes down to slits while the battering, rattling ride went on. My vision blurred. I closed my eyes entirely for a moment. When I opened them cautiously, I could see fairly well again, although the ship was still shuddering violently.

Marguerite hadn't moved since the entry began, she was still staring fixedly ahead. I wondered if her camera was getting anything or if the incandescent heat of our entry into the atmosphere had fried its lens.

The ride began to smooth out a bit. It was still bumpier than anything I had ever experienced before, but at least now I could lean my head back against the padded headrest and not have it bounce so hard it felt like I was being pummelled by a karate champion.

Marguerite turned slightly and smiled at me. A pale smile, I thought, but it made me smile back at her.

"Nothing to it," I said, trying to sound brave. It came out more like a whimper.

"I think the worst is over," she said.

Just then there was an enormous jolt and an explosion that would have made me leap out of my chair if I weren't strapped in. It took just a flash of a second to realize that it was the explosive bolts jettisoning the heat shield, but in that flash of a second I must have pumped my entire lifetime's supply of adrenaline into my blood. I came very close to wetting myself; my bladder felt painfully full.

"We're going into the clouds!" Marguerite said happily.

"Deceleration on the tick," Duchamp's voice rang out.

"Heat shield jettison complete," Rodriguez replied. "Now we're a blimp."

Rodriguez was inaccurate, I knew. A blimp has a soft envelope; ours was rigid cermet. It wasn't often I could catch Rodriguez in a slip of the tongue. I threw a superior smile to Marguerite as I popped the latch on my safety harness. The instant I stood up, though, *Hesperos* shuddered, lurched, swung around crazily, and accelerated so hard I was slammed right back into my chair.

The superrotation.

The solid body of the planet may turn very slowly, but Venus's upper atmosphere, blast-heated by the Sun, develops winds of two hundred kilometers per hour and more that rush around the entire planet in a few days. In a way, they're like the jet streams on Earth, only bigger and more powerful.

Our lighter-than-air vessel was in the grip of those winds, zooming along like a leaf caught in a hurricane. We used the engines hanging outside the gondola only to keep us from swinging too violently, otherwise we would have depleted our fuel in a matter of hours. We couldn't fight those winds, we could only surf along on them and try to keep the ride reasonably smooth.

Truax, up in a safe, stable orbit, was supposed to keep track of our position by monitoring our telemeter beacon. This was for two reasons: to stay in constant communications contact with us and to plot the direction and speed of the superrotation wind, with *Hesperos* playing the same role as a smoke particle in a wind tunnel. But *Truax* hadn't deployed the full set of communications satellites around the planet by the time we got caught in the superrotation. Without the commsats to relay our beacon, they lost almost half our first day's data.

And if anything had gone wrong, they wouldn't know it for ten–twelve hours.

Fortunately, the only trouble we had was a few bruised shins as *Hesperos* lurched and swirled in the turbulent winds. It was like being in a racing yacht during a storm: You had to hold on to something whenever you moved from one place to another.

It was scary at first, I admit. No amount of lectures, videos, or even VR simulations can really prepare you for the genuine experience. But in a few hours I got accustomed to it. More or less.

I spent most of those hours right there in the observation blister, staring out as we darted along the cloud tops. Marguerite got up and went back to her lab; crew members passed by now and then, stumbling and staggering along the passageway, muttering curses every time the ship pitched and they banged against a bulkhead.

At one point Marguerite came back to the blister, a heavy-looking gray box of equipment in her hands.

"Shouldn't you be checking the sensors up forward?" she asked, a little testily, I thought.

"They're running fine," I said. "If there were any problems I'd get a screech on my phone." I tapped the communicator in the chest pocket of my coveralls.

"Don't you want to see the data they're taking in?"

"Later on, when the ride settles down a little," I said. It had always nonplussed me that many scientists get so torqued up about their work that they have to watch their instruments while the observation is in progress. As if their being there can make any difference in what the instruments are recording.

Marguerite left and I was alone again, watching the upper layer of the cloud deck reaching for us. Long, lazy tendrils of yellowish fog seemed to stretch out toward us, then evaporate before my eyes. The cloud tops were dynamic, bubbling like a boiling pot, heaving and breathing like a thing alive.

Don't be an anthropomorphic ass, I warned myself sternly. Leave the similes to the poets and romantics like Marguerite. You're supposed to be a scientist.

Of sorts, a sardonic inner voice scoffed. You're only playing at being a scientist. A real scientist would be watching his sensors and data readouts like a tiger stalking a deer.

And miss this view? I answered myself.

We were dipping into the clouds now, sinking down into them like a submarine sliding beneath the surface of the sea. Yellow-gray clouds slid past my view, then we were in the clear again, then more mountains of haze covered the port. Deeper and deeper we sank, into the sulfuric-acid perpetual global clouds of Venus.

The ride did indeed smooth out, but only a little. Or maybe we all became accustomed to the pitching and rolling. We got our sea legs. Our Venus legs.

It was eerie, sailing in that all-enveloping fog. For days on end I stared out of the ports and saw nothing but a gray sameness. I wanted to push ahead, to go deeper, get beneath the clouds so we could begin searching the surface with telescopes for the wreckage of my brother's vessel.

But the mission plan called for caution, and despite my eagerness I understood that the plan should be followed. We were in uncharted territory now, and we had to make certain that all of *Hesperos*'s systems were performing as designed.

The mammoth cermet envelope above us had been filled (if that's the right word) with vacuum. Its hatches had been open to vacuum all the time of our flight from Earth orbit, then sealed tight when we entered Venus's atmosphere. What better flotation medium for a lighter-than-air vessel than nothingness?

Now we were slowly filling the envelope with hydrogen gas, sucked out of the clouds' abundant sulfuric acid through our equipment that separated out the wanted hydrogen and released the unwanted sulfur and oxygen. On Earth hydrogen's flammability would have been dangerous, but Venus's atmosphere contained practically no free oxygen, so there was no danger of explosion or fire. The envelope itself was a rigid shell of cermet, a ceramic-metal composite that combined toughness and rigidity yet was lighter than any possible metal alloy.

To go deeper, we would vent hydrogen overboard and replace it with atmospheric gas: mainly carbon dioxide. When the time came to rise again, we intended to break down the carbon dioxide into its component elements of carbon and oxygen, vent the carbon overboard and let the lighter oxygen buoy us upward. Higher up we intended to dissociate the sulfuric acid molecules of the clouds again and refill the envelope with hydrogen.

We had tested the equipment for splitting the carbon dioxide and sulfuric acid molecules before we ever took off from Earth, and now, inside the globe-girdling cloud deck of Venus, we put it to work to fill the gas envelope with hydrogen.

Eager as I was to go deeper, I was perfectly happy to see that the equipment worked in Venus's clouds. I had no desire to be stuck down at the surface with no way to come back up.

So we coasted along in the uppermost cloud deck, patiently filling the big shell above us and testing our equipment. Once in a while it seemed to me that we weren't moving at all, that we were stuck in place like a ship run aground on a reef. All we could see out the ports was that perpetual yellowish-gray sameness. But then some strong current in the atmosphere would grab us and the gondola would tilt and groan like a creaking old sailing ship and my insides would flutter just a little bit.

I was constantly worried about Fuchs, of course, but the IAA reports on his activity showed that he was also moving cautiously. He had entered the atmosphere several hours before we did, but so far had not gone much deeper than we had. Like us, he was floating in the upper reaches of the top cloud deck, pushed around the planet by the super-rotation winds.

"He's no fool," Duchamp told me as we sat together in the spartan little galley. "Lars takes risks, but only when he's certain the odds are in his favor."

"You know him?" I asked.

She made a thin smile. "Oh, yes. Lars and I are old friends."

"Friends?" I felt my brows hike up.

Her smile faded. "I first met him just after he had lost his business and his wife. He was a pretty desperate man then. Hurt and angry. Bewildered. Everything he had built up in his life had been snatched away from him." She exhaled a puff of air through her nostrils, something between a grunt and a sigh.

The expression on her face told me she knew perfectly well that the man who had destroyed his company and taken his wife was my father. She didn't have to say it; we both knew.

"But he pulled himself up again, didn't he?" I snapped. "He's done fairly well in asteroid mining, hasn't he?"

Duchamp looked at me for a long silent moment, the kind of look a university professor gives to an especially dense and hopeless student.

"Yes," she said. "Hasn't he."

At least, during those first days coasting through the clouds, I had an excuse to stay close to Marguerite. I was supposed to be a planetary scientist, I kept reminding myself, and even though she was a biologist we began to work together, sampling the clouds.

Marguerite's lab was too crowded for both of us to use it at the same time, and it would have been impossible for us to work together in either her quarters or mine: Each of us had nothing more than a narrow berth with a privacy screen shuttering it. We could have both fit in either berth, but no scientific research would have been done. Indeed, I found myself wondering what it would be like to have Marguerite cupped beside me in my berth. Or hers.

But she had no romantic interest in me, that was clear. Instead, we turned the observation post up in the gondola's nose into a makeshift laboratory where we took samples of the cloud droplets and analyzed them.

"There really is water in the clouds!" Marguerite exclaimed happily, after a long day of checking and rechecking the results of our spectral analyses.

"Thirty parts per million," I grumbled. "It might as well be zero for all the good—"

"No, no, you don't understand," she said. "Water means life! Where water exists, life exists."

She was really excited. I was more or less playing at being a planetary scientist but to Marguerite the search for life was as thrilling and absorbing as Michelangelo's drive to create great works of art out of rough slabs of marble.

We were sitting cross-legged on the metal decking up in the gondola's nose section because there was no room for chairs and nobody had thought to bring any cushions aboard. The transparent quartzite nose itself showed only the featureless yellowish-gray of the eternal cloud deck: It might just as well been spray painted that color for all that we could see out there. Two mass spectrometers sat to one side of us, half a dozen hand-sized computers were scattered on the deck plates, and a whole rack of equipment boxes—some gray, some black—hummed away along the bulkhead beside me.

"The presence of water," I pointed out, "does not automatically mean the presence of life. There is a good deal of water on the Moon, but no life there."

"Humans live on the Moon," she countered, with mischief in the lilt of her voice.

"I mean native lunar life, you know that."

"But the water deposits on the Moon are frozen. Wherever there's *liquid* water, like under the ice crust on Europa—"

"The water vapor in these clouds," I interrupted, jabbing a finger toward the observation port, "hardly constitutes a supply of liquid water."

"They do to microscopic organisms."

I had to hold back a laugh. "Have you found any?"

Her enthusiasm didn't waver one iota. "Not yet. But we will!"

I could only shake my head in admiration for her perseverance.

"This proves that there must be at least some volcanic activity down at the surface," Marguerite said.

"I suppose so," I agreed.

The reasoning was simple enough: Any water vapor in Venus's atmosphere quickly boiled up to the top of the clouds, where the intense ultraviolet radiation from sunlight broke up the water molecules into hydrogen and oxygen, which eventually evaporated away into space. So there had to be a fresh supply of water constantly replenishing the droplets. Otherwise they would have all been dissociated and blown off the planet ages ago. The source of the water most likely came from the planet's deep interior and was vented into the atmosphere by volcanic eruptions.

On Earth volcanoes constantly blow out steam, sometimes in explosions that tear the tops off the mountains. But the water vapor they vent into the atmosphere stays in the atmosphere, on Earth. It's not lost to space because Earth's atmosphere gets cold at high altitudes and the water condenses and falls back as rain or snow. That's why Earth has oceans and Venus doesn't. Earth's upper atmosphere is a "cold trap" that prevents the water from escaping the planet. Hothouse Venus doesn't have a cold trap in its upper atmosphere: At the altitude where on Earth the temperature dips below freezing, Venus's is almost four hundred degrees Celsius, four times hotter than water's boiling point. As a result Venus can't build up any appreciable water content in its atmosphere.

"We'll have to go deeper to find life forms in the clouds," Marguerite said, as much to herself as to me. "The UV absorber isn't that much further down."

Fuchs still worried me. Apparently he was still sailing in the clouds, as we were. But aside from his position I could get no information about him from the IAA. For a good reason: He was giving out no information, nothing but his tracking beacon and the standard telemetering data that showed his basic systems to be operating in good order. When I tried to get details about the design of his ship or the array of sensing systems he carried, I drew a blank. *Lucifer* was his ship, his design, built out in the deep darkness of the Asteroid Belt, equipped according to his specifications and no one else's. He reported the minimum required by the IAA and kept everything else to himself.

One thing I was able to do during those first days in the clouds was to begin to build up a map of the superrotation wind pattern. By recording our position from the ship's inertial navigation system I was able to generate a three-dimensional plot of where those winds blew, a sort of weather map of Venus's jet streams. Every time a powerful gust buffeted us and made me grab for a handhold, every time a sudden upwelling bounced us or a cold spot made us drop until my stomach crawled up into my throat, I thought to myself that at least I was getting useful data.

The winds fanned outward from the subsolar point, of course. That was where the Sun was directly overhead, blazing down on the planet's atmosphere like a blowtorch. Venus turns so slowly, once in 243 Earth days, that the subsolar spot gets blasted remorselessly. The atmosphere rushes away from there in a gigantic heat-driven flow, setting up currents and convection cells that span the girth of the planet. I measured wind speeds of nearly four hundred kilometers per hour: We were setting a Guinness speed record for lighter-than-air vessels.

Deeper down, where the atmosphere gets thicker and so much hotter, the winds die to almost nothing. At a pressure similar to that of an Earthly ocean a kilometer or so deep, there could be nothing that we would recognize as winds, only sluggish tidal motions.

At least, that's how the theory went.

My map of the superrotation winds was coming along quite nicely after a few days, and it made me proud to realize that I was making a real contribution toward understanding Venus. When I tried to extend my data down to a slightly lower altitude, though, in an effort to see how far down the winds might extend, the computer program glitched on me. Insufficient data, I thought, peering at the display screen.

I had coded the map with false colors, each color indicating a range of speeds. There they were, a network of jet streams all rushing out from the subsolar point, in shades of blue and green. With my VR goggles on, I saw it all in three-dimensional motion. But there was the damned glitch, a swath of red a few kilometers below our present altitude. Red should have indicated even higher wind velocity than we were in now, but I knew that was wrong. The wind velocities had to get lower as we went down in altitude, not higher. Something was wrong with the program.

I mentioned it to Duchamp and Rodriguez when we met to decide on when we would start down toward the surface.

Our conference center was the observation blister, the only place in our cramped gondola where three or four people could sit comfortably. Duchamp and I sat side by side, our chairs swivelled away from the observation ports. Rodriguez sat on the floor facing us, his back against the far bulkhead.

"All systems have performed well within their design range," Duchamp said, tapping a manicured fingernail on the screen of her handheld computer. "Unless I hear otherwise, I declare this phase of the mission completed."

Rodriguez nodded. "No complaints about that. It'll be good to get out of this wind and down to a calmer altitude."

"Calmer," Duchamp said, "but hotter."

"We can handle the heat."

She smiled at him as if they had some private joke going between them.

I spoke up. "My map of the wind system keeps throwing this glitch at me." I had brought a handheld, too, and showed it to them.

"The red indicates even higher wind velocities than we're in now," I said.

"That's an extrapolation, isn't it?" Rodriguez asked. "It's not based on observational data."

"No, we haven't gone down that far, so we don't have any data from that altitude."

"A computer extrapolation," Duchamp said, like an art critic sniffing at some child's lopsided attempt to draw a tree.

"But the extrapolation is based on pretty firm meteorological data," I pointed out.

"Terrestrial meteorological data?" asked Duchamp.

I nodded. "Modified to take into account Venus's different temperature, pressure, and chemical regime."

"An abstraction of an abstraction," Duchamp said, with a *that's-that* wave of her hand.

Rodriguez was staring at the smear of red at the bottom of my map. He handed the palm-sized computer back to me and said thoughtfully, "You don't think there could be some kind of wind shear down at that altitude, do you?"

"A supersonic wind shear?" Duchamp scoffed.

"It's not supersonic at that pressure," Rodriguez pointed out.

She shook her head. "All the planetary physicists agree that the superrotation winds die out as you go deeper into the atmosphere and the pressure builds up. The winds get swamped by the increased pressure."

Rodriguez nodded thoughtfully, then said slowly, "Yeah, I know, but if there really is a wind shear it could be a killer."

Duchamp took a breath, glanced from him to me and back again, then made her decision.

"Very well," she said. "We'll rig for intense wind shear. Check out all systems. Make everything secure and tightened down, just as we did for atmospheric entry." She turned to me. "Will that satisfy you, Mr. Humphries?"

I was surprised at the venom in her reaction. I swallowed once and said, "You're the captain."

"Good." To Rodriguez she said, "Tommy, this means you'll have to go outside and manually check all the connectors and fittings."

He nodded glumly. "Yeah. Right."

Then, smiling coldly, Duchamp turned back to me. "Mr. Humphries, would you care to assist Tom?"

"Me?" I squeaked.

"We could use the extra hand," she said smoothly, "and the inspection is actually at your behest, isn't it? You and your computer program."

You bitch, I thought. Just because my computer program showed a possible problem she's blaming me for it. Now I've either got to risk my neck or show everybody that I'm a coward.

Rodriguez leaned across the narrow passageway separating us and grabbed my knee in a rough, friendly way.

"Come on, Mr. Humphries, it won't be so bad. I'll be with you every step of the way and you'll be able to tell your grandchildren about it."

If I live long enough to have grandchildren, I thought. But I swallowed my fear and said as calmly as I could, "Sure. It ought to be exciting."

It certainly was.

Basically, our task was to check all the connectors that held the gondola to the gas envelope above us. It was a job that a plumber could do, it didn't call for any special training. But we'd be outside, in a cloud of sulfuric acid droplets that was nearly a hundred degrees Celsius, more than fifty kilometers above the ground.

Rodriguez spent two intense hours briefing me in the virtual reality simulator on what we had to do. Six main struts had to be checked out, and six secondary ones. They connected the gondola to the gas shell; if they failed under stress we would go plunging down to the red-hot surface like an iron anvil.

Akira Sakamoto, our dour life-support technician, personally helped me into my space suit. It was the same one I had used when we transferred from *Truax*, but now its exterior had been sprayed with a special heat-resistant ceramic. The suit seemed stiffer to me than before, although Sakamoto insisted the ceramic in no way interfered with limb motion.

Without a word, without any discernable expression on his chunky broad face, he slipped the safety harness around my waist and clicked it in place, then made certain both its tethers were properly looped so they wouldn't trip me as I tried to walk.

Dr. Waller helped to check out Rodriguez, who got into his suit unassisted. But you had to have somebody go around to make certain all the seals were okay and the electrical lines and life-support hoses hooked up properly from the backpack.

Marguerite came down to the airlock, too, and watched in silence as we suited up. I was trembling slightly as I wriggled into the ungainly suit, which was now sort of silvery from its new ceramic coating. But I realized with some surprise that my trembling wasn't so much fear as excitement. I knew I should have been scared out of my bleeding wits, but somehow I wasn't. I was going to *do* something, something that had to be done, and even though it was dangerous I found myself actually looking forward to it.

In the back of my mind, a jeering voice was saying, Famous last words. How many fools have looked forward to the adventure that killed them?

But with Marguerite watching me I didn't seem to care. I thought I saw a hint of admiration in her eyes. At least, I hoped it was admiration and not amusement at the foolish machismo I was exhibiting.

"Okay, we do it just the way we did in the sim." In my helmet earphones, Rodriguez's voice sounded harsh and tight, definitely more tense than his usual easygoing attitude.

I nodded, then realized he couldn't see me through the tinted fishbowl helmet, so I said, "Roger." Just like a real astronaut, I thought.

He went into the airlock ahead of me, cycled it down, and then went outside. Once the outer airlock hatch closed again and the 'lock refilled with ship's air, the inner hatch indicator light turned green.

My space suit was definitely stiff. Even with the servomotors at my elbow and shoulder joints grinding away, it took a real effort to move my arms. As the airlock cycled down and the outer hatch slid open, I had to remind myself that this was going to be different from an EVA in space. This would be more like doing steelwork at the top of a tremendously tall skyscraper. If I made a false step I wouldn't simply float away from the ship, I'd plunge screaming to the ground, fifty kilometers below.

"Take it slow and easy," Rodriguez told me. "I'm right here. Hand me your tether before you step out."

I could see his space-suited form clinging to the handgrips set into the gondola's outer hull, beside the hatch. Both his tethers were clipped to its rungs.

I handed him one end of my right-hand tether. He clipped it a rung beside his own.

"Okay now, just the way we did in the sim. Come on out."

The good thing was we were enveloped in the cloud, so I didn't have to worry about looking down. There was nothing to see out there except a blank yellow-gray limbo. But I could feel the ship shuddering and pitching in the currents of wind.

"Just like rock climbing," Rodriguez said, with an exaggerated heartiness. "Piece of cake."

"When did you do any rock climbing?" I asked as I planted one booted foot on a rung of the ladder.

"Me? Are you kidding? When I get up more than fifty meters I want an airplane surrounding me."

I had never gone rock climbing, either. Risking one's neck for the fun of it has always seemed the height of idiocy to me.

But this was different, I told myself. There was a job to be done. I was making a real contribution to the mission now, not just cowering in my bunk while others did the work.

Still, it was scary. I suppose Rodriguez could've done it all by himself, but long decades of experience dictated that it was far safer to have two people go out together, even if one of them was a neophyte. Besides, with me out there we could cut the time for the inspection almost in half; that in itself made the whole job a lot safer.

In a way, the pressure of the Venusian atmosphere helped us. In space, with nothing outside a space suit's fabric but vacuum, a space suit tends to balloon up and get stiff. That's why we had the miniature servomotors on the suits' joints and gloves, to assist our muscles in bending and flexing. Even at this high altitude, though, the atmospheric pressure was enough to make it almost easy to move around in the suits. Even the gloves flexed fairly easily; the servomotors of the spiny exoskeleton on the backs of the gloves hardly had to exert themselves at all.

One by one, Rodriguez and I checked the braces and struts that held the gondola to the gas envelope. All the welds seemed solid, to my eyes. Neither of us could find any sign of damage or deterioration. One of the hoses that fed hydrogen from the separator to the envelope seemed a bit looser than Rodriguez liked; he worked on it for several minutes with a wrench from the tools clipped to his harness, dangling from a support strut like a monkey in a banana tree.

As I watched Rodriguez working, I checked the thermometer on the wrist of my suit. To my surprise it read only a few degrees above freezing. Then I remembered that we were still fifty-some kilometers above the ground; on Earth we'd be high above the stratosphere, on the fringe of outer space. Here on Venus we were in the middle of a thick cloud of sulfuric acid droplets. Not too far below us, the atmosphere heated up quickly to several hundred degrees.

Dangling out there in the open reminded me of something but I couldn't put my finger on it until at last I remembered watching a video years ago, when I'd been just a child, about people hang gliding off some seaside cliffs in Hawaii. I had burned with jealousy then, watching them having so much fun while I was stuck in a house almost all the time, too frail to try such an adventure. And too scared, I've got to admit. But here I was, on another world, racing in the wind fifty klicks high!

"That's done," Rodriguez said as he returned the wrench to its place on his belt. But he fumbled it and the wrench dropped out of sight. One instant it was in his hand, then, "Oops!" and it was gone. I realized that's what would happen to me if my tethers failed.

"Is that it?" I asked. "Are we done?"

"I ought to check the envelope for any signs of ablation from the entry heat," Rodriguez said. "You can go back inside."

Without even thinking about it I replied, "No, I'll go with you."

So we clambered slowly up the rungs set into the massive curving bulk of the gas envelope, with that wind gushing past us. I knew the atmospheric pressure was too thin up at this altitude to really push us, yet I felt as if I was being nudged, harried, shaken by the wind.

It was slow going, climbing one rung, unclipping one tether and snapping it on a higher rung, then stepping up again and unclipping the other tether. Just like mountain climbers, we never moved a step until we had both tethers locked on safely. I could hear Rodriguez's breathing in my earphones, puffing hard with each step he took.

Duchamp was listening in on everything, of course. But I knew that if we got into trouble there was nothing she or anyone else could do about it in time. It was just Rodriguez and me out here, on our own. It was frightening and kind of exhilarating at the same time.

At last we got to the long catwalk that ran along the top of the envelope. Rodriguez knelt down and activated the switch that raised the flimsy-looking safety rail which ran the length of the metal mesh walkway. Then we fastened our tethers to the rail; it stood waist-high all the way down the catwalk, from nose to tail. A row of cleats projected up from the edge of the walkway, like the bitts on a racing yacht where you tie down the lines from the sails.

"Top of the world," Rodriguez said cheerfully.

"Yeah," I said, my voice definitely shaky.

Together we walked to the bulbous nose of the envelope, where the big heat shield had been connected. I could see the stumps of the rods that had held the shield in place, blackened from the explosive bolts that had sheared them off. Rodriguez bent over and examined the nose region, muttering to himself like a physician thumping a patient's chest during a checkup. Then we walked slowly back toward the tail, him in the lead, our tethers sliding along the safety rail.

I saw it first.

"What's that discoloration?" I asked, pointing.

Rodriguez grunted, then took several steps toward the tail. "Hmm," he mumbled. "Looks like charring, doesn't it?"

I suddenly remembered that these clouds were made of sulfuric acid.

As if he could read my mind, Rodriguez said, "Can't be the sulfuric acid, it doesn't react with the cermet."

"Are you sure?" I asked.

He chuckled. "Don't worry about it. It can't even attack the fabric of your suit."

Very reassuring, I thought. But the charred stains on the cermet skin of the gas envelope were still there.

"Could it be from the entry heat?"

I could sense him nodding inside his helmet. "Some of the heated air must've flowed over the shield and singed the butt end of the envelope a little."

"The sensors didn't record a temperature spike there," I said.

"Might've been too small to notice. If we expand the graph we'll probably see it."

"Is it a problem?"

"Probably not," he said. "But we oughtta pressurize the envelope to make certain it doesn't leak."

I felt my heart sink. "How long will that take?"

He thought before answering. "The better part of a day, I guess."

"Another day lost."

"Worried about Fuchs?" he asked.

"Yes, of course."

"Well, he's likely got problems of his—*Hey!*"

The safety rail alongside Rodriguez suddenly broke away, a whole section of it flying off into the yellowy haze, taking one of his tethers with it. He was yanked off his feet, flailing his arms and legs, the remaining tether anchoring him to the still-standing section of rail, the other one trying to pull him off the ship.

I lunged for him but he was already too far away for me to reach without taking off my own tethers.

"Pull me in!" he yelled, his voice bellowing in my earphones.

"What's happened?" Duchamp asked sharply in my earphones.

I saw him unclip the one tether from his belt. It snapped off into the clouds. I grabbed the other and began hauling him in.

But the railing itself was wobbling, shaky. It was going to tear away in another few seconds, I realized.

"Pull me in!" Rodriguez shouted again.

"What's happening out there?" Duchamp demanded.

I unclipped one of my own tethers and fastened it onto one of the cleats set into the catwalk. Then, with Duchamp jabbering in my earphones, I unclipped Rodriguez's remaining tether before the railing broke off and he went sailing into oblivion.

"What the hell are you doing?" he yelled.

His sudden weight almost tore my arms out of their sockets. Squeezing my eyes shut, I saw stars exploding against the blackness. With gritted teeth, I clumped down onto my knees and used all my strength to clamp the end of his tether to the cleat next to mine.

I saw that the broken end of the railing was fluttering now, shaking loose. And my other tether was still hooked to it. Instead of trying to reach its end I simply unsnapped it from my belt and let it flap loose, then turned back to hauling in Rodriguez's line.

He was pulling himself in as hard as he could. It seemed like an hour, the two of us panting and snorting like a couple of tug-of-war contestants, but he finally planted his boots back on the catwalk. All this time Duchamp was yelling in my earphones, "What is it? What's going on out there?"

"We're okay," Rodriguez gasped at last, down on his hands and knees on the catwalk. For an absurd instant I thought he was going to pull off his helmet and kiss the metal decking.

"You saved my life, Van."

It was the first time he'd called me anything but "Mr. Humphries." It made me feel proud.

Before I could reply, Rodriguez went on, in a slightly sheepish tone, "At first I thought you were going to leave me and go back to the airlock."

I stared at the blank fishbowl of his helmet. "I wouldn't do that, Tom."

"I know," he said, still panting from his exertion and fear. "Now," he added.

Captain Duchamp and Dr. Waller were waiting for us when we came through the airlock. I could hear her demanding questions, muffled by my helmet, directed at Rodriguez.

"What happened out there? What was that about the safety rail?" And finally, "Are you all right?"

Rodriguez started to explain as I lifted my helmet off. Waller took it from my trembling hands and I saw Marguerite hurrying up the passageway toward us.

While we both worked our way out of the space suits, Rodriguez gave a clipped but thorough explanation of what had happened to us. Duchamp looked blazingly angry, as if somehow we had caused the trouble for ourselves. I kept glancing at Marguerite, standing behind her mother. So much alike, physically. So strikingly similar in the shape of their faces, the depth of their jet-black eyes, the same height, the same curves of their figures.

Yet where the captain was truculent and demanding, Marguerite looked troubled, distressed—and something else. Something more. I couldn't tell what it was in her eyes; I suppose I subconsciously hoped it was concern for me.

Duchamp and Rodriguez headed for the bridge, Waller went without a word back toward his cubbyhole of an infirmary, leaving Marguerite and me alone by the racks of empty space suits.

"Are you all right?" she asked me.

Nodding, I said, "Fine. I think." I held out my hand. "Look, I'm not even shaking anymore."

She laughed, a delightful sound. "You've earned a drink."

We went down to the galley, passing Waller's closet-sized infirmary. It was empty, making me wonder where the doctor might hide himself.

As we took cups of fruit juice and sat on the galley bench, I realized that I did indeed feel fine. Was it Churchill who said that coming through a brush with death concentrates the mind wonderfully?

Marguerite sat beside me and took a sip of juice. "You saved Tom's life," she said.

The look in her eyes wasn't adoring. Far from it. But there was a respect in them that I'd never seen before. It felt terrifically good.

Heroes are supposed to be modest, so I waggled my free hand and said merely, "I just reacted on instinct, I guess."

"Tom would have been killed if you hadn't."

"No, I don't think so. He—"

"He thinks so."

I shrugged. "He would've done the same for me."

She nodded and brought the cup to her lips, her eyes never leaving mine.

I had to say something, so I let my mouth work before my brain did. "Your mother doesn't seem to have a molecule of human kindness in her. I know she's the captain, but she was practically chewing Tom's guts out."

Marguerite almost smiled. "That's the way she reacts when she's frightened. She attacks."

"Frightened? Her? Of what?"

"Tom nearly got killed! Don't you think that scared her? She is human, you know, underneath the stainless steel."

"You mean she really cares about him?"

Her eyes flashed. "Do you think she's sleeping with him merely to keep him satisfied? She's not a whore, you know."

"I . . ." I realized that I had thought precisely that. For once in my life, I kept my mouth shut while I tried to figure out what I should say next.

The speaker in the ceiling blared, "MR. HUMPHRIES WANTED ON THE BRIDGE." Duchamp's voice.

Saved by the call of duty, I thought.

I sat scrunched down on the metal deck plate of the bridge between Duchamp's command chair and Rodriguez's. Willa Yeats, our sensors specialist, was in the chair usually occupied by Riza, the communications tech.

The four of us were staring hard at the main display screen, which showed a graph of the heat load the ship had encountered during entry into the atmosphere.

"No blip," Yeats said, with an *I told you so* tone. She was on the chubby side, moon-faced and pale-skinned, with the kind of dirty blond hair that some people charitably call sandy.

"There was no sudden burst of heat during the entry flight," she said. "The heat shield performed as designed and the sensors show all heat loads well below maximum allowable levels."

Duchamp scowled at her. "Then what caused the charring on the envelope?"

"And weakened the safety railing?" Rodriguez added.

Yeats shrugged as if it weren't important to her. "I haven't the faintest idea. But it wasn't a pulse of heat, I can tell you that."

She had a very proprietary attitude about the ship's sensing systems. As far as she was concerned, if her sensors didn't show a problem, no problem existed.

Duchamp obviously felt otherwise. The captain looked past me toward Rodriguez. "I suppose we'll have to go out there again and see just what those charring marks are."

Rodriguez nodded glumly. "I suppose."

"I'll go with you," I said. Before either of them could object I added, with a pinch of bravado, "I'm an experienced hand at this, you know."

Duchamp did not look amused, but Rodriguez chuckled and said, "Right. My EVA lifesaver."

"You don't have to do that," Yeats said, obviously disappointed at our obtuseness. "If you simply pressurize the envelope the sensors will tell us if there's a leak."

"And what if we rip the damned envelope wide open?" Duchamp snapped. "Where are we then?"

Yeats looked abashed. She didn't have to answer. We all knew where we'd be if the envelope cracked. There was the descent module, the bathysphere-like craft that was designed to double as an escape pod. But the thought of all eight of us crammed into that tiny iron ball and rocketing up into orbit was far from comforting.

"Inspect the charring," Duchamp said with finality. "Then we can pressurize the envelope."

"Maybe," Rodriguez added, morbidly.

Gripping the arms of their two chairs, I pulled myself up to my feet. "Very well then, we'd better—"

Marguerite burst into the bridge, nearly bowling me over.

"Life!" she exclaimed, her eyes wide and shining. "There are living organisms in the clouds! Microscopic but multicelled! They're alive, they live in the clouds . . ."

She was babbling so hard I thought she was close to hysteria. Her mother snapped her out of it with a single question.

"You're sure?"

Marguerite took a deep, gulping breath. "I'm positive. They're alive."

Rodriguez said, "I've gotta see this."

I took Marguerite's arm as gently as I could and maneuvered her out into the passageway. Otherwise there was no room on the bridge for Rodriguez to get up from his chair.

We trooped behind Marguerite to her cubbyhole of a lab. As we stopped there I realized Duchamp had also left the bridge to accompany us. We stared at the image from the miniaturized electron microscope displayed on the wall screen. I saw some watery-looking blobs flailing around slowly. They were obviously multicelled; I could see smaller blobs and dividing walls pulsating inside them. Most of them had cilia fringing their outer edges, microscopic oars paddling away constantly. But weakly.

"They're dying in here," Marguerite said, almost mournfully. "It must be the temperature, or maybe the combination of temperature and pressure. It's just not working!"

Straightening up from the microscope's eyepiece, I said to her, "By god, you were right."

"It's a major discovery," Rodriguez congratulated.

"Send this to the IAA at once," Duchamp commanded. "Imagery and every bit of data you have. Get priority for this."

"But I've only—"

"Do you want a Nobel Prize or not?" Duchamp snapped. "Get this data to IAA headquarters *this instant*. Don't wait for Fuchs to get in first."

Marguerite nodded with understanding. For the first time since she'd burst into the bridge she seemed to calm down, come back to reality.

"I'll get Riza to establish a direct link with Geneva," Duchamp went on. "You bang out a written statement, two or three lines will be enough to establish your priority. But do it *now*."

"Yes," Marguerite said, reaching for her laptop computer. "Right."

We left her there in her lab, bent over the computer keyboard. Duchamp headed back toward the bridge, Rodriguez and I went toward the airlock, where the space suits were stored.

"RIZA," we heard Duchamp's voice over the intercom speakers, "REPORT TO THE BRIDGE AT ONCE." She didn't have to repeat the command; there was no room for doubt or delay in the tone of her voice.

"Bugs in the clouds," Rodriguez said to me, over his shoulder. "Who would've thought you could find anything living in clouds of sulfuric acid?"

"Marguerite did," I answered. "She was certain she'd find living organisms."

"Really?"

I nodded to his back. I had just witnessed a great discovery. Duchamp was right, her daughter would get a special Nobel for this, just like the biologists who discovered the lichen on Mars.

She expected to find living organisms on Venus, I told myself again. Maybe that's the secret of making great discoveries: The stubborn insistence that there's something out there to be discovered, no matter what the others say. Chance favors the prepared mind. Who said that? Some scientist, I thought. Einstein, most likely. Or maybe Freud.

We commandeered Dr. Waller and Willa Yeats to help us into the space suits. Waller hummed quietly as I pulled on my leggings and boots, then wormed into the torso and pushed my arms through the sleeves. Two meters away, Willa chattered like a runaway audio machine as she watched Rodriguez get into his suit. They checked out our life-support backpacks and made certain all the lines and hoses were properly connected. Then we sealed our helmets.

Rodriguez stepped into the airlock first. I waited for the lock to cycle, my heart revving up until I thought Riza at the comm console on the bridge must be able to hear it through the suit radio. Relax! I commanded myself. You've been outside before. There's nothing to be scared of.

Right. The last time Rodriguez had nearly gotten himself knocked off the ship. I had no desire to go plummeting fifty-some kilometers down to the rock-hard surface of Venus.

The airlock hatch slid open again and Rodriguez stepped back among us.

"What's the matter?" I asked. "What's wrong?"

This close, with the ship's interior lighting shining through his bubble helmet, I could see the puzzled, troubled look on his face.

"Got a red light on my head-up." The suit's diagnostic system, which splashed its display onto the helmet's inner surface, showed something was not functioning properly.

"What is it?" I asked.

"Gimme a minute," he snapped back. Then, "Huh . . . it says there was a pressure leak in the suit. Seems okay now, though."

Dr. Waller grasped the situation before I did. "But it went red when you cycled the air out of the airlock?"

"Yeah. Right."

We spent the better part of an hour pumping up the pressure in Rodriguez's suit until it started to balloon. Sure enough, there was a leak in his left shoulder joint. The suit fabric had a resin compound that self-repaired minor leaks, but the joints were cermet covered with plastic.

"It looks frayed," Dr. Waller said, his voice brimming with curiosity. "No, more like it was singed with a flame or some source of heat."

"Damn!" Rodriguez grumbled. "Suit's supposed to be guaranteed."

I remembered the old joke about parachutes: If it doesn't work, bring it back and we'll give you a new one. It was a good thing the suit's diagnostics caught the leak in the airlock. Outside, it could have killed him.

So Rodriguez unfastened his helmet and wriggled out of his suit and put on one of the backup suits. We would have to repair his suit, I thought. We only carried four spares.

Finally he was ready and went through the airlock. No problems with the backup suit. I heard him call me in my helmet earphones, "Okay, Mr. Humphries. Come on through."

I went into the airlock and got that same old feeling of being locked into a coffin when the inner hatch slid shut. The 'lock cycled down—and a red warning light started blinking on my the curving face of my helmet, flashing into my eyes like a rocket's red glare.

"Hey, I've got a problem, too," I yelled into my microphone.

The entire EVA excursion was a bust. Both our original suits were leaking and Duchamp decided to scratch the EVA until we could determine what the problem was.

I thought I knew.

"I don't know," Marguerite said, frowning with puzzlement. "It's too soon for me to tell."

Her voice was low, tired. The excitement of her discovery had worn off; now I was presenting her with its horrifying consequences.

We were walking down the passageway from her lab to the galley, where we could sit together in comfort. I was leading the way, for once.

"It can't be a coincidence," I said over my shoulder. "There's got to be a connection."

"That's not necessarily true," she objected.

We reached the galley and I punched the dispenser for a cold cup of juice, then handed it to her. After I got one for myself, I sat beside her on the bench.

"There are bugs out in the clouds," I said.

"Microscopic multicellular creatures, yes," she agreed.

"What do they eat?"

"I don't know! It's going to take some time to find out. I've spent most of the day jury-rigging a cooler for them to live in!"

"What's your best guess?" I demanded.

She ran a hand through her thick dark hair. "Sulfur oxides are the most abundant compounds in the cloud droplets. They must metabolize sulfur in some way."

"Sulfur? How can anything eat sulfur?"

Marguerite jabbed a forefinger at me. "There are bacteria on Earth that metabolize sulfur. I would have thought you'd known that."

I had to grin. "You'd be surprised at how much I don't know."

She smiled back.

I pulled my handheld computer from my pocket and punched up a list showing the composition of the fibers of our space suits. No sulfur.

"Would they eat any of these materials?" I asked, showing her the computer's tiny display.

Marguerite shrugged wearily. "It's too soon to know, Van. On Earth, organisms metabolize a wide range of elements and compounds. Humans need trace amounts of hundreds of different minerals . . ." She took a deep, sighing breath.

"It's got to be the bugs," I said, convinced despite the lack of evidence. "Nothing else could have eaten through the suits like that."

"What about the railing? That's made of metal, isn't it?"

I tapped on the handheld. "Cermet," I saw. "A ceramic and metal composite." Another few taps. "Contains beryllium, boron, calcium, carbon . . . several other elements."

"Maybe the organisms need trace elements the way we need vitamins," Marguerite suggested.

I went back to the list of suit materials and displayed it alongside the list of the safety rail's composition. Plenty of similarities, although only the cermet had any measurable amount of sulfur in it, and not much at that.

Then I realized that both suits had leaked at joints, not the self-repairing fabric. And the joints were made of cermet, covered with a thin sprayed-on layer of plastic.

"You've got to find out what they digest," I urged Marguerite. "It's vitally important!"

"I know," she said, rising to her feet. "I'll get on it right away."

I thought about the charring along the tail end of the gas envelope. "They might be chewing up the shell, too."

"I'll get on it!" she fairly shouted, then started up the passageway back to her lab. She looked as if she were fleeing from me.

So I'm pushing her, I thought. But we've got to know. If those bugs are eating our space suits and the ship itself we've got to get out of here and fast.

I stood there for a dithering moment, not certain of what I should do next. What could I do, except prod other people to do the things that I can't do myself?

I decided to go up to the bridge, but halfway there I bumped into Yeats, who was hurrying down the passageway in the opposite direction.

"Anything new?" I asked.

"All bad," she said as she squirmed past me. Her body felt soft and actually pleasurable as she pressed by. I wondered how a man's gonads could assert themselves even when his brain was telling him he's in deep trouble.

"What is it?" I called after her.

"No time," she shouted back, hurrying even faster. I'd never before seen her move at anything more than a languid stroll.

Shaking my head, in exasperation as much as disbelief, I made my way to the bridge. Duchamp and Rodriguez were both there. Good, I thought.

"We can't pressurize the gas envelope until we can determine its structural integrity," Duchamp was saying, in the kind of stilted cadence that I knew was meant for the ship's log. "The leak rate is small at present, but growing steadily. If it's not stopped it will affect the ship's trim and cause an uncontrollable loss of altitude."

She looked up at me as I stopped in the open hatchway. Jabbing a finger on the chair arm's stud that turned off the recorder, she asked impatiently, "Well?"

"We've got to get out of these clouds," I said. "The bugs out there are eating the ship."

Duchamp arched her brows. "I don't have time for theories. We've developed a leak in the gas envelope. It's minor, but it's growing."

"The shell's leaking?" My voice must have gone up two octaves.

"It's not serious," Rodriguez said quickly.

I turned to him. "We've got to get out of these clouds! You were out there, Tom. The bugs—"

"I make the decisions here," Duchamp snapped.

"Now wait a minute," I said.

Before I could go further, she said, "With all deference to your position as owner of this vessel, Mr. Humphries, I am the captain and I will make the decisions. This isn't a debating society. We're not going to take a vote on the subject."

"We've got to get out of these clouds!" I insisted.

"I totally agree," she said. "As soon as we can repair the leak in the envelope, I intend to go deeper and get below this cloud deck."

"Deeper?" I glanced at Rodriguez, but he was saying nothing.

"Have you forgotten Fuchs? The IAA just sent word that he's descending rapidly toward the clear air below the clouds."

The prize money didn't look all that enticing to me, compared to the very strong possibility that we would all be killed if the bugs chewed away enough of the ship.

Rodriguez spoke up at last. "Mr. Humphries, we can't make an effective decision until we know how badly the gas envelope's been damaged."

"It's really very minor," Duchamp said. But then she added, "At present."

"But it's getting worse," Rodriguez said.

"Slowly," she insisted.

"As long as we stay in these clouds we're going to have colonies of Venusian organisms feasting on our ship's metals and minerals," I retorted hotly.

"This is no time to panic, Mr. Humphries," she said.

I thought it over for half a second. "I could fire you and appoint Tom captain."

"That would be tantamount to mutiny," she snapped.

"Wait," Rodriguez said. "Wait, both of you. Before anybody goes off the deep end, let's repair the envelope and get back in proper condition."

"Do we have time for that?"

Duchamp said coldly, "May I point out that Fuchs is diving deeper while we fiddle around here. If your bugs are eating our ship, why aren't they eating his?"

"What makes you think they're not?"

"I know Lars," she said with a thin smile. "He's no fool. If he thought he was going into more danger by descending he wouldn't go down."

I glanced from her to Rodriguez to Riza, sitting wide-eyed at her comm console, then back to Duchamp.

"All right," I said finally. "I'm going back to the bio lab to help Marguerite determine if the bugs caused the damage to our suits. How long will it take you to repair the leak in the hull?"

"Several hours," Duchamp said.

"Yeats is suiting up now, with Akira. They're going to start the work from inside the shell," Rodriguez said. "It'll be safer that way."

"But they'll still be exposed to the bugs, won't they?" I asked. "I mean, if the outside air is leaking into the shell, the bugs are coming in with it."

Duchamp said flatly, "That's assuming you're right and it's the bugs that damaged your suits."

"You can't let them stay out too long," I insisted. "If the bugs do eat the suits—"

"The fabric is self-repairing," Duchamp said.

"The joints aren't," I pointed out.

There was one quick and dirty way to test whether the bugs were eating the suit material, Marguerite and I decided. I hacked off a small section of the cermet knee joint of my damaged suit to serve as an experimental guinea pig. It wasn't easy: The cermet was tough. I had to scrounge an electric saw from the ship's stores to do the job.

Then I brought it to Marguerite's lab, where she had set up a spare insulated cooler as an incubator for the Venusian organisms.

But when I brought the cermet sample to her, she was downcast.

"They're dying," Marguerite said, as miserable as if it was her own child expiring.

"But I thought—"

"I've tried to duplicate their natural environment as closely as I can," she said, as much to herself as to me. "I've kept the temperature inside the cooler just above freezing, right about where it was in the clouds. I've lowered the air pressure and even sprayed it with extra sulfuric acid. But it's not working! Every sample I take shows them weakening and dying."

I handed her the ragged little square of cermet I'd cut out. "Well, here, get this into the cooler with them and let's see what happens before they all die."

She had done a remarkable job of jury-rigging what had once been a spare cooler unit into a laboratory apparatus. The lid was sealed against air leaks, although there were half a dozen sensor wires and two small tubes going through the sealant into the cooler's interior.

All in all, it looked very much like the makeshift contraption that it was, the kind of thing that scientists call a kloodge. I once heard of such devices being named after someone named Rube Goldberg, but I never found out why.

Looking worried, Marguerite deftly sliced my cermet sample into hair-thin slivers with a diamond saw, then inserted half of them into the cooler through one of the tubes.

"What are you doing with a diamond saw?" I asked.

That made her smile. "What are you doing without one?" she countered.

"Huh?"

"I had hoped we'd pick up samples of Venusian rock. The saw can slice thin specimens for the microscope."

"Oh, of course," I said. I knew that; I simply didn't think of it at that moment.

"I would have thought," she went on, "that a planetary scientist would have this kind of equipment with him for geological investigations."

I felt my brow furrow. "Come to think of it, I believe I do."

She laughed. "I know you do, Van. I stole this from the equipment stores that you had marked for your use."

She'd been teasing me! To hide my embarrassment, I bent over and peered into the narrow little window in the cooler's lid. All I could see inside was a grayish fog.

"That's actual Venusian air inside there?" I asked.

"Yes," she replied, frowning slightly. "I was drawing it off from the main probe we've been using for the nephelometers and mass spectrometers."

I caught her accent on the past tense. "Was?"

She made an irritated huffing sound, very much like her mother. "The probes have been shut down. Captain's orders."

"Why would she . . . ?" Then I realized, "She doesn't want to run the risk of having the bugs break loose inside the ship."

"That's right," Marguerite said. "So I've got this sample and that's all. No replacements."

"And yet she acted as if she thought I was crazy when I told her the bugs ate the suits and the railing."

Marguerite shrugged as if it weren't important to her. But it was to me. "She's a first-class hypocrite, your mother," I said, with some heat.

"She's the ship's captain," Marguerite answered stiffly. "She might think your idea's crazy, but the safety of this ship and crew is her responsibility and she's decided not to take any unnecessary risks."

I could see the logic in that. But still . . . "She's sent Yeats and Sakamoto out to repair the shell."

"That's necessary. There's no getting around it."

"Perhaps," I admitted reluctantly. "But she shouldn't let them stay out too long."

"How long is too long?"

"How long were Rodriguez and I outside? Both our suits were damaged."

Marguerite nodded. "I'm sure she's watching their readouts."

The timer on the cooler chimed, ending our conversation. Marguerite drew out a sample of the Venusian air, rich with sulfuric acid droplets and the organisms that lived in them. Quickly she prepared a microscope slide and put the display onto the screen of the laptop computer she had plugged into the electron microscope.

"They're recovering!" she said happily. "Look at how vigorously they're swimming around!"

"But where's the suit material?" I asked.

She turned from the laptop to stare at me. "It's gone. They've digested the cermet. It's food for them."

I raced along the passageway to the bridge. Duchamp was in her command chair, as usual. I could hear Yeats's voice, puffing with exertion: ". . . going a lot slower than I expected. This is tough work, let me tell you."

"You've got to bring them back inside!" I said to Duchamp. "Now! Before the bugs kill them."

Rodriguez was not on the bridge. Riza Kolodny, at the comm console, looked at me and then the captain and finally turned her face resolutely to her screens, not wishing to get involved.

Before Duchamp could reply, I said, "The bugs eat cermet. It's like caviar to them, for god's sake!"

She levelled a hard stare at me. "You have proof of this?"

"Your daughter has the proof in her lab. It's true! Now get those two people back inside here!"

Duchamp looked as if she'd prefer to slice my throat, but she touched the communications stud on her chair arm and said crisply, "Yeats, Sakamoto, come back inside. Now. That's an order."

"Okay by me," Yeats said, with obvious relief. She was not accustomed to much physical exertion, clearly.

"Yes, captain," said Sakamoto, so even and unemotional that the words might just as well have come from a computer.

Duchamp called Rodriguez back to the bridge and Marguerite came up from her lab. She and I crowded the hatchway as she displayed her experiment's results on the main screen. Within minutes, Dr. Waller, Yeats, and Sakamoto came up, making a real crowd in the passageway. I could feel them pressing me, pushing their sweaty bodies against me. My heart was racing; I felt queasy and breathless at the same time.

"I'm still checking air samples for the signature of the cermet materials," Marguerite was telling her mother, "but so far there is none. The organisms seem to have digested every molecule."

If this information rattled our steely eyed captain, she did not show it. Turning to Rodriguez, she said, "What do you think?"

Rodriguez's brow was already deeply creased with worry. "We've got a catch-twenty-two situation here. We need to repair the shell or sink, but if we go outside the bugs will degrade our suits so badly we'll be at risk of total suit failure."

"You mean death," I said. "Someone could get killed."

He nodded, a little sheepishly, I thought.

Marguerite added, "Meanwhile the organisms are eating away at the shell. They could damage it to the point where . . . where . . ." She drew in her breath, realizing that if the shell failed, we would all go plunging into the depths of the atmosphere.

Is this what happened to Alex? I wondered. Was his ship devoured by these hungry alien bugs?

Then I realized that the organisms weren't alien at all. This was their natural environment. We were the aliens, the invaders. Maybe they were instinctively fighting against us, trying to drive us out of their world.

Nonsense! I told myself. They're just bugs. Microbes. They can't think. They can't act in an organized way.

I hoped.

Duchamp looked straight at me as she said, "This is what we're going to do. Each of us will take turns at repairing the shell. None of us will stay outside longer than Tom and Mr. Humphries did."

"But our suits were damaged," I objected.

"We will keep the excursions shorter than your EVA was," Duchamp said. "Short enough to get back inside before the bugs can damage the suits."

From behind me Yeats grumbled, "Then it's a race to see if we can plug the leaks faster than the bugs can eat through the shell."

Duchamp nodded. "In the meantime, I intend to go deeper."

"Deeper?" Riza blurted.

"There's a layer of clear air between this cloud deck and the next, about five kilometers below us," Duchamp said.

Rodriguez grinned humorlessly. "I get it. No clouds, no bugs."

I could feel Yeats start to object, but before she could the captain went on, "Willa, I want you to calculate the maximum time we can work in the atmosphere out there before we run into danger of suit damage."

"Yes, captain," Yeats said glumly.

"Tom, you take the conn. Mr. Humphries and I will take the first shift. Everyone else will take a turn at the work," she hesitated a moment, looking past me. At her daughter, I supposed. "Everyone except Dr. Waller," she said.

I felt the doctor's gusting breath of appreciation on the back of my neck. He was in no physical condition for an EVA, true enough. But I worried about Marguerite; she had no training for this sort of thing. Or did she?

Duchamp got up from her command chair. Everyone in the passageway flattened themselves out to make room for her to pass by. I followed her, fighting down the fears that were shaking me.

In a sense, of course, none of us had any training for this sort of EVA. Virtual reality simulations were all well and good, as far as they went, but nothing could prepare you for being outside in those clouds, with the wind gusting against you and the ship shuddering and bucking like a living animal. Add to that the knowledge that the bugs were chewing away on your suit . . . it scared me down to my bladder. I felt jittery, almost light-headed.

But it had to be done, and I wasn't going to back away from my share of the responsibility.

It wasn't easy, that's for certain. Even though we worked inside the shell, grappling along its curving bulkhead, dangling from the structural support beams by our suit tethers was far more demanding than climbing mountains.

And it was dark inside the shell. Outside, even in the clouds, there was always a yellowish-gray glow, a sullen twilight that was bright enough to see by, once your eyes adjusted to it. Inside the shell we had to work by the light of our helmet lamps, which didn't go far. Their glow was swallowed up by the yellowish haze pervading the shell's interior. It reminded me of descriptions of London fogs from long ages ago, groping along in the misty gloom.

"Riza," I heard Duchamp call over the suit radio, "get Dr. Waller to put together as many lamps as he can take from stores. We need working lights in here."

"Yes, captain," came the comm tech's reply.

Despite everything, I had to smile inside my helmet. Duchamp wasn't allowing our ship's doctor to sit idly while the rest of us worked.

We sprayed epoxy all across the shell's enormous interior. And it was huge in there; the vast curving space seemed measureless, infinite. The darkness swallowed the pitiful light from our helmet lamps. I began to think about Jonah in the belly of the whale or Fuchida exploring the endless caverns inside Olympus Mons on Mars.

There was no way to know precisely where the leaks were: The shell wasn't instrumented for that and the leaks weren't so big that you could see daylight through them. We concentrated our spraying on the aft end of the envelope, naturally, because that's where we had seen the charring.

Duchamp and I spent an exhausting half-hour in the shell, then Rodriguez and Marguerite replaced us. Duchamp would have had the entire crew in there at once and gotten the job over with, except for the fact that we had only two epoxy spray guns aboard.

So, two by two, the crew worked hour after hour on sealing the leaks in the gas envelope. Exhausted as I was, I took another turn, this time with Sakamoto. Rodriguez actually went out three times. So did Yeats, grumbling every inch of the way.

When my second tour was over, I half collapsed on the deck just inside the airlock, too weary even to think about peeling off my suit. I simply lifted off my helmet and sat there, not even taking off my backpack. It wasn't only the physical exertion, although just about every muscle in my body was shrieking. It was the mental strain, the knowledge that the ship was in trouble, serious trouble, and we were all in danger.

Sakamoto, standing above me, pulled his helmet off and gave me a rare smile. "Work is the curse of the drinking man," he said, then started to get out of his suit. I couldn't have been more surprised if he had sprouted wings and flown back to Earth.

Finally it was finished. I had crawled into my berth to inject an enzyme shot into my arm when the intercom blared, a scant six centimeters from my ear, "MR. HUMPHRIES TO THE BRIDGE, PLEASE."

Bleary-eyed, I finished the injection, then slid out of the berth and padded in my stockinged feet toward the bridge, not even bothering to smooth out the wrinkles in my coveralls. Somewhere in the back of my mind I knew I was sweaty and far from sweet-smelling, but I didn't care.

Duchamp was in her command chair, as flinty as ever. Rodriguez must have been grabbing a few winks of sleep. Yeats was at the comm console.

As soon as I ducked through the hatch, Duchamp said to Yeats, "Tell him, Willa."

Looking far from jocular, Yeats said, "I have good news and bad news. Which do you want to hear first?"

"The good news," I snapped.

"We stopped the leak," she said. But her face did not show any sign of joy. "The ship is back in trim and we've broken out of the clouds into the clear air."

"We're pumping out the air we took in during the descent through the cloud deck," Duchamp added, "and replacing it with the ambient air, outside."

I nodded. "Good."

"Now the bad news," said Willa. "Every one of our suits is damaged, at least slightly. Not one of them would pass a safety inspection. They all leak."

"That means we can't go EVA?"

"Not until we repair them," Yeats said cheerlessly.

"All right," I said. "That's not as bad as it might have been."

"The question is," Duchamp said, "will there be more bugs in the deeper cloud decks?"

"It gets awfully hot down there," I said. "More than two hundred degrees Celsius. And that's thirty–forty kilometers above the surface."

"So you don't think we'll have any problems from the bugs?"

"We should ask Marguerite. She's the biologist."

Duchamp nodded. "I've already asked her. She said she doesn't know. No one knows."

I heard myself say, "There can't be anything living at such high temperatures! It gets up to four hundred degrees and more at the surface."

"I wonder," she murmured.

From being a total skeptic about the bugs, the captain had swung to suspecting them to be lurking in the next cloud deck, waiting to devour us.

Then another thought struck me. "Where's Fuchs? Has he gone down into the second cloud deck yet?"

She nodded. "No. He appears to be hovering in this clear area, just as we are, according to the latest word from the IAA."

"I wonder if he . . ." Duchamp and the bridge wavered out of focus, as if someone had twisted a camera lens the wrong way. I put out a hand to grasp the edge of the hatchway, my knees suddenly rubbery.

I heard someone ask, "What's the matter?"

Everything was spinning madly around me. "I feel kind of woozy," I heard my own voice say.

That's the last thing I remember.

I opened my eyes to see Dr. Waller, Rodriguez, and Marguerite bending over me. They all looked grim, worried.

"Do you know where you are?" Waller asked, the Jamaican lilt in his voice flattened by concern.

I looked past their intent faces and saw medical monitors, green worms crawling across their screens. I heard them beeping softly and smelled antiseptic.

"The infirmary," I said. My voice was little more than a croak.

"Good!" Dr. Waller said approvingly. "Full consciousness and awareness. That's very good."

Marguerite looked relieved. I suppose Rodriguez did, too.

It didn't take much mental acumen to see that I was lying on the infirmary's one bed. Located back at the tail of the gondola, the infirmary was the only place on *Hesperos* with space enough for people to stand at bedside. Our bunks were nothing more than horizontal closets.

"What happened?" I asked, still not feeling strong enough to do anything but lie there on my back.

"Your anemia came up and bit you," said Dr. Waller.

I glanced at Marguerite. I had never mentioned my condition to her, but apparently Waller had told her everything while I was unconscious. She looked concerned, but not surprised. Rodriguez had known about it, of course, but he still looked very worried, his forehead wrinkled like corduroy.

"But I've been taking my shots," I said weakly.

"And engaging in more physical exertion than you have ever done in your life, I should think," said the doctor cheerily. "The hard work caught up with you."

"A few hours . . . ?"

"It was enough. More than enough."

Talk about depressing news. Here I thought I was doing my share, working alongside Rodriguez and even Duchamp, facing the same dangers and duties as the rest of the crew. And my god-cursed anemia strikes me down, shows everybody that I'm a weakling, a useless burden to them all. Father was right: I'm the runt of the litter, in every imaginable way.

I felt like crying, but I held myself together as Waller fussed around me and Rodriguez left, half-apologizing that he had to get back to the bridge.

"We're getting ready to enter the next cloud deck," he said. "We decided just to skim in and out, take some samples of the cloud droplets and see if there are any bugs in 'em."

I nodded weakly. "Good thinking."

"It was Dee's idea—Captain Duchamp's."

I turned my head slightly toward Marguerite. "It's a good thing we brought a biologist along with us," I said.

She smiled.

Rodriguez grabbed my hand and said, "You take care of yourself now, Van. Do what the doc tells you."

"Sure," I agreed. "Why not?"

He left. Marguerite remained at my bedside.

"How long will I have to stay here?" I asked Dr. Waller.

"Only a few hours, I should think," he replied, his face as somber as ever. "I'm running diagnostics on your red cell count and oxygen transfer to your vital organs. It shouldn't take very long."

I pushed myself up to a sitting position, expecting to feel my head spin. Instead, it felt fine. Marguerite hurriedly pushed up my pillows so I could sit back against them.

"You make a good nurse," I said to her. I actually felt pretty good. My voice was coming back to its normal strength.

"You scared the wits out of everyone, collapsing like that."

"How should I have collapsed?" I joked.

"Humor!" said Dr. Waller. "That's good. A certain sign of recovery."

"There's nothing really wrong with me," I said, "except this damned anemia."

"Yes, that's true. Except for the anemia you are in fine physical condition. But as Mercutio says to Romeo, the wound may not be as deep as a well or as wide as a church door but 'tis enough, 'twill serve."

Marguerite understood. "You have to be careful, Van. Your condition could become serious if you don't take proper care of yourself."

There was a part of me that was perfectly happy to be lying on a sickbed and having her looking so concerned about me. But how long would that last? I asked myself. I've got to get up and be active. I don't want pity. I want respect.

"What you're telling me," I said sharply to the doctor, "is that if I have to do any serious physical exertion I should take extra enzyme shots."

He nodded, but pointed out glumly, "We only have a fixed amount of the enzyme supply in our medical stores. And we do *not* have the equipment or resources to make more. Your supply is more than adequate for normal usage, with a healthy additional amount in reserve. But still—you should pace yourself more carefully than you have today, Mr. Humphries."

"Yes. Of course. Now, when can I get up and back to my work?"

He glanced at the monitors lining the infirmary's wall. "In two hours, more or less."

"Two hours," I said. "Fine."

I was actually on my feet much sooner. I had to be.

Marguerite brought me a handheld computer to work with while I sat in the infirmary bed, waiting for Dr. Waller to finish his diagnostics. He left the infirmary for a while, humming to himself as usual. I checked with IAA headquarters back in Geneva and, some twenty minutes later, got a reply that Fuchs had entered the second cloud deck more than an hour earlier.

He was ahead of us again. And apparently he had suffered no damage from the bugs that had attacked our gas envelope. Why not? Was his

Lucifer made of different materials? Had he been damaged and then repaired his ship more quickly than we had been able to do?

Sitting there staring at the printed IAA report, I began to wonder what would happen if Fuchs actually did get to the surface first and recovered Alex's remains. He'd get Father's ten billion in prize money and I'd be penniless. Totally cut off. I couldn't even afford my home in Majorca, let alone—

The ship lurched.

I mean, *lurched.* We had bounced and shuddered when we were in the superrotation winds up higher, but once we'd sunk down to the clear region between the first and second cloud decks the air pressure had become so thick that the winds were smothered and our ride had become glassy smooth.

But now everything suddenly tilted so badly that I was nearly thrown off the bed. I clutched its edges like a child riding a coaster down a snowy hillside.

Through the closed hatch of the infirmary I could hear alarm bells blaring and the thundering slams of other hatches swinging shut automatically.

The infirmary seemed to sway. For an instant I thought I was getting dizzy again, but then I remembered that I was in the tail section of the gondola and it was the gondola itself that was swinging beneath the gas envelope. Somewhere an alarm siren started shrieking.

I jumped out of bed, glad that Waller hadn't stripped off my coveralls. The floor beneath me tilted again, this time pointing downward like an airplane starting to dive. Something behind me crashed to the floor.

"ALL HANDS STRAP IN!" the intercom blared. Great advice. I had to clutch the bed to keep from sliding down to the infirmary hatch.

The hatch swung outward and banged against the bulkhead. Dr. Waller was on the other side, his red-rimmed eyes wide with terror.

"We're sinking!" he screamed. "The gas shell has collapsed!"

For a what seemed like a century and a quarter I just hung there, clutching the bed while alarms hooted and wailed all along the gondola, staring at Waller as he held onto the hatch frame with both his hands. In the hollow of my stomach I could feel the ship dropping.

"ALL HANDS TO THE AIRLOCK," the intercom speakers blared. "GET INTO YOUR SPACE SUITS. NOW."

It was Duchamp's voice, sharp as a surgeon's scalpel, not panicked but certainly urgent enough to make me move.

"Come on," I said as I stumbled past Waller. He seemed frozen, mouth gaping, eyes goggling, unwilling or unable to let go of the hatch frame and start downhill toward the airlock.

I grabbed his shoulder and shook him, hard. "Come on!" I shouted at him. "You heard the captain. That means everybody!"

"But I've never been in my space suit!" he said, almost in tears. "Never. I was told I wouldn't have to."

"That doesn't matter now," I said, yanking him free. "Come with me, I'll show you how to do it."

The ship seemed to straighten out somewhat as we staggered and weaved down the passageway. We had to manually open hatches every few meters. They automatically slammed shut behind us. At least the alarms had been silenced; their wailing was enough to scare you into cardiac fibrillation.

Rodriguez was already at the airlock, helping Riza Kolodny into her suit. The other two technicians crowded behind him, getting their own suits on.

"Where's Marguerite?" I asked him.

"I don't know. Maybe up at the bridge with her mother," he said, without looking up from his work.

"These suits are all damaged," I said, holding out the sleeve of my own. The elbow joint was obviously blackened, as if singed by a flame.

"You want to go with no suit at all?" Rodriguez snapped.

Waller moaned. I thought he was going to faint, but then I saw a growing stain across the crotch of his coveralls. The doctor had wet himself.

"What's happened?" I demanded. "What are we going to do?"

Still checking Riza's backpack, Rodriguez said, "Damned shell cracked open. We're losing buoyancy. Can't keep the ship in trim."

"So what—"

"We're going to the descent module, use it in the escape pod mode. Ride it up to orbit and hope *Truax* can find us."

"Then why do we need the suits?"

"Whole front section of the gondola's leaking like a frickin' sieve," Rodriguez said, his voice edged with fear-driven tension. "If the leaks reach the bridge before we can get everybody into the pod . . ."

He didn't have to finish the sentence. I got the picture.

I helped Dr. Waller into his suit before starting to put mine on. The ship kept dipping and then rising, making my insides feel as if I were on an elevator that couldn't make up its mind. Waller seemed almost in shock, hardly able to move his arms and legs, his eyes staring blankly, his mouth sagging open and gasping like a fish. It flashed through my mind that he had the only undamaged suit on board; all the others had developed leaks, even the spares.

By the time I got my own suit on, Marguerite and her mother were still nowhere in sight. I clomped down the slanting passageway toward the bridge.

"Where're you going?" Rodriguez yelled after me. "I gotta check you out!"

"I'll be back in a few minutes," I called back, shouting so they could hear me through the helmet. "Get everybody to the escape pod. I'll catch up with you there."

Checking out the suit was nothing more than busywork at this stage of the game. They all leaked to some degree, we all knew that. But we only needed them for the few minutes it would take to clamber into the escape pod and dog its hatch shut.

I wasn't going without Marguerite, though. What was she doing? Where was she?

Her lab was empty. The ship seemed to straighten out again; the passageway even angled upward a little, for a moment.

I pushed on to the bridge. There they were, both of them.

". . . can't stay here," Marguerite was saying, pleading really.

"Someone's got to keep the ship on as even a keel as possible," Duchamp said, her eyes fixed on the main display screen. Sitting in her command chair, she had a laptop across her knees, her fingers working the keys like a concert pianist playing a cadenza.

"But you'll—"

I broke into their argument. "Everyone's suited up and headed for the escape pod."

Duchamp looked sharply at me. Then, with a single curt nod, she turned her gaze to her daughter. "Get into your suit. Now."

"Not until you come with me," Marguerite said.

The picture is etched in my mind. The two of them, as identical as copies from a blueprint except for their ages, glaring at each other with identical stubborn intensity.

"Both of you, get your suits on," I said, trying to sound commanding. "The others are waiting for you."

The ship lurched and heaved wildly. My stomach tried to jump into my throat. I grabbed the hatch frame for support. Marguerite, standing beside her mother, staggered and fell into Rodriguez's chair with an ungainly thump.

Duchamp turned back to the main screen, banging on the laptop's keyboard again.

"We're losing the last bit of buoyancy we have," she said, not taking her eyes off the screen. I saw that it displayed a schematic of the ship's maneuvering engines.

"Then we've got to get out!" I snapped.

"Someone's got to keep the ship from diving deeper," Duchamp said. "If I don't work the engines, we'll sink like a stone."

"What about the regular trim program?" I demanded.

She barked out a single harsh, "Hah!"

I said, "The computer should be able—"

"There's no way the computer can keep this bucket on a halfway even keel without manual input," Duchamp said. "No way."

"But—"

"I'm only barely managing to hold her at altitude now."

As if to prove her words, the ship dipped down again, then popped sharply upward. I thought I could hear moaning from up forward, where the rest of the crew was waiting for us.

"It's the captain's duty," Duchamp said, glancing at me. Then she smiled thinly. "I know you didn't want me for the job, but I take the position seriously."

"You'll kill yourself!" Marguerite shrieked.

"Get her off the bridge," Duchamp said to me.

Still clinging to the rim of the hatch, I thought swiftly. "I'll make you a deal."

She arched one brow at me.

"I'll get Marguerite suited up and bring your suit here to the bridge. Then you suit up and come forward to the escape pod."

She nodded.

"Come on," I said to Marguerite.

"No," she snapped. Turning to her mother, she said, "Not without you."

Duchamp gave her a look I'd never seen on her face before. Instead of her usual stern, flint-hard stare, the captain's features softened, her eyes glistened.

"Marguerite, go with him. I'll be all right. I'm really not suicidal."

Before Marguerite could reply I grasped her wrist and literally hauled her out of the chair, off the bridge, and down the slanting passageway to the airlock where the suits were stored.

"She'll kill herself," Marguerite said in a throaty whisper, as if talking to herself. Over and over, as I helped her into her space suit, she repeated it. "She'll kill herself."

"I won't let her," I said, with a bravado I didn't really feel. "I'll get her into her suit and up to the escape pod if I have to carry her."

I only said it to make Marguerite feel better, and I'm certain that she knew it. But she let me help her put the suit on and check out the backpack.

I took the least-used-looking of the remaining suits and we staggered back up the passageway toward the bridge again. The ship's pitching and reeling seemed to calm down somewhat. Maybe we had hit a region of calm, stable air, or we were finally in equilibrium with the air pressure outside.

We got to the bridge and I offered to run the auxiliary engines while the captain got into her suit.

She gave me a pitying smile. "If I had a few days to teach you . . ."

"Then let's get Rodriguez up here," I suggested.

"I'll go get him," Marguerite said.

Raising her hand to stop her daughter, Duchamp said, "The intercom still works, dear."

"Then call him," I commanded.

She seemed to think it over for half a second, then tapped the intercom stud on her chair arm. Before she could say anything, however, the message light on the comm console flashed on.

Duchamp called out to the computer, "Answer incoming call."

Lars Fuchs's heavy, jowly face filled the screen, glowering angrily.

"I picked up your distress call," he said flatly, with no preamble.

Hesperos's command computer was programmed to beam out a distress call when safety limits were exceeded. The instant the alarms began going off and the compartment hatches were automatically shut, the computer must have started calling for help. In ten minutes or so, I realized, we would be getting inquiries from the IAA on Earth: standard safety procedure for all space flights.

"We're preparing to abandon ship," Duchamp said. "Buoyancy's gone."

"Stand by," Fuchs said, the expression on his face somewhere between annoyed and exasperated. "I'm approaching you at maximum speed. You can transfer to *Lucifer*."

Strangely, Duchamp's expression softened. "You don't have to do that, Lars."

He remained irritated. "The hell I don't. IAA regulations require any craft receiving a distress signal to render all possible assistance, remember?"

"But you can't—"

"If I don't come to your aid," he snapped, "the IAA will hang me out to dry. They'd love to make an example of me. And they won't hang me by my neck, either."

I studied his face there on the bridge's main display screen, at least two times bigger than life. There was anger there, plenty of it. Bitterness deeper than I'd ever seen before. Lars Fuchs looked like a man who'd been forced to make hard decisions all his life, iron-hard decisions that had cost him all hope for ease and joy. Joyless. That was it. That was what made his face so different from anyone I had ever seen before. There was no trace of joy in him. Not even a glimmer that a moment of happiness would ever touch him. He had abandoned all hope of joy, long years ago.

It took all of two or three seconds for me to come to that conclusion. In that time Duchamp made her decision.

"We only have a few minutes before the gondola starts breaking up, Lars."

"Get into your suits. *Lucifer* will be within transfer range in . . ." his eyes shifted to some data screen out of camera range ". . . twelve minutes."

Duchamp drew in a deep breath, then nodded once. "All right. We'll be ready."

"I'll be there," Fuchs said grimly. Strangely, I thought I heard just a hint of softening in his voice.

Rodriguez came back to the bridge and took over the conn while Duchamp struggled into her suit. She had to step out into the passageway, there was no room on the bridge to do it. Marguerite and I both checked her out. The suit had several slow leaks in it, but should have been good for at least an hour.

"We'll be aboard *Lucifer* by then," Duchamp said from inside her helmet. We were close enough so I could see her face through the tinted bubble. She wore the same hard-edged expression she usually showed. No trace of fear or even apprehension. If any of this frightened or worried her, it certainly did not show in her face.

"We'd better be," Marguerite said, barely loud enough for me to hear her. All our suits leaked a little, thanks to the bugs. I was grateful that we didn't have to pressurize them; Venus's atmospheric pressure at this altitude was slightly higher than Earth's.

It seemed to me that the ship's pitching and bobbing smoothed out somewhat under Rodriguez's hand, but that may have simply been my imagination—or the fact that I liked him a lot better than our hard-bitten captain.

Even so, the metal structure of the gondola began to groan and screech like a beast in pain. I stood out in the passageway and fought down the urge to scream out my own terror.

Marguerite didn't seem to be at all afraid. In fact, she knotted her brows in puzzlement. "Why are the bugs attacking just the one area of the gondola and not the entire structure?"

"What makes you think they're not?" I managed to gulp out.

"The only part being damaged so far is the section between airlock and the nose area," she said.

"How can you be sure of that?"

She jabbed a gloved thumb back toward the bridge. "Look at the life-support display. That's the only section that's lost air pressure."

She was right, I saw as I peered at the life-support screen. Now I furrowed my own brows. Was there any difference between that section and the rest of the gondola? I tried to remember the schematics and blueprints I had studied long months ago, when we were building *Hesperos*.

That entire section was designed around the airlock. Maybe the bugs were chewing on the plastics that we used as sealant for the outer airlock hatch?

"Is the inner airlock hatch sealed shut?" I called in to Rodriguez, who was still in the command chair.

Without stopping to think why I asked it, he flicked his eyes to the

"Christmas tree" display of lights that indicated the status of the ship's various systems. Most of the lights were bright, dangerous red now.

"No," he said, shaking his head inside his helmet.

"Seal it," I said.

"It won't do any good," Marguerite said. "If the bugs have eroded the outer hatch's sealant, they'll do the same for the inner hatch."

"It might buy us a few minutes' time," I countered.

Duchamp, fully suited up now, agreed with me. "Every second counts."

She went into the bridge and repossessed her command chair. Rodriguez came out into the passageway with us. He had to squeeze a little to get through the hatch with his suit on.

"All right," Rodriguez said. "Helmets sealed. Let's go up forward with the others."

"What about her?" Marguerite asked.

Duchamp replied, "I'm needed here. I'll leave the bridge when *Lucifer* starts taking us aboard."

"I'll stay here with you, then," Marguerite said.

"No," I said. "You're coming with us."

She had to turn her entire body toward me for me to see the flat refusal in her eyes. The same rigidly adamant expression I had seen so often on her mother's face; the same stubborn set of the jaw.

"Captain," I called out, "give the order."

"He's right, *ma petite*," Duchamp said, in a voice softer and lower than I had ever heard from her. "You've got—"

The message light began blinking again and Duchamp stopped in mid-sentence. "Answer incoming call."

Fuchs's bleakly somber face filled the comm screen. "I'll be maneuvering beneath your ship in four minutes. I won't be able to hold station for more than a minute or so. You'll have to be prepared to jump."

"Not below us!" Duchamp cried, startled. "We're breaking up. Debris could damage you."

Fuchs glowered. "Do your suits have maneuvering propulsion units?"

"No."

"Then if you can't fly, the only way to get from *Hesperos* to *Lucifer* is to drop." His wide slash of a mouth twitched briefly in what might have been the ghost of a smile. "Like Lucifer himself, you'll have to fall."

Jump from *Hesperos* onto *Lucifer*? The idea turned my innards to water. How could we do that? How close could Fuchs bring his ship to ours? I should have added maneuvering units to the space suits, I never thought of it back on Earth. We weren't planning any EVA work except for the transfer from *Truax*, and we had the cable trolley for that. Rodriguez should've known that we'd need maneuvering jets in an emergency. Somebody should've thought that far ahead.

"Three minutes, ten seconds," Fuchs said. "Be prepared to jump."

The comm screen went blank.

"Come on," Rodriguez said, nudging my shoulder to point me up the passageway.

Marguerite still hesitated.

"Go with them," Duchamp commanded. "I'll hold this bucket on course for another two minutes and then come along."

"You won't do anything foolish?" Marguerite asked, in a tiny voice.

Duchamp gave her a disgusted look. "The idea that the captain goes down with his ship was a piece of male machismo. I'm not afflicted with the curse of testosterone, believe me."

Before either of them could say anything more, I put my gloved hand on Marguerite's backpack and shoved her—gently—along the passageway.

I never found out if shutting the inner airlock hatch slowed down the bugs' destruction or not. As it turned out, it didn't matter, one way or the other.

The rest of the crew, Dr. Waller, and the three technicians were up in the nose section, already inside the descent module. As far as they knew we were still planning to use the 'sphere in its escape pod mode and rocket up into orbit, to be picked up by *Truax*.

As we hurried up the passageway toward the hatch that opened onto the airlock area, Rodriguez again ordered us to seal our helmets. "Air pressure's okay on the other side of the hatch," he said, "but there's probably a lot of Venusian air mixed in with our own. You wouldn't enjoy breathing sulfuric acid fumes."

I checked my helmet seal six times in the few steps it took us to reach the closed hatch.

Meanwhile, Rodriguez used his suit radio to tell Waller and the techs to get out of the pod and into the airlock section. They asked why, of course.

"We're going to transfer to Fuchs's ship, *Lucifer*," he said.

"How?" I heard Riza Kolodny's adenoidal voice in my helmet earphones.

"You'll see," Rodriguez said, like a father who doesn't have the time to explain.

We got the hatch open and looked into the airlock section. It seemed safe enough. I couldn't see holes in the structure. But the metal seemed to be groaning again, and I could hear thin, high-pitched whistling noises, like air blowing through a lot of pinholes.

Rodriguez stepped through the hatch first, then Marguerite. I followed. The ship lurched again and I put out my hand to rest it on the sturdy metal frame of the airlock hatch, to steady myself.

Just then the hatch on the opposite end of the section swung back. Four space-suited figures huddled there, anonymous in their bulky suits and reflective bubble helmets.

Duchamp's voice crackled in my earphones, "Fuchs is about a hundred meters below us and moving up closer. Connect your tethers to each other and start down to his ship."

Rodriguez said, "Right," then pointed at me. "You first, Mr. Humphries."

I had to swallow several times before I could answer him, "All right. Then Marguerite."

"Yessir," Rodriguez said.

There was no need to cycle the airlock. I just slid its inner hatch open and stepped inside, then punched the button that opened the outer hatch. Nothing happened. For a moment I just stood there like a fool, hearing the wind whistling around me, feeling trapped.

"Use the manual override!" Rodriguez said impatiently.

"Right," I answered, trying to recover some shred of dignity.

I tugged at the wheel and the outer hatch slowly, stubbornly inched open. Rodriguez handed me the first few tethers, clipped together end to end. He and Marguerite were hurriedly snapping the others onto one another.

"Attach the free end to a ladder rung," he told me.

"Right," I said again. It was the only word I could think of.

I leaned out the open airlock hatch to attach the tether and what I saw made me giddy with fright.

We were scudding along high above an endless layer of sickly yellowish clouds, billowing and undulating like a thing alive. And then the huge curving bulk of *Lucifer* slid in below us, so near that I thought we would crash together in a collision that would kill us all.

"*Lucifer* is on-station," I heard Duchamp's voice in my earphones.

Fuchs's ship seemed enormous, much bigger than ours. It was drawing nearer, slowly but noticeably closing the gap between us. Gasping for breath, I clicked the end of the tether onto the nearest ladder rung. Then I realized that Rodriguez was right behind me, feeding tether line out the hatch, past my booted feet. I watched the tether snake down toward the top of *Lucifer's* bulbous shell, dropping like an impossibly thin line of string down, down, down, and still not reaching the walkway that ran the length of the ship's gas envelope.

I suddenly realized that I hadn't taken any of my enzyme supply with me. Even if we made it to *Lucifer* I'd be without the medicine I needed to live.

Then *Hesperos* dipped drunkenly and the gondola groaned again like a man dying in agony. I happened to glance along the outer surface and saw that the metal was streaked with ugly dark smudges that ran from the nose to the airlock hatch and even beyond. I could see the thin metal skin cracking along those dark streaks.

Marguerite and Rodriguez were behind me, the four other space-suited figures—Waller and the technicians—stood huddled on the other side of the airlock hatch. They were all waiting impatiently for me to start the descent toward *Lucifer* and safety. I stood frozen at the lip of the open hatch. Clambering down that dangling tether certainly did not look at all safe to me.

The groaning rose in pitch until it was like a screeching of fingernails on a chalkboard. I pulled my head back inside the airlock chamber, panting as if I'd run a thousand meters.

"She's breaking up!" Rodriguez yelled, so loud that I could hear him through my helmet as well as in my earphones.

Before my eyes, the front section of the gondola tore away with a horrifying grinding, ripping sound, carrying Waller and the technicians with it. They screamed, terrified high-pitched wails that shrieked in my earphones. The front end broke entirely free and flashed past my horrified eyes, tumbling end over end, spilling the space-suited figures out into the open, empty air.

"Save meee!" one of them screamed, a shriek so strained and piercing I couldn't tell which of them uttered it.

I saw a body thump down onto *Lucifer*, below us; it missed the cat-walk and slid off into oblivion, howling madly all the time.

I could hardly stand up, my knees were so watery. Rodriguez, pressed in behind me in the airlock, whispered, "Jesus, Mary, and Joseph."

The screams went on and on, like red-hot ice picks jammed into my ears. Even after they stopped, my head rang with their memory.

"They're dead," Rodriguez said, his voice hollow.

"All of them," said Marguerite, quavering, fighting back tears.

"And so will we be," Duchamp's voice crackled, "if we don't get down those tethers *right now*."

The ship was bucking violently now, heaving up and down in a wild pitching motion. The wind tore at us from the gaping emptiness where the nose of the gondola had been. A ridiculous thought popped into my mind: We didn't need the airlock now, we could jump out of the ship through the jagged open end of the gondola.

I could hear Rodriguez panting hard in my earphones. At least, I assumed it was Rodriguez. Marguerite was there, too, and I thought Duchamp had to be on her way down to us by now.

"Go on!" Rodriguez yelled, as if the suit radios weren't working. "Down the tether."

If I had thought about it for half a millisecond I would have been so terrified I'd have frozen up, paralyzed with fear. But there wasn't any time for that. I grabbed the tether with both gloved hands.

"The servomotors will hold you," Rodriguez said. "Loop your boots in the line to take some of the load off your arms. Like circus acrobats."

I made a clumsy try at it, but only managed to tangle the tether around one ankle. The servomotors on the backs of the gloves clamped my fingers on the line, sure enough. All I had to worry about was making a mistake and letting go of the blasted line with both hands at the same time.

Down I went, hand over hand.

It was hard work, clambering down that swaying, slithering line of con-nected tethers. Drenched in cold sweat, my heart hammering in my ears, I tried to clamp my boots around the line to take some of the strain off my arms but that was a clumsy failure. I inched down the line, my powered gloves clamping and unclamping slowly, like an arthritic old man's hands.

Lucifer seemed to be a thousand kilometers below me. I could see the end of the connected tethers dangling a good ten meters or more above the catwalk that ran the length of the ship's gas envelope. It looked like a hundred meters, to me. A thousand. When I got to the end of the line I'd have to jump for it.

If I made it to the end of the line.

And all the while I crawled down the length of tethers I kept hearing the terrified, agonized screams of the crewmen who fell to their deaths. My mind kept replaying that long, wailing, "Save meee!" over and over again. What would I scream if I missed the ship and plunged down into the fiery depths of inescapable death?

"Send the others down." It was Fuchs's heavy, harsh voice in my earphones. "Don't wait. Get started *now.*"

"No," Marguerite said. I could sense her struggling, hear her breathing hard. "Wait . . ."

But Rodriguez said firmly, "No time for waiting. Now!"

I looked up and saw another figure start down the tethers. In the space suit it was impossible to see who it was, but I figured it had to be Marguerite.

She was coming down the line a lot faster than I, her boots gripping the tether expertly. Had she told me she'd done mountain climbing? I couldn't remember. Foolish thought, at that particular moment.

I tried to go faster and damned near killed myself. Let go of the line with one hand, then missed my next grab for it while my other hand was opening. There's a delay built into the servomotors that control the gloves' exoskeletons; you move your fingers and the motors resist a little, then kick in. My glove's fingers were opening, loosening my grip on the tether, when I desperately wanted them to tighten again.

There I was, one hand flailing free and the other letting go of my grip on the tether. If I hadn't been so scared I would've thrown up.

I lunged for the line with my free hand, caught it, and closed my fingers as fast and hard as I could. I thought I heard the servomotors whining furiously although that must have been my imagination, since I'd never heard them before through the suit and helmet.

I hung there by one hand, all my weight on that arm and shoulder, for what seemed like an hour or two. Then I clasped the tether with my other hand, took the deepest breath I'd ever made in my life, and started down the tether again.

"Where's my mother?" I heard Marguerite's fear-filled voice in my earphones.

"She's on her way," Rodriguez answered.

But when I looked up I saw only their two figures clambering down the tether. *Hesperos* was a wreck, jouncing and shuddering above us, falling apart. The gas envelope was cracked like an overcooked egg. The gondola was half gone, its front end torn away, new cracks zigzagging along its length even as I watched. The bugs from the clouds must have made a home for themselves in the ship's metal structure.

Well, I thought grimly, they'll all roast to death when she loses her last bit of buoyancy and plunges into the broiling heat below.

Then I caught a vision of *Hesperos* crashing into *Lucifer*, and wondered how long Fuchs would keep his ship hovering below us.

"Hurry it up!" he called, as if he could read my thoughts.

Marguerite was sobbing openly; I could hear her over the suit radio. Rodriguez had gone silent except for his hard panting as he worked his way down the tether. They were both getting close to me.

And Duchamp was still in the ship. On the bridge, I realized, working to hold the shattered *Hesperos* in place long enough for us to make it to safety. But what about her safety?

"Captain Duchamp," I called, surprised that my voice worked at all. "Leave the bridge and come down the safety tether. That's an order."

No response.

"Mother!" Marguerite sobbed. "Mama!"

She wasn't coming. I knew it with the certainty of religious revelation. Duchamp was staying on the bridge, fighting to hold the battered wreck of *Hesperos* in place long enough for us to make it to safety. Giving her life to save us. To save her daughter, really. I doubt that she cared a rat's hiccup for the rest of us. Maybe she had some feelings for Rodriguez. Certainly not for me.

And then I was at the end of the tether line. I dangled there, swaying giddily, my boots swinging in empty air. The broad expanse of *Lucifer's* gas envelope still seemed an awfully long way off. A long drop.

All my weight, including the weight of my space suit and backpack, was hanging from my hands. I could feel the bones of my upper arms being pulled slowly, agonizingly, out of my shoulder sockets, like a man on the rack. I couldn't hang on for long.

Then I saw three space-suited figures climbing slowly up the curving flank of the massive shell. They looked like toys, like tiny dolls, and I realized just how much bigger *Lucifer* was than *Hesperos*. Enormously bigger.

Which meant that it was also much farther away than I had first guessed. It wasn't ten meters below me; it must have been more like a hundred meters. I couldn't survive a jump that long. No one could.

I looked up. Through my bubble helmet I saw Marguerite and Rodriguez coming down the line toward me, almost on top of me.

"What now?" I asked Rodriguez. "It's too far to jump."

Before he could answer, Fuchs's voice grated in my earphones. "I'm bringing *Lucifer* up close enough for you to reach. I can't keep her in position for long, so when I say jump, you either jump or be damned. Understand me?"

"Understood," Rodriguez said.

"Okay."

The broad back of *Lucifer* rose toward us, slowly moving closer. The three space-suited figures were on the catwalk now, laying out long coils of tethers between them.

We were getting tantalizingly close, but each time I thought we were within a safe jumping distance *Hesperos* bobbed up or sideways and we were jerked away from *Lucifer*. My arms were blazing with pain. I could hear Rodriguez mumbling in Spanish, perhaps a prayer. More likely some choice curses.

I looked up again and saw that *Hesperos* was barely holding together. The gondola was cracked in a hundred places, the gas shell above it was missing pieces like an uncompleted jigsaw puzzle.

The only thing in our favor was that the air was thick enough down at this level to be relatively calm. Relatively. *Hesperos* was still jouncing and fluttering like a leaf in a strong breeze.

Marguerite's sobbing seemed to have stopped. I supposed that she finally understood her mother was not coming and there was nothing she could do about it. There would be plenty of time to mourn after we had saved our own necks, I thought. When your own life is on the line, as ours were, you worry about your own skin and save your sentiment for everyone else for later.

"Now!" Fuchs's command shattered my pointless musings.

I was still dangling a tremendous distance from *Lucifer*'s catwalk, my shoulders and arms screaming in agony from the strain.

"Now, dammit!" he roared. "*Jump!*"

I let go. For a dizzying instant it felt as if I hung in midair, not moving at all. By the time I realized I was falling I thudded down onto the curving hull of *Lucifer*'s envelope with a bang that knocked the breath out of my lungs.

I had missed the catwalk and the men waiting to help me by several meters. I felt myself sliding along the curve of the shell, my arms and legs scrabbling to find a grip, a handhold, anything to stop me from sliding off into the oblivion below. Nothing. The shell's skin was smooth as polished marble.

In my earphones I heard a sort of howling noise, a strangled wail that yowled in my ears like some primitive animal's shriek. It went on and on without letup. I couldn't hear anything else, nothing except that agonized howl.

If *Lucifer* had been as small as *Hesperos* I would have slid off the shell and plunged into the thick hot clouds kilometers beneath me. I sometimes wonder if I would have been roasted to death as I fell deeper into the blistering hot atmosphere or crushed like an eggshell by the tremendous pressure.

Instead, Fuchs's crewmen saved me. One of them jumped off the catwalk and slid on the rump of his suit to my side and grabbed me firmly. Even through the yowling noise in my earphones I could hear him grunt painfully when his tether stopped us both. Then he looped the extra tether he carried with him around my shoulders.

I was shaking so hard inside my suit that it took me three tries before I could control my legs well enough to follow Fuchs's crewman back up to the catwalk, where his companion already had his arms wrapped around Marguerite. I found out later that she had dropped neatly onto the catwalk and not even lost her balance.

I was on my hands and knees, gasping from the efforts of the last few minutes. My shoulders felt as if someone had ripped my arms out of them. I was beyond pain; I was numb, wooden.

The catwalk seemed to shift beneath me, tossing me onto my side. I looked up and saw *Hesperos* breaking apart, big chunks of the envelope tearing away, the gondola splitting along its length.

Marguerite screamed. I saw the line of tethers flapping wildly, empty.

Raising myself painfully to my knees, I looked for Rodriguez. He was nowhere in sight.

"Where's Rodriguez?" I demanded.

No one answered.

I looked directly at Marguerite, who had disengaged herself from the crewmen who'd held her.

"Where's Tom?" I screamed.

I couldn't see her face inside the helmet, but sensed her shaking her head. "He jumped after me . . ."

"What happened to him?" I climbed to my feet shakily.

Fuchs's voice answered in my earphones. "The third person in your party jumped too late. I had to jink the ship sideways to avoid the debris falling from *Hesperos*. He missed us and fell into the clouds."

That was the long, terrified scream I heard in my earphones: Rodriguez falling, falling all that long way down to his death.

I stayed there on my knees until two of the crewmen yanked me up roughly by the armpits of my suit. I could hardly breathe. Every muscle and tendon in my body was in agony. And Rodriguez was dead.

Marguerite sobbed, "My mother . . ." She sounded exhausted, as drained physically and emotionally as I felt.

I looked up. *Hesperos* was gone. No sign of the ship. Nothing above us but swirling sickly yellow-gray clouds. Nothing below us but more of the same.

One of the crewmen motioned me toward a hatch set into the catwalk. I nodded inside my helmet and headed for it, Marguerite following me.

Rodriguez, Captain Duchamp, Waller, and the three technicians— all dead. Venus had killed them. But then I realized that was not true. It was my fault. I had brought them to this hellish world. I had made them intrude into this place where humans were never meant to be. I had killed them.

And myself, as well, I thought. Without my medication I'd be dead soon enough.

But I was still alive. Venus had tried to kill me and failed. I had survived. I still lived.

That which does not kill us makes us stronger. I remembered reading that somewhere. All right, I thought; as long as I'm still alive I'm going to push on. No matter what lies ahead, I'm going to get down to the surface of this hellish world and find what's left of my brother.

And I'm not doing it for Alex, or for the prize money, or even to prove to my father that I'm more than a Runt. I'm doing it for *me*, because I want to, because I have to.

Venus might very well kill me, in the end. But even so, I'll die trying.

Not everyone who leaves Earth for a life in space will be an adventurer or scientist. As habitats grow off-planet, inevitably people will be attracted to them for more personal reasons. One of those reasons may well be the gentler pull of gravity to be found in orbit, or on the Moon.

The immediate inspiration for "The Man Who Hated Gravity" sprang from personal experience: I wrecked my knee playing tennis and had to hobble around on crutches for a while. Yet, now that I think about it, I had written about the advantages of the Moon's one-sixth g as far back as my 1976 novel, Millennium. I thought then that my secret ambition to dance like Fred Astaire—a hopeless passion on Earth—might just be realizable if only I could get to the gentler gravity of the Moon.

The Great Rolando is no dancer, but—like me—he longs for a way to escape the clutches of Earth's gravity.

THE MAN WHO HATED GRAVITY

The Great Rolando had not always hated gravity. As a child growing up in the travelling circus that had been his only home he often frightened his parents by climbing too high, swinging too far, daring more than they could bear to watch.

The son of a clown and a cook, Rolando had yearned for true greatness, and could not rest until he became the most renowned aerialist of them all.

Slim and handsome in his spangled tights, Rolando soared through the empty air thirty feet above the circus's flimsy safety net. Then fifty feet above it. Then a full hundred feet high, with no net at all.

"See the Great Rolando defy gravity!" shouted the posters and TV advertisements. And the people came to crane their necks and hold their breaths as he performed a split-second ballet in midair high above them. Literally flying from one trapeze to another, triple somersaults were workaday chores for the Great Rolando.

His father feared to watch his son's performances. With all the superstition born of generations of circus life, he cringed outside the Big Top while the crowds roared deliriously. Behind his clown's painted grin Rolando's father trembled. His mother prayed through every performance until the day she died, slumped over a bare wooden pew in a tiny austere church far out in the Midwestern prairie.

For no matter how far he flew, no matter how wildly he gyrated in midair, no matter how the crowds below gasped and screamed their delight, the Great Rolando pushed himself farther, higher, more recklessly.

Once, when the circus was playing New York City's huge Convention Center, the management pulled a public relations coup. They got a brilliant young physicist from Columbia University to pose with Rolando for the media cameras and congratulate him on defying gravity.

Once the camera crews had departed, the physicist said to Rolando, "I've always had a secret yearning to be in the circus. I admire what you do very much."

Rolando accepted the compliment with a condescending smile.

"But no one can *really* defy gravity," the physicist warned. "It's a universal force, you know."

The Great Rolando's smile vanished. "*I* can defy gravity. And I do. Every day."

Several years later Rolando's father died (of a heart seizure, during one of his son's performances) and Rolando married the brilliant young lion tamer who had joined the circus slightly earlier. She was a petite little thing with golden hair, the loveliest of blue eyes, and so sweet a disposition that no one could say anything about her that was less than praise. Even the great cats purred for her.

She too feared Rolando's ever-bolder daring, his wilder and wilder reachings on the high trapeze.

"There's nothing to be afraid of! Gravity can't hurt me!" And he would laugh at her fears.

"But I *am* afraid," she would cry.

"The people pay their money to see me defy gravity," Rolando would tell his tearful wife. "They'll get bored if I keep doing the same stunts one year after another."

She loved him dearly, and felt terribly frightened for him. It was one thing to master a large cage full of Bengal tigers and tawny lions and snarling black panthers. All you needed was will and nerve. But she knew that gravity was another matter altogether.

"No one can defy gravity forever," she would say, gently, softly, quietly.

"I can," boasted the Great Rolando.

But of course he could not. No one could. Not forever.

The fall, when it inevitably came, was a matter of a fraction of a second. His young assistant's hand slipped only slightly in starting out the empty trapeze for Rolando to catch after a quadruple somersault. Rolando almost caught it. In midair he saw that the bar would be too short. He stretched his magnificently trained body to the utmost and his fingers just grazed its tape-wound shaft.

For an instant he hung in the air. The tent went absolutely silent. The crowd drew in its collective breath. The band stopped playing. Then gravity wrapped its invisible tentacles around the Great Rolando and he

plummeted, wild-eyed and scream
below.

"His right leg is completely shatte
wife. She had stayed calm up to that
while her husband lay unconscious in

"His other injuries will heal. But t
suited man shook his dignified head sad
him like an honor guard, shook their he
their leader.

"His leg?" she asked, trembling.

"He will never be able to walk again," the famous surgeon pronounced. The petite blond lion tamer crumpled and sagged into the sleek leather couch of the hospital waiting room, tears spilling down her cheeks.

"Unless . . ." said the famous surgeon.

"Unless?" she echoed, suddenly wild with hope.

"Unless we replace the shattered leg with a prosthesis."

"Cut off his leg?"

The famous surgeon promised her that a prosthetic bionic leg would be "just as good as the original—in fact, even better!" It would be a *permanent* prosthesis; it would never have to come off, and its synthetic surface would blend so well with Rolando's real skin that no one would be able to tell where his natural leg ended and his prosthetic leg began. His assistants nodded in unison.

Frenzied at the thought that her husband would never walk again, alone in the face of coolly assured medical wisdom, she reluctantly gave her assent and signed the necessary papers.

The artificial leg was part lightweight metal, part composite space-manufactured materials, and entirely filled with marvelously tiny electronic devices and miraculously miniaturized motors that moved the prosthesis exactly the way a real leg should move. It was stronger than flesh and bone, or so the doctors confidently assured the Great Rolando and his wife.

The circus manager, a constantly frowning bald man who reported to a board of bankers, lawyers, and MBAs in St. Petersburg, agreed to pay the famous surgeon's astronomical fee. "The first aerialist with a bionic leg," he murmured, dollar signs in his eyes.

Rolando took the news of the amputation and prosthesis with

. He agreed with his wife: Better a strong and reliable arti-
n a ruined real one.
wo weeks he walked again. But not well. He limped. The leg
, with a sullen stubborn ache that refused to go away.

"It will take a little time to get accustomed to it," said the physical therapists.

Rolando waited. He exercised. He tried jogging. The leg did not work right. And it ached constantly.

"That's just not possible," the doctors assured him. "Perhaps you ought to talk with a psychologist."

The Great Rolando stormed out of their offices, limping and cursing, never to return. He went back to the circus, but not to his aerial acrobatics. A man who could not walk properly, who had an artificial leg that did not work right, had no business on the high trapeze.

His young assistant took the spotlight now, and duplicated—almost—the Great Rolando's repertoire of aerial acrobatic feats. Rolando watched him with mounting jealousy, his only satisfaction being that the crowds were noticeably smaller than they had been when he had been the star of the show. The circus manager frowned and asked when Rolando would be ready to work again.

"When the leg works right," said Rolando.

But it continued to pain him, to make him awkward and invalid.

That is when he began to hate gravity. He hated being pinned down to the ground like a worm, a beetle. He would hobble into the Big Top and eye the fliers' platform a hundred feet over his head and know that he could not even climb the ladder to reach it. He grew angrier each day. And clumsy. And obese. The damned false leg *hurt* no matter what those expensive quacks said. It was *not* psychosomatic. Rolando snorted contempt for their stupidity.

He spent his days bumping into inanimate objects and tripping over tent ropes. He spent his nights grumbling and grousing, fearing to move about in the dark, fearing even that he might roll off his bed. When he managed to sleep the same nightmare gripped him: He was falling, plunging downward eternally while gravity laughed at him and all his screams for help did him no good whatever.

His former assistant grinned at him whenever they met. The circus manager took to growling about Rolando's weight, and asking how long he expected to be on the payroll when he was not earning his keep.

gravity, he was certain. Inwardly, he was eager to find out, too. But he let no one know that, not even his wife.

To his utter shame and dismay, Rolando was miserably sick all the long three days of the flight from Texas to Moonbase. Immediately after takeoff the spacecraft carrying the circus performers was in zero gravity, weightless, and Rolando found that the absence of gravity was worse for him than gravity itself. His stomach seemed to be falling all the time while, paradoxically, anything he tried to eat crawled upward into his throat and made him violently ill.

In his misery and near-delirium he knew that gravity was laughing at him.

Once on the Moon, however, everything became quite fine. Better than fine, as far as Rolando was concerned. While clear-eyed young Moonbase guides in crisp uniforms of amber and bronze demonstrated the cautious shuffling walk that was needed in the gentle lunar gravity, Rolando realized that his leg no longer hurt.

"I feel fine," he whispered to his wife, in the middle of the demonstration. Then he startled the guides and his fellow circus folk alike by tossing his cane aside and leaping five meters into the air, shouting at the top of his lungs, "I feel *wonderful!*"

The circus performers were taken off to special orientation lectures, but Rolando and his wife were escorted by a pert young redhead into the office of Moonbase's chief administrator.

"Remember me?" asked the administrator, as he shook Rolando's hand and half-bowed to his wife. "I was the physicist at Columbia who did that TV commercial with you six or seven years ago."

Rolando did not in fact remember the man's face at all, although he did recall his warning about gravity. As he sat down in the chair the administrator proffered, he frowned slightly.

The administrator wore zippered coveralls of powder blue. He hiked one hip onto the edge of his desk and beamed happily at the Rolandos. "I can't tell you how delighted I am to have the circus here, even if it's just for a month. I really had to sweat blood to get the corporation's management to okay bringing you up here. Transportation's still quite expensive, you know."

Rolando patted his artificial leg. "I imagine the bionics company paid their fair share of the costs."

The administrator looked slightly startled. "Well, yes, they have picked up the tab for you and Mrs. Rolando."

"I thought so."

Rolando's wife smiled sweetly. "We are delighted that you invited us here."

They chatted a while longer and then the administrator personally escorted them to their apartment in Moonbase's tourist section. "Have a happy stay," he said, by way of taking his leave.

Although he did not expect to, that is exactly what Rolando did for the next many days. Moonbase was marvelous! There was enough gravity to keep his insides behaving properly, but it was so light and gentle that even his obese body with its false leg felt young and agile again.

Rolando walked the length and breadth of the great Main Plaza, his wife clinging to his arm, and marveled at how the Moonbase people had landscaped the expanse under their dome, planted it with grass and flowering shrubs. The apartment they had been assigned to was deeper underground, in one of the long corridors that had been blasted out of solid rock. But the quarters were no smaller than their mobile home back on Earth, and it had a video screen that took up one entire wall of the sitting room.

"I love it here!" Rolando told his wife. "I could stay forever!"

"It's only for one month," she said softly. He ignored it.

Rolando adjusted quickly to walking in the easy lunar gravity, never noticing that his wife adjusted just as quickly (perhaps even a shade faster). He left his cane in their apartment and strolled unaided each day through the shopping arcades and athletic fields of the Main Plaza, walking for hours on end without a bit of pain.

He watched the roustabouts that had come up with him directing their robots to set up a Big Top in the middle of the Plaza, a gaudy blaze of colorful plastic and pennants beneath the great gray dome that soared high overhead.

The Moon is marvelous, thought Rolando. There was still gravity lurking, trying to trip him up and make him look ridiculous. But even when he fell, it was so slow and gentle that he could put out his powerful arms and push himself up to a standing position before his body actually hit the ground.

"I love it here!" he said to his wife, dozens of times each day. She smiled and tried to remind him that it was only for three more weeks.

At dinner one evening in Moonbase's grander restaurant (there were only two, not counting cafeterias) his earthly muscles proved too strong for the Moon when he rammed their half-finished bottle of wine back into its aluminum ice bucket. The bucket tipped and fell off the edge of the table. But Rolando snatched it with one hand in the midst of its languid fall toward the floor and with a smile and a flourish deposited the bucket with the bottle still in it back on the table before a drop had spilled.

"I love it here," he repeated for the fortieth time that day.

Gradually, though, his euphoric mood sank. The circus began giving abbreviated performances inside its Big Top, and Rolando stood helplessly pinned to the ground while the spotlights picked out the young fliers in their skintight costumes as they tumbled slowly, dreamily through the air between one trapeze and the next, twisting, tumbling, soaring in the soft lunar gravity in ways that no one had ever done before. The audience gasped and cheered and gave them standing ovations. Rolando stood rooted near one of the tent's entrances, deep in shadow, wearing a tourist's pale green coveralls, choking with envy and frustrated rage.

The crowds were small—there were only a few thousand people living at Moonbase, plus perhaps another thousand tourists—but they shook the plastic tent with their roars of delight.

Rolando watched a few performances, then stayed away. But he noticed at the Olympic-sized pool that raw teenagers were diving from a thirty-meter platform and doing half a dozen somersaults as they fell languidly in the easy gravity. Even when they hit the water the splashes they made rose lazily and then fell back into the pool so leisurely that it seemed like a slow-motion film.

Anyone can be an athlete here, Rolando realized as he watched tourists flying on rented wings through the upper reaches of the Main Plaza's vaulted dome.

Children could easily do not merely Olympic, but Olympian feats of acrobatics. Rolando began to dread the possibility of seeing a youngster do a quadruple somersault from a standing start.

"Anyone can defy gravity here," he complained to his wife, silently adding, Anyone but me.

It made him morose to realize that feats which had taken him a lifetime to accomplish could be learned by a toddler in half an hour. And soon he would have to return to Earth with its heavy, oppressive, mocking gravity.

I know you're waiting for me, he said to gravity. You're going to kill me—if I don't do the job for myself first.

Two nights before they were due to depart they were the dinner guests of the chief administrator and several of his staff. As formal an occasion as Moonbase ever has, the men wore sport jackets and turtle-neck shirts, the women real dresses and jewelry. The administrator told hoary old stories of his childhood yearning to be in the circus. Rolando remained modestly silent, even when the administrator spoke glowingly of how he had admired the daring feats of the Great Rolando—many years ago.

After dinner, back in their apartment, Rolando turned on his wife. "You got them to invite us up here, didn't you?"

She admitted, "The bionics company told me that they were going to end your consulting fee. They want to give up on you! I asked them to let us come here to see if your leg would be better in low gravity."

"And then we go back to Earth."

"Yes."

"Back to *real* gravity. Back to my being a cripple!"

"I was hoping . . ." Her voice broke and she sank onto the bed, crying.

Suddenly Rolando's anger was overwhelmed by a searing, agonizing sense of shame. All these years she had been trying so hard, standing between him and the rest of the world, protecting him, sheltering him. And for what? So that he could scream at her for the rest of his life?

He could not bear it any longer.

Unable to speak, unable even to reach his hand out to comfort her, he turned and lumbered out of the apartment, leaving his wife weeping alone.

He knew where he had to be, where he could finally put an end to this humiliation and misery. He made his way to the Big Top.

A stubby gunmetal gray robot stood guard at the main entrance, its sensors focusing on Rolando like the red glowing eyes of a spider.

"No access at this time except to members of the circus troupe," it said in a synthesized voice.

"I am the Great Rolando."

"One moment for voiceprint identification," said the robot, then, "Approved."

Rolando swept past the contraption with a snort of contempt.

The Big Top was empty at this hour. Tomorrow they would start to dismantle it. The next day they would head back to Earth.

Rolando walked slowly, stiffly to the base of the ladder that reached up to the trapezes. The spotlights were shut down. The only illumination inside the tent came from the harsh working lights spotted here and there. Rolando heaved a deep breath and stripped off his jacket. Then, gripping one of the ladder's rungs, he began to climb: Good leg first, then the artificial leg. He could feel no difference between them. His body was only one-sixth its earthly weight, of course, but still the artificial leg behaved exactly as his normal one.

He reached the topmost platform. Holding tightly to the side rail he peered down into the gloomy shadows a hundred feet below.

With a slow, ponderous nod of his head the Great Rolando finally admitted what he had kept buried inside him all these long anguished years. Finally the concealed truth emerged and stood naked before him. With tear-filled eyes he saw its reality.

He had been living a lie for all these years. He had been blaming gravity for his own failure. Now he understood with precise, final clarity that it was not gravity that had destroyed his life.

It was fear.

He stood rooted on the high platform, trembling with the memory of falling, plunging, screaming terror. He knew that this fear would live within him always, for the remainder of his life. It was too strong to overcome; he was a coward, probably had always been a coward, all his life. All his life.

Without consciously thinking about it Rolando untied one of the trapezes and gripped the rough surface of its taped bar. He did not bother with resin. There would be no need.

As if in a dream he swung out into the empty air, feeling the rush of wind ruffling his gray hair, hearing the creak of the ropes beneath his weight.

Once, twice, three times he swung back and forth, kicking higher each time. He grunted with the unaccustomed exertion. He felt sweat trickling from his armpits.

Looking down, he saw the hard ground so far below. One more fall, he told himself. Just let go and that will end it forever. End the fear. End the shame.

"Teach me!"

The voice boomed like cannon fire across the empty tent. Rolando felt every muscle in his body tighten.

On the opposite platform, before him, stood the chief administrator, still wearing his dinner jacket.

"Teach me!" he called again. "Show me how to do it. Just this once, before you have to leave."

Rolando hung by his hands, swinging back and forth. The younger man's figure standing on the platform came closer, closer, then receded, dwindled as inertia carried Rolando forward and back, forward and back.

"No one will know," the administrator pleaded through the shadows. "I promise you; I'll never tell a soul. Just show me how to do it. Just this once."

"Stand back," Rolando heard his own voice call. It startled him.

Rolando kicked once, tried to judge the distance and account for the lower gravity as best as he could, and let go of the bar. He soared too far, but the strong composite mesh at the rear of the platform caught him, yieldingly, and he was able to grasp the side railing and stand erect before the young administrator could reach out and steady him.

"We both have a lot to learn," said the Great Rolando. "Take off your jacket."

For more than an hour the two men swung high through the silent shadowy air. Rolando tried nothing fancy, no leaps from one bar to another, no real acrobatics. It was tricky enough just landing gracefully on the platform in the strange lunar gravity.

The administrator did exactly as Rolando instructed him. For all his youth and desire to emulate a circus star, he was no daredevil. It satisfied him completely to swing side by side with the Great Rolando, to share the same platform.

"What made you come here tonight?" Rolando asked as they stood gasping sweatily on the platform between turns.

"The security robot reported your entry. Strictly routine, I get all such reports piped to my quarters. But I figured this was too good a chance to miss!"

Finally, soaked with perspiration, arms aching and fingers raw and cramping, they made their way down the ladder to the ground. Laughing.

"I'll never forget this," the administrator said. "It's the high point of my life."

"Mine, too," said Rolando fervently. "Mine, too."

Two days later the administrator came to the rocket terminal to see off the circus troupe. Taking Rolando and his wife to one side, he said in a low voice that brimmed with happiness, "You know, we're starting to accept retired couples for permanent residence here at Moonbase."

Rolando's wife immediately responded, "Oh, I'm not ready to retire yet."

"Nor I," said Rolando. "I'll stay with the circus for a few years more, I think. There might still be time for me to make a comeback."

"Still," said the administrator, "when you do want to retire . . ."

Mrs. Rolando smiled at him. "I've noticed that my face looks better in this lower gravity. I probably wouldn't need a facelift if we come to live here."

They laughed together.

The rest of the troupe was filing into the rocket that would take them back to Earth. Rolando gallantly held his wife's arm as she stepped up the ramp and ducked through the hatch. Then he turned to the administrator and asked swiftly: "What you told me about gravity all those years ago—is it really true? It is really universal? There's no way around it?"

"Afraid not," the administrator answered. "Someday gravity will make the Sun collapse. It might even make the entire universe collapse."

Rolando nodded, shook the man's hand, then followed his wife to his seat inside the rocket's passenger compartment. As he listened to the taped safety lecture and strapped on his safety belt he thought to himself: So gravity will get us all in the end.

Then he smiled grimly. But not yet. Not yet.

Of all the stories that were written about the first human flight to the Moon during science fiction's "golden age" of the 1930s and '40s (including Robert A. Heinlein's script for the 1950 movie Destination Moon) not one author foresaw that the lunar landing would be televised back to Earth.

Television was not a common household fixture when those tales were written. By the time broadcast TV became as commonplace as commercial radio, the major science fiction authors had moved on to the other subjects: The first lunar landing was old-hat in science fiction circles.

When the first humans set foot on Mars, their landing will be transmitted back to Earth not only by television, but by virtual reality systems, so that people on Earth with the proper equipment will be able to see, feel, experience the thrill of setting foot on the red planet.

"Appointment in Sinai" is about that moment, and although the tale is told from several different viewpoints, it is really the story of astronaut Debbie Kettering, who was passed over for the Mars mission, and her eventual realization that, as the poet John Milton put it, "They also serve who only stand and wait."

APPOINTMENT IN SINAI

Houston

No, I am not going to plug in," Debbie Kettering said firmly. "I'm much too busy."

Her husband gave her his patented lazy smile. "Come on, Deb, you don't have anything to do that can't wait a half hour or so."

His smile had always been her undoing. But this time she intended to stand firm. "No!" she insisted. "I won't."

She was not a small woman, but standing in their living room next to Doug made her look tiny. A stranger might think they were the school football hero and the cutest cheerleader on the squad, twenty years afterward. In reality, Doug was a propulsion engineer (a real rocket scientist) and Deborah an astronaut.

An ex-astronaut. Her resignation was on the computer screen in her bedroom office, ready to be e-mailed to her boss at the Johnson Space Center.

"What've you got to do that's so blasted important?" Doug asked, still grinning at her as he headed for the sofa, his favorite Saturday afternoon haunt.

"A mountain of work that's been accumulating for weeks," Debbie answered. "Now's the time to tackle it, while all the others are busy and won't be able to bother me."

His smile faded as he realized how miserable his wife really was. "Come on, Deb. We both know what's eating you."

"I won't plug in, Doug."

"Be a shame to miss it," he insisted.

Suddenly she was close to tears. "Those bastards even rotated me off the shift. They don't *want* me there!"

"But that doesn't mean—"

"No, Doug! They put everybody else in ahead of me. I'm on the bottom of their pecking order. So to hell with them! I won't even watch it on TV. And that's final!"

Los Angeles

"It's all set up, man. All we need's a guy who's good with the 'lectronics. And that's you, Chico."

Luis Mendez shifted unhappily in his desk chair. Up at the front of the room Mr. Ricardo was trying to light up some enthusiasm in the class. Nobody was interested in algebra, though. Except Luis, but he had Jorge leaning over from the next desk, whispering in his ear.

Luis didn't much like Jorge, not since first grade when Jorge used to beat him up at least once a week for his lunch money. The guy was dangerous. Now he was into coke and designer drugs and burglary to support his habit. And he wanted Luis to help him.

"I don't do locks," Luis whispered back, out of the side of his mouth, keeping his eyes on Mr. Ricardo's patient, earnest face.

"It's all 'lectronics, man. You do one kind you can do the other. Don't try to mess with me, Chico."

"We'll get caught. They'll send us to Alcatraz."

Jorge stifled a laugh. "I got a line on a whole friggin' warehouse full of VR sets and you're worryin' about Alcatraz? Even if they sent you there you'd be livin' better than here."

Luis grimaced. Life in the 'hood was no picnic, but Alcatraz? More than once Mr. Ricardo had sorrowfully complained, "Maybe you *bufóns* would be better off in Alcatraz. At least there they make you learn."

Yeah, Luis knew. They also fry your brains and turn you into a zombie.

"Hey." Jorge jabbed at Luis's shoulder. "I ain't askin' you, Chico. I'm tellin' you. You're gonna do the locks for me or you're gonna be in the hospital. *Comprende?*"

Luis understood. Trying to fight against Jorge was useless. He had learned that lesson years ago. Better to do what Jorge wanted than to get a vicious beating.

Washington

Senator Theodore O'Hara fumed quietly as he rolled his powerchair down the long corridor to his office. The trio of aides trotting behind him were puffing too hard to speak; the only sound in the marble-walled corridor was the slight whir of the powerchair's electric motor and the faint throb of the senator's artificial heart pump. And obedient panting.

He leaned on the toggle to make the chair go a bit faster. Two of his aides fell behind but Kaiser, overweight and prematurely balding, broke into a sprint to keep up.

Fat little yes-man, O'Hara thought. Still, Kaiser was uncanny when it came to predicting trends. O'Hara scrupulously followed all the polls, as any politician must if he wants to stay in office. But when the polls said one thing and Kaiser something else, the tubby little butterball was inevitably right.

Chairman Pastorini had recessed the committee session so everybody could plug into the landing. Set aside the important business of the Senate Appropriations Committee, O'Hara grumbled to himself, so we can all see a half-dozen astronauts plant their gold-plated boots on Mars.

What a waste of time, he thought. And money.

It's all Pastorini's doing. He's *using* the landing. Timed the damned committee session to meet just on this particular afternoon. Knew it all along. Thinks I'll cave in because the other idiots on the committee are going to get all stirred up.

I'll cave them in. All of them. This isn't the first manned landing on Mars, he thought grimly. It's the last.

Phoenix

Jerome Zacharias—Zack to everyone who knew him—paced nervously up and down the big room. Part library, part entertainment center, part bar, the room was packed with friends and well-wishers and media reporters who had made the trek to Phoenix to be with him at this historic moment.

They were drinking champagne already, Zack saw. Toasting our success. Speculating on what they'll find on Mars.

But it could all fail, he knew. It could be a disaster. The last systems check before breaking orbit had shown that the lander's damned fuel cells still weren't charged up to full capacity. All right, the backups are okay, there's plenty of redundancy, but it just takes one glitch to ruin everything. People have been killed in space and those kids are more than a hundred million miles from home.

If anything happens to them it'll be my fault, Zack knew. They're going to give me the credit if it all works out okay, but it'll be my fault if they crash and burn.

Twenty years he'd sweated and schemed and connived with government leaders, industrial giants, bureaucrats of every stripe. All to get a team of twelve men and women to Mars.

For what? he asked himself, suddenly terrified that he had no real answer. To satisfy my own ego? Is that why? Spend all this money and time, change the lives of thousands of engineers and scientists and technicians and all their support people, just so I can go to my grave saying that I pushed the human race to Mars?

Suppose somebody gets killed? Then a truly wrenching thought hit him. Suppose they don't find anything there that's worth it all? Suppose Mars is just the empty ball of rusty sand and rocks that the unmanned landers have shown us? No life, not even traces of fossils?

A wasted life. That's what I'll have accomplished. Wasted my own life and the lives of all the others. Wasted.

Houston

Debbie was sorting through all the paperwork from her years with the agency. Letters, reports, memos, the works. Funny how we still call it paperwork, Debbie thought as she toiled through her computer files.

Her heart clutched inside her when the official notification came up on her screen. The final selection of the six astronauts who would be the American part of the Mars team. Her name was conspicuously absent.

"You know why," she remembered her boss telling her, as gently as he could. "You're not only married, Deb, you're a mother. We can't send a mother on the mission; it's too long and too dangerous."

"That's prejudice!" Debbie had shrilled. "Prejudice against motherhood."

"Buffalo chips. The mission is dangerous. We're not talking about a weekend camping trip. They're going to Mars, for chrissake! I'm not going to be the one who killed some kid's mother. Not me!"

She had railed and fumed at him for nearly half an hour.

Finally, her boss stopped her with, "Seems to me you ought to be caring more about your kid. Two and a half years is a long time for him to be without his mother—even if nothing goes wrong with the mission."

Suddenly she had nothing left to say. She stomped out of his office before she broke into tears. She didn't want him or anybody else see her cry.

Pecking at her keyboard, Debbie pulled up the stinging memoranda she had fired off to Washington. She still felt some of the molten white heat that had boiled within her. Then she went through the lawyers' briefs and the official disclaimer from the agency's legal department: They denied prejudice against women who had children. The agency's choice had been based on "prudent, well-established assessments of risks, performances, and capabilities."

"Jeez, Deb, are you going to take this to the Supreme Court?" Doug had asked in the middle of the legal battle.

"If I have to," she had snapped at him.

Doug merely shook his head. "I wonder how the rest of the crew would feel if the Supreme Court ruled you have to go with them on the mission."

"I don't care!"

"And little Douggie. He'd sure miss his mother. Two and a half years is a long time. He won't even be five yet when the mission takes off."

She had no reply for that. Nothing except blind fury that masked a deeply hidden sense of guilt.

The Supreme Court refused to hear the case, although the news media splashed the story in lurid colors. Astronaut mother denied chance to be part of Mars crew. Space agency accused of anti-mother bias. Women's groups came to Debbie's aid. Other groups attacked her as an unfit mother who put her personal glory ahead of her son's needs.

Her work deteriorated. Sitting in front of her computer screen, scanning through her performance appraisals over the three years since the Mars crew selection, Debbie saw that the agency wasn't going to suffer grievously from her loss. She had gone into a tailspin, she had to admit.

They'll be happy to see me go, she thought. No wonder they don't even want me at mission control during the landing. They're afraid I'll screw up.

"Mommy?"

Douggie's voice startled her. She spun on her little typist's chair and saw her five-year-old standing uncertainly at the bedroom doorway.

"You know you're not allowed to bother me while I'm working, Douggie," she said coldly.

He's the reason I'm stuck here, she raged to herself. If it weren't for him I'd be on Mars right now, this instant, instead of looking at the wreckage of my career.

"I'm sorry, Mommy. Daddy said I should tell you."

"Tell me what?" she said impatiently. The boy was a miniature of his father: same eyes, same sandy hair. He even had that same slow, engaging grin. But now he looked frightened, almost ready to break into tears.

"Daddy says they're just about to land."

"I'm busy," she said. "You watch the landing with Daddy."

The boy seemed to draw up all his courage. "But you said you would watch it with me and 'splain what they're doing for me so I could tell all the kids in school all about it."

A little more gently, Debbie said, "But I'm busy here, honey."

"You promised."

"But . . ."

"You *promised*, Mommy."

Debbie didn't remember making any promises. She looked into her son's trusting eyes, though, and realized that he wasn't the reason she wasn't picked to go to Mars. It's not his fault, she realized. How could it be? Whatever's happened is my responsibility and nobody else's.

Her anger dissolved. She was almost sorry to see it go; it had been a bulwark that had propped her up for the past three years.

With a reluctant sigh she shut down her computer and headed off to the living room, her son's hand clasped in hers.

Los Angeles

"Luis!" Mr. Ricardo called as the teenagers scrambled for the classroom door the instant the bell sounded.

Luis scooped up his books and made his way through the small stampede up to the front of the classroom. He walked slowly, reluctantly. Nobody wanted his friends to think that he liked talking to the teacher.

Mr. Ricardo watched Luis approaching him like a prizefighter watches the guy coming out from the other corner. He looked tight around the mouth, like he was expecting trouble. Ricardo was only forty or so, but years of teaching high school had made an old man out of him. His wiry hair was all gray; there were wrinkles around his dark brown eyes.

But when Luis came up to him, the teacher broke into a friendly smile. "Have you made up your mind?" he asked.

Luis had been afraid that Ricardo would put him on the spot. He didn't know what to say.

"I don' know, Mr. R."

"Don't you want to do it?" Ricardo asked, sounding kind of disappointed; hurt, almost. "It's the opportunity of a lifetime."

"Yeah, I know. It'd be cool, but . . ." Luis couldn't tell him the rest, of course.

Ricardo's demanding eyes shifted from Luis to Jorge, loitering at the classroom door, watching them intently.

"He's going to get into a lot of trouble, you know," the teacher said. He kept his voice low but there was steel in it.

Luis shifted his books, shuffled his feet.

"There are only ten rigs available at the planetarium. I've reserved one. If you don't use it I'll have to let some other student have it."

"Why's it gotta be now?" Luis complained.

"Because they're landing now, *muchacho*! They're landing on Mars today! This afternoon!"

"Yeah . . ."

"Don't you want to participate in it?"

"Yeah, sure. I'd like to."

"Then let's go. We're wasting time."

Luis shook his head. "I got other things to do, man."

"Like running off with Jorge, eh?"

"Obligations," Luis muttered.

Instead of getting angry, as Luis expected, Ricardo sat on the edge of his desk and spoke earnestly to him.

"Luis, you're a very bright student. You have the brains to make something of yourself. But only if you use the brains God gave you in the right way. Going with Jorge is only going to get you into trouble. You know that, don't you?"

"I guess so."

"Then why don't you come with me to the planetarium? It could be the turning point of your whole life."

"Maybe," Luis conceded reluctantly. He knew for certain that if he went to the planetarium, Jorge would be furious. Sooner or later there would be a beating. Jorge had sent more than one kid to the hospital. Everybody knew that sooner or later Jorge was going to kill somebody; it was just a matter of time. He had no self-control once he started beating up on somebody.

"Are you afraid of Jorge?" Ricardo asked.

"No!" Luis said it automatically. It was a lie and they both knew it.

Ricardo smiled benignly. "Then there's no reason for you not to come to the planetarium with me. Is there?"

Luis's shoulders sagged. If I don't go with him he'll know I'm chicken. If I do go with him, Jorge's gonna pound the shit outta me.

Ricardo got to his feet and put one hand on Luis's shoulder. "Come on with me, Luis," he commanded. "There's a much bigger world out there and it's time you started seeing it."

They walked past Jorge, hanging in the hallway just outside the classroom door. Mr. Ricardo went past him as if he wasn't even there. Luis saw the expression on Jorge's face, though, and his knees could barely hold him up long enough to get to Ricardo's ancient Camaro.

Washington

The outer office of Senator O'Hara's walnut-panelled suite had been turned into something of a theater. All the desks had been pushed to one side of the generous room and the central section filled with folding chairs. Almost his entire staff was seated there, facing the big hologram plate that had been set up on the wall across from the windows. On a table to one side of the screen rested a single VR helmet, a set of data gloves, and the gray box of a computer.

The staff had been buzzing with anticipation when the senator pushed in through the hallway door. Instantly, though, all their talk stopped. They went silent, as if somebody had snapped off the audio.

All excited like a bunch of pissant children, the senator grumbled to himself. Half of 'em would vote in favor of another Mars mission, the young fools.

O'Hara snorted disdainfully as he wheeled up the central aisle among the chairs. Turning his powerchair smartly to face his staffers, he saw that they were trying to look as blank and uninvolved as possible. Like kids eager to see a forbidden video trying to mask their enthusiasm as long as he was watching them.

"I know what you all think," he said, his voice a grating bullfrog's croak. "Well, I'm going to surprise you."

And with that, he guided his chair to the VR rig and the two technicians, both women, standing by it.

"I'm going to use the rig myself," he announced to his staff. Their shock was visible. Even Kaiser looked surprised, the fat sycophant.

Chuckling, he went on, "This Mars hoopla is the biggest damned boondoggle pulled over on the American taxpayer since the days of the Apollo project. But if *anybody* in this room plugs himself into the landing, it's going to be me."

Kaiser looked especially crestfallen. He's the one who won the lottery, Senator O'Hara figured. Thought you'd be the one to plug in, did you? O'Hara chuckled inwardly at the disappointment on his aide's face.

"You all can see what I'm experiencing on the hologram screen," the senator said as the technicians began to help him worm his bony, emaciated hands into the data gloves.

An unhappy murmuring filled the room.

"I've always said that this Mars business is hooey. I want to experience it for myself—see what these fancy astronauts and scientists are actually going to *do* up there—so's nobody can say that I haven't given the opposition every possible opportunity to show me their point of view."

One of the technicians slipped the helmet over the senator's head. He stopped her from sliding down the visor long enough to say, "I always give the other side a fair break. Then I wallop 'em!"

The visor came down and for a brief, terrifying moment he was in utter darkness.

Phoenix

For nearly half an hour the oversized TV screen had been split between a newscaster chattering away and an unmoving scene of a rusty-red, rock-strewn landscape of Sinai Planum on Mars. Zacharias kept pacing back and forth in the back of the big room, while his guests seemed to edge closer and closer to the giant screen.

"We are seeing Mars as it was some eleven minutes ago," the newscaster intoned solemnly, "since the red planet is so distant from Earth that it takes that long for television signals to reach us."

"He's only told us that twenty-six times in the past five minutes," somebody in the crowd muttered.

"Hush! They should be coming down any moment now."

"According to the mission schedule," the newscaster went on, "and taking into account the lag in signal transmission time, we should be seeing the parachute of the landing craft within seconds."

The unmanned landers had been on the ground for days, Zacharias knew, automatically preparing the base camp for the ten astronauts and scientists of the landing team. Over the past half hour the news broadcast had shown the big plastic bubble of the main tent, the four unmanned landers scattered around it, and the relatively clear, level section of the Sinai plain where the crewed landing craft would put down.

If all went well.

No sonic boom, Zack knew. The Martian air's too thin and the lander slows down too high up, anyway. The aerobrake should have deployed by now; the glow from the heat shield should be visible, if only they had programmed the cameras to look for it.

What am I saying? he asked himself, annoyed, nervous. It all happened eleven minutes ago. They're on the ground by now. Or dead.

"There it is!" the announcer yelped.

The crowd of guests surged forward toward the TV screen. Zacharias was drawn, too, despite himself. He remembered the two launch failures that he had witnessed. Put the project back years; almost killed it. After the second he vowed never to watch a rocket launch again.

Yet now he stared like any gaping tourist at the TV image of a beautiful white parachute against the butterscotch Martian sky. He was glad that the meteorologists had been able to learn how to predict the planet-wide dust storms that turned the sky pink for months afterward. They had timed the landing for the calmest possible weather.

The chute grew until he could see the lander beneath it, swaying slightly, like a big ungainly cylinder of polished aluminum.

They all knew that the landing craft would jettison the chute at a preset altitude but they all gasped nonetheless. The lander plummeted downward and Zack's heart constricted beneath his ribs.

Then the landing rockets fired, barely visible in the TV cameras, and the craft slowed. It came down gracefully, with dignity, kicking up a miniature sandstorm of its own as its spraddling legs extended and their circular footpads touched gently the iron rust sands of Mars.

Everyone in the big rec room cheered. All except Zack, who pushed his way to the bar. He felt badly in need of fortification.

Houston

"Nuthin's happ'nin," Douggie complained. "Can't I watch *Surfer Morphs?*"

"Wait a minute," his father said easily. "They're just waiting for the dust to settle and the rocket nozzles to cool down."

Debbie saw the two virtual reality helmets on the coffee table in front of them. Two pairs of gloves, also. Doug and Douggie can use them, she thought. Not me.

"Look!" the child cried. "The door's open!"

That should be me, Debbie thought as she watched the twelve-person team file down the lander's impossibly slim ladder to set their booted feet on the surface of Mars. I should be with them.

Douggie was quickly bored with their pretentious speeches: Men and women from nine different nations, each of them pronouncing a statement written by teams of public relations experts and government bureaucrats. Debbie felt bored, too.

But then, "Two of us have virtual reality sensors built into our helmets and gloves," said Philip Daguerre, the astronaut who commanded the ground team.

Debbie had almost had an affair with the handsome French Canadian. Would things have worked out differently if I'd had a fling with him? Probably not. She knew of three other women who had, and all three of them were still as Earthbound as she.

"Once we activate the VR system, those of you on Earth who have the proper equipment will be able to see what we see, feel what we feel, experience what we experience as we make our first excursion onto the surface of Mars."

Doug picked up one of the VR helmets.

"Can't I watch *Surfer Morphs?*" their son whined.

Los Angeles

It wasn't until Mr. Ricardo handed him the VR helmet that Luis realized his teacher had sacrificed his own chance to experience the Mars team's first excursion.

There were only ten VR rigs in the whole planetarium theater. The nine others were already taken by adults. Maybe they were college students, Luis thought; they looked young enough to be, even though almost everybody else in the big circular room was his teacher's age or older.

"Don't you want it?" Luis asked Ricardo.

His teacher made a strange smile. "It's for you, Luis. Put it on."

He thinks he's doin' me a big favor, Luis thought. He don' know that Jorge's gonna beat the crap outta me for this. Or maybe he knows an' don' care.

With trembling hands, Luis slipped the helmet over his head, then worked the bristly gloves onto his hands. Ricardo still had that strange, almost sickly smile as he slid the helmet's visor down, shutting out Luis's view.

As he sat there in utter darkness he heard Ricardo's voice, muffled by the helmet, say, "Enjoy yourself, Luis."

Yeah, Luis thought. Might as well enjoy myself. I'm sure gonna pay for this later on.

Washington

Senator O'Hara held his breath. All he could hear from inside the darkness of the helmet was the faint chugging of his heart pump. It was beating fast, for some reason.

He didn't want to seem cowardly in front of his entire staff, but the dark and the closeness of the visor over his face was stifling him, choking him. He wanted to cry out, to yank the damned helmet off and be done with it.

With the abruptness of an eyeblink he was suddenly looking out at a flat plain of rust red. Rocks and boulders were littered everywhere like toys scattered by an army of thoughtless children. The sky was a strange butterscotch color, not quite pink, not quite tan. A soft hushing sound filled his ears, like a distant whisper.

"That's the wind," said a disembodied voice. "It's blowing a stiff ninety knots, according to our instruments, but the air here is so thin that I can't feel it at all."

I'm on Mars! the senator said to himself. It's almost like actually being there in person.

Phoenix

It's just like we expected it to be, Jerome Zacharias thought. We could have saved a lot of money by just sending automated probes.

"Over that horizon several hundred kilometers," Valerii Mikoyan was saying in flat Midwestern American English, "lies the Tharsis bulge and the giant shield volcanoes, which we will explore by remote-controlled gliders and balloons later in this mission. And in *this* direction . . ."

Zack's view shifted across the landscape quickly enough to make him feel a moment of giddiness.

". . . just over that line of low hills, is the Valles Marineris. We are going to ride the rover there as soon as the vehicle is checked out."

Why don't I feel excited? Zack asked himself. I'm like a kid on Christmas morning, after all the presents have been unwrapped.

Houston

For a moment Debbie was startled when Doug solemnly picked up one of the VR helmets and put it on her, like a high priest crowning a new queen.

She was sitting in the springy little metal jump seat of the cross-country rover, her hands running along the control board, checking out all its systems. Solar panels okay. Transformers. Backup fuel cells. Sensors on and running. Communications gear in the green.

"Okay," said the astronaut driving the buggy. "We are ready to roll." It might as well have been her own voice, Debbie thought.

"Clear for canyon excursion," came the mission controller's voice in her earphones. The mission controller was up in the command spacecraft, hanging high above the Plain of Sinai in a synchronous orbit.

With transmission delays of ten to twenty minutes, mission control of the Mars expedition could not be on Earth; it had to be right there, on the scene.

"Go for sightseeing tour," Debbie acknowledged. "The bus is leaving."

Los Angeles

Luis watched the buggy depart the base area. But only for a moment. He had work to do. He was a geologist, he heard in his earphones, and his job was to take as wide a sampling of rocks as he could and pack them away in one of the return craft.

"First we photograph the field we're going to work in." Luis felt a square object in his left hand, then saw a digital camera. He held it up to the visor of his helmet, sighted, and clicked.

"What we're going to be doing is to collect what's called contingency samples," the geologist was saying. "We want to get them aboard a return vehicle right away, the first few hours on the surface, so that if anything happens to force us to make an unscheduled departure, we'll have a decent sampling of surface materials to take back with us."

At first Luis had found it confusing to hear the guy's voice in his head when it looked like he himself was walking around on Mars and picking up the rocks. He could *feel* them in his hands! Feel their heft, the grittiness of their surfaces. It was like the first time he had tried acid; he'd been inside his own head and outside, looking back at himself, both at the same time. That shook him up so much he had never dropped acid again.

But this was kind of different. Fun. He was the frigging geologist. He was there on Mars. He was doing something. Something worthwhile.

Washington

Collecting rocks, Senator O'Hara growled inwardly. We've spent a hundred billion dollars so some pointy-headed scientists can add to their rock collection. Oh, am I ever going to crucify them as soon as the committee reconvenes!

Phoenix

Zack felt as if he were jouncing and banging inside the surface rover as it trundled across the Martian landscape. He knew he was sitting in a comfortable rocking chair in his big library/bar/entertainment room. Yet he was looking out at Mars through the windshield of the rover. His hands were on its controls and he could feel every shudder and bounce of the six-wheeled vehicle.

But there's nothing out there that we haven't already seen with the unmanned landers, Zack told himself, with mounting despair. We've even brought back samples, under remote control. What are the humans on this expedition going to be able to accomplish that will be worth the cost of sending them?

Houston

Easy now, Debbie told herself. Don't let yourself get carried away. You're *not* on Mars. You're sitting in your own living room.

Los Angeles

Luis could feel the weight of the rock. It was much lighter than a rock that size would be on Earth. And red, like rust. Holding it in his left hand, he chipped at it with the hammer in his right.

"Just want to check the interior," he heard the geologist say, as if he were saying it himself.

The rock cracked in two. Luis saw a tracery of fine lines honeycombing the rock's insides.

"Huh. Never saw anything like that before." And the geologist/Luis carefully put both halves of the split rock into a container, sealed it, then marked with a pen its location in the photograph of the area he had taken when he had started collecting.

This is fun, Luis realized. I wish I could do it for real. Like, be a real astronaut or scientist. But reality was something very different. Jorge was reality. Yeah, Luis said to himself, I could be on Mars myself someday. If Jorge don' kill me first.

Washington

Bored with the rock-sampling task, Senator O'Hara lifted the visor of his VR helmet.

"Get me out of this rig," he told the two startled technicians. Turning to Kaiser, he said, "You can try it if you like. I'm going into my office for a drink."

Phoenix

The ground was rising slightly as the rover rolled along. "Should be at the rim in less than a minute," the driver said.

Zack felt his hand ease back on the throttle slightly. "Don't want to fall over. It's a long way down."

Nothing ahead of them but the dull, rock-strewn ground and the butterscotch sky.

Houston

Debbie checked the time line on the dashboard computer screen and slowed the rover even more. "We ought to be just about . . . there!"

The rim of the grandest canyon in the solar system sliced across her field of view. Craning her neck slightly, she could see the cliffs tumbling away, down and down and down, toward the valley floor miles below.

Phoenix

Mist! The floor of the valley was wreathed in mists that wafted and undulated slowly, rising and falling as Zack watched.

It's the wrong time of the year for mists to form, he knew. We've never seen this before.

As far as the eye could see, for dozens of miles, hundreds of miles, the mist billowed softly, gently along the floor of Valles Marineris. The canyon was so wide that he could not see the opposite wall; it was beyond the horizon. Nothing but gentle, whitish mist. Clouds of mystery. Clouds of excitement.

My gosh, Zack thought, do they extend the whole three-thousand-mile length of the valley?

Los Angeles

Luis roamed across the rust-colored sandy landscape, staring at more rocks than he had ever seen in his whole life. Some the size of pebbles, a few bigger than a man. How'd they get there? Where'd they come from?

And what was over the horizon? The geologist said something about big volcanoes and mountains higher than anything on Earth. Luis thought it'd be great to see them, maybe climb them.

Houston

Debbie stared at the mists billowing along the valley floor. They seemed to be breathing, like something alive. They've got to be water vapor, she thought. Got to be! And where there's water there could be life. Maybe. Maybe.

We've got to get down onto the valley floor. Got to!

Phoenix

Zack felt like a child, the first time his father had taken him up in a helicopter. The higher they went, the more there was to see. The more he saw, the more eager he was to see more.

Staring out at the mist-shrouded rift valley, he finally realized that this was the difference between human explorers and machines. What's beyond the horizon? What's beneath those mists? He wanted to know, to explore. He *had to* seek the answers.

He realized he was crying, tears of joy and wonder streaming down his cheeks. He was glad that none of the others could see it, inside the VR helmet, but he knew that neither embarrassment nor disapproval mattered in the slightest. What's beyond the horizon? That was the eternal question and the only thing that really counted.

Los Angeles

Yeah, this is great, Luis thought. For these guys. For scientists and astronauts. It's their life. But it's not for me. When I leave here tonight it's back to the 'hood and Jorge and all that crap.

Then a powerful surge of new emotion rose within him. Why can't I go to Mars for real someday? Mr. Ricardo says I'm smart enough to get a scholarship to college.

Fuck Jorge. Let him do what he wants to me. I'll fight him back. I'll kick the shit outta him if that's what I gotta do to get to Mars. He'll have to kill me to keep me away from this.

Washington

Senator O'Hara was mixing his third martini when Kaiser came in, looking bleary-eyed.

"You been in the VR rig all this time?" O'Hara asked. He knew Kaiser did not drink, so he didn't bother offering his aide anything.

"Mostly," the pudgy little man said. O'Hara could see his aide's bald head was gleaming with perspiration.

"Bad enough we have to waste a hundred billion on this damned nonsense. Is it going to tie up my entire staff for the rest of the day?"

"And then some," Kaiser said, heading for the bar behind the senator's desk.

O'Hara watched, dumbfounded, as his aide poured himself a stiff belt of whiskey.

He swallowed, coughed, then swallowed again. With tears in his eyes, he went to the leather sofa along the side wall of the office and sat down like a very tired man.

O'Hara stared at him.

Holding the heavy crystal glass in both hands, Kaiser said, "You're going to have to change your stand on this Mars business."

"What?"

"You've got to stop opposing it."

"Are you crazy?"

"No, but you'd be crazy to try to stand against it now," Kaiser said, more firmly than the senator had ever heard him speak before.

"You're drunk."

"Maybe I am. I've been on Mars, Teddy. I've stood on fuckin' *Mars!*"

Kaiser had never used the senator's first name before, let alone called him "Teddy."

"You'd just better watch your tongue," O'Hara growled.

"And you'd better watch your ass," Kaiser snapped. "Do you have any idea of how many people are experiencing this Mars landing? Not just watching it, but *experiencing* it—as if they were there."

O'Hara shrugged. "Twenty million, maybe."

"I made a couple of phone calls before I came in here. Thirty-six million VR sets in the U.S., and that's not counting laboratories and training simulators. There must be more than thirty million voters on Mars right now."

"Bullcrap."

"Yeah? By tomorrow there won't be a VR rig left in the stores. Everybody's going to want to be on Mars."

O'Hara made a sour face.

"I'll bet that half the voters in dear old Pennsylvania are on Mars right this instant. You try telling them it's all a waste of money."

"But it is!" the senator insisted. "The biggest waste of taxpayer funds since SDI."

"It might be," Kaiser said, somewhat more moderately. "You might be entirely right and everybody else totally wrong. But if you vote that way in the committee you'll get your ass whipped in November."

"You told me just the opposite no more'n ten days ago. The polls show—"

"The polls are going to swing around one hundred and eighty degrees. Guaranteed."

O'Hara glared at his aide.

"Trust me on this, Teddy. I've never let you down before, have I? Vote for continued Mars exploration or go out and find honest work."

Houston

With enormous reluctance, Debbie pulled the helmet off and removed the data gloves. Doug was still in his rig, totally absorbed. He might as well be on Mars for real, Debbie thought.

Shakily, she got up from the living room sofa and went to Douggie's room. Her son was watching three-dimensional cartoons.

"Come with me, young man," she said in her not-to-be-argued-with voice. The boy made a face, but turned off his 3D set and marched into the living room with his mother.

She helped him into the gloves and helmet.

"Aw, Ma," he whined, "do I hafta?"

"Yes," she whispered to her son. "In a few years, you would never forgive yourself if you didn't."

And she left her son and her husband on Mars and went back to her computer to erase her letter of resignation.

There's a lot of work to be done, she told herself. The exploration of Mars is just beginning.

I believe it was Michelangelo (or maybe Rodin?) who said that the finished sculpture is waiting inside the raw stone; the sculptor's task is to remove the overlying layers and reveal the sculpture to our waiting eyes.

It works that way for writing fiction, as well. The finished story is there, deep inside the writer's mind. The physical labor of writing is the task of revealing the story in its finished form.

When I first wrote "Sepulcher" I had no idea it was part of the Grand Tour. The billionaire who brought Elverda Apacheta to the asteroid and its alien artifact was not named Martin Humphries. Only years afterward did I understand that it was indeed Humphries, and this short tale is not only a part of the Asteroid Wars, it is a pivotal moment in the ongoing saga of the Grand Tour itself.

SEPULCHER

was a soldier," he said. "Now I am a priest. You may call me Dorn."

Elverda Apacheta could not help staring at him. She had seen cyborgs before, but this . . . person seemed more machine than man. She felt a chill ripple of contempt along her veins. How could a human being allow his body to be disfigured so?

He was not tall; Elverda herself stood several centimeters taller than he. His shoulders were quite broad, though; his torso thick and solid. The left side of his face was engraved metal, as was the entire top of his head: Like a skullcap made of finest etched steel.

Dorn's left hand was prosthetic. He made no attempt to disguise it. Beneath the rough fabric of his shabby tunic and threadbare trousers, how much more of him was metal and electrical machinery? Tattered though his clothing was, his calf-length boots were polished to a high gloss.

"A priest?" asked Martin Humphries. "Of what church? What order?"

The half of Dorn's lips that could move made a slight curl. A smile or a sneer, Elverda could not tell.

"I will show you to your quarters," said Dorn. His voice was a low rumble, as if it came from the belly of a beast. It echoed faintly off the walls of rough-hewn rock.

Humphries looked briefly surprised. He was not accustomed to having his questions ignored. Elverda watched his face. Humphries was as handsome as cosmetic surgery could make a person appear: chiselled features, earnest sky-blue eyes, straight of spine, long of limb, athletically flat midsection. Yet there was a faint smell of corruption about him, Elverda thought. As if he were dead inside and already beginning to rot.

The tension between the two men seemed to drain the energy from Elverda's aged body. "It has been a long journey," she said. "I am very tired. I would welcome a hot shower and a long nap."

"Before you see it?" Humphries snapped.

"It has taken us months to get here. We can wait a few hours more." Inwardly she marveled at her own words. Once she would have been all fiery excitement. Have the years taught you patience? No, she realized. Only weariness.

"Not me!" Humphries said. Turning to Dorn, "Take me to it now. I've waited long enough. I want to see it now."

Dorn's eyes, one as brown as Elverda's own, the other a red electronic glow, regarded Humphries for a lengthening moment.

"Well?" Humphries demanded.

"I am afraid, sir, that the chamber is sealed for the next twelve hours. It will be imposs—"

"Sealed? By whom? On whose authority?"

"The chamber is self-controlled. Whoever made the artifact installed the controls, as well."

"No one told me about that," said Humphries.

Dorn replied, "Your quarters are down this corridor."

He turned almost like a solid block of metal, shoulders and hips together, head unmoving on those wide shoulders, and started down the central corridor. Elverda fell in step alongside his metal half, still angered at his self-desecration. Yet despite herself, she thought of what a challenge it would be to sculpt him. If I were younger, she told herself. If I were not so close to death. Human and inhuman, all in one strangely fierce figure.

Humphries came up on Dorn's other side, his face red with barely-suppressed anger.

They walked down the corridor in silence, Humphries's weighted shoes clicking against the uneven rock floor. Dorn's boots made hardly any noise at all. Half machine he may be, Elverda thought, but once in motion he moves like a panther.

The asteroid's inherent gravity was so slight that Humphries needed the weighted footgear to keep himself from stumbling ridiculously. Elverda, who had spent most of her long life in low-gravity environments, felt completely at home. The corridor they were walking through was actually a tunnel, shadowy and mysterious, or perhaps a natural chimney vented through the rocky body by escaping gases eons ago when the asteroid was still molten. Now it was cold, chill enough to make Elverda shudder. The rough ceiling was so low she wanted to stoop, even though the rational side of her mind knew it was not necessary.

Soon, though, the walls smoothed out and the ceiling grew higher. Humans had extended the tunnel, squaring it with laser precision. Doors lined both walls now and the ceiling glowed with glareless, shadowless light. Still she hugged herself against the chill that the others did not seem to notice.

They stopped at a wide double door. Dorn tapped out the entrance code on the panel set into the wall and the doors slid open.

"Your quarters, sir," he said to Humphries. "You may, of course, change the privacy code to suit yourself."

Humphries gave a curt nod and strode through the open doorway. Elverda got a glimpse of a spacious suite, carpeting on the floor, and hologram windows on the walls.

Humphries turned in the doorway to face them. "I expect you to call for me in twelve hours," he said to Dorn, his voice hard.

"Eleven hours and fifty-seven minutes," Dorn replied.

Humphries's nostrils flared and he slid the double doors shut.

"This way." Dorn gestured with his human hand. "I'm afraid your quarters are not as sumptuous as Mr. Humphries's."

Elverda said, "I am his guest. He is paying all the bills."

"You are a great artist. I have heard of you."

"Thank you."

"For the truth? That is not necessary."

I was a great artist, Elverda said to herself. Once. Long ago. Now I am an old woman waiting for death.

Aloud, she asked, "Have you seen my work?"

Dorn's voice grew heavier. "Only holograms. Once I set out to see *The Rememberer* for myself, but—other matters intervened."

"You were a soldier then?"

"Yes. I have only been a priest since coming to this place."

Elverda wanted to ask him more, but Dorn stopped before a blank door and opened it for her. For an instant she thought he was going to reach for her with his prosthetic hand. She shrank away from him.

"I will call for you in eleven hours and fifty-six minutes," he said, as if he had not noticed her revulsion.

"Thank you."

He turned away, like a machine pivoting.

"Wait," Elverda called. "Please. . . . How many others are here? Everything seems so quiet."

"There are no others. Only the three of us."

"But—"

"I am in charge of the security brigade. I ordered the others of my command to go back to our spacecraft and wait there."

"And the scientists? The prospector family that found this asteroid?"

"They are in Mr. Humphries's spacecraft, the one you arrived in," said Dorn. "Under the protection of my brigade."

Elverda looked into his eyes. Whatever burned in them, she could not fathom.

"Then we are alone here?"

Dorn nodded solemnly. "You and me—and Mr. Humphries, who pays all the bills." The human half of his face remained as immobile as the metal. Elverda could not tell if he was trying to be humorous or bitter.

"Thank you," she said. He turned away and she closed the door.

Her quarters consisted of a single room, comfortably warm but hardly larger than the compartment on the ship they had come in. Elverda saw that her meager travel bag was already sitting on the bed, her worn old drawing computer resting in its travel-smudged case on the desk. Elverda stared at the computer case as if it were accusing her. I should have left it at home, she thought. I will never use it again.

A small utility robot, hardly more than a glistening drum of metal and six gleaming arms folded like a praying mantis's, stood mutely in the farthest corner. Elverda stared at it. At least it was entirely a machine; not a self-mutilated human being. To take the most beautiful form in the universe and turn it into a hybrid mechanism, a travesty of humanity. Why did he do it? So he could be a better soldier? A more efficient killing machine?

And why did he send all the others away? she asked herself while she opened the travel bag. As she carried her toiletries to the narrow alcove of the bathroom, a new thought struck her. Did he send them away before he saw the artifact, or afterward? Has he even seen it? Perhaps . . .

Then she saw her reflection in the mirror above the washbasin. Her heart sank. Once she had been called regal, stately, a goddess made of copper. Now she looked withered, dried up, bone thin, her face a geological map of too many years of living, her flight coveralls hanging limply on her emaciated frame.

You are old, she said to her image. Old and aching and tired.

It is the long trip, she told herself. You need to rest. But the other voice in her mind laughed scornfully. *You've done nothing but rest for the entire time it's taken to reach this piece of rock. You are ready for the permanent rest; why deny it?*

She had been teaching at the university on Luna, the closest she could get to Earth after a long lifetime of living in low-gravity environments. Close enough to see the world of her birth, the only world of life and warmth in the solar system, the only place where a person could walk out in the sunshine and feel its warmth soaking your bones, smell the fertile earth nurturing its bounty, feel a cool breeze plucking at your hair.

But she had separated herself from Earth permanently. She had stood at the shore of Titan's methane sea; from an orbiting spacecraft she had watched the surging clouds of Jupiter swirl their overpowering colors; she had carved the kilometer-long rock of *The Rememberer*. But she could no longer stand in the village of her birth, at the edge of the Pacific's booming surf, and watch the soft white clouds form shapes of imaginary animals.

Her creative life was long finished. She had lived too long; there were no friends left, and she had never had a family. There was no purpose to her life, no reason to do anything except go through the motions and wait. At the university she was no longer truly working at her art but helping students who had the fires of inspiration burning fresh and hot inside them. Her life was one of vain regrets for all the things she had not accomplished, for all the failures she could recall. Failures at love; those were the most bitter. She was praised as the solar system's greatest artist: The sculptress of *The Rememberer*, the creator of the first great ionospheric painting, *The Virgin of the Andes*. She was respected, but not loved. She felt empty, alone, barren. She had nothing to look forward to; absolutely nothing.

Then Martin Humphries swept into her existence. A lifetime younger, bold, vital, even ruthless, he stormed her academic tower with the news that an alien artifact had been discovered deep in the Asteroid Belt.

"It's some kind of art form," he said, desperate with excitement. "You've got to come with me and see it."

Trying to control the long-forgotten longing that stirred within her, Elverda had asked quietly, "Why do I have to go with you, Mr. Humphries? Why me? I'm an old wo—"

"You are the greatest artist of our time," he had snapped. "You've *got* to see this! Don't bullshit me with false modesty. You're the only other person in the whole whirling solar system who *deserves* to see it!"

"The only other person besides whom?" she had asked.

He had blinked with surprise. "Why, besides me, of course."

So now we are on this nameless asteroid, waiting to see the alien artwork. Just the three of us. The richest man in the solar system. An elderly artist who has outlived her usefulness. And a cyborg soldier who has cleared everyone else away.

He claims to be a priest, Elverda remembered. A priest who is half machine. She shivered as if a cold wind surged through her.

A harsh buzzing noise interrupted her thoughts. Looking into the main part of the room, Elverda saw that the phone screen was blinking red in rhythm to the buzzing.

"Phone," she called out.

Humphries's face appeared on the screen instantly. "Come to my quarters," he said. "We have to talk."

"Give me an hour. I need—"

"Now."

Elverda felt her brows rise haughtily. Then the strength sagged out of her. He has bought the right to command you, she told herself. He is quite capable of refusing to allow you to see the artifact.

"Now," she agreed.

Humphries was pacing across the plush carpeting when she arrived at his quarters. He had changed from his flight coveralls to a comfortably loose royal blue pullover and expensive genuine twill slacks. As the doors slid shut behind her, he stopped in front of a low couch and faced her squarely.

"Do you know who this Dorn creature is?"

Elverda answered, "Only what he has told us."

"I've checked him out. My staff in the ship has a complete file on him. He's the butcher who led the *Chrysalis* massacre, fourteen years ago."

"He . . ."

"Eleven hundred men, women, and children. Slaughtered. He was the man who commanded the attack."

"He said he had been a soldier."

"A mercenary. A cold-blooded murderer. He was working for Toyama then. The *Chrysalis* was their habitat. When its population voted for independence, Toyama put him in charge of a squad to bring them back into line. He killed them all; turned off their air and let them all die."

Elverda felt shakily for the nearest chair and sank into it. Her legs seemed to have lost all their strength.

"His name was Harbin then. Dorik Harbin."

"Wasn't he brought to trial?"

"No. He ran away. Disappeared. I always thought Toyama helped to hide him. They take care of their own, they do. He must have changed his name afterward. Nobody would hire the butcher, not even Toyama."

"His face . . . half his body . . ." Elverda felt terribly weak, almost faint. "When . . . ?"

"Must have been after he ran away. Maybe it was an attempt to disguise himself."

"And now he is working for you." She wanted to laugh at the irony of it, but did not have the strength.

"He's got us trapped on this chunk of rock! There's nobody else here except the three of us."

"You have your staff in your ship. Surely they would come if you summoned them."

"His security squad's been ordered to keep everybody except you and me off the asteroid. He gave those orders."

"You can countermand them, can't you?"

For the first time since she had met Martin Humphries, he looked unsure of himself. "I wonder," he said.

"Why?" Elverda asked. "Why is he doing this?"

"That's what I intend to find out." Humphries strode to the phone console. "Harbin!" he called. "Dorik Harbin. Come to my quarters at once."

Without even an eye blink's delay the phone's computer-synthesized voice replied, "Dorik Harbin no longer exists. Transferring your call to Dorn."

Humphries's blue eyes snapped at the phone's blank screen.

"Dorn is not available at present," the phone's voice said. "He will call for you in eleven hours and thirty-two minutes."

"God-*damn* it!" Humphries smacked a fist into the open palm of his other hand. "Get me the officer on watch aboard the *Humphries Eagle*."

"All exterior communications are inoperable at the present time," replied the phone.

"That's impossible!"

"All exterior communications are inoperable at the present time," the phone repeated, unperturbed.

Humphries stared at the empty screen, then turned slowly toward Elverda. "He's cut us off. We're really trapped here."

Elverda felt the chill of cold metal clutching at her. Perhaps Dorn is a madman, she thought. Perhaps he is my death, personified.

"We've got to do something!" Humphries nearly shouted.

Elverda rose shakily to her feet. "There is nothing that we can do, for the moment. I am going to my quarters and take a nap. I believe that Dorn, or Harbin or whatever his identity is, will call on us when he is ready to."

"And do what?"

"Show us the artifact," she replied, silently adding, I hope.

Legally, the artifact and the entire asteroid belonged to Humphries Space Systems. It had been discovered by a family—husband, wife, and two sons, ages five and three—that made a living from searching out iron-nickel asteroids and selling the mining rights to the big corporations. They filed their claim to this unnamed asteroid, together with a preliminary description of its ten-kilometer-wide shape, its orbit within the Asteroid Belt, and a sample analysis of its surface composition.

Six hours after their original transmission reached the commodities market computer network on Earth—while a fairly spirited bidding was going on among four major corporations for the asteroid's mineral rights—a new message arrived at the headquarters of the International Astronautical Authority, in Geneva. The message was garbled, fragmentary, obviously made in great haste and at fever excitement. There was an artifact of some sort in a cavern deep inside the asteroid.

One of the faceless bureaucrats buried deep within the IAA's multilayered organization sent an immediate message to an employee of Humphries Space Systems. The bureaucrat retired hours later, richer than he had any right to expect, while Martin Humphries personally contacted the prospectors and bought the asteroid outright for enough money to end their prospecting days forever. By the time the decision makers in the IAA realized that an alien artifact had been discovered they were faced with a fait accompli: The artifact, and the asteroid in which it resided, were the personal property of the richest man in the solar system.

Martin Humphries was not totally an egomaniac. Nor was he a fool.

Graciously he allowed the IAA to organize a team of scientists who would inspect this first specimen of alien existence. Even more graciously, Humphries offered to ferry the scientific investigators all the long way to the asteroid at his own expense. He made only one demand, and the IAA could hardly refuse him. He insisted that he see this artifact himself before the scientists were allowed to view it.

And he brought along the solar system's most honored and famous artist. To appraise the artifact's worth as an art object, he claimed. To determine how much he could deduct from his corporate taxes by donating the thing to the IAA, said his enemies. But during their voyage to the asteroid, Elverda came to the conclusion that buried deep beneath his ruthless business persona was an eager little boy who was tremendously excited at having found a new toy. A toy he intended to possess for himself. An art object, created by alien hands.

For an art object was what the artifact seemed to be. The family of prospectors continued to send back vague, almost irrational reports of what the artifact looked like. The reports were worthless. No two descriptions matched. If the man and woman were to be believed, the artifact did nothing but sit in the middle of a rough-hewn cavern. But they described it differently with every report they sent. It glowed with light. It was darker than deep space. It was a statue of some sort. It was formless. It overwhelmed the senses. It was small enough almost to pick up in one hand. It made the children laugh happily. It frightened their parents. When they tried to photograph it, their transmissions showed nothing but blank screens. Totally blank.

As Humphries listened to their maddening reports and waited impatiently for the IAA to organize its hand-picked team of scientists he ordered his security manager to get a squad of hired personnel to the asteroid as quickly as possible. From corporate facilities on Ceres and the moons of Mars, Humphries Space Systems efficiently brought together a brigade of experienced mercenary security troops. They reached the asteroid long before anyone else could, and were under orders to make certain that no one was allowed onto the asteroid before Martin Humphries himself reached it.

"The time has come."

Elverda woke slowly, painfully, like a swimmer struggling for the air and light of the surface. She had been dreaming of her childhood, of the village where she had grown up, the distant snow-capped Andes, the warm night breezes that spoke of love.

"The time has come."

It was Dorn's deep voice, whisper-soft. Startled, she flashed her eyes open. She was alone in the room, but Dorn's image filled the phone screen by her bed. The numbers glowing beneath the screen showed that it was indeed time.

"I am awake now," she said to the screen.

"I will be at your door in fifteen minutes," Dorn said. "Will that be enough time for you to prepare yourself?"

"Yes, plenty." The days when she needed time for selecting her clothing and arranging her appearance were long gone.

"In fifteen minutes, then."

"Wait," she blurted. "Can you see me?"

"No. Visual transmission must be keyed manually."

"I see."

"I do not."

A joke? Elverda sat up on the bed as Dorn's image winked out. Is he capable of humor?

She shrugged out of the shapeless coveralls she had worn to bed, took a quick shower, and pulled her best caftan from the travel bag. It was a deep midnight blue, scattered with glittering silver stars. Elverda had made the floor-length gown herself, from fabric woven by her mother long ago. She had painted the stars from her memory of what they had looked like from her native village.

As she slid back her front door she saw Dorn marching down the corridor with Humphries beside him. Despite his slightly longer legs, Humphries seemed to be scampering like a child to keep up with Dorn's steady, stolid steps.

"I *demand* that you reinstate communications with my ship," Humphries was saying, his voice echoing off the corridor's rock walls. "I'll dock your pay for every minute this insubordination continues!"

"It is a security measure," Dorn said calmly, without turning to look at the man. "It is for your own good."

"My own good? Who in hell are you to determine what my own good might be?"

Dorn stopped three paces short of Elverda, made a stiff little bow to her, and only then turned to face his employer.

"Sir: I have seen the artifact. You have not."

"And that makes you better than me?" Humphries almost snarled the words. "Holier, maybe?"

"No," said Dorn. "Not holier. Wiser."

Humphries started to reply, then thought better of it.

"Which way do we go?" Elverda asked in the sudden silence.

Dorn pointed with his prosthetic hand. "Down," he replied. "This way."

The corridor abruptly became a rugged tunnel again, with lights fastened at precisely spaced intervals along the low ceiling. Elverda watched Dorn's half-human face as the pools of shadow chased the highlights glinting off the etched metal, like the Moon racing through its phases every half minute, over and again.

Humphries had fallen silent as they followed the slanting tunnel downward into the heart of the rock. Elverda heard only the clicking of his shoes, at first, but by concentrating she was able to make out the softer footfalls of Dorn's padded boots and even the whisper of her own slippers.

The air seemed to grow warmer, closer. *Or is it my own anticipation?* She glanced at Humphries; perspiration beaded his upper lip. The man radiated tense expectation. Dorn glided a few steps ahead of them. He did not seem to be hurrying, yet he was now leading them down the tunnel, like an ancient priest leading two new acolytes—or sacrificial victims.

The tunnel ended in a smooth wall of dull metal.

"We are here."

"Open it up," Humphries demanded.

"It will open itself," replied Dorn. He waited a heartbeat, then added, "Now."

And the metal slid up into the rock above them as silently as if it were a curtain made of silk.

None of them moved. Then Dorn slowly turned toward the two of them and gestured with his human hand.

"The artifact lies twenty-two point nine meters beyond this point. The tunnel narrows and turns to the right. The chamber is large enough to accommodate only one person at a time, comfortably."

"Me first!" Humphries took a step forward.

Dorn stopped him with an upraised hand. The prosthetic hand. "I feel it my duty to caution you—"

Humphries tried to push the hand away; he could not budge it.

"When I first crossed this line, I was a soldier. After I saw the artifact I gave up my life."

"And became a self-styled priest. So what?"

"The artifact can change you. I thought it best that there be no witnesses to your first viewing of it, except for this gifted woman whom you have brought with you. When you first see it, it can be . . . traumatic."

Humphries's face twisted with a mixture of anger and disgust. "I'm not a mercenary killer. I don't have anything to be afraid of."

Dorn let his hand drop to his side with a faint whine of miniaturized servomotors.

"Perhaps not," he murmured, so low that Elverda barely heard it.

Humphries shouldered his way past the cyborg. "Stay here," he told Elverda. "You can see it when I come back."

He hurried down the tunnel, footsteps staccato.

Then silence.

Elverda looked at Dorn. The human side of his face seemed utterly weary.

"You have seen the artifact more than once, haven't you?"

"Fourteen times," he answered.

"It has not harmed you in any way, has it?"

He hesitated, then replied, "It has changed me. Each time I see it, it changes me more."

"You . . . you really are Dorik Harbin?"

"I was."

"Those people of the *Chrysalis* . . . ?"

"Dorik Harbin killed them all. Yes. There is no excuse for it, no pardon. It was the act of a monster."

"But why?"

"Monsters do monstrous things. Dorik Harbin ingested psychotropic drugs to increase his battle prowess. Afterward, when the battle drugs cleared from his bloodstream and he understood what he had done, Dorik Harbin held a grenade against his chest and set it off."

"Oh my god," Elverda whimpered.

"He was not allowed to die, however. The medical specialists rebuilt his body and he was given a false identity. For many years he lived a sham of life, hiding from the authorities, hiding from his own guilt. He no longer had the courage to kill himself; the pain of his first attempt was far stronger than his own self-loathing. Then he was hired to come to this place. Dorik Harbin looked upon the artifact for the first time, and his true identity emerged at last."

Elverda heard a scuffling sound, like feet dragging, staggering. Martin Humphries came into view, tottering, leaning heavily against the wall of the tunnel, slumping as if his legs could no longer hold him.

"No man . . . no one . . ." He pushed himself forward and collapsed into Dorn's arms.

"Destroy it!" he whispered harshly, spittle dribbling down his chin. "Destroy this whole damned piece of rock! Wipe it out of existence!"

"What is it?" Elverda asked. "What did you see?"

Dorn lowered him to the ground gently. Humphries's feet scrabbled against the rock as if he were trying to run away. Sweat covered his face, soaked his shirt.

"It's . . . beyond . . ." he babbled. "More . . . than anyone can . . . nobody could stand it . . ."

Elverda sank to her knees beside him. "What has happened to him?" She looked up at Dorn, who knelt on Humphries's other side.

"The artifact."

Humphries suddenly ranted, "They'll find out about me! Everyone will know! It's got to be destroyed! Nuke it! Blast it to bits!" His fists windmilled in the air, his eyes were wild.

"I tried to warn him," Dorn said as he held Humphries's shoulders down, the man's head in his lap. "I tried to prepare him for it."

"What did he see?" Elverda's heart was pounding; she could hear it thundering in her ears. "What is it? What did *you* see?"

Dorn shook his head slowly. "I cannot describe it. I doubt that anyone could describe it—except, perhaps, an artist: A person who has trained herself to see the truth."

"The prospectors—they saw it. Even their children saw it."

"Yes. When I arrived here they had spent eighteen days in the chamber. They left it only when the chamber closed itself. They ate and slept and returned here, as if hypnotized."

"It did not hurt them, did it?"

"They were emaciated, dehydrated. It took a dozen of my strongest men to remove them to my ship. Even the children fought us."

"But—how could . . ." Elverda's voice faded into silence. She looked at the brightly lit tunnel. Her breath caught in her throat.

"Destroy it," Humphries mumbled. "Destroy it before it destroys us!

Don't let them find out. They'll know, they'll know, they'll all know." He began to sob uncontrollably.

"You do not have to see it," Dorn said to Elverda. "You can return to your ship and leave this place."

Leave, urged a voice inside her head. Run away. Live out what's left of your life and let it go.

Then she heard her own voice say, as if from a far distance, "I've come such a long way."

"It will change you," he warned.

"Will it release me from life?"

Dorn glanced down at Humphries, still muttering darkly, then returned his gaze to Elverda.

"It will change you," he repeated.

Elverda forced herself to her feet. Leaning one hand against the warm rock wall to steady herself, she said, "I will see it. I must."

"Yes," said Dorn. "I understand."

She looked down at him, still kneeling with Humphries's head resting in his lap. Dorn's electronic eye glowed red in the shadows. His human eye was hidden in darkness.

He said, "I believe your people say, *Vaya con Dios*."

Elverda smiled at him. She had not heard that phrase in forty years. "Yes. You, too. *Vaya con Dios*." She turned and stepped across the faint groove where the metal door had met the floor.

The tunnel sloped downward only slightly. It turned sharply to the right, Elverda saw, just as Dorn had told them. The light seemed brighter beyond the turn, pulsating almost, like a living heart.

She hesitated a moment before making that final turn. What lay beyond? What difference, she answered herself. You have lived so long that you have emptied life of all its purpose. But she knew she was lying to herself. Her life was devoid of purpose because she herself had made it that way. She had spurned love; she had even rejected friendship when it had been offered. Still, she realized that she wanted to live. Desperately, she wanted to continue living no matter what.

Yet she could not resist the lure. Straightening her spine, she stepped boldly around the bend in the tunnel.

The light was so bright it hurt her eyes. She raised a hand to her brow to shield them and the intensity seemed to decrease slightly, enough to make out the faint outline of a form, a shape, a person . . .

Elverda gasped with recognition. A few meters before her, close enough to reach and touch, her mother sat on the sweet grass beneath the warm summer sun, gently rocking her baby and crooning softly to it.

Mamma! she cried silently. Mamma. The baby—Elverda herself— looked up into her mother's face and smiled.

And the mother was Elverda, a young and radiant Elverda, smiling down at the baby she had never had, tender and loving as she had never been.

Something gave way inside her. There was no pain; rather, it was as if a pain that had throbbed sullenly within her for too many years to count suddenly faded away. As if a wall of implacable ice finally melted and let the warm waters of life flow through her.

Elverda sank to the floor, crying, gushing tears of understanding and relief and gratitude. Her mother smiled at her.

"I love you, Mamma," she whispered. "I love you."

Her mother nodded and became Elverda herself once more. Her baby made a gurgling laugh of pure happiness, fat little feet waving in the air.

The image wavered, dimmed, and slowly faded into emptiness. Elverda sat on the bare rock floor in utter darkness, feeling a strange serenity and understanding warming her soul.

"Are you all right?"

Dorn's voice did not startle her. She had been expecting him to come to her.

"The chamber will close itself in another few minutes," he said. "We will have to leave."

Elverda took his offered hand and rose to her feet. She felt strong, fully in control of herself.

The tunnel outside the chamber was empty.

"Where is Humphries?"

"I sedated him and then called in a medical team to take him back to his ship."

"He wants to destroy the artifact," Elverda said.

"That will not be possible," said Dorn. "I will bring the IAA scientists here from the ship before Humphries awakes and recovers. Once they see the artifact they will not allow it to be destroyed. Humphries may own the asteroid, but the IAA will exert control over the artifact."

"The artifact will affect them—strangely."

"No two of them will be affected in the same manner," said Dorn. "And none of them will permit it to be damaged in any way."

"Humphries will not be pleased with you."

He gestured up the tunnel, and they began to walk back toward their quarters.

"Nor with you," Dorn said. "We both saw him babbling and blubbering like a baby."

"What could he have seen?"

"What he most feared. His whole life has been driven by fear, poor man."

"What secrets he must be hiding!"

"He hid them from himself. The artifact showed him his own true nature."

"No wonder he wants it destroyed."

"He cannot destroy the artifact, but he will certainly want to destroy us. Once he recovers his composure he will want to wipe out the witnesses who saw his reaction to it."

Elverda knew that Dorn was right. She watched his face as they passed beneath the lights, watched the glint of the etched metal, the warmth of the human flesh.

"You knew that he would react this way, didn't you?" she asked.

"No one could be as rich as he is without having demons driving him. He looked into his own soul and recognized himself for the first time in his life."

"You planned it this way!"

"Perhaps I did," he said. "Perhaps the artifact did it for me."

"How could—"

"It is a powerful experience. After I had seen it a few times I felt it was offering me . . ." he hesitated, then spoke the word, "salvation."

Elverda saw something in his face that Dorn had not let show before. She stopped in the shadows between overhead lights. Dorn turned to face her, half machine, standing in the rough tunnel of bare rock.

"You have had your own encounter with it," he said. "You understand now how it can transform you."

"Yes," said Elverda. "I understand."

"After a few times, I came to the realization that there must be thousands of my fellow mercenaries, killed in engagements all through the

Asteroid Belt, still lying where they fell. Or worse yet, floating forever in space, alone, unattended, ungrieved for."

"Thousands of mercenaries?"

"The corporations do not always settle their differences in Earthly courts of law," said Dorn. "There have been many battles out here. Wars that we paid for with our blood."

"Thousands?" Elverda repeated. "I knew that there had been occasional fights out here—but wars? I don't think anyone on Earth knows it's been so brutal."

"Men like Humphries know. They start the wars, and people like me fight them. Exiles, never allowed to return to Earth again once we take the mercenary's pay."

"All those men—killed."

Dorn nodded. "And women. And children, too. The artifact made me see that it was my duty to find each of those forgotten bodies and give each one a decent final rite. The artifact seemed to be telling me that this was the path of my atonement."

"Your salvation," she murmured.

"I see now, however, that I underestimated the situation."

"How?"

"Humphries. While I am out there searching for the bodies of the slain, he will have me killed."

"No! That's wrong!"

Dorn's deep voice was empty of regret. "It will be simple for him to send a team after me. In the depths of dark space, they will murder me. What I failed to do for myself, Humphries will do for me. He will be my final atonement."

"Never!" Elverda blazed with anger. "I will not permit it to happen."

"Your own life is in danger from him," Dorn said.

"What of it? I am an old woman, ready for death."

"Are you?"

"I was . . . until I saw the artifact."

"Now life is more precious to you, isn't it?"

"I don't want you to die," Elverda said. "You have atoned for your sins. You have borne enough pain."

He looked away, then started up the tunnel again.

"You are forgetting one important factor," Elverda called after him.

Dorn stopped, his back to her. She realized now that the clothes he wore had been his military uniform. He had torn all the insignias and pockets from it.

"The artifact. Who created it? And why?"

Turning back toward her, Dorn answered, "Alien visitors to our solar system created it, unknown ages ago. As to why—you tell me: Why does someone create a work of art?"

"Why would aliens create a work of art that affects human minds?"

Dorn's human eye blinked. He rocked a step backward.

"How could they create an artifact that is a mirror to our souls?" Elverda asked, stepping toward him. "They must have known something about us. They must have been here when there were human beings existing on Earth."

Dorn regarded her silently.

"They may have been here much more recently than you think," Elverda went on, coming closer to him. "They may have placed this artifact here to *communicate* with us."

"Communicate?"

"Perhaps it is a very subtle, very powerful communications device."

"Not an artwork at all."

"Oh yes, of course it is truly an artwork. All works of art are communications devices, for those who possess the soul to understand."

Dorn seemed to ponder this for long moments. Elverda watched his solemn face, searching for some human expression.

Finally he said, "That does not change my mission, even if it is true."

"Yes it does," Elverda said, eager to save him. "Your mission is to preserve and protect this artifact against Humphries and anyone else who would try to destroy it—or pervert it to his own use."

"The dead call to me," Dorn said solemnly. "I hear them in my dreams now."

"But why be alone in your mission? Let others help you. There must be other mercenaries who feel as you do."

"Perhaps," he said softly.

"Your true mission is much greater than you think," Elverda said, trembling with new understanding. "You have the power to end the wars that have destroyed your comrades, that have almost destroyed your soul."

"End the corporate wars?"

"You will be the priest of this shrine, this sepulcher. I will return to Earth and tell everyone about these wars."

"Humphries and others will have you killed."

"I am a famous artist, they dare not touch me." Then she laughed. "And I am too old to care if they do."

"The scientists—do you think they may actually learn how to communicate with the aliens?"

"Someday," Elverda said. "When our souls are pure enough to stand the shock of their presence."

The human side of Dorn's face smiled at her. He extended his arm and she took it in her own, realizing that she had found her own salvation. Like two kindred souls, like comrades who had shared the sight of death, like mother and son they walked up the tunnel toward the waiting race of humanity.

Jupiter is the largest of all the solar system's planets, more than ten times bigger and three hundred times as massive as Earth. Jupiter is so immense it could swallow all the other planets easily. Its Great Red Spot, a storm that has raged for centuries, is itself wider than Earth. And the Spot is merely one feature visible among the innumerable vortexes and streams of Jupiter's frenetically racing cloud tops.

Yet Jupiter is composed mainly of the lightest elements, hydrogen and helium, more like a star than a planet. All that size and mass, yet Jupiter spins on its axis in less than ten hours, so fast that the planet is clearly not spherical: Its poles are noticeably flattened. Jupiter looks like a big color-fully striped beach ball that's squashed down as if some invisible child were sitting on it.

Spinning that fast, Jupiter's deep, deep atmosphere is swirled into bands and ribbons of multihued clouds: pale yellow, saffron orange, white, tawny yellow-brown, dark brown, bluish, pink, and red. Titanic winds push the clouds across the face of Jupiter at hundreds of kilometers per hour. What gives those clouds their colors?

What lies beneath them?

The indications are that some fifty thousand kilometers—nearly four times Earth's diameter—beneath those clouds lies a boundless ocean of water, an ocean almost eleven times wider than the entire Earth and some five thousand kilometers deep. Heavily laced with ammonia and sulfur compounds, highly acidic, it is still an ocean of water, and everywhere else in the solar system where there is water, life exists.

Is there life in Jupiter's vast, deep ocean?

In my novel Jupiter I postulated that there is not merely life in the giant planet's vast ocean, but gigantic creatures of a high order of intelligence. It was a challenge to depict truly alien life forms, extraterrestrials that are more than actors in funny makeup. Leviathan is a creature of its environment, an otherworldly giant that consists of a huge colony of many different semi-independent components, a creature that communicates with others of its kind mainly through light, by flashing pictures on its luminescent flanks. Alien.

The following excerpt from the novel Jupiter *is told from the viewpoint of Leviathan, down in that dark and turbulent Jovian ocean; it deals — in part — with Leviathan's first fleeting encounter with the puny, strange, alien explorers from another world: Earth.*

t is a boundless ocean, more than ten times wider than the entire planet Earth. Beneath the swirling clouds that cover Jupiter from pole to pole, the ocean has never seen sunlight, nor has it ever felt the rough confining contours of land. Its waves have never crashed against a craggy shore, never thundered upon a sloping beach, for there is no land anywhere across Jupiter's enormous girth: Not even an island or a reef. The ocean's billows sweep across the deeps without hinderance, eternally.

Heated from below by the planet's seething core, swirled into a frenzy by Jupiter's hyperkinetic spin rate, ferocious currents race through this endless sea, jet streams howling madly, long powerful waves surging uninterrupted all the way around the world, circling the globe over and again. Gigantic storms wrack the ocean, too, typhoons bigger than whole planets, hurricanes that have roared their fury for century after century. It is the widest, deepest, most powerful, most dynamic and fearsome ocean in the entire solar system.

Leviathan followed an upwelling current through the endless sea, smoothly grazing on the food that spiraled down from the abyss above. Far from the Kin now, away from the others of its own kind, Leviathan reveled in its freedom from the herd and their plodding cycle of feeding, dismemberment, and rejoining.

To human senses the boundless ocean would be impenetrably dark, devastatingly hot, crushingly dense. Yet Leviathan moved through the surging deeps with ease, the flagella members of its assemblage stroking steadily as its mouth parts slowly opened and closed, opened and closed, in the ancient rhythm of ingestion.

To human senses Leviathan would be staggeringly huge, dwarfing all the whales of Earth, larger than whole pods of whales, larger even than a good-sized city. Yet in the vast depths of the Jovian sea Leviathan was merely one of many, slightly larger than some, considerably smaller than the eldest of its kind.

There were dangers in that dark, hot, deep sea. Glide too high on the soaring currents, toward the source of the bountiful food, and the waters grew too thin and cold; Leviathan's members would involuntarily disassemble, shed their cohesion, never to reunite again. Get trapped in a treacherous downsurge and the heat welling up from the abyss below would kill the members before they could break away and scatter.

Best to cruise here in the abundant world provided by the Symmetry, between the abyss above and the abyss below, where the food drifted down constantly from the cold wilderness on high, and the warmth from the depths below made life tolerable.

Predators swarmed through Leviathan's ocean: Swift voracious Darters that struck at Leviathan's kind and devoured their outer members. There were even cases where the predators had penetrated to the core of their prey, rupturing the central organs and forever destroying the poor creature's unity. The Elders had warned Leviathan that the Darters attacked solitary members of the Kin when they had broken away from their group for budding in solitude. Still Leviathan swam on alone, intent on exploring new areas of the measureless sea.

Leviathan remembered when the abyss above had erupted in giant flares of killing heat. Many of Leviathan's kind had disassembled in the sudden violence of those concussions. Even the everlasting rain of food had been disrupted and Leviathan had known hunger for the first time in its existence. But the explosions dissipated swiftly and life eventually returned to normal again.

Leviathan had been warned of another kind of creature in the sea: A phantasm, a strange picture drawn by others of the Kin, like nothing Leviathan had ever sensed for itself: small and sluggish and cold, lacking flagella members or any trace of community. It was pictured to have appeared once in the sea and once only, then vanished upward into the abyss above.

None of the others had paid much attention to it. It was so tiny that it could barely be sensed at all, yet for some reason the vision of its singular presence in the eternal ocean sent a chilling note of uneasiness through Leviathan's entire assemblage. It was an unnatural thing, alien, troubling.

Cruising through the eternal sea, Leviathan's sensory members warned of the storm ahead. Leviathan's eye parts could not see the storm, it was much too far away for visual contact, but the pressure-sensing members along Leviathan's immense bulk felt the tug of currents that wanted to draw the whole world ocean into the storm's voracious maw.

It was a huge vortex, its powerful spiral generating currents that grew stronger and stronger until even creatures as powerful as Leviathan and its kind could no longer resist and would be sucked into a whirling, shattering dismemberment.

Leviathan felt no anxiety about the distant storm, no dread of its insatiable lure. At this distance the storm was too weak to be dangerous, and Leviathan had no intention of approaching any closer. Yet it felt a tendril of curiosity. No member of the Kin had ever gone close enough to the storm to actually see it. What would that experience be like?

The food that sifted down from the cold abyss above seemed to be concentrated more thickly the closer Leviathan cruised to the storm's vicinity. The inward-pulling currents generated by the storm's powerful spinning vortex were sucking in the drifting particles until they became veritable streams, thick torrents of food flooding into the storm's maelstrom, impossible to ignore and difficult to resist. The Elders should be shown this, Leviathan thought.

Far, far off on the horizon Leviathan's eye parts detected a faint flickering, nothing more than the slightest rippling of light, barely discernible. Yet it alerted Leviathan to the fact that it was getting close enough to the storm to actually see it. Leviathan felt a strange thrill, a mixture of excitement and apprehension.

Darters! the sensory members warned.

Leviathan's eye parts focused on them, the Darters were that close. Swift, streamlined shapes, lean and efficient, heading straight toward Leviathan. There were dozens of them, spreading out in a globe to surround Leviathan, intent on pressing their attack home. They would not be content with a quick nip at Leviathan's outer hide; an armada of this size meant to kill and feast on all of Leviathan's members.

Escape lay in retreat, but retreat was in the direction of the storm. The Darters had hatched a clever hunting strategy, knowing that if they pursued Leviathan close enough to the swirling storm front, Leviathan's members would instinctively disassemble and become easy prey for the voracious hunters.

Leviathan estimated the distance to the storm's towering ringwall of turbulence, tested the pull of the currents plunging into the storm, and planned a strategy of its own. It commanded its flagella members to row as fast as they could toward the ceaseless streaks of lightning that showed where the storm raged. No questions, no doubts came back from the flagella; they were blindly obedient, always.

Now it was a race, and a test of strength. The Darters chased after the fleeing Leviathan, eager to chew through its thick outer armor and puncture the vital organ-members deep within. Leviathan felt the storm's currents tugging, pulling it closer and closer to the cloud wall. Lightning stroked the clouds and Leviathan's sensor members cringed at the storm's mindless, endless roar. Members sent signals of alarm to Leviathan's central brain: Soon they would automatically begin to disintegrate; they had no control over their hard-wired instincts.

Darters were close enough now to nip at the thickened dead tissue of Leviathan's outer hide. Leviathan swatted at them, turning the faithful mindless flagella into brutal clubs that could rupture flesh, crush bone.

Driven to frenzy by the scent of torn flesh, the Darters redoubled their attack. Leviathan felt their teeth tearing into its hide, all its members flashed signals of pain and fear as the ever-growing pull of the storm's mighty currents dragged Leviathan closer to involuntary dissociation.

Now! Leviathan suddenly shifted course, moving to parallel the spinning currents of the storm, battering its way through the net of Darters surrounding it. The Darters were too close to the lightning-wracked storm to be able to resist the inward-pulling currents. Like helpless specks of food they were sucked into the storm, one after another, struggling futilely against the storm's overwhelming power, shrieking their death howls as they spun into the raging clouds.

Leviathan struggled, too, straining mightily to slide around the face of the lightning-streaked cloud wall, gradually spiraling away from the storm.

When at last it was free of danger, Leviathan felt drained, exhausted—and hungry. But there was no food here; on this side of the storm the sea was empty, barren. Only gradually did it realize that it had been swept far from its usual haunts, into a region of the all-encompassing ocean that it had never seen before.

Leviathan flashed out a call to the others of its kind. There was no response. Alone, weak, and bleeding, Leviathan began to search for food, desperately hoping to build enough strength to swim far from the storm, wondering how it could find its way back to the familiar haunts of the Kin.

• • •

Weakened by its battle against the Darters, slowly starving in this barren region of the sea, Leviathan allowed the powerful currents surging out of the eternal storm to drive it farther from the towering, roaring wall of seething water and its menacing bolts of lightning.

Its wounded members flared with pain signals. Leviathan needed food, and plenty of it, to heal the flesh torn and shredded by the Darters' teeth. Yet there was no food to be found.

At least there were no Darters in this empty part of the ocean. Leviathan doubted its members would have the strength to fight them.

Food. Leviathan had to find food. Which meant it had to circle the immense storm, and return to the side where the currents flowed into it and the food streamed thickly.

Riding the circling currents, drifting rather than propelling itself through the ocean, Leviathan wondered if there might be some food—any food—up higher. It was dangerous to rise too high into the cold abyss above, but Leviathan knew it would be death to remain at this depth, where no food at all was available.

Slowly, cautiously, Leviathan made its flotation members expand. The immense creature drifted higher, nearing exhaustion, nearing the moment when its members would instinctively disintegrate and begin their individual buddings, in the last desperate hope of survival by spawning offspring.

The old instincts would be of no avail now, Leviathan knew. The members could separate and reproduce themselves in the hope of uniting into renewed assemblies, but what good would that do where there was not enough food even for one? Even if a few individual members survived temporarily, how could they live without the unity of all the others? Apart they were helpless. What could flagella members do without a brain to guide them? How could a brain member exist without sensor members and digestive members and—

Leviathan halted its pointless musing. There *was* food drifting in the currents above. The sensor members felt its faint echo vibrating through the water. The storm's merciless flow swept the particles into its own mindless vortex before they could sift down to the comfortable level where Leviathan swam.

It would be cold up there, numbingly cold. Leviathan's kind traced tales of foolish youngsters who rose too high in their haughty search to outdo their elders and never returned, disintegrated by the cold and their members devoured by Darters or the eerie creatures that haunted the abyss above.

But remaining at this level meant starvation. Leviathan needed enough food to allow it to circle around the great storm and return to the familiar region where the food rained down without fail.

Upward Leviathan rose, straining against the growing cold, heading toward the meager trickle of food that its sensor members had detected.

It was not food, Leviathan realized. Despite the numbing cold and the continuing pain signals from its wounded members, Leviathan's eye parts showed that the echoes the sensors detected came not from a thin stream of food particles but from one single particle, much larger than any food Leviathan had ever known, yet puny compared to Leviathan or even to the Darters.

It was that alien thing that had been seen before. Far, far off in the distance, up so high that Leviathan dared not even try to approach it, a strange circular object was struggling through the abyss above, sending out eerie signals that made no sense whatsoever.

Is this real? Leviathan wondered. Or are we so close to disintegration that our brain is beginning to fail?

The alien continued to flash signals mindlessly into the empty ocean, totally oblivious to Leviathan drifting in the cold empty sea, far out of range of its sensing systems.

Starving, dying, Leviathan drifted in the cold empty abyss high above its usual level in the ocean. It took an effort of will to hold its parts together, to prevent them from spontaneously disintegrating.

We must stay together, Leviathan kept repeating. If we break apart each component of us will die, whether we bud or not. We will become food for the scavengers who wait below in the hot darkness of the depths. Together we might survive. If we can stay together long enough we might find food.

But the ocean was cold and barren at this level. Legends pictured monsters up in this frigid emptiness, slithering beasts that preyed on each other and any of Leviathan's kind foolish enough to drift this high.

Leviathan thought that the legends were mere tales, stories flashed by elders to frighten young ones away from climbing too far from the safe levels of the sea.

It is time for us to return to the warmer region, Leviathan knew. But it could not force its flotation members to contract. They no longer had the strength to expel the gas that filled them. It took energy to make their muscles contract, and starving members had no energy to work with.

Cold. Cold and empty. Leviathan could sense its control of its outer members begin to fade. A unit of armored hide peeled away spontaneously. Instead of the promised joy of budding, Leviathan felt a wave of uncontrollable grief wash through its mind. We are disintegrating. We will all die here, alone, never to bud, never to generate new life.

Unbidden, three of the flagella members broke loose, fluttering mindlessly in the frigid current. Leviathan realized that the end was near. Once the vital organ members dissociated, Leviathan's existence would be finished, without even the knowledge that its parts would generate new buds, create new members that would associate into offspring.

The Symmetry would be disrupted. The eternal cycle of life budding new life would end. It was not meant to be so, Leviathan knew. It had failed to maintain the Symmetry.

A sense organ shuddered, then began to quiver violently, the first step in its dissociation. There was nothing Leviathan could do to prevent it. Not now.

And yet . . .

The sense organ suddenly stopped fluttering and became still. It flashed a picture to Leviathan's brain. A monster. A long, flat, many-armed creature was quietly slithering toward Leviathan, grasping its dissociated members in its wriggling tentacles and pushing them into a circular, snapping mouth ringed with sharp teeth.

For a flash of a second Leviathan thought its sensor member was hallucinating, hysterical on the edge of starvation and dissociation. But no, other sense members flashed the same picture. The creature was huge, almost as large as Leviathan itself, and it was nearly transparent, difficult to see until it was very close. It glided through the sea with hardly a ripple, making it impossible to detect at long range.

It was one of the mindless beasts that the old legends warned of. It was trailing Leviathan, gobbling up its members as they dissociated and drifted helplessly in the cold abyss.

It was heading for Leviathan itself, tentacles weaving, round tooth-ringed mouth snapping open and shut, open and shut.

Leviathan's first instinct was to flee. But in its weakened condition, could it outrun this scavenger? The monster slowed as it approached Leviathan, stretched out two of its longest tentacles and barely touched Leviathan's hide.

Pain! Leviathan had never felt an electric shock before, but the jangling, burning pain of the monster's touch made Leviathan recoil instinctively. The monster pursued leisurely, in no hurry to do battle with Leviathan. It seemed content to wait until more of Leviathan's members dissociated. It was more of a scavenger than a predator, Leviathan thought.

Weak, almost helpless, Leviathan studied the monster. Its main body was a broad flat sheet, undulating like jelly. That gaping mouth was on the underside; its top was studded with dome-like projections that must be sensory organs. Dozens of tentacles weaved and snaked all around the central body's periphery. Two of them were much longer than the others, and ended in rounded knobs.

Can all the tentacles cause pain when they touch? Leviathan wondered. Cautiously, it backed away from the creature. The monster followed at the same pace, keeping its distance, waiting patiently.

A new thought arose in Leviathan's mind. This monster could be *food*. The old legends pictured these beasts eating one another when they had no other food available. It wants to eat my members. Perhaps we could eat it.

But first, Leviathan knew, it would have to kill the monster. And to do that, it would have to avoid those painful tentacles.

If Leviathan had not been weakened and starving there would be no contest. Leviathan's speed and strength would have made short work of this gossamer creature. Except for those pain-dealing tentacles. We must avoid them.

Leviathan conceived a plan. It was part desperation, part cunning. It called for a sacrifice.

Deliberately, Leviathan willed three more of its flagella members to dissociate. Faithful, mindless, they peeled away from Leviathan's body and began propelling themselves down toward the warmer depths.

The monster immediately dived after them, so fast that Leviathan realized his plan could not possibly work. But there was nothing else to do. He dived after the beast.

The monster's two longer tentacles touched the first of the flagella, instantly paralyzing it. They passed the immobilized member to the shorter tentacles so quickly that their motions seemed a blur to Leviathan. The tentacles, in turn, relayed the inert flagellum to that snapping, hideous mouth.

The two other flagella were instinctively fleeing, diving blindly toward the warmth of the lower levels of the sea. The monster pursued them singlemindedly. Which gave Leviathan its opportunity. With its last reserves of strength Leviathan dove after the beast and rammed into it. Waves of concussion rippled through the jelly-like body of the monster; its tentacle writhed in pain.

Quickly, Leviathan fastened as many of its mouth parts as possible onto that broad, flat body. The monster's longer tentacles snaked back and stung Leviathan again and again, searching blindly for the parts where the armored hide members had dissociated and the more vulnerable inner organs were exposed.

Despite the pain that flared through it, Leviathan tore through the monster's body, its mouth parts crushing the beast's flimsy body. The monster's tentacles went limp at last and Leviathan fed on its dead body. It tasted awful, but it was food.

Feeling stronger despite the strangely acid sensation simmering through its digestive organs, Leviathan resumed its course around the great storm, heading for the deeper waters where — it hoped — it would find plentiful food and others of its own kind.

Leviathan had a tale to portray to them.

AFTERWORD: THE ROADS AHEAD

Obviously, the Grand Tour is far from finished.

There is at least one more novel I need to write about Jamie Waterman, on Mars. At the conclusion of *Return to Mars*, Jamie and the woman he loves, Vijay Shektar, have decided to remain on Mars while the other members of the second expedition return to Earth. Jamie is determined to preserve Mars, its microscopic life forms and its ancient artifacts, from those who would despoil the planet and try to alter its environment to make it more Earthlike.

Then there is Grant Archer in the research station orbiting Jupiter, and the giant creatures he discovered swimming in Jupiter's planet-girdling ocean. Can humans and the utterly alien Leviathans make meaningful contact with one another? Are the Leviathans truly as intelligent as we are? Or more so?

And of course, Lars Fuchs and Martin Humphries are still fighting their deadly war in the cold and dark depths of the Asteroid Belt. They hate each other, and they both love Amanda Cunningham.

I do not intend to write a novel about each one of the solar system's planets. Yet . . . what of the giant solar power stations to be built near the planet Mercury? Are the particles that make up Saturn's beautiful rings actually alive? What is happening in the petrochemical sea that slithers across Titan like a living beast? Beneath the ice crust of Europa? In the frozen wastes of Pluto and the icebergs of the Kuiper Belt?

Will we journey even farther, to the stars themselves?

And what of the alien artifact discovered in "Sepulcher"? How recently were the aliens visiting our solar system? Are they still here? If so, what do they want of us?

There is plenty more to write about!

It makes me think of the rocket pioneer Robert Goddard, who, nearly a century ago, wrote to a friend: "There can be no thought of finishing, for 'aiming at the stars,' both literally and figuratively, is a problem to occupy generations, so that no matter how much progress one makes, there is always the thrill of just beginning."